Contingency

BOOK ONE: COVENANT OF TRUST SERIES

PAULA WISEMAN

MINDSTIR MEDIA

Published by Mindstir Media
PO Box 1681 | Hampton, New Hampshire 03843 | USA
1.800.767.0531 | www.mindstirmedia.com

Printed in the United States of America

ISBN-10: 0-981964-82-6
ISBN-13: 978-0-9819648-2-9

Library of Congress Control Number: 2010941896

Book design by Find The Axis
www.findtheaxis.com

Visit Paula Wiseman on the World Wide Web:
www.paulawiseman.com

For Jon, who lives true love daily

Acknowledgements

Thank you. . .

To Jon for your unwavering confidence in me and in the story. I would have quit long ago without you.

To Amanda for the endless hours of plotting, and revising. The book is better, deeper and stronger because of your help. And so am I.

To Kristi for your emotional investment from the beginning, and for the inside look at second grade.

To Mary for your photos, your comments and your awesome proofreading.

To countless others who read and gave feedback.

To J.J. for his enthusiasm for the book and his help and encouragement.

All glory to God, who gives the story, who opens doors, who accomplishes His purposes in all things.

CHAPTER 1
REVELATION

Thursday, July 28

> Chuck,
> I'm meeting Chad and Michelle for drinks at Baker Street
> Pub at 6. Can you join us? My whole evening is free again.
> *wink*
> --Tracy

Bobbi Molinsky stared at the e-mail. Yes, it was addressed to her husband. Yes, it automatically forwarded from his account at the law firm since he was out of town again. But it didn't make any sense.

Her fingers hovered over the mouse as she grasped for the "logical explanation." Chuck never mentioned a Tracy. Who was this woman, and why was she inviting Chuck to a pub, when he didn't drink? Why would Tracy say 'again'? Unless . . .

She swiveled the chair around, grabbed the cordless handset, and punched in the speed dial number for Chuck's cell phone. She'd hear it straight from him. He would clear up everything, and they would laugh about it. What's more, he would rib her for her jealous paranoia for the next twenty years.

His cell rang once, then rolled over to voice mail. *Strike one.* Now what? Chuck's office must have a number where he could be reached, but if she interrupted him in the middle of the biggest deal in the firm's history . . .

"Benton, Davis, & Molinsky, how may I direct your call?"

"This is Bobbi Molinsky, Chuck's wife. I need to get in touch with him." The receptionist gave her Chuck's hotel number and three different client numbers. She also promised to have Chuck call home if he called in.

Bobbi pulled her notepad closer. Eight, one, three . . . then she froze. The receptionist. Was that Tracy? She hit redial with both thumbs.

"Is this Tracy?"

"No, it's Christine. Tracy Ravenna is no longer with the firm, and I don't have a number where she can be reached. If you're a client of hers, I can put you through to Mr. Davis."

Tracy . . . an attorney . . . but no longer with the firm. Did Christine know anything about Chuck and Tracy? Office gossip?

"Ma'am? Is there anything else I can help you with?"

Bobbi switched the phone to her left ear and hunched over the desk. "Maybe there is. This is Bobbi Molinsky again. We received an e-mail from Tracy Ravenna, and I'm almost positive it should go to someone else. Is there anyone else there named Chuck?" *Please God, let there be another Chuck.*

"No, ma'am, I'm sorry. If you want to forward the e-mail to our IT guy, I'm sure he could help you."

Strike two.

One e-mail doesn't mean anything. Besides, why was a Monday e-mail just now showing up in their inbox three days later?

If this Tracy person e-mailed him, did she call him, too? Bobbi knew she could call in to Chuck's voice mail, and find out in thirty seconds. She bought the phone for him and set up the voice mail. She pulled the cordless phone closer, but hesitated. Was she ready to admit her marriage had slid to the place where she would cross that line of trust, that she could, or rather would, doubt her husband?

She dropped the phone back on its cradle and closed her eyes, envisioning last year's Christmas party. Why hadn't she paid more attention to the endless stream of clients, attorneys, and guests Chuck paraded before her that night?

Wait! She remembered Chad. He joined the firm last fall, and his wife was named Michelle. Chad and Michelle from the e-mail! Had they introduced Tracy to Chuck? But they knew he was married. None of this added up.

Chuck was a lot of things, but an adulterer? All those other girls, he knew them in college, before they even met, before he discovered his parents' faith, before he committed himself to follow Jesus Christ. A shared faith drew them to each other in the first place. Shouldn't that faith stop him from . . .?

Just because they'd had another argument Monday morning, that didn't justify monitoring his phone calls. People have arguments all the time. She and Chuck still slept in the same bed. Most nights, anyway. They were going through a phase, that's all.

She glanced up at the e-mail again and dialed.

The factory-set PIN no longer worked. Why would he change his PIN? She tried 1234, but the system rejected it. She tried their house number, then his birthday. Still no access. What would he have chosen? *My birthday?* Bingo. He had four messages. The first two were work–related, but the third was from a woman.

"Now I know why you never gave me a home phone number!"

The message continued with a profanity-laced tirade about being used and lied to by a married man until the machine cut her off. On the fourth message, Tracy picked up where she had left off.

Bobbi watched the phone slide out of her hand, unable to will her fingers to close around it before it dropped onto the carpet under the desk. She had run out of straws to grasp. It *was* true. Chuck had been unfaithful. With Tracy. The e-mail was from Chuck's mistress.

Bobbi pushed the chair back, leaving a sweaty handprint on the desk. Perspiration beaded across her back and her jaws tingled with an odd hollowness. She grabbed the wastebasket the instant before she threw up.

She staggered around the desk and across the hall to the downstairs bathroom, dragging the wastebasket with her. Her brain, misfiring on all cylinders, managed to put two coherent words together—*how long?* How long had she been blind? How long had she been a failure? How long had Chuck . . .?

"NO! No, no, no, no, no!"

She snatched the hairbrush lying by the sink and slammed it to the floor. It echoed in the tiny room as it hit the tile, then ricocheted up and knocked the wastebasket over. Seizing the basket before it could spill, she set it in the shower, then turned the hot water on full blast.

If Chuck was cheating, she would know it. He couldn't hide that from her. How could he have taken her out for their anniversary if he broke his marriage vows? How could he kiss her goodbye in the morning? *When he kissed me goodbye . . .*

Would Chuck try to smooth things over with Tracy and continue their affair? Was Tracy the first or just the latest? Gagging on the acid rising in the back of her throat, she tried to vomit again, but her stomach was empty.

Dizzy and lightheaded, she flipped the toilet lid closed so she could sit down. She rested her forehead on the sink and concentrated on each breath. *Don't pass out . . . Breathe . . .* She rubbed the back of her neck, her icy fingers soothing the flush of heat that washed over her. Long moments passed before she felt steady enough to sit up. *Dear God, how could he? How could You let him? How . . . how are we supposed to recover from this?*

How?

She would give him the chance to come clean, that's how. Back in the study, she kicked the cordless out from under the desk, then punched in Chuck's cell phone number. "Your call has been forwarded to a voice mailbox."

If she left a message, he would have time to prepare, time to get his story straight before he faced her. She considered waiting for him to get home, then broadsiding him the way he had done her. No, she needed to keep the high ground, but when the beep sounded, her throat closed off.

"Chuck, we have to talk . . . about Tracy."

Chuck Molinsky snapped his briefcase shut. *Mission accomplished.* Mentally spending his portion of the ServMed fees, he checked his watch on his way out of the hotel conference room. *A Rolex. That's what I need. I've earned it.* A quarter past eleven meant he could grab a quick lunch before boarding his plane and getting out of Kansas City. He threw his briefcase onto the passenger seat of his rental car, yanked his necktie off, and powered up his cell phone. A tweet indicated a missed call.

"Bobbi, there's nothing wrong with your car, and no, I won't let you apologize." Hers wasn't the only call he missed, though.

He halfway listened to the first two messages from Walter Davis and Gina Novak. The third one hit like a slap in the face. "Now I know why you never gave me a home phone number! How long were you going to lie to me about being married? Did you think you could just use me as a little side distraction?" Tracy sprayed accusations and epithets like a verbal machine gun, spitting words Chuck hadn't heard since the high school locker room, and even a few new ones.

"I never lied . . . not to you." Everybody knew he was married. If she missed that, it wasn't his fault. And he never used her. She had him all wrong. Didn't they have an understanding? All they had was an intense, physical . . . whatever, not even a relationship.

He shook his head, as if that would disrupt the memories. As if. He saw her, saw himself with her every time he closed his eyes. He leaned back in the driver's seat and played Bobbi's message.

In that one searing moment, the choking anguish in her voice ripped away his carefully constructed fantasy world. "Chuck, we have to talk . . . about Tracy."

Dear God, she knew. The only woman who ever really loved him, and she knew. At some point, he dropped his phone, probably when the crushing pressure hit his chest, followed by waves of panic. He was having a heart attack. His Grandpa Bradley died at forty-two of a heart attack.

He was forty-two, and now he was going to die in a hotel parking lot far away from home. He was going to die without ever seeing Bobbi again.

He slapped at the key until he got the car started and blasted the air conditioner in his face. Chuck rested his forehead on the steering wheel and took long, slow breaths. Sweat dripped from his forehead and his pulse throbbed in his neck. He closed his eyes and waited. Finally, the pain in his chest subsided. Not a heart attack. Not that kind, at least.

Bobbi knew. But how much did she know? How did she find out? Maybe she thought he was in love with Tracy. Maybe if he could reassure her that he never considered leaving, that it wasn't about her at all. Tracy was just . . . whatever.

Time. He could convince Bobbi to forgive him if he had enough time. If forgiveness was asking for too much, he had to keep her from divorcing him. A divorce meant failure. A negotiator who couldn't work things out with his own wife—that looked bad. If they stayed together, that would be enough to keep Walter Davis from blowing a gasket. Keep his wife, his sons, and his job. Buy time and don't let Bobbi divorce him, no matter what.

Bobbi leaned her forehead against the window in the study and stared out into the empty street. She hadn't spoken to Chuck since Monday morning. She resolved then, after she dropped him off at the terminal, that he could find his own way home. If he was still coming home. In six hours, she'd have her answer. She tugged the cord and drew the drapes.

Their most recent family photograph sat on the bookcase. She walked over and picked up the picture, cradling it like a fragile heirloom. Her necklace, the eighteenth anniversary diamond necklace, shifted against her. It went with the fifteenth anniversary bracelet she wore in the photo. Those went along with the twelfth anniversary earrings and the tenth anniversary diamond ring. Always diamonds. Cold, hard diamonds.

Bobbi studied Chuck's face, her finger tracing his square jaw line. She searched his eyes, trying to wring some sign of dissatisfaction or unhappiness from them. She couldn't see it.

Chuck had one just like it on his desk at work. What was missing from the picture, from Chuck's life, that would push him to another woman?

I've been a good wife. I've supported him, been understanding. I've always given him the benefit of the doubt. Was that my mistake? Have I set him up to take advantage of me?

If they had any hope of salvaging their marriage, that had to change. She couldn't be passive and reactive. She had to be ready for him when he came home.

Chuck piled his bags against a no-parking sign and stood on the airport curb, scanning the incoming traffic. He checked his watch again. Bobbi had his itinerary and the plane landed on time. Granted, he never called her to confirm he needed a ride, but she knew exactly when to be here, and she was never late. She wasn't coming.

Bobbi didn't do public confrontation. Fine. He'd do this her way. He reached in his jacket pocket for his necktie and tied it in a crisp knot. She bought this shirt and tie for him. She would remember that, and that would work to his advantage. He caught his reflection in the terminal's plate glass window and smoothed his hair. The suit jacket was all wrong, so he folded it and slipped it in his garment bag. He stood up straight, picked up his bags, and hailed a taxi.

He ran through his approach one more time. Let her vent, agree with her, then bring up the deeper issues in their marriage. He had to be careful that he didn't come across like he blamed her at all. That would be a disaster. She would agree the best thing for the boys, for the family, was finding some way to work through this. He was willing to go to counseling for as long as it took to satisfy her. Counseling would keep everybody else out of it, the law firm, the church, and especially Rita.

When the taxi turned onto his street, Chuck could feel his adrenaline kick in. His pulse quickened. The back of his neck warmed, and every muscle tensed. It was go time.

He heard the front door open as he paid the cab driver and he could feel Bobbi's eyes on him. Should he speak first, or wait for her? He had to be proactive. He had to make the first move. He picked up his bags, and when he turned around, his eyes met hers. His wife of eighteen years, the mother of his sons, stood in silent dignity, never blinking, never flinching, and he . . . looked away.

He watched his feet step up to the porch, all the while trying to remember some shred of the things he wanted to tell her.

"Did you get your phone messages?" she asked with an icy edge on each word. Before Chuck could answer, she slammed the door, then came the crash of shattering glass.

He eased the door open and slid his carry-on bag inside. Silence greeted him. The mangled frame for Brad's first grade picture lay in the entry hall floor among glass shards of all sizes. Chuck carefully picked up the largest pieces and placed them on the console table.

He set his briefcase down and straightened the other pictures in the entry hall, the boys' baby photos, Joel's first grade picture, sports teams, and Cub scouts. With lingering care, he leveled their wedding picture. Bobbi looked stunning in her grandmother's wedding dress. Her jet-black hair framed her face and her ready smile lit up the room. Her dark eyes even had an extra sparkle.

Bobbi's question finally registered with him. The phone messages. If Bobbi heard Tracy's messages . . .

She sat at the breakfast table with her back to him. "Bobbi, where are the boys?" He didn't want his sons to hear any of this.

"Don't you even say my name." She spoke without turning around, her voice low with the same intense anger. "I hate you. I hate what you've done, and I hate you."

Chuck didn't dare join her at the table. Instead, he moved over, and leaned against the sink so he could face her. She folded her hands in front of her and looked past him. "Are the boys here?" he asked again.

"They're at Rita's. And no, she doesn't know."

"Look, I—"

"Just give me the whole speech, Chuck. I'm sure you practiced it all the way home."

She locked her eyes on his. That seething emotion wasn't anger at all. It was humiliation and betrayal. He wanted her to be angry. He could face anger. He could fight that. But he couldn't fight hurt. He never wanted to hurt her. For the first time in his life, his swaggering self-confidence evaporated, and he bolted.

"I can't do this right now," he muttered, stepping around the table. "I'm going to go. We'll talk about this later."

"This?" She slammed her hand on the table, and he froze. "Can't you even say it?" She pushed back from the table and jerked herself to her feet. "Here, let me do it for you. You slept with another woman, Chuck! You had an affair! You committed adultery! You cheated on me." She closed the gap between them until she stood mere inches away.

"For God's sake, Bobbi—"

"God? Don't drag Him into this! He didn't have anything to do with it." Bobbi pointed her finger right at Chuck's heart. "It was all you!"

"I know!" His instincts told him to unload on her, to match her yelling and slamming, but he couldn't. "I'm going."

"Can't you face me? You didn't have any trouble facing me while you were having an affair behind my back! Why should now be any different?"

"Because you're upset. I can't talk to you when you're upset." He couldn't think of anything better than that lame excuse. His points, his concessions, his action plan vanished.

"Upset? I just found out my husband is having an affair! How did you expect me to act when you got home?"

"Maybe coming home was a mistake!" he shouted as he walked back to the front hallway to get his bag and briefcase.

Chuck twisted the last screw in the last outlet in the last upstairs bedroom of the biggest house in the subdivision. His knees popped as he stood up. At least this was just a summer job.

"Got those outlets wired, college boy?" Gene Thomas, the head contractor, stepped in between the studs of the unfinished wall. Chuck enjoyed the good-natured ribbing.

"Just finished."

"All right. I can get the drywallers in here." He scribbled a note on his clipboard. "Get packed up, and you can get out of here."

"But it's not four yet."

"Son, when your boss tells you to go home, you go."

"I just wanted to make sure it wasn't a test." Chuck grinned and walked over to close the bedroom windows.

"You're too smart for this job." Gene shook his head.

As Chuck slid the front window closed, an old Buick Electra, a little old lady's car, pulled up out front. He was ready to walk away when he caught sight of tanned legs. That was no little old lady. Then he got a full view of the woman the legs belonged to. She rounded the front of the car and pushed her sunglasses up on her head. She wore her hair pulled back and pinned up. Her shirt flattered her without being tight or revealing, and she had an easy grace when she walked. "Hey, Gene, who's that?" Chuck motioned for his boss then pointed out the window.

"The plumber's daughter . . . Brenda, maybe . . . no . . . something with a 'B'."

"I gotta go." Chuck pushed around Gene and clamored down the stairs, trying to catch the woman before she got in the house. He yanked the door open and found her standing on the porch.

"You startled me," she said. Even at six-foot-two, he didn't tower over her. She had a perfect Mediterranean complexion and the most beautiful deep brown eyes.

"I'm sorry. I just finished up, getting ready to go home."

"Yeah, I'm here to get my dad. He's a plumber."

"He doesn't drive?"

"His car's in the shop. Now, if you'll excuse me . . ."

"Wait, can I take you for a burger or something?"

"No, I don't even know your name."

He held out his hand. *"I'm Chuck Molinsky."*

She smiled. *"Yours is almost as bad as mine. I'm Bobbi—Bobbi with an 'i'—Petrocelli."* She shook his hand with a firm, confident grip. *"What is that, Polish?"*

"Russian, actually. Somewhere along the way the Slavs got mixed up some blue-eyed blondes, though. I'm not sure when that happened. Now, can I take you somewhere?"

"I don't think so. Daddy doesn't like for me to date construction types."

"Oh, I'm not. I mean, I'm going to law school this fall." He took his Missouri hat off. *"See, I've already got a lawyer haircut. I just work for Gene in the summer."*

"You've . . . already finished college."

"Is that bad?"

"I haven't graduated high school yet. I only have a couple of weeks left, but . . ."

"You're kidding me. I thought . . . Never mind."

"You thought I was older?"

"At least my age." He looked into those eyes again. *"The age thing, it doesn't matter to me if it doesn't bother you."*

"I don't know." Her eyes sparkled. *"Usually when an older guy wants to go out it's because all the girls his own age know he's a loser."* At least she smiled when she said it.

"You're harsh!" He put a hand over his heart. *"I swear I'm not a loser."*

"And you expect me to take your word for it?" She smiled again, and he thought he'd melt right into the unfinished floor.

"I can get you some references. Please? I'd love to spend some time with you."

"But if I say yes on such short notice, it looks like I'm pathetic and have nothing else to do."

"Not at all. If you're free, I'll figure that it's God arranging things."

"So, you're a Christian?"

"Yeah, about a year now. I'm still learning."

"Tell you what." She took the pen from his shirt pocket, then raised his hand, and wrote her address in his palm. "Come by about seven. We'll go for ice cream or something."

CHAPTER 2
COUNSEL

Chuck let reflex take over and drove to his office. In the parking lot, he shut the car off and slid his seat all the way back. *She's going to divorce me. She hates me and she's going to divorce me.* In spite of all his preparations, the battle never materialized. Once he saw Bobbi with his own eyes, he couldn't fight her. He couldn't sit back and let her leave, either.

Think. There's gotta be a way out of this. Who would Bobbi listen to? Besides Rita. Phil! Phil and Donna. Their pastor and his wife would never go along with divorce and Bobbi trusted Phil. Donna Shannon could convince a cat to give up chasing mice and make the cat think it was his idea all along. They were perfect. If he could get the Shannons involved, he may have hope after all.

He fished his cell phone out of his pants pocket, but he didn't have the Shannons' phone number saved anywhere. *New plan. Get a hotel room, then call Phil from the hotel.*

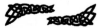

With her tears exhausted, Bobbi opened her eyes to a darkened house. Chuck hadn't returned. That meant he wasn't coming back. *Of course he's not coming back. I said I hated him. Here, my marriage is dying, and I took it off life support.*

Her head throbbed, and turning on the kitchen light made it explode with pain. Bobbi snapped the light back off and called her sister.

"Hello?" Brad answered the phone.

"Honey, let me talk to Aunt Rita."

"Mom, are you okay? You sound sick or something."

"I'm fine." *Get him off the phone before I lose it.*

"Did Dad make it home?"

"Yeah," Bobbi whispered. She hated lying to him. How was that any different from what Chuck did to her? Because she lied to protect her son. Brad had no way to grasp the upheaval coming in his life, and she was shielding him. That was completely different, wasn't it? "Honey, could you get Rita?"

"Sure, Mom."

"Bobbi, what's wrong?" Rita asked. "Is Chuck okay?"

"Chuck . . ." Bobbi took a deep breath and tried again to choke out the words. "Chuck . . . I found . . . he had an affair, Rita. He cheated on me."

"What?" A heavy silence followed. "Are you sure?"

"I'm sure."

"Are you at home now?"

"Yes."

"I'll be right there."

Rita Heatley drove to her sister's house, her foot heavier on the accelerator with each passing mile. A block away, the light changed. "I don't have time for red lights," she muttered, jamming the brake pedal to the floor. How many times had she tried to warn Bobbi about him? She knew it was only a matter of time before he did something like this. "The golden boy's not going to be able to talk his way out of this one."

She screeched to a stop in front of Bobbi's house, but before getting out, Rita sat in her car and counted. "One, two, three," she whispered, with a breath after every number. *Can't lose my temper. Have to be calm for Bobbi's sake.* "Thirty-one, thirty-two." Gavin questioned her self-control, but she could do this. "Sixty-seven, sixty-eight, sixty-nine." She could keep her own feelings in check at least for tonight. "Ninety-eight, ninety-nine, one hundred."

Rita let herself in the front door and called Bobbi's name. She tiptoed from room to room until she found Bobbi in the kitchen, a wastebasket full of used tissues in the floor beside her. "Baby, I am so sorry," she whispered, as she knelt and wrapped her arms around Bobbi's shoulders. "So sorry."

Bobbi twisted away from her sister. "What did I do wrong? I don't understand."

"Baby, don't talk that way." She took Bobbi's hands and once again became the surrogate mother. "You didn't do anything to deserve this, or cause this. If Chuck had an affair, it is one hundred percent his fault. Do you understand me? His fault."

"There's no 'if' about it," Bobbi said, motioning toward the study. "Read the e-mail. Chuck didn't deny it when he came home."

"He came home?" Rita pulled a chair around and sat down.

"Briefly. Then he left again."

"Did he go to . . . her?" *If he's with that woman right now . . .*

"I doubt it. She didn't know about me, either."

"Who is she?"

"Someone from the law firm. I don't know her."

"I can't imagine what today's been like for you. You should have called me earlier."

"I wanted to talk to Chuck first." She dropped her head and fidgeted with the corner of a paper napkin. "I didn't want him to know how much he hurt me. I exploded on him."

"You should have!" Rita tapped the table to get Bobbi to look up. "You were completely justified."

"But I didn't give him a chance to explain."

"You can't trust anything that comes out of his mouth now. Chuck is a liar . . ."

"He's never lied to me!"

Rita closed her eyes and tried to focus on relaxing her clenched jaw. "I'm not going to argue that with you tonight." She concentrated on keeping her voice low. "Does Chuck want a divorce?"

Bobbi's lips started to form words, but she made no sound. She rolled her eyes up toward the ceiling and let a long breath escape. "I think he does." Her words were so soft and weak that Rita strained to hear them over the hum of the refrigerator.

"Then there's no sense fighting him." The sooner Bobbi grasped that, the better.

"I want to talk to Phil before I do anything."

"Phil will want you to drag this out for months and months."

Bobbi snapped upright in her chair. "This is going to end up my fault. No matter what I do, Chuck will spin it until he's the victim. At least I can say with a clear conscience that I tried everything I could."

Good girl. "You want me to call Phil now?"

Bobbi nodded. "I don't want Chuck to get to him first."

When the doorbell rang, Bobbi spit the mouthful of Listerine into the bathroom sink. Rita convinced her to eat something, but the soup and toast wouldn't stay down. Now she had to look her pastor in the eye and explain, try to explain, how her marriage imploded in the last twelve hours. If she survived that, then she had to convince Phil that divorce was the most rational alternative.

"Bobbi? They're here. You okay?"

"I'll be right out. Go ahead and let them in." She splashed cold water on her face and took one last deep breath. *God, forgive me.* She slipped out of the bathroom and met everyone in the entry hall. "Thanks for coming," she said, hugging Donna, and then Phil. "Come in and sit down."

Bobbi motioned them into the living room and sat on the sofa with Donna and Rita, while Phil sat in the armchair, facing them. He leaned forward, resting his elbows on his knees, engaged, but not pressing . . . yet.

"Bobbi, Donna and I are just heartbroken for you." Phil's years of ministering in the Midwest hadn't robbed him of his gentle Tennessee accent. He often reminded Bobbi of Andy Griffith, and she expected that 'now Opie' tone of voice any minute. "I understand this is very personal, but what can you tell me?"

"We got an e-mail from Chuck's office from a woman named Tracy. I tried to call Chuck. When he came home, he didn't bother denying it." She smoothed the fringe on the throw pillow to avoid Phil's eyes. "Oh, I listened to his phone messages. He lied to her, too. She never knew Chuck was married." As a tear made its way down her cheek, Rita reached over and squeezed her hand.

"Do you want to end your marriage?" Phil asked without shaming her or rebuking her, and she raised her eyes.

"I don't have any other option. He doesn't love me—"

"I know it looks that way."

"He never said it, Phil." She slammed the pillow against the arm of the sofa. "He had hours to prepare his statement before he got home. There was no, 'Bobbi, I love you', no 'please forgive me.' Nothing. He's through, and the quicker we can . . ." She blinked several times, then dropped her eyes. *Don't cry. Not in front of Phil and Donna.* "There's no sense dragging things out. I'll give him his divorce." Bobbi felt Rita's hand on her back.

"I don't blame you," Phil said.

"Really? I didn't think you'd go for that."

"I didn't say I agreed with you, I just don't blame you for drawing that conclusion. Bobbi, can I ask you some hard questions?"

She nodded and let a deep breath escape.

"Do you want a divorce? Not what you think Chuck wants. Do *you* want a divorce?"

"I don't think so. No."

"Do you love Chuck?"

"I did."

"That's a great answer." Phil smiled at her. "Would you be willing to accept, at least for right now, that your marriage might be restored through the grace and power of God?"

"That's up to Chuck. I'm not going to fight him."

"But are you going to fight God?"

"Depends on what God says." Bobbi folded her arms across her chest, bracing for the sermon.

"I appreciate your honesty. Here's what I've heard in your answers, but don't hesitate to correct me. You love your husband. You hate the idea of divorce, but he's backed you in a corner. However, if he could prove himself, you'd consider giving him another chance."

"You're good. I didn't realize I'd said all that."

"I was inferring." Phil smiled. "So I was close?"

"Dead on."

"Then I want you to do a couple of things for me." He leaned forward and counted on his fingers. "First, don't *do* anything. Don't file papers. Don't sell his stuff. Don't get a tattoo, okay?"

Bobbi managed a smile and nod.

"This is a real shock to your life, and I don't want either of you to do anything rash. Second, I'm going to ask you to let this sit for about three weeks."

"That long? Why?"

"Because you've had a death in the family. I hope we're not looking at the death of your marriage, but a lot of your ideas and beliefs about your marriage have died, along with the trust you had in Chuck."

"That's an understatement."

"Take some time to mourn, process your emotions, before we address what happens next. I also want to spend some time counseling Chuck one-on-one, if he'll agree to it, before we start working with the two of you. When does school start?"

"The twenty-third. The kids start on the twenty-fifth."

Phil pulled his calendar from his back pocket, unclipped the pen, and scribbled a quick note. "Rita, is Gavin working full days, now?"

"Yes, but I'm sure he'll help however you need him." Phil nodded and made one more note before returning the calendar and pen to his pocket.

"So, what am I supposed to do in the meantime?" Bobbi asked. "Pretend like this never happened?"

"Not at all. It's going to take you two or three times longer to get ready for school than you expect. Your boys are going to need you . . . I'm asking for three weeks to counsel Chuck. If he and I don't make any progress, we can revisit your decision to divorce him."

"You can fix him in three weeks?"

"No," Phil said, raising a hand. "I didn't say that, but we'll know if there's anything worth fighting for in that time."

"You don't think he wants a divorce?"

"I haven't talked to him, but I'd be very surprised if he did."

Bobbi sat in silence for several moments. Three weeks. Chuck could lay all the groundwork to ruin her in a divorce court in three weeks. "You're asking a lot."

"I know it, and I'm going to add one more. Don't let what's happened with Chuck get between you and God. God's going to take care of this and He's going to take care of you. I promise you that He wants to walk every step of this road with you. Don't shut Him out."

Bobbi averted her eyes again. "Where was God, Phil? Chuck's supposed to be a believer. I don't understand how God could let this happen."

Phil pushed his fists together in front of his chest. "There's an irresolvable tension that exists between God's sovereignty and man's free will. He never forces man to act or prevents him from acting. God is never caught off guard by our choices, and His purposes are always fulfilled in spite of our interference."

Bobbi nodded and answered with an unsatisfied, "I see."

"That's seminary talk for 'I don't know.'" He dropped his hands and smiled at her. "I don't doubt that you're angry with God right now, too. I'd be naïve to think otherwise. However, the fact is, I can't help you if you won't let Him guide the process."

She knew he was waiting for her to agree, to promise she'd go along with that, but she couldn't. Not yet. At least Phil let it drop.

"Is there anything else Donna or I can do for you or the boys right now?" he asked. "Get your groceries? Cut your grass? Anything."

Bobbi shook her head and shifted on the sofa. "I don't mean to come across angry with you. I appreciate you coming. I just . . . How could he hurt me like this?" She clenched her jaw. She refused to let the Shannons see any tears. Chuck wouldn't get that victory.

Donna slipped an arm around Bobbi's shoulder. "Honey, I don't know about Chuck, but I will tell you that you don't have to worry about our feelings. We love you and we understand." Bobbi pushed away. She didn't want pity. She wanted someone to tell her she should be furious, that she should want to kick something or throw something, that not even God Himself expected her to absorb this.

Phil knelt between the coffee table and the sofa and held out his hands. "Can we pray with you?" Bobbi reached her hands out as Rita and Donna moved to join hands as well. Phil let out a long, slow breath before beginning.

"Father, You are good, and You know all things. Help us see Your hand at work, and follow Your leading. We know it's never Your will for families and marriages to be destroyed, but we also know that they're some of the enemy's favorite targets.

"Dear God, we need Your wisdom, Your grace. Help Bobbi in her pain, in her uncertainty. Give her rest tonight and in the coming days, and a clear focus on her boys and her job. Help all of us hold her up and show her Your love and comfort. Protect her from unkind words and accusations and help her to feel Your presence with her. Amen."

When Bobbi raised her head, she was startled to meet Phil's eyes. "Did you pray?" She nodded, thankful he didn't ask for details. "Do you know where Chuck is now?"

"No, he left a while ago."

"I'm going to call him after we leave here."

"I know."

"Do you want me to give him any messages?"

"None I'd care to repeat," Bobbi said, as Phil stepped back out of the way.

As Donna reached to hug Bobbi, she said, "This will work out. It will be hard and it will hurt, but Bobbi, if anyone can weather this storm, it's you and Chuck."

"Donna, I don't have your confidence."

"We're going to get out of here," Phil said. "Try to get some rest." He and Donna hugged Rita and Bobbi once more. "Call us if you need anything," Phil offered, and then they slipped out the door.

As Rita turned the deadbolt behind them, Bobbi asked, "Want some coffee?"

Warm temperatures with a light breeze made it a perfect summer night. Occasionally, the scent of freshly mowed grass would drift in through the open sunroof of Chuck's car. Stars twinkled in the clear sky, and Bobbi could tell Chuck was up to something. He knocked over a glass of water at dinner, and she'd never heard him stutter before.

He reached over and took her hand as he turned onto the road out to Dixson Lake. She was relieved when he suggested the drive. Her father would be passed out, so she had nothing to go home to. Chuck listened to her, made time for her, enjoyed being with her. She loved the easy way they got along. Tonight, he even wore a tie. Nobody ever wore a tie on a date with her. Every time she thought about him leaving, though, she got queasy.

"We should move somewhere where you can wear sundresses like that all the time." Chuck kissed the back of her hand. "I never knew a woman's shoulders could be so beautiful."

"You should have a very fine career as a smooth talker." She shook her head at him. He said 'we'. 'We should move.' "I'll move anywhere you want to."

"How 'bout Evanston?"

"Evanston? I thought you were going to Chicago."

"Yeah, Northwestern's in Evanston."

"What's the deal with that? Missouri's got a law school."

"My dad went to Northwestern. He set up some fund for me to go there right after I was born."

"And what if you hadn't chosen law school?"

"Now, that's crazy talk." He grinned at her and his blue eyes twinkled. "So, are you coming with me?"

"You paying for my college?"

"I'll figure out something."

"Your mom and dad don't like me, anyway. That would cinch it."

"They love you."

"If you say so. My dad needs somebody, though. I probably should stick close."

"I had to give it a shot. At least try and convince you." He whipped his car into Dixson Lake State Park and navigated around to the boat ramp. "Wanna look at the stars?"

"It'd be a shame not to."

He parked the car and got out, but he stopped and opened the trunk before he came around to her door. He was definitely up to something. A moment later her door clicked open, and he offered her his hand. He carried a blanket draped across his other arm.

"I figured it would be more comfortable sitting on the grass and I'd hate for you to get your dress dirty."

"What a gentleman." And she meant it. He was. They wandered over to a spot of grass beside the asphalt ramp. He spread the blanket out and steadied her as she eased down, then he dropped in beside her. He nuzzled her neck, kissing her just behind her ear. "Okay, that's too much." She leaned forward.

"Tickles?"

"Yes!"

"I'll quit. That'll spoil the mood."

"What mood is that?"

"This one." He brought his leg around so he could sit up and face her. "Bobbi, this has been the most incredible summer of my life. I've never known *anybody like you, and I am hopelessly, eternally in love with you."*

He took both of her hands and electricity shot through her. Could he be ready to . . .? No . . . It was way too soon for that, although she'd imagined marrying him since that first day.

"I don't want you to ever question how much I love you." He leaned back and pushed a hand into the front pocket of his Dockers, and her heart flipped. When she saw the ring box, she thought she might faint. He smiled and pulled a diamond solitaire out of the box, and held it up. "Bobbi . . ." He had tears in his eyes, and she couldn't stop her own eyes from brimming. "Bobbi, would you marry me?"

"Yes . . . Yes! YES!" She threw her arms around his neck and kissed him. "Yes!" She held her hand up so he could slip the ring on. It fit perfectly. Of course. Mrs. Chuck Molinsky. She was going to be Mrs. Chuck Molinsky.

*"**Then we went** out to the lake." Bobbi watched her sister's eyes, but Rita's expression never changed. "And it was absolutely perfect. The stars were out and there was a breeze . . . So anyway, he says, 'I'm hopelessly eternally in love with you and I don't want you to ever question that.' And he pulls out this ring box. I thought I'd die right there."*

"What did Daddy say?" Rita tipped her hand. She didn't approve, and now she was looking for ammunition to make her case.

"He said he's a good boy, and if I was happy, that's what mattered."

"And he was sober when he said that?"

"I caught him before work this morning."

Rita chewed her bottom lip. "This . . . this is really fast. You've only known him a couple of months, and you're just barely eighteen."

That one she could answer. "First of all, we're not getting married until we get through school. And second, you were seventeen when you got married! Not just engaged, married." No sense dragging this out. May as well jump right in. "Why don't you like him?"

"He's a spoiled brat. I've seen the labels on his pants. We could buy two

weeks' worth of groceries for each pair."

"His parents quit giving him money once he started this summer job. He pays all his own living expenses."

"Doesn't matter. He still has that mindset."

"Being poor doesn't make you a better person. There are as many poor jerks as rich ones."

"Bobbi, here's the thing. I know him. He's a playboy. He'll say anything to get what he wants from a girl, then . . ."

"Was."

"Was what?"

"Was a playboy. He's a believer, now. He hasn't even had a date since he became a Christian. Well, until me."

"He told you this?"

"Yeah, he's been very open about things."

"Did he also mention he asked Lisa Mellon to marry him, then dumped her after she slept with him?"

"That's not what happened. He never . . ."

"Bobbi, that's his story. Andrea and I are best friends. I think she'd know what happened with her little sister."

"It doesn't matter, now. He's different."

Before he started his car, Phil called Chuck. "Do you think he'll talk to you?" Donna asked.

"I'll find out." Chuck answered on the second ring, and Phil smiled at his wife. "Chuck, this is Phil Shannon. Can I come and see you?"

"That'd be great. Thanks. Lobby of the Embassy. I left a message on your machine. I hoped—"

"I'll be there in twenty minutes."

Phil dropped Donna off at home before heading to the Embassy Hotel. "I'll be praying," she promised as she slid out of the car.

"I'll need it." Phil pulled in a parking spot right on schedule. He turned the car off and prayed as he walked across the lot. *Father, I need You again. Help me give Chuck wise counsel. Please let him have a listening heart. Give him the courage and resolve to do what he needs to do now. In Jesus' name.*

The Embassy strived to emulate the luxury hotels downtown. Glistening marble floors, rich wood, and shiny brass fixtures trimmed out the expansive lobby. The big screen television broadcast CNN to the sofas, chairs, and plants. On a Thursday night, everyone had a better place to be. Everyone but Chuck Molinsky. Phil spotted him, in his Brooks Brothers suit and tie, trying his best to appear successful and in command.

Chuck stood well before Phil made it across the lobby, but he never raised his eyes. Phil stopped an arm's length away and extended his hand. Chuck hesitated, but as soon as he made a move to shake hands, Phil pulled him into a hug. "How are you, Chuck?"

"You've talked to Bobbi?" Chuck took a seat, and Phil followed his lead.

"I just came from there."

"Then you know what I'm up against. How do I keep her from leaving me?"

He watched Chuck perched on the edge of his seat, ready to hear a failsafe strategy, some quick, three-step plan to restoration. Phil intended to shatter that idea. "Do you want to leave Bobbi?"

"What? Leave? Does she think I want—?"

Phil's raised hand to cut him off. "Do you want to restore your marriage?"

"Of course, Phil, I—"

"Will you listen to me and do what I advise you to do?" Phil softened his tone. "Or at least consider my advice?"

"How was Bobbi?" Chuck asked. "Do I have any hope?"

"You've got a hard road ahead. She's hurt . . . bewildered . . . angry." Phil leaned back in the chair. "But, I don't think it's hopeless by any means. Although Biblically speaking, Bobbi may be within her rights to divorce you, she didn't say she wanted a divorce outright."

"Thank God."

"Speaking of God, have you approached God about this?"

"Kind of."

"That's your first priority. Until you confess this adultery to God, and repent and get His forgiveness, you're not going to get anywhere." He leaned forward again. "Let me back up a step." He fixed his eyes on Chuck's. "Do you genuinely believe in Jesus Christ?"

"Of course. Just because . . . That doesn't mean . . . Why?"

"It's different when an unbelieving man cheats on his wife. The approach to restoration is different. Plus, a believer has additional accountabilities." As he spoke, Phil began to count on his fingers. "To the Lord first, but also to his church."

"What are you talking about?"

"I mean as a believer, you answer to the church as well. Your sin was public, or soon will be, so you've got to make it right . . . publicly." Phil let that statement hang. Chuck's eyes widened as it sunk in.

"You want me to go in front of the church? I'll get eaten alive! I can just see me up there trying to stammer through a confession with a hundred freelance judges scowling at me. With all due respect, Phil, that's beyond crazy."

"You might be surprised." Phil leaned all the way back in the over-stuffed chair, sliding his hands behind his head.

"I might not."

"You asked me how to keep your wife from leaving you." Phil dropped his hands down to the armrests. "That's where you start. You confess it, renounce it, and get your church family behind you."

"What about Bobbi? This is between us. Shouldn't I be dealing with her?"

"You can't demand grace, Chuck. You have to wait until she offers it."

"How do I get her to do that?"

"You're not listening to me. You can't." Phil leaned forward and looked Chuck in the eye. "In this short time, I've noticed something very significant. In fact, it's going to be the key to what happens next." He had Chuck's undivided attention now. "You don't love your wife."

Chuck jerked himself to his feet. "Of course I do! Where do you get off—?"

"Then why didn't you tell Bobbi you loved her when you got home?"

"She wouldn't let me! She unloaded on me as soon as I walked in!"

"Since I got here, the focus of your conversation has been on yourself, and you never mentioned to me that you loved her."

Chuck dropped back in the chair. "That's not fair. All I can think about is making sure I still have a wife."

"And you won't, unless you give up this self-centered imitation love, and learn how to love her sacrificially. We can't restore the marriage you had. We have to rebuild it from scratch." Chuck nodded. Maybe he did understand. "You have to rebuild your credibility with her. In three weeks."

"Three weeks?" Chuck jumped up and paced away from Phil. "I have to make her trust me in three weeks?"

"No, but you have to show her that you're making progress toward change, or she's not going to invest herself emotionally in counseling. She *will* divorce you."

"I guess you're going to tell me how to do that." Chuck shoved his hands deep in the pockets of his slacks.

"There's nothing mysterious about it. In a nutshell, you have to get past the guilt and shame and learn to live in Christ's grace, and you have to make yourself worthy of Bobbi's trust. That's where the confession comes in. Also, you have to accept that there are some things in your marriage, in your life even, that will never be the same."

"I know."

"Let me throw out some things you may not have thought of yet. You can't be alone with a woman again, ever. No meetings, no taxis, no elevators."

"That's going overboard, isn't it?"

"No such thing, anymore. I'd recommend you not work late at your office, but bring it home." Chuck didn't protest. "You can't give Bobbi the slightest reason to doubt you ever again. Your integrity has got to be beyond reproach."

"Yeah," Chuck whispered, easing back into his seat.

"This other woman, is she a Christian?"

"I doubt it."

"You need to apologize to her for how you've treated her, and then break off all contact with her. I imagine she's not going to be very forgiving."

"That's putting it mildly. She found out I was married about the same time Bobbi found out about her."

"How could a woman you worked with not know you were married?"

"It never came up."

"What about your wedding ring?" Phil asked, pointing to the finger where the ring should have been.

"Oh, it's not what you're thinking," Chuck said, holding his hand up for Phil to see. "About four years ago, Gavin wanted to take his son-in-law, John, you know, Kara's husband, and Danny deer hunting, and he asked me and Brad to go. I fell out of a tree and broke my wrist and these two fingers on my left hand," he said, indicating his little finger and ring finger. "See, they're kind of crooked." Phil nodded. "I just never got my wedding band resized." Then his voice grew quiet. "I never made it that much of a priority."

"Don't you have any pictures of Bobbi at work?"

"Yes, right on my desk!"

"I'm getting off the subject," Phil said. "We don't need to get into all this tonight. Bottom line, Chuck, is you're going to have to let Bobbi set the pace here. Don't force her toward reconciliation before she's ready. It may take a long time, but she deserves to do this on her terms. Answer every question she asks, but don't volunteer things yet."

"Isn't that deceitful?"

"No, it's giving her time to absorb things. While Donna and I help her work through things, you and I will focus on how this happened in the first place. Then, we'll get to counseling you together about where the two of you go from here. Well, the four of you. The boys will have to be a part of the healing."

"I haven't talked to the boys yet." Chuck mumbled.

"Brace yourself. It'll be almost as difficult as facing your wife. For the next couple of weeks, you may feel like that's all you get done, admitting your adultery."

"How many people do I have to tell? If I confess it at church, won't that take care of it?"

"You have coworkers. You're going to have to be straight with them. There's your mother. Then there's going to be gossip, embarrassment, and even when you and Bobbi reconcile, this is a specter that won't go away. Ever."

Chuck nodded, and Phil hoped his words registered. "Years from now, it may rear its ugly head, and you'll feel like you have to prove yourself all over again."

"I will do anything it takes to make this right." Tears began to fill his eyes. "I really do love Bobbi."

If Chuck was lying now, he was making a good show of it. Phil put his hand on Chuck's shoulder and bowed his head. "Father, You see Your son here. You know his heart and You know what he has to face. Honor his sincerity and help him to honor You in his life. Restore his marriage and the trust between him and Bobbi. Help us come alongside him during this time." Before Phil could say amen, Chuck began to pray.

"God in heaven, I'm not worthy to call You, Father. I have sinned . . . I broke my marriage vows . . . I've dishonored You . . . and my wife . . . my family and my church. God, I am so sorry. God, I need Your forgiveness again. Dear Jesus . . ." Chuck dissolved into sobs.

Phil squeezed Chuck's shoulder and picked up the prayer. "Thank

You, Jesus. Bless Chuck and help him to know You've heard his prayer. Let him feel Your love and forgiveness. In Jesus' name, amen." When Phil opened his eyes, he saw Chuck with his head bowed, tears spotting his designer slacks. *Dear God, he is sincere. Thank You.*

When Phil stood to leave, Chuck hugged him with a backslap that echoed through the empty lobby, causing the desk clerk to look up. He let go a deep sigh, and said, "Thanks, Phil."

Phil smiled. "Ninety percent is showing up." He took a step toward the lobby door to leave. "You golf?"

"It's almost a job requirement. I keep my clubs in the car."

"Let's go tomorrow, say, one o'clock. I'll call Gavin, and we can talk more then."

"At Billings or Milford Glen?"

"Billings. I can't afford to lose that many golf balls." Phil shook Chuck's hand. "Think about what I said, and try to get some sleep."

Silence hung over the kitchen as Bobbi made the coffee. Could Phil Shannon really get Chuck to change in three weeks? No. No one could pull that off. Chuck was a good guy, but he was the center of his own universe. She loved Chuck—she did this morning, anyway, but she wouldn't beg him to stay.

When the coffeemaker kicked off, she turned to Rita. "So, should I divorce him?"

"Maybe . . . probably . . . I don't know." Rita sighed. "See if he's willing to be straight with you and tell you everything."

"Everything?"

"If you're ever going to trust him again . . ."

"What if I don't want to know everything?" Bobbi set a coffee cup in front of Rita, and sat across the table from her.

"It'll be worse if you're left to fill in the details yourself." Rita stirred sweetener into her black coffee.

Worse? How could it possibly be any worse? "Here, see if you can figure this out. That e-mail was sent Monday. Why is it just now showing up in our inbox on Thursday?"

"That's strange." Rita took a long, slow sip from her coffee. "Do you check your e-mail every day?"

"Every morning."

"What about Chuck? When does he check it?"

"Who knows. He gets tons of mail from work through that account when he travels."

"Have you gone through it?"

"No. I would never . . ." Maybe she should. Maybe Tracy had e-mailed before.

Rita thought for a moment. "I think God did it."

"Did what?"

"The e-mail. I think God wanted you to find out, so He held that e-mail up until you were the one checking."

"He had to do something, because I was too stupid to figure it out for myself."

"Bobbi, you're a very trusting person, and trusting people aren't suspicious."

"I never had reason not to trust Chuck. Good grief, all the traveling he does, the late nights he works . . . he's had plenty of opportunities."

"Don't. Don't unleash your imagination. That's the last thing you need. Besides, he can't keep your Christmas presents a secret. How on earth could he hide a long-running affair or a series of affairs from you?"

"Maybe you're right." She twisted her cup on the table in front of her. "You know what today is?"

"The twenty-eighth? What?"

"The day Chuck asked me to marry him. Twenty-one years ago today. Now we're on the brink of divorce." Bobbi looked up at the ceiling to keep the brimming tears from spilling onto her cheeks. "The last thing he said to me was that coming home was a mistake. Rita, if he divorces me, I can't maintain this house and everything on a teacher's salary."

"If he divorces you? Listen, if that jerk—"

"The jerk is still my husband."

"If he has the nerve to file for divorce after what he did," Rita said, tapping the table for emphasis, "you take him for everything he's worth, and you do it with a clear conscience."

"That doesn't sound very Christ-like."

"This is about protecting yourself and the boys."

"The boys. How am I supposed to explain this to Brad and Joel?"

"Make him do it."

"I can't wait for that. I need to tell them tomorrow." She took a long drink from her coffee. "They look up to their dad so much. I hate . . . I hate to destroy that."

"Chuck destroyed it."

As they sat in silence, Bobbi mulled over everything Phil and Donna had said, along with Rita's advice. Forgive and reconcile, or divorce. She couldn't decide without hearing from Chuck himself. "Saturday," Bobbi blurted out.

"Saturday, what?"

"I want to talk to Chuck on Saturday. Alone. Here."

CHAPTER 3
FALLOUT

Friday, July 29

Chuck gave up trying to sleep and dragged himself out of bed before his alarm buzzed. 'Think about what I said,' Phil told him, as if he could think about anything else. Phil was wrong. He loved his wife. Just because he didn't say it yesterday, or Monday before he left, or . . .

People can't be married for eighteen years and not love each other. He loved his wife, and he would prove it to her and everybody else. Everyone was overreacting, blowing things way out of proportion. It wasn't like he was unfaithful to his wife, he just had sex with . . .

Chuck, you idiot, that's what unfaithful means. Phil's right.

But he didn't love Tracy. He didn't want to be with her. Didn't that count for anything?

He took a long, hot shower, but he didn't feel any cleaner afterwards. He wiped the condensation from the bathroom mirror so he could shave, but seeing his reflection, he wished he could re-fog the mirror. He, Chuck Molinsky, cheated on his wife. He hadn't imagined it. He hadn't dreamed it. He'd done it. What did that say about him as a man? If he would sink to committing adultery, what else was he capable of?

He had a meeting with Walter Davis, senior managing partner of the firm, at eight o'clock to discuss ServMed. Yesterday, he couldn't wait for this meeting. He visualized Walter saying, 'You are the key member of my team here at BD&M. No one else could have handled ServMed.' That tone would be a little different now.

As he tied his necktie, watching himself in the mirror, he rehearsed the rest of the conversation. He planned to ask for a leave of absence. He had no choice. Bobbi would be watching to see if he would take Phil's advice.

If Walter wouldn't agree to it, he would threaten to resign.

Granted, he was gambling, but if he overplayed, Walter would take a step or two back. The old man would think he was being gracious, and Chuck would end up with what he wanted. Everybody won. Then Bobbi had to believe he was serious about making things right.

Bobbi showered and dressed, thankful for the comfort of her morning ritual. In the early hours of the morning, she protested when Rita suggested she come up to bed to get some sleep. It wasn't that simple. It wasn't just her bed. She shared that bed with Chuck. His affair swept aside every memory of late nights, early mornings, lazy Saturdays, private jokes, intimate conversations. The very bed itself was defiled.

Before she started with the moisturizer, she stopped to study her face in the mirror. What changed? What was so undesirable that Chuck would look for someone else?

Granted, gray hairs stood out against the black ones, but her shorter, trendy haircut took a few years off. The wrinkles around her eyes betrayed more than a poor night's sleep. She carried the extra pounds of a two-time mother. Chuck bought his midlife crisis car. Was he ready to move on to a trophy wife as well?

Dear God, what is going on with Chuck? Has he changed, or have I been blind all these years? How do we even begin to work through this?

Opening her eyes from her prayer, Bobbi reached for the bottle of moisturizer, but there beside it, her engagement ring and wedding band lay in a small crystal dish. Sometimes during the summer, the rings were tight, so she wouldn't wear them. Yesterday, after her morning shower, when the rings didn't slide on, she left them in the dish.

Should she leave them in the dish until she resolved things with Chuck? "I am still married," Bobbi said, pushing both rings on. She vowed not to take them off again unless Chuck divorced her.

Walter Davis welcomed Chuck into his office with a hearty handshake. "So, I understand things went well." Walter outlived the firm's other, much younger, founding partners, Jim Benton and Jim Molinsky, and attributed his longevity to bourbon and cigars.

Walter's suits were black, his ties striped, and his cuffs French. He was sour, difficult, and humorless. Several of the firm's attorneys remarked that after interviewing with Walter, facing a judge was a piece of cake.

"Very smooth," Chuck said. "We got everything squared away quickly. I think both sides were closer than they realized." He slid into one of Walter's office chairs, the very same chairs Walter had when Chuck visited his dad's office as a little boy.

"Very good. Your hard work paid off. Let's see, Gina assisted on that one, correct?"

"She handled everything on this end while I was in Kansas City."

"I'm glad to see you finally found someone who measured up," Walter said, with just a hint of sarcasm. "After Eva and Jeanette refused to work with you again, my list was getting short."

Walter leaned forward and folded his hands. "We had a personnel situation while you were gone. Tracy Ravenna gave notice in an e-mail and took her vacation."

"She resigned?" *Why would she . . .? Because of their . . . whatever it was?* "When?"

"Yesterday. Her office is empty and I found her files outside my door yesterday morning. Did she have any personal issues you know about?"

There was the rope. Walter sat, watching, waiting for him to hang himself. Chuck shifted in his chair. *Say it. You have to tell him.* "Tracy and I had . . . we had an affair, Walter. It blew up in the last couple of days." An uncomfortable silence squeezed him. He was dead.

Walter tipped his chair back, but his eyes stayed fixed on Chuck. "Your personal life is your business, but . . ."

The tension in the office intensified, so Chuck went on the offensive. "Since you brought it up, I need some time to try and put my life and my marriage back in order." Walter's expression didn't change. Chuck tried not to stammer, annoyed that he let Walter intimidate him. "If you can give Blackburn to Pete and Will, and Ryder to Gina, I can handle the rest of my load."

"What about Burke county, though? You and Tracy were handling that one."

"You have her files. I can finish it up."

Again, unnerving silence settled over the office and Walter glared at him a moment too long. "I don't care what society says these days, this kind of behavior is despicable." Chuck bristled at the lecture. "Your father was such an honorable man, a man of integrity, a good man. How could you do this to your wife?" As the indignation in the old man's voice grew shriller, Chuck could feel the heat rising on the back of his neck.

"I can't justify this." Chuck matched Walter's tone and volume. "I'm not trying to, and I'm not trying to get your sympathy. If you won't give me the time I need to make this right with Bobbi . . ." Chuck hesitated, then lowered his voice, negotiating the way Walter taught him. "Then I'll get my resignation letter together."

When Walter didn't respond, Chuck feared he'd miscalculated, and his resignation was exactly what Walter wanted.

"Tuesday after Labor Day," Walter said, running his finger down his calendar. "I want to see you in here, with some progress on the home front to report." He leaned back in his chair, scowling. "Now, are we facing any liability in this situation?"

"Liability?"

"Is Tracy Ravenna going to sue you, or us, for harassment or anything like that?"

"I don't think so."

"You'd better make sure." He made several notes in his appointment book. "Get this straight. I don't care if it takes your last dime to keep her quiet. I will not have this firm's name, my name, dragged through the muck because of this. Do we understand each other?"

"Completely," Chuck said as he stood to leave.

"I can't tell you how disappointed I am." Walter glared over the top of his glasses at him. "I cannot tolerate men of low character. If it weren't for your father, you'd be at the unemployment office right now. Is that clear?"

"Yes, sir." Chuck nodded.

Without taking his eyes off Chuck, Walter punched a button on his intercom. "Christine, is Gina Novak here?"

"Yes, sir."

"Have her meet with me in fifteen minutes." He leaned back in his chair again. "Chuck, I'm giving Gina Homebuilders and Missouri Securities to Cary Morgan."

"But I brought those clients in. They're mine."

"I'm also making Pete Weinberg a partner."

"Are you replacing me, Walter?"

"I have to have men and women I can trust in the leadership positions in my firm."

"Did you look at the numbers for ServMed?" Chuck jabbed a finger at the sheet lying on the desk in front of Walter. "That's more than Gina, Pete, and Cary have brought in put together. I have never been anything but a consummate professional. You can't penalize me for what's going on in my personal life."

"I can't risk your next lapse in judgment coming with one of our clients."

"You think I'm going to hit on a client? That's outrageous!"

"The second line is always easier to cross. Now, if you'll excuse me, I have another meeting."

Chuck couldn't get out of the building quickly enough. How could Walter . . . how could he even think something so ridiculous? *Can we just stick with the real sin, and not some intangible, worst-case scenario?*

The real sin. With his leave of absence following on the heels of

Tracy's resignation, the wags would soon put two and two together. Maybe they would forget in the five weeks he was out of the office. Right now, though, it was eight fifteen, and he had nowhere to go.

"This was a great idea, coming to the lake, Mrs. Molinsky. We've both been working way too hard." Chuck dumped the charcoal in the grill, and carefully touched a match to the corner. "I don't feel like we've had a decent conversation in months."

"Yeah. Graduate school's nuts. Project after project." Bobbi wore his old, faded Missouri sweatshirt. Just one more thing that looked great on her. "Can you believe how warm it is? It's almost November."

"And Missouri's playing Oklahoma State today. Just so you know what you're worth to me."

"You're taping the game, though, aren't you?" She crossed her arms and raised an eyebrow.

"All right, yes, I'm taping the game, but I'm here."

"As long as your brain's here, too."

He took her hand and they walked down to the lake while the charcoal heated. "I know I've been . . ."

"A jerk."

"That bad?"

"Yes. Your fuse is about this long." She held her thumb and forefinger an inch apart. "Chuck, nobody expects you to make partner the first year after you pass the bar exam."

"I know. It's just . . . I want to make it on my own. I don't want people to think I just got my spot because of my dad."

"But you're a very good attorney, very conscientious, thorough."

"Thanks." He knew she was trying to help, but she couldn't begin to comprehend what his days were like. He sat down on the ground and steadied her as she nestled in beside him. "So, you picked out any school systems yet?"

"Good grief, no. They won't know what openings they have until spring anyway."

"But you'll have your master's. You'll be all set."

"I'll have no experience, though. That could hurt me. They'd have to pay me more."

"Good. You should be paid more."

She leaned her head over on his shoulder and sighed. "You know, we've never had a break."

"What do you mean?"

"From the stress. School, the wedding, more school for me, law firm for you."

"Honey, that's the way life is."

"I just . . . I don't know . . . I don't want to lose 'us', you know?"

"Never happen." He squeezed her close and they sat for a long time, not saying anything. No one ever needed him, needed to connect, the way she did. Maybe that came from losing her mom so early. She craved security, and he was doing his best to provide that. That's what the long hours, the lunches, the dinners, the golf games were for. Building their future.

He leaned over and kissed her neck, inhaling deeply. The vanilla scent of her shampoo fit her. He kissed her again, and again, following her jaw line around to her lips, when she pushed away. "What's wrong?"

"My stomach's upset."

"Since when?"

"I don't know, all day."

"You never said anything before now. Maybe you're just hungry. Did you have breakfast?"

"No."

"There you go. Let's go check the grill."

"Chuck, I don't . . ."

He pulled her to her feet and walked her back to the grill. The coals were white hot. "I'll have the steaks ready in no time." He opened the cooler, and threw two T-bones on. They sizzled as flames licked around them. "I love that smell, don't you?"

Bobbi was backing up toward the car.

"Where are you going?"

"I can't . . . the smell . . . it's making me nauseous."

"You're kidding."

"No . . ."

Before he knew it, she rounded the bumper, and threw up in the weeds. "Bobbi!" He stood by, not sure if he should help, or what exactly he could do. "Why didn't you tell me you were sick? I thought when you wanted to come out here . . ."

"I did," she said weakly, then heaved one last time. "I'm fine. Really." She pulled a tissue from the pocket of her jeans, and wiped her mouth. "It's . . . it's nothing."

"It's not nothing. I need to get you home. As soon as the steaks finish, we'll get out of here."

"No, I don't want to go. It's over now. It's got to be over now."

"What's over?"

"The morning sickness. Sometimes it lasts all day."

He spun around in front of her and took her shoulders. "What? What did you say?" A grin spread across his face and tears welled up in his eyes. "Morning sickness? Are you . . .? Are we . . .?"

She nodded, tears streaming down her face. "May, I think. Possibly June."

"That's . . . that's fantastic!" He hugged her, kissed her, hugged her again. "A baby . . . I'm gonna be a daddy . . ." He laughed out loud, but saw she was still crying. "Honey, what's wrong?"

"I wanted it to be . . . I didn't want to tell you like this. I wanted it to be special."

"It is! Bobbi, this is . . . this is . . . Wow! I can't wait to tell Mom and Dad!" He hugged her again. "I love you. I'll be a good dad. I promise." He put a hand on her belly and spoke to the baby. "You hear that? I promise you, I'll be the best daddy I can be."

Bobbi drove to Rita's house, her eyes glued to the taillights of her sister's car, making the turns without ever engaging her brain. She felt like the executioner, preparing to put innocence and idealism to death. She had to admit to her sons that she and their father were frauds, keeping up appearances while their marriage languished. Now that marriage was dying, it was going to take the boys' security and stability with it.

The parenting books never dealt with this one. No sermons, no small group studies, no daily devotionals could walk her through it. She'd have to wing it. *You can't fall apart in front of them. Be strong, and they'll be strong. Simple, straightforward, honest . . . You can do this. You have to do this. They have to hear it from you . . . and not Chuck.*

Rita's husband, Gavin, opened the front door before Bobbi got out of her car. She checked herself in the rearview mirror, took a deep breath, and strode up to the porch with as much calm control as she could fake.

Gavin, God bless him, didn't have any sad pity in his eyes. He reached out and hugged her the way he always did, but he whispered, "Don't choke him yet." She had to smile.

"Not until tomorrow at the earliest."

"I'll get the guys," he said.

"What did Gavin say to you?" Rita asked, following Bobbi into the house.

"Not to choke Chuck yet."

"Yet. Remember that part."

Gavin came back with two bleary-eyed boys. "Staying up too late, I see," Bobbi said, brightening a little.

"Won't have that option once practice starts," Brad said, then he yawned.

"Guys, we need to talk." Bobbi directed her sons to the living room, as Rita and Gavin faded back into kitchen.

"It's about Dad, isn't it?" Brad asked, slumping onto the sofa. "I knew it when I heard you on the phone. I knew something was up."

"Yeah." *He couldn't know. If I didn't know, Brad couldn't.* She pulled the ottoman close, taking a seat on it as Joel slid in beside his brother.

"This is just like when you told us about Grandpa Jim," Brad said. "Has Dad got cancer or something?"

"No, if you'll let me talk . . ." she said in mock aggravation. Bobbi swallowed hard and looked into Brad's eyes and then Joel's, lingering over that last moment of 'before.' "Yesterday . . . your dad . . . I mean, I found out . . . your dad has had an affair."

"What!" Brad jumped to his feet. "With who?"

"Sit down!" Bobbi said, with a sharpness she never intended. "That's irrelevant." She laid a hand on Joel's knee. "Honey, do you understand what I'm saying?"

"Yes, Mom."

"Of course you do," Bobbi whispered. "You're not a baby anymore, are you?" She patted his knee, giving him a half smile. Joel inherited his dad's unruly, dark blond hair, his square jaw, and his blue eyes that sparkled with just a hint of mischief.

"Where is Dad?" Joel asked.

"I guess he's at work. We were both too upset to talk last night when he got home, so he spent the night somewhere else."

"Alone?" Brad asked through clenched teeth.

"Brad, stop it!" Bobbi took a deep breath to calm down. *Control. Don't take it out on the boys. This is between Chuck and me.*

"Why didn't he have the guts to tell us himself?" Brad pulled at a loose string on his shorts. "Why did he make you do it? The jerk." The pout was already settling over him.

"All right, that's enough." She lost control of the discussion and she risked losing control of her own emotions. *Pick up the thread again. Be a parent.* "I don't have any answers right now." She sighed and tried her best to relax her fists and her jaw. "Uncle Gavin is going to tell Dad that I want to talk to him tomorrow afternoon. I'm sure he'll be anxious to talk."

"I've got nothing to say to him," Brad grumbled.

"I know how hard this was to hear. I know you're hurt and angry, and I'm so sorry." Did Chuck ever consider this moment, his sons wrestling with the reality that he cheated on their mother? Did this ever cross his mind when he chose another woman?

"Guys, I'll be real honest with you. I don't know what's going to happen. I don't know if your dad wants to leave us, and I don't know if I want him to, but it's going to be tough to pull us all back together—"

"Mom! What is there to pull back together? How can you even consider—?"

"Brad, please . . . I've spent the last day crying and puking my guts out." Tears began to form. "Right now, I'd like to take my sons out for breakfast, because I could really use the company." Bobbi tried to smile through the tears. She felt a hand sweep across her back, and then a gentle pat as Joel reached over and hugged her.

When Joel let go, she glanced at Brad, but he twisted around her and out of the living room. "Go get your gear," she said to Joel. The boys returned moments later. "We can talk about this any time you need to. Don't keep things all bottled up, okay?" Joel nodded. Bobbi waited until Brad made eye contact. "Okay?" she prompted. He nodded and then looked away.

She was failing again. She had failed as a wife and now she was failing as a mother. "Head on out to the car. I'll be right there." Bobbi walked back into the kitchen to let Rita know they were leaving.

"We're going to get out of here. Thanks for everything."

"I wish I could do more." Rita hugged her again. "How did it go?"

"I've got a volcano and an iceberg."

"You sound more upset for telling the boys than Chuck is for committing adultery in the first place."

"Chuck is upset."

"Then where is he? Why wasn't he on your doorstep this morning begging you for forgiveness?"

"Probably because Phil told him to back off and give me some space," Bobbi shot back. "Listen, I can't fight him and you and Brad."

"I'm not trying to fight you, Baby. Don't cut him any slack, all right?"

"I'm not." Bobbi headed toward the front door with Rita following. "I'm sure we'll need you again before this is all resolved." Bobbi opened the front door and stepped out onto the porch.

"Gavin and I will be here."

"How's the Pancake Place sound?" Bobbi called to Brad and Joel as they got into the car. For once, Joel didn't challenge Brad for the front seat.

CHAPTER 4

COMPANY

Brad passed the ride in sullen silence, his bottom lip curling. He slouched into a booth at Pancake Place, but instead of picking up a menu, he took a packet of sweetener and flipped it back and forth on the table in front of him.

"Brad, what are you thinking?" Bobbi asked.

He pressed his lips together and shook his head.

"I wish you wouldn't hold it in. You're not gonna shock me, no matter how angry you are."

"Not now."

"Later?"

"Mom . . . just . . . drop it, okay?" He spun the sweetener packet between his thumb and forefinger, without ever looking up.

She couldn't let him brood like this, but across the table, Joel squirmed, bursting to talk. She smiled at him. "You know what you're gonna get?"

"Strawberry waffles!" Joel's shoulders relaxed and he grinned. "And bacon, and can I get hash browns?"

"Sure," Bobbi said. "Brad?"

"I'm not hungry," he mumbled.

"Brad," Bobbi said. When he didn't answer, she spoke his name again with a parental edge. "I don't feel like eating either." The strong aromas of bacon and sausage triggered a fresh round of nausea.

"Mom, is Dad moving out?" Joel asked. Brad shot him a 'don't ask stupid questions look,' which he ignored.

"I think that would be best for a little while," Bobbi said. "When the waitress comes, order strawberry waffles for me, too." She slid out of the booth and excused herself to the ladies' room.

Bobbi washed her hands in cold water, splashing a little on her face. *God, how do I parent them? How do I get Brad to open up? How do I make Joel understand I can't answer his questions?*

After her mother died, Bobbi craved stability and security. Maybe Brad and Joel needed those same things, the stability of a routine and the security of the familiar. *Focus on those.* She dried her hands, fluffed her bangs, and went out to rejoin her sons. Before she reached the booth, she overheard Brad arguing with his brother.

"Don't you get it? It's over! They're splitting up."

"Mom didn't say that." Joel spoke with a calm and matter-of-fact tone. She wished he could bottle some of that up for her.

"This is not some stupid movie where everybody lives happily ever after. Dad chose somebody else. He's a liar, and I don't care if I ever see him again."

"I think you're wrong. And I can see you crying."

Dear God, Joel is so naïve and simplistic. What's going to happen to him if he's wrong? Bobbi eased into the booth, careful not to look in Brad's direction. She didn't want to embarrass him or tip him off that she'd heard the argument.

"I ordered for you," Joel said, then nodded toward his brother. "He ordered, too." Brad stared across the restaurant at nothing in particular.

Bobbi took a long drink from the coffee in front of her. Since Brad vented to Joel, maybe she could pull a little more out of him. "We may be in for some changes, guys, but no matter what happens, we'll be okay. We love each other, and we'll get through."

"Dad doesn't love us," Brad said, without anger, just indifference.

"He does. He loves you guys more than anything."

Brad looked her in the eye for the first time. "How could he love me, and then do this?"

She wondered the same thing. "You're asking for answers I don't have right now." She watched him disengage, folding over every other scallop on his paper placemat, and she gave up. "So, what time does football practice start Monday?"

Still feeling the sting of Walter Davis' insinuations, Chuck caught himself two exits away from driving into Illinois. He pulled off the highway and backtracked through the downtown and toward the suburbs once again.

Tracy found out Wednesday. But she didn't call until Thursday. Wednesday night she could have talked to him, but she knew he had a meeting Thursday morning. She knew she'd get his voice mail. Why'd she wait?

What'd she do in the meantime? Besides clean out her office. Which didn't make any sense either. But had she confronted Bobbi Thursday morning? Was that how this all went down? Some strange woman showing up on the doorstep . . . No wonder Bobbi exploded on him.

Bottom line, he secured some time off. That counted as a win. Bobbi knew what his job meant to him. She had to see that as a sacrifice on his part. She knew that he talked with Phil, too. This afternoon, he planned to get to her through Gavin.

Bobbi trusted Gavin's judgment without reservation. If he could persuade Gavin to see his side, then that would get back to Bobbi, and this whole thing would be over.

Now, how to approach Gavin? He had to be simple and straightforward. Gavin would cut through any pretenses. *I made a mistake.* No, it was a sin. Gavin would be listening for that. *I'll do whatever Bobbi says to make this right. Let her set the pace, Phil said. She needs time. I need to know that she's willing to try to work this out. That's all I'm asking for.*

It sounded fake. What if he just went to the golf course and let the conversation develop naturally? That terrified him. But he did it all the time. When he negotiated, his intuition kicked in, and the discussion never came across scripted.

He still wanted to practice. At the next red light, he popped his cell phone off his belt, and dialed the other woman who hated him, then he held his breath until Tracy's machine picked up.

"Uh, Tracy . . ." *Get a grip. Be a man.* "Tracy, this is Chuck. I got your messages. Everything you said was true. I took advantage of you and that was wrong. I'm sorry you felt that you had to resign from the firm. You're an excellent attorney and I'm sure Walter will give you a favorable recommendation to any other firm you choose." He sounded like a disappointed boss firing her. Proof positive he needed a script. *Say something, Stupid. It's still recording.* "Look Tracy, I . . . uh, I gotta put things back together with my wife. I'm sorry."

Bobbi fumbled with the house key, trying to get the door unlocked before the phone stopped ringing, but the machine kicked on. "You have reached the Molinskys," Chuck's voice said. "You'll never catch us if you don't leave a message." *Gotta change that message.*

"Brad, this is Cooper DeWitt. You wanna go shoot a round? Call me." Bobbi appreciated the invitation from the youth minister for Brad's sake, but Cooper called because he knew. How many other people knew?

"Did you get that?" Bobbi slipped into the downstairs bathroom for an aspirin.

"Not interested," he called, already upstairs. The door to his room banged shut.

"Joel," she called, "do you want to help me laminate?"

"Be right there, Mom," Joel answered.

In the study, school papers fanned out across the floor, just where Bobbi left them Wednesday evening. The familiar and the routine. She picked through the papers, trying to reestablish where she had left off, when the phone rang.

"Bobbi, good morning." Chuck's mother, Ann, called at least every other day since moving to South Carolina after Jim died. "Did Chuck make it home?"

"Yes, he got in last night." *Which is not a lie.*

"Good. He should be home for a while, shouldn't he?"

Lie or drop the bomb? She needed Ann as an ally. She had to tell her. Bobbi took a deep breath and thanked God she couldn't see Ann's face. "Chuck and I are having some problems right now."

"Oh, I'm so sorry. I know Chuck can be difficult. He takes after his dad that way."

"It's more serious than that. He . . . While he was gone on this trip, I found out he was having an affair. I confronted him, and he didn't deny it." After a long, uncomfortable silence, Bobbi continued. "I don't know much more right now. I'm sorry to be the one to tell you."

"Oh, Honey." The energy, the life had drained from her voice. "Who was it?"

"Someone from the law firm. I have her name, that's it. I don't have any idea how long it's been going on . . . if this is the first time—"

"Bobbi, no. I can't imagine. Does he want a divorce?"

"I don't know. Things got too heated last night, so we're taking some time to cool off. I think we'll talk tomorrow."

"So Chuck walked out?"

"Chuck spent the night somewhere else. I'm trying not to read anything else into it."

"What can I do? I feel helpless being so far away."

"Pray for us, Ann, and for Brad and Joel."

"Oh, of course. Those poor boys. They know, I guess."

"I told them this morning. Brad took it much harder." Again, silence. "I don't want to give you the impression things are hopeless. Chuck and I have both met with our pastor individually, and I think Chuck is meeting with him again today. Until he and I can talk, though, I can't say what's going to happen."

"That's wise. I'm sure you're still in shock."

"I'm going to try to work on some things for school today to keep my mind occupied."

"What was he thinking?" Ann asked with whispered disbelief.

"That's the sixty-four thousand dollar question. I wish I knew."

"I won't keep you on the phone." Now Ann's voice wavered. "You are the best thing that ever happened to Chuck. Please don't give up on him."

Give up on him? Bobbi dropped the phone back on its cradle. *He gave up on me.* Did Ann not hear what she said? Chuck had the affair. Chuck walked away from the marriage. But of course, Ann sided with her only son.

Bobbi eased down to the floor, then snatched the nearest stack of papers and slung them across the room. She always gave in and smoothed things over. Not this time. She was right, he was wrong and she wasn't going to give him an inch. She could picture Chuck, this very minute, laying out his points, preparing to maneuver her into a corner emotionally so she'd let it all go. Never again.

Chuck found a parking spot and pulled his golf bag out of the trunk without glancing toward Gavin and Phil. He wiped his sweaty palms on his slacks and then swung the bag up to his shoulder. His marriage, his future, his life hinged on this meeting. He could not screw this up. Joining the others, Chuck shook Phil's hand, but then he broke one of his own first rules of negotiation. He couldn't look Gavin in the eye.

"I'll get us a cart." Phil abandoned him and walked into the clubhouse.

Gavin held out his hand. "This is going to be a long afternoon if you won't face me. I'm your brother, you know."

Chuck shook hands with his brother-in-law. "I, uh, I wasn't sure you'd see it that way."

"I'll be real straight with you." He took a step closer and leveled a finger. "What you did was disgusting."

Chuck flinched. *This isn't a meeting. It's a set-up, a chance for Gavin and Phil to team up against me.*

"You callously hurt people I care deeply for and you trashed vows that I heard you make before God to your wife." After that last jab, he dropped his hand, and his tone softened. "The only way any good can ever come from this, though, is for me to love you as my brother, and do everything in my power to help you."

Chuck dropped his eyes. *He's going to be a tough sell, but sounds like he wants to get us back together.* "I've never felt so helpless . . . I . . . I'm afraid I've ruined my life." He kicked at piece of gravel on the sidewalk.

"Let me give you some hope, then. Bobbi wants to talk to you tomorrow afternoon."

"Phil convinced her?" *ThankGodthankGodthankGod.*

"No, she told Rita last night to see to it that I passed the message along to you."

Yes! A chance to talk to his wife. He and Bobbi could work this out if they just had some time and space.

"Gentlemen, we are all set." Phil rejoined them and swung his bag up to his shoulder. "Just let me go after Chuck, so I can see how these holes are supposed to be played." He grinned and wrote their names on the scorecard.

On the first green, watching Phil line up his putt, Gavin said, "Chuck, Phil mentioned to you about going before the church, didn't he?"

"I need to get things settled with Bobbi, first. It's between us."

"It is, and we can't make you do anything, but you can't serve in any capacity until you deal with it publicly. This wasn't just Phil's idea. All the deacons and Cooper agree."

"I can't face these people and admit this. I'll look like the biggest hypocrite in the world."

"You're a hypocrite if you don't." Phil dropped his putter back in his bag. "All of us are broken, fallen, with nothing except what God gives us in Christ. This is not for the church to shame and humiliate you. It's a chance for us as your family to come alongside and stand with you while you go through the restoration process."

"In the twenty-some years I've been in church, I don't recall anybody making a public confession. You can't tell me I'm the first guy who did anything wrong."

"I give everybody the same counsel," Phil said.

"You think that might say something about your advice?"

"Do it Sunday night then," Phil offered. "There will be fewer people there, and a more relaxed atmosphere."

"Have you told anyone yet?" Gavin asked.

"I told my boss this morning. He gave me five weeks off to work things out with Bobbi, which is more time than Phil gave me."

"I didn't say you had to have it all worked out in three weeks. I said Bobbi needs to see committed progress very soon."

"She will." Chuck jerked his bag off the ground and climbed into the golf cart.

"You want to get some of this out of your system?" Gavin asked when he joined Chuck in the cart. "I think the secrecy is wearing on you."

"There's nothing to tell. We had a new attorney join in February. She's very attractive. She came onto me and I fell for it. It's that simple."

"It's never that simple. How were things between you and Bobbi?"

"Okay."

"Everything?"

"Yeah, everything." Chuck rolled his eyes. "Can we drive to the next hole please?"

"I should probably wait for Phil."

Chuck crossed his arms and frowned. "This thing with Tracy, it's got nothing to do with my marriage. That wasn't why it happened. I never considered leaving Bobbi. It was purely physical."

"I don't think so," Gavin argued. "I can believe you never wanted to split with Bobbi, but I think this woman met some emotional need, or you wouldn't have gone back to her."

"And your psychology degree is from where?" Chuck's voice dripped with sharp sarcasm.

"The ugly truth is that you wanted this to happen and you allowed a situation to develop that made it possible."

Chuck's eyes narrowed in anger, but he didn't answer Gavin.

"You have to be honest with yourself first," Gavin said, "or Bobbi will never believe you."

"Have you told her all your theories, Dr. Freud?"

"Of course not."

"Then don't. I hoped that you, of all people, would extend some grace."

"If your definition of grace is condoning what you did, or letting it slide, then no, I can't."

Chuck played the final holes in silence and mumbled through his goodbyes. Gavin was way out of line, totally off base. He didn't have any 'emotional needs.' Why was it so hard to understand that he simply gave in to a seductive coworker? He and Bobbi were fine. They were just 'settled,' that's all. They had their own lives now. Isn't that what happens to everybody after fifteen or twenty years?

At any rate, tomorrow afternoon, he would get his chance to sit down and talk with Bobbi, and all this going before the church and emotional needs talk would be irrelevant. He stuffed his golf bag in the trunk of his car just as his cell phone rang. Plucking it off his belt, he saw his mother's phone number.

"Not now. I don't have the energy to go through this with her." He answered with all the cheerfulness he could muster, hoping to get her off the phone quickly. "Mom, how are things?"

"Chuck, I talked to Bobbi this morning." He'd heard that kind of grief in her voice only once before, the morning she called after his dad's death.

"I see."

"Don't you have anything to say?"

"What can I say, Mom? You want me to say I didn't do it. Or maybe it's not my fault? The fact is, yes, I cheated on my wife and, yes, it's all my fault!" He realized he was shouting. His voice dropped to a near whisper.

"I'm sorry."

"What happened? Why would you . . .?"

"I don't know."

"That's garbage! Why didn't you just ask Bobbi for a divorce instead of hurting her this way?"

"Because I don't want a divorce!" Chuck yelled, then tears formed. He glanced toward the clubhouse, hoping nobody was watching the lunatic in the parking lot, ranting one minute, crying the next. Going for the only privacy available, he opened his car door, and collapsed in the driver's seat.

"Mom, I love Bobbi, but I can't explain what happened. I'm scared to death she's going to leave me. I'm afraid she's going to leave and take the boys with her." His voice trailed off, and he dissolved into sobs.

"Listen to me." Her voice invited, rather than commanded. "Bobbi is afraid that you're through with the marriage. If she knows there's something to save, she'd be willing to give you another chance."

"You think so?" Chuck lifted a little.

"Yes, but . . ."

"I knew it. There's always a 'but'."

"Yes, but," Ann repeated, "you're going to have to drop that Molinsky 'I know everything—I can do it all myself' attitude. That might work in the courtroom, but not in this situation."

"I know."

"There you go again with the 'I know.' Son, you don't have this kind of humility in you. God is going to have to give it to you."

Chuck thought of his resistance to going before the church and his simmering anger at Gavin for speaking the truth to him. His mother nailed him. With Phil last night, he prayed out of humiliation, not humility. The discovery embarrassed him far more than the sin shamed him.

"Phil wants me to go before the church and confess this."

"Then you should do it. Give up the fight, Chuck, or you're going to lose your family."

"Have you got a few minutes now?"

Chuck looked up from his desk and saw Bobbi standing in the doorway of the study. He didn't, but she said she needed to talk days ago and he'd put her off. *"Sure. What's on your mind?"*

She frowned, and slipped a hand across her belly. The baby was kicking again. *"Can we . . . I don't want the desk in between us."*

He laid his pen down and walked around the desk. *"Is everything okay?"*

"Yeah . . . It's just . . . The baby will be here in a few months."

"You're gonna be a great mother." He took her hand and smiled.

"That's just it." She pulled her hand back. Her eyes darted past him, then to the floor. *"Chuck . . . I'm . . . I want to stay home with the baby. I'm not going to look for a teaching job for the fall."*

"What?" Her words stung like a slap in the face. *"After everything you've worked for? Why would you throw that away?"* This was crazy.

"I'm not throwing it away."

"Yes, you are! What brought this on? Did you have a bad day at school or something?"

"You don't give me any credit at all. Just because I'm not a lawyer . . ."

"That's ridiculous. I'm upset because you made this decision just like that!" He snapped his fingers. *"Without even talking to me about it."*

"I beg your pardon! I've tried to talk to you about this for three months! You're never here, and when you are here, you're holed up in this study! I feel like your roommate, not your wife."

"I have some ambition. I'm not going to apologize for that."

"And I do, too!"

"Not like you should!" He lowered his voice and took a long deep breath. *"You're brilliant, for crying out loud. I don't know anybody that finished their undergraduate degree in three years, and you're wasting that reading Clifford the Big Dog all day long. You belong in medical school, or in a research lab or something. At the very least, you should be looking at being a principal."*

"It's not about me. This our child. He's a gift God's entrusting to us."

"I realize that."

"But you don't think he's worth my time?"

"Anybody can change diapers and wipe noses. Anybody can sing the ABC song. You should be doing more. My mom's around. She's already asked me what we're doing with the baby."

"And what'd you tell her?"

"I told her we haven't made a final decision. And we haven't."

"I have."

"This is an epic mistake. I'm not going to go along with this."

"Then divorce me."

He waved a hand at her. "That's your hormones talking."

"You're insufferable." She turned and walked out of the study.

He groaned. Why was she making this so difficult? He didn't have time for this today, but he knew better than to let her walk away. "There's no way you're gonna convince me you really want me to divorce you," he called after her. "You're being dramatic to make a point."

She whipped around and they stood inches apart in the narrow hallway. "And you're being a patronizing jerk. Again."

"You're only hearing the 'no'."

"The no? You're not going to 'let' me stay home? You're going to drag me to work?"

"Just stop for five seconds. You're not listening to the reason behind it. I want the best, the very best for you . . ."

"No, Chuck, you want to do things your way." She jabbed at him, almost touching his chest. "If it'd been your idea for me to stay home, it would've been the greatest solution to childcare this century."

"That's not true!"

"Did your mother stay home?"

"Yes, but . . ."

"Then why are you bucking this? Your mother is extremely gifted. Why was she not a failure for staying home?"

"I did not say you'd be a failure." He took a deep breath and dropped his head. *You can't negotiate when emotions take over. He had to be calm. He had to be the rational one.* "Bobbi, Mom's situation is different. She lost two babies before I was born, and another one after me. It messed with her, I think."

"Then you should be able to grasp where I'm coming from." She'd quit yelling at him. *His way worked.* "I lost my mother when I was twelve, and I may as well have lost my dad then, too. I don't want my son to grow up without me."

He drew her close, as close as her belly would allow, and kissed her. He wouldn't push it today, but this wasn't over. Not by a long shot.

CHAPTER 5
CONFRONTATION

Bobbi punched in numbers on her calculator, double-checking the check-book entries. Since the clock in the study slid past noon, she battled to stay focused on paying bills and budgeting for August. She regretted not giving Chuck a definite time to show up. He could come any minute now, or not at all.

She reached for her mug and finished her fourth cup of the strong Turkish coffee she brewed this morning. The caffeine hadn't bothered her for years and the warmth always soothed and relaxed her.

Pushing the empty mug out of the way, she pulled the payment book for Chuck's BMW from her stack. She hated that car. Things hadn't been the same between them since he bought it. Was Chuck cheating then? Did Tracy have a thing for BMWs? If she was the reason he bought the car, was he also buying her things? *God, please tell me I haven't spent eighteen years managing our finances so Chuck could keep a mistress.*

She made a couple of changes to the budget sheet and recalculated. The house would be paid off next summer, but if they divorced . . . If she started shifting more money there now, that might be enough to pay off the mortgage by the time everything was finalized.

The doorbell rang. Bobbi caught sight of Chuck's car in the driveway. *He's here. God help us all.*

Chuck stood on his own front porch wavering between walking in or ringing the doorbell. Starting the meeting well was critical. No, this was his wife—it was a conversation, not a meeting. Even so, if he lost his temper the way he did Thursday night, he stood a zero chance of reconciling with Bobbi. She wanted to talk, so let her run things, and that meant not assuming any rights. He wiped his palm on his slacks and rang the bell.

Joel opened the front door and broke into a huge grin. He threw his arms around Chuck and squeezed. "I love you, Dad."

Chuck kissed the top of the boy's head. "I love you, too. I needed to hear that."

"Mom's in the kitchen, but Brad doesn't want to talk to you," Joel said as he passed his dad to go outside.

"You're not going to stick around?"

"I don't want to hear you yell."

"Who said we were going to yell? Mom didn't say that, did she?"

"No, Brad did."

"Well, Brad's wrong."

"What else is new?" Joel grabbed his bike and pedaled away.

Suddenly a stranger in his own house, Chuck stepped into the entry hall. Brad's first grade picture hung in its place in a new frame. Bobbi's pillow and blankets lay in the corner by the sofa. She couldn't sleep. He wished lost sleep was all he had to atone for.

Chuck followed the exotic coffee aroma and found Bobbi in the same spot at the kitchen table where he had last seen her on Thursday. He wanted to go to her, pour out his heart, beg for her forgiveness, but the coolness hanging over the room stopped him. As their eyes met, he saw resolve and determination. He debated whether to sit or stand. "Have a seat," she said, her voice steady and firm.

He dropped into the chair opposite her. "Thanks for letting me . . . uh . . . come by."

"Do you want to be with this woman?" She looked at him, not flinching or blinking, no warmth or compassion in her deep brown eyes, and he looked away.

"No." His wife's bluntness flustered him as she seized control of the conversation.

"Do you want out of this marriage?"

"No, of course not. I didn't go looking for this. I . . . I was stupid, and put myself in a . . . well, in a situation where I would be tempted, and then I gave in."

"Who is she?"

Bobbi heard the phone message. She knew exactly who Tracy was. Every lawyer knows you don't ask a question unless you already know the answer. He could pass this test. "An attorney at the firm. She's been there a few months."

"Well, she certainly didn't waste any time. Very ambitious."

"What are you talking about?"

"Chuck, your name is on the side of the building! Do you honestly think she came on to you because of your charm and good looks?"

"She's not like that." Tracy wanted him as much as he wanted her . . . didn't she?

"Whatever." Bobbi rolled her eyes in disgust. "How old is she?"

"I don't know, thirty or thirty-five."

"Is she married?"

"No."

"How many times?"

"What?" The questions were coming so fast, he couldn't catch his breath. She should have been a prosecutor.

"How many times . . . did you . . . sleep . . . with her?"

"Three." He dropped his eyes. *Please, don't make me tell you any more than that.*

"In my house?"

"Never."

"How long has this been going on?"

"About three weeks."

Bobbi paused a moment in her questioning, then murmured, "When the boys and I were in Detroit."

Chuck fought back tears. "I swear, that's not why I stayed home. It's just . . . that's when it started." He knew every word hurt her, but only the blinking of her eyes betrayed it.

"Is she pregnant?"

"No."

"How do you know that for sure?"

"She told me she used a patch." Chuck shifted in his chair and went on offense. "Bobbi, I can never explain this or justify myself. I know I can't begin to understand how much I've hurt you, but you and the boys are my life. I am sorry and I promise you before God that I'll do whatever it takes to make this right."

"You made me a promise before God eighteen years ago, Chuck." She spoke his name with such hopelessness that he feared it might already be too late.

"Bobbi, please. I love you. Give us a chance."

She didn't answer him, but went to the refrigerator for a bottled water. He watched her slowly twist the cap off, then sip from the bottle. He knew she was debating, weighing her options. She rejoined him at the table, and his chest tightened. Here it came—her terms.

"I trust Phil for counseling," she said. "Do you?"

"Absolutely."

"Are you committed to counseling with him?"

"Are you?"

"I'm asking the questions."

"I will do whatever Phil tells me is in our best interest. He wants me to tell the church."

"Are you going to?"

"I don't know."

"You're not going to do the first thing he tells you to do?"

"That's not what I said. It's more complicated than that."

Bobbi took a long drink from her water. He blew it on her first demand. No matter what second condition she laid down, he vowed to accept it unequivocally. "You can't stay here," she said.

"What?" If he let her kick him out . . . "This is my home."

"Then the boys and I will go."

"No. No, you stay. I'll find a place."

"One last thing."

"Name it." He let himself breathe again and tried to reassure himself terms were good. Terms meant they could reach an agreement.

"I want you to see a doctor."

"Why?"

"I have to know that you haven't picked up some disease."

"Good grief, Bobbi, I wasn't with some cheap hooker!" She arched her eyebrow, and folded her hands on the table in front of her. "I mean . . . of course. I'll take care of that."

"That's all for now. Goodbye, Chuck."

"Just like that?"

"We've been civil and we've talked. That's good enough for now."

"Sure," he said, rising from his chair. "I'll let myself out." He proved he was an idiot, a naïve idiot who thought he could walk in here and explain away his adultery, then have everything go back to normal.

When he got to the kitchen doorway, he caught Bobbi's eye once more. She hadn't softened. "Take care," he said. Even if she didn't divorce him, had he lost her forever?

The front door weighed more than he remembered, forcing him to brace himself before swinging it open. That woman in the kitchen wasn't the Bobbi he'd married. He'd never seen such strength, such toughness out of her. She wore her wedding band. That had to be a good sign, but she asked him to move out. What if that was the first step to divorce?

Joel skidded his bike to a stop in the driveway. "Are you coming home tonight, Dad?"

Chuck smiled and motioned for Joel to join him on the porch steps. "It's not that easy, Son."

"Are you getting a divorce?"

"No. Mom and I are not getting a divorce." Chuck could see Joel's shoulders relax so he kept talking. "I really hurt Mom. I spent some time with another woman, giving her the kind of attention that is reserved only for Mom, and that was wrong."

Joel nodded. "I get that part. What I don't get is why you did it. Don't you love Mom anymore?"

"Of course I love Mom. I just . . . what I did was beyond stupid."

"Does Mom love you?"

"I think so."

"So why would you want to be with someone else if Mom loves you and you love Mom?"

"It's a grown-up thing, Joel. I don't think I can explain it."

"Try me."

Chuck let a deep sigh escape. He'd alienated every member of his family but Joel. How could he answer him without destroying what respect the boy still held for him?

"It made me feel good that this other woman liked me." *She met some emotional need, or you wouldn't have gone back to her . . .*

"Mom likes you."

"Yeah, but this was somebody different . . . it was new . . ." He dropped his head. "It sounds stupid when I try to explain it to you."

"That's what I was thinking, too." He scowled and looked out across the street. "So . . . what happens if some other woman likes you?"

"Nothing. Nothing happens. I will never hurt Mom like this again. Ever."

"Did you tell Mom that?"

"Yeah, but she can't just take my word for it. I hurt her way too much for that."

"Is that why you can't come home?"

"For now. It's going to take some time, Buddy. You know, when Brad makes you mad, and you just want to be by yourself for a while?"

"Yes!"

"Well, Mom's going to need some time to work through being mad at me. I deserve to have her mad at me." Chuck patted Joel's knee and stood up. "Same with Brad. Let him be mad, okay?"

"Okay," Joel shrugged. "You're not divorcing. That's all I was worried about."

"See you at church, Buddy," Chuck said as he got in his car.

"Bye, Dad!" Joel called. "Love you!"

Chuck smiled and waved as he backed out of the driveway. Before he turned off his block, he dialed Phil Shannon's number. "Have you got a few minutes? I won't take long, but I'm in big trouble."

Before Chuck even pulled out of the driveway, Bobbi rushed to the downstairs bathroom to throw up again. The details were too much. The less she knew, the better.

Chuck didn't say he wanted out, but what did he want? Did he even know? A thirty-year-old lawyer. She couldn't compete with that.

You got every answer you asked for. He seemed contrite, penitent. He was hurting, too. She'd seen Chuck's reflection in the microwave, and watched as he wiped his eyes.

God help me. I believe him. Now what? She wanted to run after him so he could take her in his arms, tell her everything would work out, and let her cry on his shoulder. It would be so much easier that way. But that would make her a fool. Only a fool would absorb the hurt and the anger. Only a fool would trust him again. He said he loved her, finally, but that wasn't enough. Things had to change, and Chuck had to change.

She swished a mouthful of mouthwash and spit it in the bathroom sink. *If I get through this with any of my sanity left, it'll be a miracle.*

"Brad!" she called upstairs. "He's gone. Do you want to go to the mall? I'll even drop you at a different door!" Bobbi wanted to get out of the house, to do something normal, and forget she was a victim of infidelity.

Brad tromped down the stairs. "You don't have to do that," he said with a sly grin. "Just wait about ten minutes before you follow me in."

"You rotten kid," Bobbi said with a smile. She rummaged through her purse, making sure she had her keys and phone.

"So how did it go?" Brad asked. "More lies?"

So much for thinking about something else. Setting her purse down on the console table, she turned to face her son. "Do you want us to split up?"

"Well, no, but what other choice do you have? I don't know how you can forgive him. He's done youth retreats with us on dating, and sex, and stuff, and then he does this. He's a phony."

"Have you ever done anything wrong?"

"Yeah, everybody has." He rolled his eyes and bobbed his head, repeating what he heard many times before. "Since everybody makes mistakes, everybody should forgive everybody. Blah, blah, blah, but Mom—"

"This is serious. Have you ever done anything you said you wouldn't?" Bobbi paused, but when Brad didn't answer, she continued. "Like . . . ever cheated on a test?"

"No way!"

"Ever 'compared answers' after you couldn't finish your algebra?" Brad scowled. "I'll take that as a yes. You took something that didn't belong to you. You cheated. Copying homework problems is a much smaller scale, and has much smaller consequences, but it's the same as what your dad did. He took something that didn't belong to him. He cheated."

"Why are you defending him?"

"I'm not. I'm just saying be careful when you level judgment. Make sure you don't catch yourself."

"You didn't cheat. He did. You can't just take him back like it never happened."

"Is that what you think I'm doing? Just because I asked to talk to your dad doesn't mean this is over." *How much do I tell him?* "Your dad is moving out, and we have a hard road ahead of us. Lots of counseling. It's going to be a much longer process than deciding to marry him in the first place." Bobbi smiled, but Brad didn't soften. "You're right to be angry and hurt. Believe me, I am. Just don't write your dad off."

"I'm not making any promises," Brad replied, his jaw set.

When Chuck rang the Shannons' doorbell, the thirty seconds it took Phil to answer the door seemed ten times that long. "Come on in," Phil said, extending his hand to shake Chuck's.

"Thanks for letting me come by on such short notice," Chuck said, stepping inside. "I hate to bother you on a Saturday."

"Then consider this a visit to a friend's house. You can always stop by a friend's house on Saturday." Phil ushered Chuck to the living room sofa. "Now, what can I do for you?" He eased into the recliner across from the sofa.

"I'm an idiot, Phil. I've just come from talking to Bobbi. Things are worse than I thought."

"I'm sorry to hear that. What happened?"

"She wants me to move out."

"Did she ask you for a divorce?"

"No, she wants to go through counseling. I told her I would do anything to make it up to her, but I'm not sure it mattered. She was nothing like the Bobbi I fell in love with."

"What can I do?"

"I talked to my mom yesterday, and she said I should do the confession thing." Chuck took a deep breath. "It's just . . . Phil, I've worked so hard, to be successful, and to look successful. It mattered a lot to me. I even hounded Bobbi a few years back about moving out to The Arbors, you know, a better neighborhood. None of that matters if I lose her. If she doesn't believe that I'm sorry, that I love her, and I want to be a good husband, everything else is just pointless." He raised his head and looked Phil in the eye.

"Are you sorry?"

"Of course I am."

"And you love your wife, and you want to be a good husband?"

"That's what I said."

"No, you said you wanted Bobbi to believe those things. There's a difference."

"Phil . . ."

"You can't fake this, Chuck. You have to be one hundred percent sincere for your own sake as much as for Bobbi's. You have to be open and honest about everything from now on."

"Then let me be straight with you. I understand that I have sinned against God and against my wife. I realize that I did far more damage than I thought, and if I have any hope of getting Bobbi back, I need your help." He closed his eyes and pinched the bridge of his nose, trying to keep himself from dissolving into tears. "Please, Phil, I'm begging you."

"Now we're getting somewhere." Phil slid to the edge of his seat. "First of all, I need you to understand that God intends for marriage to show how Christ loves and cares for His church. It's a serious insult to God to tear it down, and He's going to vindicate Himself."

"So, even if I do this, I'm still facing some kind of judgment?"

"Think of it like this. Say you drive a nail into a two-by-four, and then come back later and pull the nail out. The nail may be gone, but the hole is there. Even if you fill it, maybe so it's unnoticeable, it's still going to be there. The two-by-four will never be the same."

"My marriage," Chuck nodded.

"God removes the sin when you ask for forgiveness," Phil continued, "but the effects of the sin never go away."

"So how do I fill in the hole?"

"Now, that's God's business, working that miracle of restoration, but He often lets us have a hand in it."

"Which brings me back to confessing this to the church."

"Exactly."

"Tell me how to do it then," Chuck said, grasping for that hope.

"You sure?"

"I want my wife back."

"What are you doing?" Bobbi found Chuck facing the mirror in their bathroom, whipping his tie around into a perfect knot.

"Getting ready for work."

"Today?"

"I do this almost every day."

She took his hand, and he frowned. "Chuck, your dad's funeral was yesterday. Nobody expects you . . ."

He jerked his hand away. "What am I supposed to do here? Sit and stare at the walls, or waste my time on something stupid?"

"Not at all. You've never lost anybody. This is . . ." The lines in his forehead grew deeper, and she risked him walking out. "You need some time. Trust me on this, and your mother needs you. She's alone today."

"She's got friends there."

"It's not the same, and you know it."

"Look, I've got commitments to clients." His jaw twitched ever so slightly "And I intend to keep them. That's uh . . . that's what my dad . . . he taught me that. Honor your commitments." He closed his eyes and clenched his jaw so tightly it shook.

She touched his face, and a single tear escaped from his eyes. She slipped her hand behind his head, and he let her guide it to her shoulder. "I love you," she whispered, and he let go and sobbed. She held him, rubbed his back, and cried with him. "You are so much like your dad . . ."

He raised up and shook his head. "I'll never be half the man my dad was." He shifted and looked at the floor in front of him for several moments. When he finally spoke, the words came softly and tentatively. "Walter and Jim are giving me Dad's spot."

"As a managing partner? That's wonderful."

"It's kind of a junior manager. They still have final oversight."

"Still, at thirty-six, that's an amazing accomplishment."

"But I didn't earn it."

"You did. They didn't have to give it to you." He frowned again and wiped his eyes. "I know how hard you work, Chuck—"

"I gotta go." He eased around her, and reached for his suit jacket.

"Why doesn't it matter when I say it?"

"What?" He slipped his arm in the jacket sleeve.

"When I say you work hard, or you're a good attorney, you blow it off."

"Bobbi, don't start on me right now." He straightened his tie and adjusted the silk in his breast pocket.

He was grieving and he had no idea how to process it. She had to believe that, to push down the hurt and anger welling up inside her. If he felt safe with her, venting it to her, then she'd be safe for him. "All right, should I plan on you for dinner?"

"Go ahead and feed the boys. Don't wait on me."

She took his hand in hers. "I'll be here when you get home. I'll help you anyway I can."

"You can't help me."

CHAPTER 6
CONFESSION

Sunday, July 31

When Phil Shannon smiled at her, Bobbi dropped her eyes, wanting to avoid another round of tears. Chuck hadn't come for Bible study and he had yet to appear in the worship service. He failed the first test of his sincerity and commitment. Counseling was going to be a sham. Chuck would go through all the motions, make a good show, and then they would split. He would walk away without any guilt. He tried, after all.

Stop thinking about Chuck! I'm here for worship. Concentrate.

But he told her about the confession. He said he would do anything, whatever Phil said. Maybe after she kicked him out of the house, he didn't feel free to come to church anymore. She hadn't meant that at all.

She flinched when Joel touched her and asked for a pen. She fished one out of her purse, then slipped an arm around her son. Joel talked with Chuck yesterday afternoon, but he hadn't relayed the details to her. Had it gone badly? Maybe Chuck wanted to speak to Brad privately before risking a public encounter with his son.

Bobbi mumbled her way through the first hymn, then settled back in the pew. She already deflected several questions about where Chuck was this morning. 'He was in Kansas City this week,' she said, which was the truth, just not the whole truth.

The truth is, I'm in church. It's not going to do me any good if I'm zoned out through the whole service.

Pastor Phil Shannon stepped into the pulpit and welcomed everyone. He smiled at her when he passed. Maybe he knew how awkward it would be for her, so he had cautioned Chuck to stay out of sight.

Did Chuck even have church clothes? Was he still living out of his suitcase? Suddenly, she felt harsh and coldhearted for not letting him get his things yesterday. She should at least call him this afternoon and arrange a time when he could do that. Monday would work. She'd be at school all day Monday.

As the ushers stepped up to collect the offering, she thought she caught sight of her husband out of the corner of her eye. She turned to double check, but it wasn't Chuck. She tried to visualize him at the front of the church, admitting to everyone that he'd been unfaithful. It made the heat rise on the back of her neck. If he confessed, did she have to sit through it?

Late Saturday afternoon, Chuck secured a furnished apartment, and now he needed his things. Bobbi left for church right on time, so Chuck had the house to himself. He gathered up clothes, toiletries, a few books and files from the study, and his Bible. He grabbed a couple of sturdy boxes from the attic and began carrying things to his car. He hoped, for Bobbi's sake, none of the neighbors drew the inevitable conclusion.

He had one last box to load when his cell phone rang. He answered it without checking the ID.

"Don't hang up, Chuck. I got your message, and I didn't want that to be goodbye."

Tracy. All at once, shame burned through his chest. It felt so good to hear her voice. A thousand images flashed through his mind. He could smell her perfume, her shampoo, even the air freshener in her house.

Chuck switched his phone to his left hand and wiped his palm on his pants. "Tracy, uh, this is not good idea."

"I won't take much time, but I think I have a right to be heard."

"I'm listening."

"I would have never gotten involved with you if you hadn't given off some strong signals that you were interested. You invited me to lunch. You stopped by my office. You came to my house."

Gavin's words roared back at him. *The ugly truth is that you wanted this to happen, and you allowed a situation to develop that made it possible.* "I shouldn't have. That was wrong."

"No, having an extramarital affair, cheating on your wife, that was wrong. This has been very hard on her, I'm sure, especially since she's not back at school yet. These empty days must be especially difficult."

"How did you—?"

"Then having to tell Brad and Joel—a mother's worst nightmare."

"You knew all along." A sucker punch in the kidney would have been easier to take. Tracy wasn't interested in him at all. She played him.

"Of course I knew," she laughed. "You know, I would have given anything to have seen your face Thursday morning."

"Where is all this hostility coming from? I never—"

"You don't deserve this? Is that your point? You don't deserve to have your reputation self-destruct because you can't control your ego or your impulses? You're a liar, and in your limitless arrogance, you've convinced yourself that everyone around you is too stupid to figure that out. I'm sure your wife would agree with me. She and I should have a cup of coffee sometime."

"You wouldn't."

"Why not? You want to be completely truthful with her now, don't you?"

"Wait just a minute! You're going to tell me about being truthful? After that phone message? After the 'scorned lover' act?"

"Lover? Is that what you thought? Chuck, I'm touched."

"But you said—"

"Exactly what you wanted to hear. I am not the wicked woman who led you astray. You had both eyes wide open, and I am not taking the blame."

"I know. It was my fault." How could she deceive him, turn on him this way?

"If you ever figure out what you're looking for, call me. Your wife is still the same woman she was when you lost interest in her." The line went dead.

Chuck sunk into the living room armchair and waited for his heart rate to return to normal. The back of his neck heated and sweat beaded across his lip. His marriage was in ruins because he primed himself to believe every line she fed him. Every single line.

Chuck dragged the last box to the door, then left a note for Bobbi on the console table explaining that he'd stopped by. He included a crude map to his apartment and hoped that hint would be enough to prompt her to change her mind. Making one last sweep of the house before leaving, he opened his top dresser drawer and found the box containing his wedding band. He carefully took the ring out and tried to slip it on his finger. It still didn't fit.

A lump rose in his throat as he read the inscription, MRP to CJM, For Always. He couldn't remember the inscription in his wife's ring. *I'm such a jerk.* He returned the ring to its box and dropped it into his pocket.

The hall clock chimed eleven. Now it was too late to slip into church, so he opted for lunch, and an afternoon of preparing to face everyone tonight.

Chuck slipped into a pew in the back as the last chorus of the evening praise music swelled through the auditorium. He hoped folks didn't notice, didn't realize that he wasn't with Bobbi. She was here and that was all that mattered. He only needed to touch her heart tonight. Bobbi knew he was doing this for her.

All afternoon he went over the things Phil told him. "Keep it to three S's," Phil said, "simple, short and sincere. Nobody needs details, just name it, renounce it, and promise to make things right."

As the praise band moved off the podium, Phil stepped up for the opening prayer. He made eye contact with Chuck and gave him the subtlest nod. Chuck never heard the prayer or the songs that followed. His pulse pounded in his neck and a wave of heat rose across his chest. *God,*

I'm going to do the right thing, I promise.

"All right, folks," Phil began the evening sermon. "We'll pick up where we left off last week in Matthew, chapter five, looking at the Beatitudes. We've covered the poor in spirit, the mourners, the meek, the merciful, and those who hunger and thirst for righteousness. Tonight, we want to consider the pure in heart."

As Phil spoke of pure motives and an inner man cleansed from any corruption and hypocrisy, Chuck's chest tightened with the weight of guilt. He wasn't just an adulterer, he was a liar and a fraud besides. His face flushed, and sweat beaded across his forehead. He dropped his head and hoped no one noticed him squirming.

God, I get the message. My motives, my heart . . . they're not pure. He swallowed hard, and wiped his eyes. *I told Phil what I had to in order to get him to help me, and I planned to say whatever Bobbi needed to hear. God, I'm so scared . . . I'm scared I'm going to lose her. Please, don't let her leave me. Please.*

The invitation music began and Chuck raised his head. Phil's eyes pulled at him. He wanted to move, but the nerve impulses died somewhere between his brain and his feet. With blood thundering in his ears, Chuck took a deep breath and screamed within himself, *Go!*

Phil Shannon met him with extended arms and drew him into a hug. "I'm proud of you. It'll be okay, I promise." He directed Chuck to the front pew.

When the music stopped, Phil stood and spoke in measured, somber tones. "Please be seated for a moment. My friends, it is fitting that the Bible often refers to believers as a family. Families face trials that strain the very relationships that bind them together. I want each of you to hear Chuck out so that we can help him and his family as they face perhaps the greatest of trials." With a subtle wave, Phil signaled Chuck and stepped out of the way.

Chuck stood and faced the congregation in time to see Donna Shannon leave. A check to his right confirmed the reason. Bobbi was gone.

Fighting the impulse to run after her, he looked out at the people he'd gone to church with for years. He caught the eyes of his parents' closest friends, Jack and Gloria Bond. He graduated with their son, Marty. Mary Ellen Cantrell, Joel's Sunday school teacher, sat four rows behind Joel. If she saw Bobbi leave, she could piece together what he was about to say. Lorraine Kinney sat down front, almost close enough for him to touch. Everyone knew her husband had run off with his secretary, leaving her with a mortgage and three children.

Before his resolve wavered any further, he wiped his eyes, cleared his throat, and addressed his church.

"I, uh . . . well, the Bible says in James to confess your faults to one another, and I need to confess to you, not just a fault, but a sin, a gross sin." Tears threatened to choke the words off, but he took a deep breath and fought them back. "I sinned against God, my wife and family, and you, my church. I broke my marriage vows and had an affair with another woman."

A gasp, then a murmur filtered through the crowd. "I had the capacity and responsibility to overcome the temptation, but I made the conscious decision to give in. I am sorry beyond my ability to express it. I have repented before God, asked for, and I believe, received God's forgiveness. I am asking for yours as well."

Chuck swallowed hard, thankful no one but Phil Shannon could see the tremor in the back of his pant leg as he spoke. "I don't want you to see this as trying to get you to 'take my side.' There is no 'side.' I am completely wrong. Bobbi is entirely innocent. I hope for your understanding and support, and for your prayers for God's help to put my family and my marriage back together."

Nobody spoke, nobody moved.

After a long moment, Chuck saw Joel slip up to the pew with his aunt, Rita. She put her arm around his shoulder and gave him a little squeeze.

Chuck glanced at Phil, looking for a cue. Now what? Should he sit down? Across the aisle from him, the front pew creaked as George

McLaughlin pulled himself to his feet. The old man embraced Chuck, without ever saying a word, and the other deacons followed his lead. Last in line, Gavin smiled at Chuck, and whispered, "God's going to honor this. Hang in there, and see this through to the end."

Chuck relaxed his shoulders. He'd gotten past the deacons. Now, it had to be over. The floor appeared to tilt away from him, so he took a step to sit down, but Lorraine Kinney moved. He forgot to breathe as she eased out into the aisle toward him. *Here it comes.* She stood before him, her head held high. In the stillness, she said, "If Dean had done what you just did, I would have taken him back."

The simple statement electrified the congregation. Tears flowed as Preston Road Community Church came together as a family. In the blur of faces and hugs, Chuck heard 'Bless you,' and 'that took a lot of courage,' and 'we'll be praying.'

Rita Heatley remained planted in her spot, with Joel at her side, watching Chuck. Even when Gavin returned to the seat beside her, she never took her eyes off him.

Gavin whispered to her, and she shook her head, pointing in Chuck's direction. Finally, Gavin nodded toward Joel and she rolled her eyes. She took Joel by the shoulders and ushered him into the aisle. The boy threaded his way through everyone to get to his father. When Joel hugged him, Chuck smiled for the first time.

Then Rita stepped closer and his smile withered. Chuck squeezed Joel's shoulder and sent his son back to his seat. "I meant what I said, Rita. I am sorry, and I—"

Rita took his hand and leaned in close, her eyes bored into his, her voice tight. "You may have fooled everyone in this building, even Phil Shannon, but I'm not buying it. You don't deserve Bobbi. You . . . never . . . have."

As she marched away, Phil Shannon strode to the center aisle. "This has been an extraordinary worship service," he said, with a nod toward her. "Before we close, I want to caution you on two things. Bobbi chose not to be here. Don't read anything into her decision. This is very painful for her. She deserves this same love and compassion from you, just respect her privacy."

Rita nodded, glancing around the sanctuary.

"Second," the pastor continued, "bad news travels fast enough. Don't help it along. This is a family matter and I want us to keep it that way." He surveyed the congregation one last time, and then slipped his arm around Chuck's shoulder. "Let's pray," he said, and bowed his head. "Father," he began, letting a long sigh escape, "we praise You for Your spirit with us. Thank You for letting us be a part of Your grace. Thank You for Chuck's obedience to Your Word as he made his confession before his brothers and sisters. As You are the God of reconciliation, bring this family back together. Heal their pain, and help them be a powerful testimony to Your power to redeem broken lives and marriages through Your great grace. Thank You, Jesus. Amen."

Heavy emotional and physical exhaustion seemed to settle on Phil. "Tomorrow morning, nine o'clock, my office," he said, before he let Chuck walk away. "And don't go after Bobbi right now."

"But Phil—"

He raised a finger. "I mean it. Don't press her."

Chuck's stance relaxed. "I lived," he said. "Thanks for your help."

"That's what I'm here for. Get some sleep. You've had a hard day."

Bobbi jammed her car in reverse, but as she turned to check the passenger mirror, she caught sight of Donna Shannon. Donna motioned for her to roll down the passenger window. "Can I go with you?" she asked.

Bobbi turned off the car and unlocked the passenger door. "I don't even know where I was going. I can't leave. The boys are still inside."

Donna sat down in the passenger seat. "We can just sit, but if you want to talk, I'd be glad to listen."

Bobbi slid her hands down to the bottom of the steering wheel and leaned her head back against the headrest. "Donna, I couldn't sit through it. Not only did Chuck take something intimate and sacred and give it to another woman, but now he's thrown it out there for anybody who's interested. I feel so violated. It's humiliating." Her voice trailed to a whisper and tears began to run from the corners of her eyes.

Donna turned in the seat so she could face Bobbi. "Honey, Phil advised Chuck to go before the church."

"I know," Bobbi answered, sniffling and wiping her eyes. "I know it was the right thing to do. It was going to get out anyway." Bobbi sighed. "Brad is so angry. So bitter. Cooper took him to lunch today, and Brad's only concern is making sure his dad pays. He's lost all respect for his dad, and if I forgive Chuck, Brad won't respect me either. I'm afraid we'll lose him."

"Lose him how?"

"I'm afraid he'll turn into some rebellious punk who throws away his future just because I did the right thing and forgave his dad."

"You've already forgiven Chuck, then?"

"I love him. What else can I do?"

"Honey, you could do any number of things—hate him forever, divorce him, run over him with your car . . ." Bobbi managed a slight smile. "But the fact that you've chosen, and it is a choice, to love and forgive is a great thing. I admire you for it."

"Thanks, but it doesn't help with the pain. It hurts . . . so . . . much."

"I know it does," Donna said, taking Bobbi's hand. "I'm afraid it will for a long time, but you are doing the right things . . . and so is Chuck."

Bobbi closed her eyes and exhaled slowly. "I wonder . . . how many times has Chuck cried over this?"

"Not as many as he's going to, I'm sure." They sat for several minutes before Donna spoke again. "Honey, can I pray with you real quick? Then I promise I'll leave you alone." She winked and squeezed Bobbi's hand.

Bobbi sat up straighter in her seat and bowed her head. If God heard anybody, He heard Donna Shannon.

"Dear Jesus, I know I don't have to tell You anything about Bobbi. She's Yours and You know all about her, including this crisis. Honor her decision to follow Your word and Your example of love and forgiveness, and Jesus, be her big brother. Defend her from anyone who would add to her burdens right now, from that other woman, and guard her thoughts so her imagination doesn't get the best of her. Help us, help me, know how to support her. Thank You, Jesus. Amen." Donna patted Bobbi's arm. "I'll send the boys out so you don't have to go hunt them."

"Thank you. For everything."

"You bet," Donna said with another wink, while opening the car door. She disappeared inside the church building, and within a few moments, Bobbi's sons made their exit.

Bobbi watched them walk down the sidewalk. Joel bounded toward the car, while Brad shuffled along, his hands shoved in his jeans pockets.

Joel reached the car first and jumped in the front seat, "Mom! You missed it! Dad told everybody!"

Squashing Joel's enthusiasm, Bobbi said, "I know. That's why I walked out."

"You walked out of church, Mom?" Brad asked from the backseat.

"Yeah, Dad told everybody about the affair," Joel answered.

"Joel, I think I can take it from here," Bobbi said. "Your dad went before the church tonight to confess what he did, and it's a little too painful for me to hear again, so yes, I walked out of church." Bobbi started her car and pulled out of the parking lot.

"Hasn't he done enough damage?" Brad snarled.

"Brad, it's Biblical to confess things that way. Dad did the right thing, and he was following what Pastor Phil counseled him to do—"

"Mom! It doesn't change anything. He can make a thousand confessions, but it doesn't change the fact that he had the affair!"

"No, but you can't have forgiveness until you have confession."

"He better not ask me for forgiveness."

As soon as Chuck walked through the front door at Benton, Davis, & Molinsky he spotted the redhead in Walter Davis' office. No surprise the old man was handling her case personally.

"Mr. Molinsky, Mr. Davis wants to see you." Christine Gardner nodded toward the office.

"Now? He's in with a client."

"Not a client. New attorney."

"He didn't tell me . . ." Chuck knocked on Walter's door before easing it open. "Christine said you wanted to see me."

"Yes, come in. Chuck, this is Tracy Ravenna. I've hired her to take some of your load off."

She uncrossed her long legs, and stood to shake Chuck's hand. "I'm pleased to meet you." She locked her eyes on his and shook his hand with firm confidence. Her eyes, almost the same deep, dark brown as Bobbi's, danced when she smiled.

"Tracy comes to us from Anheuser-Busch by way of University of Virginia." Walter slid a folder toward Chuck. "She has tremendous credentials."

"What made you leave Busch?" Chuck flipped through the papers in the folder.

"I love business law, but frankly, I got tired of the beer industry. I wanted some variety."

"We don't do anything on that scale."

"No, but this firm has an excellent reputation, and I like new challenges." She smiled and sat down again, smoothing her skirt across her lap. Her suit, what Bobbi called winter white, perfectly complemented her hair. He caught himself before his eyes drifted to that hint of a curve in her tailored suit jacket.

"Chuck, I want Tracy to work with you on the Beckham case to orient her to our system."

"Sure. Let me get settled, and I'll brief you."

"I look forward to it." She pushed her hair behind her ear and flashed that *smile again.*

Chuck walked to his office. Was she flirting with him? Of course not. Professionals didn't flirt.

Chuck knocked on *the doorframe of Tracy's office and she looked up and smiled. "Finally, a friendly face."*

"Bad day?"

"Just dealing with idiots all day. What's up?"

"Thought you'd like to see these." He crossed to her desk and handed her a folder. "Beckham's resolved. The cease and desist was enough. Your instincts were right."

"They usually are." She scanned the pages, then straightened them, and flipped the folder closed. "We make a good team."

"I'd like to take you to lunch, you know, to celebrate. If you're free."

"I'd like that. Give me about twenty minutes to wrap up a couple of things."

Exactly twenty minutes later, she stood in the doorway of Chuck's office, pulling her coat on. He grabbed his suit jacket and followed her through the lobby. He waved to the receptionist on his way out the door. "Christine, we're gonna grab some lunch. I've got my cell."

He led Tracy around to his gleaming black Lincoln Navigator and unlocked her door. "I'm surprised," she said as she climbed inside.

"Why's that?"

"I would've figured you for something sporty, a convertible even."

"Funny you should say that. I'm looking to trade, just waiting on a deal." He pushed her door closed and walked around to the driver's side. Bobbi would kill him for trading a year-old car.

"What are you in the mood for?" he asked as he started the car.

She blinked slowly and smiled. "For lunch? How about Mexican?"

"Santiago's?"

"Perfect."

"So, you're not from St. Louis. How long have you been here?"

"I worked at a firm in Charlottesville until I passed the Virginia bar, then I took the job with Anheuser-Busch."

"You're from Virginia, then?"

"No, just went to school there. But you're a local boy, right?"

"Yeah. Went to Missouri, then law school at Northwestern like my dad."

"The founding partner?"

"One of three. Dad, Walter, and Jim Benton started the firm. They could see St. Louis growing as a business center and realized very few companies could afford a legal department. No one ever questioned that I'd follow him."

"I think it's your calling."

"How so?"

"You get this . . . intensity whenever you talk about anything to do with law. Even saying 'my dad started the firm,' your voice changes, you sit up straighter."

"I do not."

"You do. I bet you'd make an incredible trial attorney."

"No desire. Crooks are enough for me. No real criminals, thanks."

"You don't work for crooks, do you?"

"Not on purpose."

"I was going to say . . ."

Inside the restaurant, he held her chair for her before taking his seat. "Listen, I don't drink, but if you want a margarita or whatever, feel free."

"Not on a work day," she said, flipping the menu open. "Want to split this fajita deal?"

"Sure, that'll simplify things."

She laid her menu aside and took a long sip from her water. "So, I bought my first house."

"That's exciting."

"And frustrating."

For the next hour, all through the meal, they talked about tile and wainscoting, skylights and countertops. It reminded him of the easy, no-pressure conversation he used to have with Bobbi. The third time the waiter asked to take their plates, Chuck pushed away from the table. "I guess I should take the hint."

"I can't tell you how much I enjoyed lunch." Tracy held out her hand and Chuck reached to shake it. Her fingers folded around his and she looked into his eyes just as she had that first day. That was no business handshake. He hadn't imagined it. She was interested in being much more than a colleague.

CHAPTER 7
GROUNDWORK

"Something changed last night, Chuck, even before you spoke. What happened?" Phil Shannon sipped from a cup of tea.

"I had a little reality check." Chuck shifted in his seat. He couldn't recall ever being in Phil's office before this moment. "I never intended to confess, exactly. I planned to say what you told me Bobbi needed to hear."

"But you meant it. You weren't negotiating your way out of a divorce, after all. You sacrificed your reputation and credibility to win back the woman you love."

"That pure in heart stuff you said . . . that got me."

"For the record, God said it, not me."

"Thing is, once I got started, it didn't matter as much that Bobbi wasn't there. I wish she had stayed, but I wasn't trying to impress her anymore."

"You have hit the core issue for everything we are going to do." Phil set his cup down and leaned forward in his chair. "This is about you and your relationship with Jesus Christ."

"I thought this was about my marriage."

"The trouble in your marriage is a symptom. I asked Bobbi to give me some time to work with you alone so we can establish a foundation for everything else."

"I messed up, but adultery doesn't take away my salvation."

"I'm not questioning that, but if you'd been where you should have been spiritually, this would have never happened." Chuck shifted and frowned. He preferred interrogations to lectures. "I'm not going to pull any punches with you, and I expect you to be completely honest with me."

"I know," Chuck mumbled. *Nobody's pulling any punches on me.*

"Tell me about this other woman." Phil picked up his cup and took a long drink from his tea. "When did the attraction start?"

"I can't nail it down to a specific event or anything. I just gravitated towards her." Chuck looked down at his shoes, avoiding Phil's eyes. "Pathetic as it sounds now, she reminded me of Bobbi."

"No, that's helpful. In what way?"

"She's very bright and articulate. Focused on her job. Very professional."

"And Bobbi is all those things, too?"

"Yeah, in her own way. Bobbi doesn't have the presence Tracy does."

"Presence?"

"You can't ignore Tracy if she's in the room. There's . . . something about her that draws your attention." Phil scowled. "Did I say something wrong?" *If Phil frowns every time I mention Tracy—.*

"Making mental notes. Nothing to worry about."

"I love my wife, Phil," Chuck said.

"Who are you trying to reassure?"

"I don't want you to think that I have any lingering feelings for Tracy. Because I don't." *I never had any feelings . . . I didn't.* "I only got involved with her after I stopped by her house to fix a light."

"Involved physically, you mean?"

Chuck nodded, again averting his eyes.

"Chuck, what were you thinking?"

"I don't know. She flirted with me all evening, but the instant she kissed me, it didn't matter that I had a wife and kids. Nothing else mattered. When I got home, I swore I'd never be around her again." He dropped his voice and looked away. "I couldn't stop thinking about her, though."

"Then you saw her again that same week?"

"Yeah, I, uh, left my toolbox at her house, and I thought it would start gossip if she brought it to me at work, so I arranged to stop by her place and pick it up." Phil shook his head, and Chuck felt perspiration bead in the small of his back. This sounded so bad. "She, uh . . . she met me at the door looking like a . . . a lingerie model." The heat of guilt swept over him. "Bobbi and the boys got home from Detroit that night."

"What did you say to your wife?"

"Nothing. She was so tired from her trip. I was always working late, crazy hours. She never questioned it." Chuck swallowed hard. "Walter put Tracy on a new case with me. I asked her to work late the Thursday before my last trip to Kansas City and waited for the building to clear out."

"What about Bobbi that night?" Phil asked. Grief replaced any trace of accusation in his voice.

"She, uh, asked me if I got everything finished. I said 'yes' and kissed her goodnight." Chuck wiped his eyes. "Then I laid there beside my wife and wondered how I could see Tracy one more time before I left town."

Admitting this, saying it out loud, made Chuck's stomach roll. He couldn't blame Bobbi if she filed for divorce. "How did I get to that point? I was a good husband, Phil. How could I slide so fast?"

Phil said nothing for several long moments, then he leaned forward and dropped his head, almost apologizing. "There are a number of factors involved, and we'll get into them in much more depth as we counsel. The one thing that strikes me, though, is how God protected you through this."

"Protected me?"

"Don't you see? It was God's grace that this blew up in your face before it destroyed your marriage, and maybe even you. Bad as this is, your wife is willing to forgive you, and to restore the marriage. That may not have been the case after a year, or two, or five. Things could have been much, much worse."

"I don't think I could have stopped the affair."

"Very few people ever do until they're found out," Phil said. "Even if you ended things with this woman, you would've been tangled up with somebody else very soon."

Chuck shifted in his chair. If Phil was right, then his affair wasn't just a case of giving in to a temptation. It was an indication of who he was as a man, a deeply flawed, failed man.

"Are you still with me?" Phil asked.

"I was thinking about what you said."

"Believe me, there is a ready supply of women who wouldn't think twice about getting involved with a married man, especially one with your income and position."

"Yeah, Tracy wasn't all that upset that I was married, just that I didn't tell her up front."

"When did she say that?"

"Yesterday morning—"

"Have you lost your mind? You cannot have any contact with that woman!"

"She called me to have her last word, that's all."

"It had better be." Phil took a deep breath and closed his eyes for a moment. "I lost my train of thought . . . What about pornography?"

How much do I have to admit today? "Not long after I met Tracy, I started surfing the Internet. Except for that, I hadn't bought any magazines or anything since college."

"Late night television?"

"Sometimes."

"Have you ever been unfaithful to your wife before this?"

"Of course not!" Finally, something he had the right answer for.

"You travel a good deal. You ever watch any of those pay per view movies at a hotel?"

"Yes."

"Ever have dinner with another woman?"

"A few times. So?"

"Just stick with me," Phil answered. "Here's the tough one. Have you thought about being with someone else, or even wondered what it would be like to be with another woman? Maybe not any particular woman?"

"Yes." He was ruined. Phil had to think the absolute worst about him now.

"Thank you for being honest," Phil said. "I know it's hard, but we have to face all this head-on."

We? I'm the one doing all the 'facing.'

"Let's switch gears now. What was your marriage like a year or so ago, before any of this was even on the horizon?" He leaned back and picked up his tea again.

"Good."

"Not great?"

"It's been almost twenty years. We're settled into our routines. With our schedules, and now the boys' schedules, we're lucky to have a cup of coffee together."

"So, 'comfortable,' 'safe,' and 'routine?'"

"You make it sound bad."

"I'm not trying to make it sound like anything. I just want to make sure I'm hearing what you're saying. Did you date much in high school and college?"

"Not so much in high school, but I bounced around from girlfriend to girlfriend in college."

"Did you ever get physical with any of them?"

"I had sex before I was married if that's what you're asking." Chuck said. *After everything else, what's a little premarital sex?* "But not after I got serious about Jesus. Bobbi knows all that."

"Give me a rough timeline between meeting Bobbi and marrying her."

"I made a commitment to Christ between my junior and senior year in college, and I met Bobbi the summer after I graduated. I was working for a contractor then, and her dad was a master plumber. She came to pick him up one afternoon at a house we were working on. I'll never forget it."

He smiled, visualizing it once again. "I thought she was five years older than me. Just the way she walked up the sidewalk . . . I had to meet her. She was going to start college in the fall when I went to law school. We got engaged before the summer ended. She worked extra hard to get her bachelor's degree in the three years I was at Northwestern. You baptized me that spring, and we got married that summer after we finished school."

"How were those years being apart?"

"Tough, but I think it helped us both focus on our studies. Plus, Bobbi got to make her own friends and be on her own for a while before getting married." Chuck shifted in his chair again. "Did you talk to her last night?"

"Donna did. She's grappling with quite a bit emotionally. Bobbi's also especially concerned about Brad. He's taking this very hard."

"Joel says Brad doesn't want to speak to me. So what do I need to do to fix things?"

"You can't."

"Then why am I here if it's hopeless?"

"I didn't say it was hopeless. I said *you* can't fix things. You let God make the changes in you that need to be made, and things with Bobbi and Brad will heal. You need to think in terms of months, not weeks."

Chuck dropped his eyes. "That's not what I wanted to hear."

"With your confession, you've laid this huge burden down, and things feel better to you already, but Bobbi's not going to heal until she can't hurt anymore."

Was that possible? "Can I call her?"

"Just take it slow, be patient, and don't push her."

"I see a theme developing."

"You *have* been listening. Let me give you an overview of what to expect from me, and then we'll be finished for today." Phil leaned up to his desk. "I have found that sin, especially big sin, happens when we get lax in our spiritual lives. Our relationship with God becomes mechanical, cold, indifferent, and this leaves us susceptible to attacks or temptations that wouldn't merit a second glance otherwise.

"So, first off, I want you to rediscover your relationship with Jesus Christ, that foundation we talked about. Then we'll look at what's in your makeup that made you vulnerable to an affair, and build a hedge against it ever happening again. From what you've told me, purity issues have been a consistent problem for you, and it's going to take a conscious, active commitment to change that."

"You make it sound like I was an affair waiting to happen." He couldn't mask the frustration. He didn't have time for Phil to drag him through some Bible study designed to point out how rotten he was while Bobbi drifted further and further away.

"Everyone has an area of weakness—"

"You have a problem with women? I find that hard to believe."

"No, mine is anger. I have an explosive, bitter temper."

"That's even less believable."

"Thirty-four years ago, Donna left me. She wouldn't come home, wouldn't talk to me until I got myself under control." He leaned across the desk. "I know where you're at, Chuck. I know how it feels to lose control and have everything you care about in a heap at your feet."

"I'm sorry. I never dreamed—"

"Well, that just shows you the kind of changes God can accomplish when we get desperate enough to let Him." Phil took a long drink from his tea. "Trust me, you can recover from this, and my, it will be worth it." He leaned back in his chair. "Now, Mr. Hot Shot Lawyer, tell me what a contingency fee is."

Chuck smiled. "It's a fee built in to cover unforeseen circumstances or events."

"An extramarital affair was a contingency you never considered, so there was no protection in your marriage against it. I want us to fix that." Chuck nodded. "Okay, your homework, then, is to read the gospels. I want you to note every person Jesus comes in contact with, what their issues were, and how He dealt with them."

"Homework, huh?"

"Yes, I'm very serious about this. I want you to write out a list."

"It's a good thing I'm off work." Chuck said with a slight grin.

"I took that into account. Now, do you have any questions, need anything else from me?"

"Not right now."

"Why don't you pray for us, then?"

"Father God, thank You for Phil and for his time and counsel. Thank You for Your mercy, and for grace and forgiveness. Dear God, help me follow where You lead, and be patient and teachable. In Jesus' name, amen." Chuck stood and shook hands with Phil. "Thanks again."

"Not at all. Let's meet again Wednesday morning."

Ann Molinsky waited as long as she could stand it before calling her son. "How did it go last night?" she asked as soon as Chuck picked up the phone.

"I lived."

"But?"

"Bobbi walked out before I even started."

"Now, it may not be as bad as you think. Did you talk to her Saturday?"

"I don't know what good it did. She was cold and distant. I didn't get to say much."

"She's hurting. She's maintaining that distance because it makes her feel a little safer, don't you think?"

"I'd feel a lot more confident about us if she'd talk to me. Maybe you could talk to her—"

"No. As much as I hurt for you both, as much as I would like this to be over, I don't think it's wise for me to get in the middle. You need to talk directly to each other, not through a third party." Chuck gave her the same silent response he'd used since grade school. "Did you start counseling?"

"This morning. Phil . . . Phil's going to be a big help. More than I realized. I took a five-week leave of absence, too."

"Really?" Maybe Chuck did realize what was at stake.

"I think Walter would have fired me if I hadn't."

"Walter Davis would not have fired you."

"You didn't see his face. He was close."

"Well, he would have made a terrible mistake if he had," Ann said. "I'm proud of you, and the steps you're taking. God's going to honor this."

"That's exactly what Gavin said."

"It's a consensus then." Silence. "You don't agree?"

"Mom, am I a bad person?"

"I think you've done a bad thing, but that doesn't make you a bad person."

"I think I might be." He sighed deeply. "I've got some phone calls to make. I'll talk to you soon."

Later that evening, Chuck unpacked a box of fried chicken and coleslaw, and set it on the coffee table along with his Bible and a legal pad. "Okay, Matthew, what have we got?" he asked, flipping in his Bible to the first gospel. "Chapter one, Jesus isn't born yet. Chapter two, He's a baby. So chapter three, John the Baptist." He scribbled on his legal pad. "John didn't have any issues," he said, writing his observations down. "Treated John with respect, validated John's ministry." He flipped the page in his Bible. "Chapter four. Oh wait. I should pray first."

Father, it hasn't even been a week yet. I don't have the patience for this. I want Bobbi to forgive me and have it over with, but I know she needs time. I can't thank You enough that she's willing to try to work through this.

Be with her and help her see how sorry I am, and that I want to make up for what I've done. Forgive me for being such a jerk with Phil.

CHAPTER 8
ROUTINE

Bobbi stopped in the school office to pick up her mail, then she led Joel to her classroom. She was grateful to have his company for the day. He would keep things light and, best of all, wouldn't give her any advice.

"It's bare!" he said, looking around at the blank walls and empty bulletin boards.

"Now you see how much work I have ahead of me. You may regret coming with me instead of going to Aunt Rita's today."

"Nah, it'd just be me and her. This is better."

Surveying the room, she muttered, "Okay, where to start . . . Joel, why don't you get the desks in groups of four while I go through my mail and try to get a plan."

Joel swept his hand up to his forehead in an exaggerated salute and started dragging desks across the floor. Fighting the impulse to chide Joel for making so much noise, Bobbi turned on the computer on her desk and shuffled through a handful of memos while she waited.

"Wow."

"What is it?" Joel asked.

"I was checking my class list. I have a Kelsey, with an 'ey,' a Kelsee, with an 'ee,' and a Chelsea, plus I have a Tanner and a Tannen."

"Mr. Henneke is messing with you," Joel smiled.

"No doubt. Hey, the desks look good. Now, I'll put you to work on the calendar cut-outs, the weather cut-outs, and the numbers. Then we'll laminate them and cut them all out again. You'll love that part."

"What's Aunt Rita's phone number again?" Joel teased. "Do you have any big people scissors?" Bobbi handed Joel a pair of scissors, along with a stack of construction paper and patterns, then she returned to her computer and began setting up her electronic grade book. Typing in students' names, addresses, and phone numbers was exactly the kind of mechanical task she needed today. No thinking, no reasoning, just read the name and type it in. She flipped the sheet over to get the last child's name and she froze.

The last student on her list was Tracy Caroline Wexler. Tracy. Every day, dozens of times a day, Tracy . . . It wouldn't matter that the little girl was innocent . . .

"Mom, did you hear me?" Bobbi hadn't noticed Joel at her side until he touched her arm.

"I'm sorry, Honey, what did you say?"

"I said I'm done cutting. You can laminate these now."

"Good . . . great."

"Are you okay, Mom?"

"Yes." Bobbi patted Joel's arm, trying to reassure herself most of all. "I'm fine."

"Oh, I looked at your list. That's Seth Wexler's sister. She goes by Caroline. Tracy is her dad's name, too, so it was too confusing."

"Are you sure?"

"Seth has been in my class twice. I'm sure."

"Well, thanks for catching that." Bobbi corrected her list, and thanked God for small graces. "Now, the laminator is around in the next hallway." Bobbi dropped her voice to a whisper. "In the teachers' lounge." Joel gave her a conspiratorial smile.

Bobbi and Joel spent the rest of the morning working on more cutouts and labels. His presence kept her attention on the job at hand and prevented her mind from drifting. A little after noon, Joel spoke up. "So what time is lunch around here?"

"Oh, lunchtime slipped up on me. I bet you're starved. You want to go for a burger?"

"I thought you'd never ask!"

Settled in a booth at Wendy's, Joel devoured his cheeseburger and fries, while Bobbi pushed her salad around on its plastic plate. Joel chattered in between bites about a sequel playing at the multiplex he wanted to see, Cardinals baseball statistics, and an Internet rumor about somebody finding a live frog in their salad. Bobbi struggled to stay engaged in the conversation. After he finished his lunch, he folded his wrapper in a tight square, then spoke without looking up. "Mom, I don't want to upset you . . ."

"But what?"

"I miss Dad." He pushed the wrapper out of the way and lifted his head, with the same tilt Chuck had. "When can he come home?"

"That's hard to say."

"I don't think you could be any sadder with him there than you are without him."

"It's not that simple, Joel." Bobbi boxed up her salad.

"I didn't mean to make you mad."

"You didn't make me mad, but I don't know how I can explain to you how much your dad hurt me. It's going to be a while before seeing him or even talking about him doesn't stir it all up again. I need you to be patient with me, because it's going to seem like forever." Joel nodded, but frowned.

He doesn't understand. He thinks I'm being difficult. God, how do I . . .?

"Here, think of it like this. If a person breaks his leg, and it's all gross, bones hanging out and stuff, he's going to be in the hospital for a while, right?"

Joel sat up straight and nodded. She had his attention now.

"Then he gets a cast and has to wear it for weeks. Even after the cast comes off and everything looks like it's back to normal, he's going to have to go to therapy and do special exercises. It might take years for him to regain all his strength in that leg. If he's old like me, he'll have trouble with it the rest of his life."

Joel nodded again and slurped the last of his Coke.

"It's kind of that way for me, only the hurt is all on the inside. Not having your dad around is like putting a cast on and giving me time to heal. Does that make sense?"

"I guess so." Joel slumped back in his seat and stared out the window. He looked so much like Chuck, with the same irritated squint, the same mouth downturned in a pout. She could never rationalize coping at Joel's expense.

"You're right to miss your dad and want to see him. It's not fair for me to keep you apart, so what if I have Dad come for dinner tomorrow?"

"Really?" Joel leaned up to the table, his eyes wide. "That would be great! I mean, if you're sure."

"Not completely, but I think it'll be okay. It's kind of a compromise. Can we keep it quiet, though, until I get it all arranged?" Joel nodded as he crumpled the neatly folded wrapper. "I'm glad you spoke up, Honey. We all have to work through this, so we have to be able to talk to each other." Bobbi took out her cell phone. "Now let's see if Brad made it to Aunt Rita's." She punched the number in and Rita answered on the second ring. "Hey! Did the boys make it to your house?"

"Not yet. Danny called though. They went for pizza. Hey, what are you doing for dinner?"

"I hadn't thought about it."

"Eat with us then. That'll save you from having to cook. I've got to show a house at six-thirty, so we'll eat early, like five o'clock."

"You've convinced me. We'll finish up at school and be over." Bobbi snapped the phone closed and thanked God for a reason not to go straight home.

The rest of the afternoon, Bobbi sorted through the books she inherited from Mrs. Atwater. She showed Joel how to set the classroom television to pick up regular cable channels. Between TV and the handheld video game he carried everywhere, he had a typical afternoon. Just after four o'clock, Bobbi spoke up. "Hey, let's call it a day."

"I was beginning to wonder if I should have brought a sleeping bag."

"You've been hanging around your sarcastic brother too much."

At Rita and Gavin's house, Bobbi knocked as she pushed the front door open. "We smelled food and came to investigate."

"Come on in," Rita called from the kitchen. "Joel, the guys are out back." Joel turned and went back out the front door while Bobbi made her way to the kitchen.

Rita stood at the island, slicing carrots amid devastation. Open spice bottles, very few of them still upright, littered the counter. Used bowls filled the sink and random cabinets and drawers were opened. "Everything smells great," Bobbi said. "Spaghetti or lasagna?"

"Spaghetti. Who has time to make lasagna anymore?" Rita laid her knife down, and looked Bobbi in the eyes. "You look tired. How are you doing?"

"I'm okay. We stayed busy today. That helped."

"You still sleeping on the sofa?"

"Rita, don't start." Bobbi sighed, then curiosity took over. "How was the speech last night?"

"Simple," Rita answered, slicing a tomato. "He didn't give any details, was very, um, what's the word? Contrite."

"You didn't believe him."

"Why would you say that?" Rita never looked up, but slid the knife through the next tomato, clicking it against the cutting board at the end of each stroke.

"I can tell from the way you cut the tomato."

"Let me put it this way." She laid the knife down. "I think *he* believed what he said. I believe he's sorry. He may even be sorry he hurt you, but he's not going to change, and I don't see how he can make this up to you."

"He agreed to do everything I asked him to when we talked Saturday afternoon."

"And what did you ask him to do?"

"To counsel with Phil, to see a doctor, and to move out."

"Do you think that's wise? He can see her whenever he wants now."

"He doesn't want to be with her."

"He says."

"Living with me wasn't stopping him."

"Do you think Phil will be tough enough?"

"Tough? I want Biblical, wise advice. If I wanted tough, I'd call a divorce attorney."

"You might hold on to that idea." She dumped the sliced tomato into the salad bowl. "So is Phil smart enough for Chuck? None of the rest of us ever have been, so I wonder how Phil is suddenly qualified."

"Just say it, Rita. You hate Chuck, and you think I made a mistake when I married him."

"I don't hate him." She rinsed a bell pepper and began slicing it.

Bobbi decided there would never be a good time to tell her sister. "I'm going to ask Chuck to come for dinner tomorrow night."

"What?" Rita dropped her knife. "Just like that?"

"Joel and I had a talk at lunch. He needs his dad around. It's just dinner, two or three hours."

"So how long before you take him back like nothing ever happened?" It was a rebuke, not a question.

"*I* was the one hurt. Chuck cheated on *me*. Isn't it my decision when and how to forgive?"

"Has he asked you for forgiveness?" Bobbi dropped her eyes. "He hasn't, has he?" Rita tapped the knife on the counter. "Bobbi, you make it easy for him to come back and the next affair is guaranteed."

"You're wrong. I know Chuck."

"You think you know him, but frankly, you're a little blinded right now. You're hurting and you'll do whatever you need to do to ease that hurt regardless of the long-term consequences." Before Bobbi could respond, the back door swung open.

"Who's the old man now?" Gavin announced, his arms raised high. Danny and Brad came in behind him, shaking their heads, with Joel following, a broad grin on his face. "Ask these boys what the final score was!"

"Danny, thank you for letting your dad win," Rita said, with a teasing glance at Gavin. "Wash up, guys."

Gavin gave Bobbi a hug as he walked by. "It's good to see you."

"Thanks." With the guys out of earshot, Bobbi turned back to Rita. "I appreciate you trying to protect me, but I have to do this my way."

"What is your way, Bobbi? Letting Chuck take advantage of you? Make a fool out of you?"

"Rita . . ."

"No! He doesn't deserve that opportunity. I won't let you do this."

"I don't recall asking you for permission," Bobbi said.

"I didn't mean it like that." Rita backtracked, but it was too late. Gavin and the boys returned, cutting the conversation off. Throughout the meal, Bobbi refused to make eye contact with Rita. After dinner, she kept Joel and Brad close as they gathered their things to leave, denying Rita any opportunity to apologize or explain further.

Rita was wrong. She had to be. Chuck would never cheat on her again. *I never dreamed he would cheat in the first place.* Now, in his apartment, it would be much easier for him to get away with it. *Stop! Don't even go there.* For now, she believed Chuck, whether he deserved it or not.

Chuck stretched and flipped the sheet on his legal pad, ready for the second half of Matthew. His cell phone chirped, showing a call from his home. He dived to answer it. "Hello?"

"Are you alone?" It was Bobbi.

"Of course." *How could she think . . .?*

"Sorry, it's just, Rita . . . Never mind. Forget I said anything." He loved her soft, gentle voice. "Listen, the reason I called . . . ummm . . . Why don't you come for dinner tomorrow evening?"

"Are you serious?"

"Joel misses you."

"What about you?"

"It was my idea."

"Will Brad be there tomorrow night?"

"He will. I wouldn't expect much more than that out of him, though."

"There is nothing in the world I would rather do than join you for dinner tomorrow evening."

"Say six o'clock?"

"I can't wait." He heard her take a deep breath. She had more to say.

"I'm sorry I walked out of church last night."

"Don't apologize, please. I understand." Realizing how much he missed her, he wanted to keep her on the line. "Thank you . . . for dinner. I know you're taking a risk."

"I thought about that, but I think it's worth it." Chuck felt a lump in his throat. "Um, I guess that's all I needed to talk to you about."

"I'll see you tomorrow then."

"Goodnight," Bobbi whispered and hung up.

What on earth had changed? Saturday, Bobbi couldn't speak to him without clenching her jaw, and last night she couldn't stand to be in the church service with him. Tonight, she asked him to dinner. It couldn't be over already, could it?

Bobbi stood in her closet, pulling out blouses and holding them up against her, checking herself in the full length mirror. Ordinarily content to let her birthday pass without fanfare, she decided turning thirty-nine was a bigger reason not to draw attention to it, but Chuck wanted to take her out. After the long hours he'd been putting in, she had him all to herself. Brad and Joel were sleeping over at Rita's house, so there wouldn't be any excuses tonight.

She heard the front door open and she glanced at the clock. "Good grief, he's on time."

"Anybody home?"

She heard him coming up the stairs. "In here."

He smiled when he saw her, then crossed the room to the walk-in closet. He kissed her and then straightened the strap on her camisole. "I love what you're wearing."

"Not quite appropriate."

"Depends on what you're talking about." He pulled his tie loose and dropped onto the bed. "Do you care if I don't wear a tie?"

"I'm not wearing one." She settled on a burgundy sweater and gray slacks. It had been an unseasonably warm day for early March, but the weatherman predicted a cold front would pass through later in the evening. "We have seven o'clock reservations at Santiago's."

"Bobbi, you made your own birthday reservations?" he whined.

"I was just trying take one little thing off your list."

"I think I can handle dinner reservations. I set us up at The Stockyard at seven."

"Fine. Last I heard we were going to Santiago's."

"Yeah, I know, but I ate there for lunch."

"You went out to lunch?"

"So?"

"Nothing. I didn't think you had time." All she heard from him these days was a list of things he didn't have time for.

"I still have to eat. We started going out on Fridays last month." He pulled a sweater on over his dress shirt. "Do you care if we make a stop before we get to the restaurant? I'll try to make it fast."

"Where are we going?"

"You'll see." He grinned.

She stopped him before they headed downstairs. "Hey, I want you to know . . ." She put a hand on his arm. "It means a lot to me that you got home on time to take me out to dinner."

"I'm glad it made you happy." He kissed her cheek and headed downstairs.

She glanced around the bedroom before turning out the light. She thought about suggesting that they take advantage of the empty house, but she was half dressed when Chuck got home. If he had wanted to make love, he would have started something then. No matter. They had the whole night, after all.

As they drove, Chuck tapped the steering wheel and sang to the radio, switching the station any time they played a song he didn't know. She couldn't remember the last time she'd seen him in such a good mood. Then he pulled into a new car dealership, a luxury dealer who sold Jaguars, BMWs, Audis, and Acuras. He absolutely was not buying her a car for her birthday.

"Chuck?"

"I want to get your opinion on something." He parked the car and hopped out. She had to take long strides to catch up to him. He stopped in front of a pair of convertible BMWs, a red one and a navy one. "What do you think?" He smiled and held his arms out in front of the cars.

"About what?"

"The car. Pretty sweet, isn't it?" He peered in the window of the red one. "Just two seats."

"Sounds a little impractical. There are four of us."

"Well, we're not all going to be riding in it."

"We aren't."

"No, you always have the boys with you."

"The car's for you?"

"Yeah, what'd you think?" He turned and looked at her with patronizing amusement, the same look he got right before he patted one of the boys on the head when they were little.

"Uh . . . I figured it was for you . . . I was . . . I was kidding with you."

"So, you're okay with me getting it?"

"Now? You just traded cars."

"Over a year ago. Besides, we don't need that monster."

"At least you can drive that monster in snow."

"BMWs are known for their handling."

"But it's a convertible. We do not live in convertible country."

"The days we can put the top down will make it worthwhile, though."

She walked around and checked the sticker in the window. "Chuck! We can't afford this."

"We just add a year to the loan for the Lincoln. Besides, I'm expecting a very good year."

"We can't spend money you haven't earned."

"Bobbi, you don't have any faith in me." He stood in front of the cars again. "I think the blue one."

"You're not listening. We cannot buy this car."

"I appreciate your sense of fiscal responsibility, but we can afford the car."

Knowing she had lost already, she still had to register her protests, just for the record. "What about the insurance?"

"Reasonable, especially for somebody my age." He waved for a salesman. "Yep, this is definitely the one. A sporty convertible."

"Chuck, is something else going on?"

"Of course not. I just have a huge client I'm trying to land, and you even said that my car was one the best ways to make an impression."

"I said . . .?" She shook her head and walked away while Chuck chattered with the salesman. She climbed back in the Navigator and watched the dashboard clock as seven o'clock came and went.

CHAPTER 9
INTRANSIGENCE

Tuesday, August 2

Bobbi lay on the sofa, waiting for the alarm. Wide awake now, she slipped off to sleep soon after talking to Chuck last night. It reminded her of dating Chuck in college. He called every Monday and Thursday evening, always after eleven when the rates went down so they could talk longer. His voice sounded just like that Chuck, the Chuck who was crazy about her, the Chuck she fell in love with.

Rita didn't believe *that* Chuck existed anymore. Bobbi hated fighting with her sister, but dinner was the right thing to do, not just for Joel. Brad needed to deal with his anger, and facing his dad would be the first step, although she'd need a minor miracle for Brad to see that.

She switched the alarm clock off before it had a chance to buzz and grabbed her clothes from the laundry basket. Whispering a blessing on the one who decided to put a shower in the downstairs bath, she got ready for the day. Twenty minutes later, she sat nursing her first cup of coffee when Brad came in the kitchen.

"Morning, Brad," she said, teasing her night owl son. "Does the coach understand how much you love football? That you wake up early for it?"

Brad grunted and shook his head, then opened the refrigerator. He pulled the orange juice out, and gathered four granola bars.

"Breakfast of champions?"

"I'm not real hungry, but I figure it's this, or throw up or something at practice. It's just conditioning this week. I'll be fine." Then he grinned. "Next week, however, I'll be needing a full, home-cooked breakfast. You know eggs, pancakes, the works."

"Will I get to meet the cook you've hired for this before next week?"

Brad rolled his eyes at her. "Get your stuff, then come and sit down. I need to talk to you."

"You know, the last time you needed to talk to me, it was really bad." He slouched in the corner chair.

"Brad, I invited your dad for dinner this evening."

"What?" He snapped up in his seat. "Did he talk you into this? Or was it Pastor Phil's idea?"

"It was *my* idea. You can't hide from him the rest of your life."

"It's not hiding. It's refusing to associate with him."

Bobbi leaned across the table. "I am not divorcing your father, so you and I need to figure out a way to deal with what he's done."

"You can't let him get away with this! He can't waltz back in here like nothing happened. I won't let him."

"Wait just a minute. I'm not asking for your permission. I'm telling you. Your father will be here for dinner. You will eat dinner with the rest of the family, and you will be civil. I don't expect you to pretend nothing happened, but you will be respectful. Is that understood?" Brad didn't respond. "I said, is that understood?"

"Yes, ma'am." Brad forced the words out between his teeth. He ate his breakfast, and passed the ride to football practice in silence.

"I'll see you at twelve-thirty," Bobbi said as she let him out of the car. Brad gave her a half nod and slammed the car door. She watched him trudge the long sidewalk to the practice field and wished she could explain to him that she agreed with most of what he said. She heard herself in every one of his outbursts, and twenty-five years ago, she would have said the very same things.

Bobbi straightened the knives, forks, and spoons at each place setting on the dining room table. *Breathe. It's just Chuck.* She hadn't been this nervous about a meal since the day Chuck took her home to meet his parents. Would he try to make his case tonight? Would he press Brad, or use Joel as leverage against her? Was she playing into Chuck's hands by inviting him in the first place?

She called Donna Shannon after dropping Brad at football practice, desperate for reassurance. "Dinner is a beautiful step," Donna said. "A wonderful idea." Someone finally agreed with her.

Joel bounded into the dining room. "He's here!"

"Let him in. I'll get Brad." Bobbi made it halfway up the stairs before the doorbell rang. *I've got to tell him to stop doing that.*

She knocked on Brad's door. "It's dinner time. Wash up." He didn't answer, but she heard movement, so she headed back downstairs.

Chuck stood in the entry hall and as soon as their eyes met, her reflexes took over, and she moved to kiss him. She'd already leaned in a little too close before she caught herself. "Things . . . are nearly ready." She stumbled backward, then took Joel by the shoulders, and steered him between them. "Go wash up."

"Why are we eating in the dining room?" Joel grumbled. "It's not even a holiday."

"Just go." *Because the kitchen is too intimate. I want some formality between us.*

Chuck followed her into the kitchen and leaned against the sink. "Everything smells great," he said.

"Thanks." Things felt oddly out of balance with Chuck there for dinner on a weeknight, dressed in jeans and sneakers. It had been months since the four of them sat down for dinner. Since before ServMed.

Bobbi filled the plates and set them on the table, and Chuck and Joel took their seats. "Brad?" She called, then shook her head as he slipped into his chair. He'd been watching, waiting for the last possible moment. "Joel, why don't you say grace?"

"Dear God, thank You for this food, for Mom fixing it, and for Dad being here with us. Let him be back with us all the time real soon. Amen."

Brad kicked him under the table, but Joel took it without a word. Bobbi glared at Brad and he dropped his head and began to eat.

Flatware scraped across dishes and glasses clinked, but no one dared speak. After several uneasy minutes, Chuck laid his fork down and looked into Bobbi's eyes. "How are preparations for school going?"

Bobbi sighed with relief. "Good. There's plenty to do, but I think I have a good class. I have twenty-five kids, and I know most of them from either working with them or testing them." Talk of lesson plans and orientation materials filled the dinner hour. Chuck attempted to engage Brad, but the teenager only spit out one-word replies.

After the meal, Chuck folded his napkin and laid it on his plate. "Bobbi, that was great. Brad and I will clean up." He stood and began stacking plates.

Bobbi wanted to check for identification. Chuck never cleared a table in their entire married life. Anytime she had been ill, Chuck's mother took care of the housework. Was this a show, or a genuine change? "Joel, come on. Let's give them room to work."

Chuck stopped in the kitchen doorway and turned back to Brad, seething at the table. "Bring in the glasses, Son." Brad stomped into the kitchen with the glasses and a handful of flatware. "I'm impressed, Brad. I know you didn't want to be here."

"What do you know?" Brad's eyes flashed.

"I know you have a lot on your mind." Chuck set the dishes by the sink, then faced his son. "Let me have it."

"What?"

"Say it, Brad. Get it off your chest."

Brad stared at him for a moment, then he spoke with an arrogant sneer. "All right, I'll tell you what I think. You're a lousy, no-good liar who doesn't deserve to be in the same room with my mother, let alone be her husband! I'm ashamed to admit you're my dad. I don't care how many confessions you make, I'll *never* forgive you." He whipped a dishtowel across the room. "There! Are you satisfied? Is that what you wanted to hear?"

"Yeah, it is." Chuck knelt, picked the dishtowel up, and laid it beside the stack of dishes. "Now how about this? I agree with you." Chuck locked eyes with Brad, and only the teenager's blinking betrayed his surprise. "I don't blame you for being ashamed. What I did was shameful—"

"Why don't you say it?" Brad spit out. "Or can you?"

"I committed adultery. I slept with another woman. I had sex with somebody besides your mother. I betrayed my wife. Good enough?"

Brad stood motionless, white-knuckled fists hooked on the waistband of his baggy shorts.

"Brad, if I could turn back time and undo everything, I would. Nothing is worth causing this much pain to the people I love." Brad stepped back as Chuck got down on his knees. "Breaking my vow to be faithful to my wife was a despicable thing to do. I'm sorry I shamed and hurt you because of it." He swallowed hard. "You've made your feelings on forgiveness crystal clear, and I understand. All I'm asking for is that you to help your mom heal."

"Get up," Brad said at last. "You look ridiculous."

"Not yet. Your anger's justified. It's a man's anger, and you deserve a man's apology."

"Whatever," Brad said, with a dismissive wave. He brushed past Chuck, toward the back stairs that led from the kitchen to the hallway outside his bedroom. Before disappearing, he turned for one last word. "You're not welcome at my football games."

Chuck put a hand on the counter and pulled himself to his feet. Failure sapped his energy and made his body heavy. He opened the dishwasher and began rinsing the dinner dishes and placing them inside. He didn't expect to win Brad over in one night, but he hoped for a little more progress.

Chuck never heard Bobbi come in to help him with the dishes. When she set her tea glass down, he flinched. "Did you accomplish what you set out to?" she asked.

"I've got a lot of work to do," Chuck said.

"This isn't going to be fixed in one evening."

"I didn't expect to fix it."

"But you thought you could come in and lay out your case, and convince him. That's not going to work. He's too emotional right now."

"What about his mother?"

"Chuck, I can't discuss it," she said, turning away from him.

"We don't have to, at least not tonight." He closed the dishwasher and stepped toward her. "I, uh, started counseling with Phil yesterday. He gave me a lot to think about, and some things to study. I made the doctor's appointment you wanted, and I took a six-week leave of absence to work on all this." He paused, hoping in vain to get a response. "I love you and the boys, and I want you to know that I'm not taking this second chance lightly. I'm going to make this right."

She never moved. At least Brad faced him. Chuck waited another uncomfortable moment before giving up. "Thank you for dinner," he said. "I'll, uh, let myself out."

Chuck struggled to contain his excitement on the phone. "Don't worry, Tom. I'll handle everything from here on out . . . This'll be wrapped up by the first of August. I guarantee it . . . No, thank you. I'll be in touch." He dropped the phone onto its base and jumped out of his chair, pumping his fist. "Yes! Yes! Yes!"

ServMed Insurance agreed to let him, or the firm actually, handle their end of the collective bargaining talks between the state university system and the employees' union. ServMed would save the universities money on the coverage, but he had to reassure the union they weren't losing anything in the deal.

A two thousand dollar-a-day deal, and he projected it would run four months. Nearly a quarter of a million dollars, and as the lead and a partner, he'd net a big chunk of that. He pulled up his proposal on the computer. He'd slated two or three attorneys. His choice.

He picked up his phone and dialed Tracy's extension, but it rolled to voice mail. He ended the call and dialed Christine. "Yes, Mr. Molinsky?"

"Is Tracy in with a client?"

"Yes, sir."

"Have her call me as soon as she's free." *He turned back to his desk and started making notes and outlines, losing himself in the details.*

"You wanted to see me?"

"What?" *He looked up and Tracy stood in his office doorway.* "Yeah, come on in, and shut the door." *He pulled a chair around for her. He tried to be patient, waiting for her to sit down.* "I just got off the phone with Tom Conrad at ServMed. He wants me to represent them in the negotiations."

"Chuck!" *She reached over and squeezed his hand.* "That's fantastic. Congratulations. How long have you courted him?"

"Couple of months."

"And you got him. I'm thrilled for you. This is major."

"Single biggest client we've ever had. If we pull this off . . ."

"If *you* pull this off," *she corrected.* "You've done this. You deserve all the credit."

"Thanks. I told Tom this would take two or three attorneys. Would you be interested in working on this? Granted, it would be almost full time."

"Thank you, but no."

"Why not?" *He made a conscious effort to keep his disappointment from showing.*

"It's nothing personal, Chuck. I love working with you, but I have absolutely no interest in labor law."

"And there's no way I can persuade you?"

She stood and smiled. "I made myself a promise long ago not to waste my time on anything that didn't arouse my interest." *He watched her walk to his door, but her hand lingered on the knob.* "Oh, I love your new car. It suits you."

"Thanks. I'm still getting used to it."

"Congratulations again. The old man might even smile over this one."

He laughed and watched her walk back down the hallway toward her office. Her perfume still hung in the air, a spicy scent, so different from anything Bobbi ever wore. Things had been a little tense between them since her birthday. At least the sofa in the study was comfortable to sleep on. He sighed and started packing up his stuff.

Bobbi had to be too young for menopause, but something was going on with her. He never said the right thing. Her mood changed more often than springtime weather. If he didn't know better, he'd say she was pregnant, but he knew better.

Maybe now, with ServMed, he could finally make her see what drove him. He created the opportunity to take the firm to a new level, to build a regional reputation. No, she wouldn't get it. He was tempted not to mention it at all. She would minimize it, and he would get angry. At least Tracy understood. He shut down his computer and turned out the light. He did the right thing, telling Tracy first.

When he got home, he pushed the front door open. "Bobbi? Are you home?"

"Hey!" She came in from the kitchen and threw her arms around his neck. This was more like it. "I have fabulous news!"

"So do I." He set his briefcase down. "ServMed gave me the go-ahead today. I'm going to handle their end in the bargaining this summer."

"ServMed?"

"The insurance company. They're going to be the provider for the university employees' union if the union will go for it. It's my job to make sure that happens."

"This is the one you've been working on for . . .?"

"Months. I contacted Tom Conrad after the first of the year."

"This is the huge one, right?"

He nodded. Huge. "Quarter of a million dollars in fees." Her jaw dropped. Yes. "But this is gonna be my life now. I need you to understand that."

"Just through the summer, though."

"My plan is to be done by August first, so three and a half, four months."

"You don't have any help?"

"Yeah, we'll have a team, another lawyer or two and the support people. I haven't picked them yet."

"You haven't picked them? Walter's letting you pick! It's about time he let you make some management decisions. I don't know why he doesn't retire and just let you have it."

"Thank you for the vote of confidence." He took her hand and they walked back to the kitchen. "Where are the boys?"

"Outside. Don't you want to hear my news?"

"Of course." He crossed his arms and leaned against the sink.

"Okay, Mary Atwater, one of our second grade teachers, announced her retirement at the end of last year, right?"

He nodded, but no, he had no idea.

"Ted offered me her spot today." Her eyes danced. "I'm gonna have my own class!"

"Hey, that's great." He kissed her cheek and reached in the refrigerator for a Coke.

"That's it?"

"What'd you expect?" And now she started.

"Chuck, this is what I've wanted since I started teaching. It's like when you made partner."

He almost spit his Coke out. "You're not serious. Making partner in a law firm is nothing like teaching a roomful of kids."

"No . . . It's about reaching a goal."

"You need to set your goals a little higher, Bobbi." She dropped her arms. Now she was going to light into him.

"You are the most arrogant—"

"Stop. Let's just stop with calling me names, all right? I had a great day, and I don't deserve to come home to this."

"Oh . . . my . . ." She gripped the back of one of the kitchen chairs. "You don't . . . deserve—"

"No, I don't. You don't have any respect for how hard I work, how much skill it takes."

"*And you refuse to recognize that anybody else ever does anything worthwhile!*"

"*I did not say that teaching wasn't worthwhile. You're extrapolating.*"

"*If kids don't learn how to read and do math, they won't grow up to be business people who need lawyers.*"

"*So you're keeping me in a job? That's rich.*" *He shook his head.* "*There's nothing magical about teaching. Anybody could do it.*"

"*You've known since the first day we met that I wanted to teach.*" *She dropped her head and stared at the floor for a moment. He watched her, trying to judge whether she was finished or not. Life would be a lot easier if he let her have the last word. He sipped his Coke, trying hard not to make a sound. He suspected no one ever had to tell Tracy that she wasn't reaching her full potential. No, they probably had to tell her to rein it in a little.*

Bobbi spoke his name and brought him back to the present argument. "*So Chuck, I'm through.*"

"*Wait! Through with what?*"

"*You weren't listening!*"

"*Of course I was listening. I just wanted a clarification.*"

"*You're lying.*"

"*No . . .*"

"*I'm sure someone as skilled and brilliant as you got it the first time.*"

CHAPTER 10
COUNTERPOINT

Wednesday, August 3

Bobbi pulled a pizza from the oven and checked the kitchen clock. Football practice ended twenty minutes ago, so Rita should be there with Brad any minute now. She could finally smooth things over with her sister.

A moment later, she heard the front door open, and soon after Brad shuffled into the kitchen. "Hey, how was practice?"

"Hot." Brad took a bottle of water and a can of Coke from the refrigerator. "Is that my pizza?"

"I just took it out." Bobbi slid the pizza onto a plate for him. He balanced the plate on his Coke can and headed toward the family room. "Where's Aunt Rita?"

"She was right behind me."

Bobbi shook her head and was about to search for her sister when Rita came in the kitchen. "I got a phone call right as we got here. Did Brad disappear already?"

"Yeah, I had his lunch waiting."

"He didn't say two words in the car. I worry about him."

"He's exhausted from practice, and he doesn't talk that much anyway." Rita scowled. "Dinner went well. Thank you for asking."

"Bobbi—"

"You know, I wish you would just support me in this."

"I do support you. You. Not you and Chuck." Rita pulled out a kitchen chair and sat down. Bobbi took the chair across from her. "I love Phil to death, but he sees things very black and white. Gavin is the same way about divorce. That's fine as long as you're dealing with hypotheticals, but when it comes to real people in real situations, things get very gray in a hurry."

"You think I should consider divorcing Chuck?"

"I don't know if that's the right thing or not, but everyone is pressuring you to resolve this too quickly. It hasn't even been a week yet. You need space, and you need to think long term."

"I am. It's in everyone's long-term best interests if we hold this family together."

"If you say so," Rita said. "Are the utilities in Chuck's name or yours?"

"Chuck's. Why?"

"You should change them to your name."

"Because he moved out? That's temporary."

"You don't know that for sure."

"I am not divorcing him!"

"But he may still divorce you. You need to take steps to protect yourself financially and legally."

"Like what?"

"Like opening a checking account in your own name, re-titling your car, and changing the locks. Making him move out was very smart, by the way."

"You watch too much television."

"And you are too naïve! Any lawyer would tell you to take these kinds of steps."

"Any lawyer?" Bobbi folded her arms across her chest and arched an eyebrow. "Or just the one you called?"

"All right, yes, I called a lawyer."

"I don't need this kind of help," Bobbi muttered. "You always, always think the worst, especially about Chuck."

"I think I've been vindicated."

"And that's what counts, isn't it?" Bobbi got up from the table and pushed her chair in. "I'll pick Brad up tomorrow."

"I overstepped—"

"I don't have the energy to second-guess everything I do because you don't approve. From now on, my marriage is a closed subject."

Rita mumbled a weak apology, promising to call in a day or two, and then she slipped out.

Divorcing Chuck was wrong. It had to be. The thoughts of going to court and airing their private life made Bobbi queasy. The alternative wasn't so simple either. She loved Chuck, and would always love him, but how could she put her marriage back together when she couldn't stand to be around him?

Rita overreacted about Brad, too. Teenage boys never discussed their feelings. Granted, he had it out with Chuck, but he vented.

Still . . . Was she playing with Brad's well-being by working toward reconciliation before he had a chance to process everything? He would never give her a straight answer and he had no interest in talking to his youth pastor. Maybe it was time to get Phil involved.

Thursday, August 4

It's two-fifteen," Phil said. "We did say Thursday, right?"

"That's what I told Bobbi," Donna said.

Across the office from Donna, Cooper DeWitt stood up. Phil asked him to sit in, hoping the boys, especially Brad, might be more comfortable. "I'll check the parking lot," he said.

Before he could cross the room, the outer door opened and Brad said, "Just shut up, Joel! I'm here, all right!"

"Brad, straighten up!" Bobbi reprimanded. She shepherded her sons into the study, her face flushed. "I apologize for making you wait."

"Brad didn't want to come," Joel said.

"I don't blame him," Phil said, robbing Brad of the opportunity to snap back at his brother. "Have a seat." Three empty chairs faced Phil's desk, between Donna and Cooper. "Having to sit in your pastor's office and discuss your dad's affair is a rotten place to be."

"Pastor Phil," Brad said. "I don't want you to take this wrong, but I don't see what we're doing here. My dad can't take back what he did. I never want to speak to him again."

"What about you, Joel?"

"Dad said he was sorry. It's supposed to be over, right?"

Phil caught just a glimpse of Brad rolling his eyes.

"In the simplest terms, yes," Phil agreed.

"That's not right!" Brad jumped in. "Mom, tell him!"

"Brad, listen to Pastor Phil," Bobbi said.

"No! If you won't stand up for yourself, I will!"

"Brad! Sit down!" Bobbi said. The boy locked eyes with his mother, hesitated, then slumped into his chair. "Phil, I'm sorry, maybe we should try another day."

"No, he's fine," Phil said, trying to reassure her. "Let's try a different approach." He reached in his desk and pulled out three pads of paper with pens attached. He handed one to Cooper. "Cooper, take Joel down the hall like we discussed."

"Sure thing," Cooper said, taking the pad. "Come on, Buddy. Let's blow this popcorn stand." Joel grinned, clearly thankful to be leaving.

As they left, Phil handed his wife the second notepad and pen. "Donna, you and Bobbi find someplace quiet."

"You sure you want to be in here with him?" Bobbi asked before she left.

"Positive," Phil said.

"Brad, behave," Bobbi said, but he wouldn't look up.

Phil listened for doors down the hall to close. "All right, it's just me and you. What else is on your mind?"

Brad sighed. "Look, I came because of my mom, but no one on God's green earth, not even you, can talk me into forgiving my dad."

"Because?"

"Why doesn't anybody understand this?" Brad said. "My dad is a liar and a phony. My mom should divorce him now before he does something else."

"Divorce him?"

"Yes. It says that in the Bible for adultery. I looked it up."

"The Bible says divorce is allowed, not required, in cases of adultery," Phil clarified.

"Whatever."

"Your dad has always been an adulterer?"

"I don't think so, but who knows?"

"So he changed once, from a non-adulterer to an adulterer. Could he change again?"

"Can a murderer change back into a non-murderer? He can't undo it."

Brad argued like a lawyer's son. Phil had to give him credit. "Then who has he hurt?" Phil slid the pad across the desk. "Make me a list." Brad took the pad, yanked the pen from the top, scribbled some names, then slid the tablet back.

"You, your mom, and your brother," Phil read. "Well, you left a lot of names off this list." He took the pen from his shirt pocket. "What about the other woman?"

"What?" Brad yelled. "Don't you dare put her name down!"

"Your dad took advantage of her, used her, and she may never see that she needs Jesus because of your dad." Phil continued to write. "Then there's me and my wife. I married your mom and dad. How does this reflect on my ability to counsel the couples in my charge?"

"This is *not* your fault."

"I didn't say it was my fault. It's your dad's fault. I'm just saying I got hurt. Then of course, there's your Aunt Rita and Uncle Gavin, Danny, Kara, John, and Kelly, and your grandmother."

Phil never looked up at Brad even as the list grew longer. "Everybody your grandpa knew, every client at the law firm, the parents of every student your mom teaches, all your friends and their parents, Boy Scouts, little league baseball players, Cooper and the other kids in the youth group, my church and my Lord."

Brad sat up straighter in his chair. "Oh, I agree with you that my dad hurt way more people than he realizes. He has no idea how much damage he's done."

"Let's start at the bottom of the list." He pushed the tablet back to Brad. "Jesus Christ. He was beaten, spit on, and crucified for your dad. And here, your dad goes out and humiliates him all over again."

"Exactly," Brad said.

Phil smiled, and set the trap. "You know what 1 John 1:9 says?"

"Not right off."

"A hundred years ago, when I was nine, I learned it like this. 'If we confess our sins, He is faithful and just to forgive us our sins and to cleanse us from all unrighteousness.'"

He saw Brad grip the arms of the chair. The boy knew what was coming. The forgive part.

"Your dad has done that very thing, and God has forgiven him. You understand justice, right?"

"That's what I want," Brad said.

"Then that verse says it's just, fair, and right for God to forgive and cleanse us if we confess."

Brad lowered his eyes.

"More than that, after doing one of the most despicable things a man could do, your dad did one of the most courageous things I've ever seen." Phil leaned forward. "See, you missed it Sunday evening. He stood up in front of the whole church, told them what he had done, then asked for their forgiveness."

"He lied to them, too," Brad said.

"A man's hands don't shake when he's lying. He confessed and he begged for forgiveness. It was the most incredible church service I've ever been in . . . because they forgave him."

Phil pointed at the list. "Your brother has already forgiven him."

"That's because Joel doesn't get it."

"Your mom surely gets it, and she forgives him."

Brad shifted, stretching his long legs in front of him.

"This is not about your mom, is it?" Phil asked.

Brad sat, biting his bottom lip, and Phil knew then, he'd hit the issue.

"Your dad is not the man you thought he was and you're disappointed, embarrassed, and even ashamed of him. He let you down."

Brad never looked up, and wrestled with each word. "Do you know how furious that makes me? Or how stupid I feel for thinking my dad was such a great guy?" After a long pause, he raised his eyes. "I just can't do it, Pastor Phil. I can't forgive him."

"Son, I'm not trying to badger you into saying something you don't mean just to get me off your back. Promise me you'll think about what I said, and pray about it. At least consider the possibility that you might forgive him."

"A very slim possibility."

"Fair enough."

"Your office is a lot smaller than Pastor's Phil's," Joel said, as Cooper closed the door.

"Yeah, I inherited a broom closet," Cooper said with a smile. "But it's big enough for my bookcase, my laptop, my couch, and my refrigerator from college. You want something to drink?"

"Thanks," Joel said, taking a can of Mountain Dew from Cooper. He flopped onto Cooper's couch and stretched his legs out.

Cooper pulled out a folding chair for himself, opened his soft drink, and set the can on the floor. "Okay, Joel, your dad cheats on your mom. He's not at home anymore. Everybody's on edge, and it's not too clear what's going to happen next. Does that about sum it up?"

"I guess."

"How are you with all that?"

"I'm okay. Dad said he was sorry, and when everybody's gotten over being mad, Mom will let him come home."

"You mad?"

"No."

"Afraid?"

"Not now."

"What *were* you afraid of?"

"That Mom and Dad would get a divorce." He downed his Mountain Dew, and debated whether he should rat out his brother. "Brad says they're gonna split."

"But you don't think so. What's the difference?"

"Brad won't talk to Dad. Dad told me they're not getting a divorce. He said he loves Mom, but he was an idiot. Mom told me that too, the 'no divorce' part, not the 'idiot' part."

"So, you're good?" Cooper asked.

"I'm good."

"Sleeping and eating like you should?"

"Yep."

"That was easy," Cooper said, drinking from his Coke. "Anything else you want to talk about? Any questions?"

"Yeah, what's the paper for?"

"To make Brad think everybody was doing the same thing he was so he'd cooperate."

"Sweet."

At the end of the hallway, Bobbi and Donna settled in a classroom, taking corner seats at the end of a long table. "Phil may be through counseling us after this meeting with Brad," Bobbi said, shaking her head.

"Nonsense. We raised two boys. Phil can handle him. So, how was dinner with Chuck?"

"Fair," Bobbi said. "He and Brad had it out after we ate."

"That's not necessarily a bad thing," Donna said. "What about you?

Did you and Chuck talk?"

"He tried. Chuck would've talked all night if I'd let him."

"But you didn't."

"I can't. I can't even look at him."

"How did you get through the dinner then?"

"We talked about school. That's a whole different part of my brain."

"Honey, you need to talk to Chuck. I know it's hard, but you have to work at this together. Have you talked to him at all?"

"Saturday, he came to the house, and I, uh, interrogated him."

"Did he crack?" Donna smiled, but it didn't lighten the mood.

"I nearly did. He told me everything . . . everything I asked him, anyway. She's a thirty-year-old lawyer. He started seeing her when I was out of town the second week of July."

"Oh, Bobbi," Donna murmured.

"There. That's it. If I go any further, my imagination goes berserk, and I start wondering what he said to her . . . how he kissed her . . ." She squeezed her eyes shut, and tapped a clenched fist on the table, trying to push the thoughts from her mind. "Can we change the subject? Please?"

"Well, it's not much of a change. Phil wants you to write down anything you want him to go over in counseling, either when he's talking to Chuck, or when he meets with you both."

Bobbi took the pad of paper and pen Donna offered. Where to begin? Questions swirled through her thoughts every waking moment. She pondered for several moments, then she distilled everything into one simple question. 'How can I trust Chuck again when I can't separate him from what he did?'

Bobbi straightened chairs and put away the crayons and markers after her preschoolers cleared out of the Sunday school room. As she dropped her teacher's guide in her tote bag, she spotted Chuck walking across the church parking lot, his hands stuffed deep in the pockets of his slacks. She ducked out

the door close to nursery and caught up with him in several long strides. "Is everything okay?"

"Fine," he said, but never raised his head or broke stride.

"You're not staying for the worship service?"

"I've got a couple things I need to get done before I leave this afternoon."

"You're leaving today? I didn't think you were leaving until tomorrow morning."

"This will be easier on me. I won't have to get up at three-thirty."

"But you were going to slip out of church, and not say goodbye?"

"I didn't want to interrupt your class."

She pulled at him until he turned to face her. "Chuck, what is going on?"

"Nothing. I told you ServMed would be my life until it was settled."

She studied his face for a moment. Something else troubled him. She knew it. "You feel okay?"

"Yeah, why?"

"You're not sleeping. I can tell you've lost weight. You're short-tempered—"

"Bobbi . . ." He shook his head slowly. "I'm fine. Everything's fine."

"Did you decide about the trip to Detroit? The All-Star game?"

"There's no way."

"We haven't had a vacation in a couple of years. This is perfect. Why don't you want to go with us?"

"I can't afford the time away right now."

"You love baseball . . ." She glanced back toward the church to make sure no one else was leaving. "So you were gonna sneak out of church without telling me. You're leaving early for Kansas City, and you don't want to go on a vacation with us. It makes . . . It makes me think it's me, Chuck, like you're avoiding me."

"Bobbi . . ." he whined. "If it was in September or October, I'd go."

"So it's just work?"

"Yes."

"And you feel fine?"

"Yes, can I go now?" He flipped his wrist over and checked his watch.

"*I'm not through, yet. I know it's getting close to the time of year when your dad died. I know for me . . .*"

"*I'm not you. Dad died six years ago. I don't even think about it anymore.*"

"*What do you think about?*"

"*What kind of question is that?*"

"*Because you used to tell me. You used to tell me everything. Now, you don't care what's going on with me, and you won't open up—*"

"*This is ridiculous. I've got to go.*"

He started to walk away, but she reached for his arm. "*While you're in the car this afternoon, I want you to think long and hard about what your priorities are. I'll put up with this while you're on this case, but come September, things have got to change.*"

"*Don't lecture me.*" He jerked his arm out of her grip. "*My priorities are right where they should be! Providing for my family!*" He paced away, but turned back and leveled a finger at her. "*I'll tell you what's got to change! You, Bobbi! You used to support me one hundred percent. You used to build me up, encourage me, but now you hit me as soon as I walk in the door with a list of everything I failed to do.*"

He raised his hand, holding it inches from her, counting with more anger and intensity with each point. "*I'm not home enough. I don't spend enough time with the boys. I spend too much money. I don't meet every single emotional need you manufacture—*"

"*What? You're mad because I want to spend time with you?*"

"*It's not spending time! You want to control me. You weren't like this when we got married.*"

"*And you weren't a paranoid workaholic! I wish you could hear yourself. Who else is against you, Chuck, or is it just me?*"

"*And now you're mocking me. Very helpful.*"

"*I'm not mocking, I love you. I will always love you, but right now, I can't stand to be in the same room with you.*"

"*The feeling's mutual, Sweetheart.*" He stalked away, got in his car, and squealed his tires before speeding away.

As soon as he was out of sight, her hands began to shake and she had to brace herself against the nearest car. "Lord God, I don't know who he is anymore."

CHAPTER 11
EXAMINATION

FOUR WEEKS LATER
Friday, September 2

"Mr. Tennant," the nurse called, and Chuck watched yet another seventy-year-old man make his way back to see Dr. Andy Hokoana. Even so, Chuck preferred the discretion of private practice to the speed of a clinic. The check-up was the last thing on Bobbi's list, and meeting Bobbi's requirements while protecting her privacy was just what he wanted.

Tuesday, he'd resume his normal work schedule and rejoin society. He ate with his family three precious nights and he met with Phil at least twice each week, but he spent the rest of his time alone. The loneliness gnawed at him.

He checked into a gym membership just to get out of his apartment, but after spending the trial evening surrounded by young women in workout gear, he dropped that idea. Far too dangerous.

Instead, he bought running shoes. Each morning he poured out his heart to God during his run, then he hit the books like a seminary student. In the afternoons, he worked at the small mountain of paperwork from BD&M, keeping Walter Davis happy.

Since he'd destroyed his reputation at Preston Road Community Church, he never hesitated to make his way to the altar during the invitation to pray. He confessed his pride, his failure to love Bobbi selflessly, and his undeniable refusal to listen to anyone who suggested he was wrong.

The more he learned from Phil, the more he marveled that Bobbi stayed with him, even before the affair. He took her for granted, never listened to her, and bossed rather than led, but she loved him in spite of it all. Every day he prayed for the opportunity to love her the way she deserved.

A nurse entered from one of the side doors and called his name. She smiled and held the door for him. "Follow me," she said, with a bright smile. Leading him into an exam room, she scanned his file. "They didn't write down the reason for your visit." She looked up at Chuck with her pen ready to write.

"That's because I didn't tell them." Chuck relaxed when she laid her pen down.

"Let me get your blood pressure then." She quickly took a reading. "One thirty-two over eighty-six," she said, and wrote the number down. "Is that typical for you? It's on the high end of normal."

"Stress."

"You might keep an eye on it." She straightened his paperwork, then closed the folder. "He'll be right in," she said and then slipped out.

Within minutes, an enormous Polynesian man came in the exam room. He stood at least six-and-a-half-feet tall, with his long hair pulled back into a ponytail. His glasses hung on a chain around his neck. "Hi, I'm Andy Hokoana," he said, extending his hand. After the handshake, he flipped Chuck's file open and slid his glasses on. "Well, Mr. Molinsky, when you won't say what you're here for, I know it's got to be about sex. So what is it?"

Chuck felt the heat rising on the back of his neck as Dr. Hokoana looked straight into his eyes. Shame stirred inside him. *Just get it over with.*

"I had an extramarital affair and my wife requested that I have an exam and get tested for sexually transmitted diseases."

The doctor sat down and began writing. "Do you have reason to suspect you have a disease?"

"No."

"No symptoms?"

"No."

"Any other partners besides your wife and the other woman? I'm assuming it was a woman." He looked at Chuck over the top of his glasses.

"Yes, it was a woman." *Sheesh! I don't need this.* "What else did you ask me?"

"Any other partners?"

"You mean ever?"

"Yes."

"Twenty . . . twenty-five years ago. That doesn't matter though, right?"

"That remains to be seen. How long has it been since you had sex with this other woman?"

"Five weeks."

"Have you had sex with your wife since then?"

"No. Well, I mean, I was with my wife during the affair."

Dr. Hokoana finished writing, closed the folder, and took his glasses off.

"Mr. Molinsky, your wife is wise to ask for this. She should consider getting tested as well. Should any results come back positive you'll need to inform your lover . . ."

"She's not my lover." Chuck said.

"What you call her is irrelevant to me. My part in this is medical, not moral. Should any of the tests come back positive, you have an obligation to inform her, and these other women as well."

"There won't be any positive results."

"If you knew that, Mr. Molinsky, you wouldn't be here. Now then, I'll do a physical exam, take some samples, and draw some blood. I'll have you come back in for an HIV screen because that takes six weeks to show up. Then in a week or two after that, all your results will be back, and we'll go from there. Any questions?"

"No, I guess not." *Inform my 'lover?' God . . . please. Spare us that much.*

The doctor stood and slid open a drawer in a small metal cabinet. He took out a folded paper gown and tossed it to Chuck, smiling ever so slightly. "I'll give you a few minutes. That opens in the front."

Bobbi drove to the church for her four o'clock appointment with Phil and Chuck for their first joint session. Throughout the day, twinges of hope welled up inside her, but reality choked them away. Chuck cheated, but he confessed. It hurt with relentless freshness every time she saw him, but she forgave him. In time, she would exhaust her store of protests, then he would come home, and life would go on.

In some ways, that appealed to her. Isolated and abandoned by her friends and church family, at odds with Rita, she questioned whether she was accomplishing anything by holding out.

She pulled into a parking place near the church's side door. If she could get out of Phil's office without losing her composure, it would be a major victory.

Chuck pulled in and parked his car beside hers. He smiled at her, then got out of his car and waited at her front bumper to walk inside with her. "How does it feel to have your first full week over with?" he asked.

"Great," she said, brushing past him to open the door.

"Here. Let me." He held the door for her. She eyed him with suspicious surprise before stepping through the door. Phil Shannon sat behind his desk with a half dozen books open in front of him. Chuck knocked on the doorframe.

"Wow, is it four already?" Phil asked, looking at his watch. He stood to shake hands with Chuck and Bobbi. Immediately, he grabbed the corner of his desk and sat down again.

"Phil? Are you okay?" Chuck took two steps around the desk toward the pastor.

"I'm fine. The doctor changed some of the medication I take for my blood pressure. He said to expect some dizziness for a little while." He released his grip on his desk one finger at a time. "I just stood up too fast. It's happened before."

"We can reschedule," Bobbi said, hoping.

"No need. I've worked all day. I'll not stand up so fast next time."
Then with a smile, he said, "Come and sit."

Chuck waited for her to sit before taking the other chair. She never
looked in his direction.

Phil closed up his books and set them on the floor. "Let's pray first," he
said and bowed his head. "Father God, we need You as we try to help
Chuck and Bobbi heal their marriage. We know that it's Your will for us
to have strong marriages and families. Give us wisdom, compassion and
patience. Glorify Yourself through all this. In Jesus' name. Amen."

He leaned back in his chair. "First off, let me say, Bobbi, you and
Chuck have already made great advances toward restoration and healing."
He glanced at Chuck, then spoke to her. "He's taken this very seriously.
In all the counseling I've done, I doubt if I've had two out of a hundred
take it to heart and follow what I tell them. So far, Chuck is one of those."

Bobbi heard Chuck shift in his chair and knew he was soaking in the
compliment. How could she avoid being cast as the bad guy now? *Chuck
did everything he could, but she was unreasonable . . .*

Phil continued, "I also appreciate your willingness to forgive. You've
fought half the battle by separating the issue of forgiveness from the pain
of the affair."

His eyes darted back and forth between her and Chuck. "However,
now it will get challenging. We're going to get personal. I don't want to
mislead you. It's going to be hard and it's going to hurt. You're both
going to come up against some painful truth about yourselves and your
marriage, but that's how you heal. As long as we deny or ignore things, we
can't heal them."

Bobbi crossed her legs. *Personal, painful truth . . . great. Just what I
need.*

"I commend you both on being so honest and open through this. I also
want you to know that nothing you say will cause me to think less of you,
or shake my desire to see you work this out. All right?"

She nodded. Everyone wanted to see them work this out. They never spoke to her, but they supported her completely.

"Bobbi, how old were you when your mother died?"

Phil caught her off guard with the question. "Twelve. It was right after Rita married Gavin. Mama was growing weaker all the time, but she seemed determined to make it until the wedding."

"Then it was just you and your dad?"

"Yes, but he had a lot of trouble coping with losing Mama. He withdrew from everything, and at some point, he started to drink. He was never a violent or abusive alcoholic. He hurt, and dealing with a teenage daughter was beyond his ability."

She never talked much about her dad, and out of the corner of her eye, she could see Chuck lean forward, listening. "I never saw him. He came home from work and went to his room. Rita shopped and cooked for us. I took care of the house and raised myself."

"You did a very good job," Phil said. "Tell me about your spiritual life growing up."

"We were raised Catholic, but Rita came here with Gavin after they married, and I came to some of the youth events. I got more involved and everything clicked when I was fourteen."

"Then your dad died before you and Chuck were married, right?"

She nodded. "He died in February before we got married in July."

"So why'd you marry Chuck?" Phil asked with a smile, glancing toward Chuck.

Bobbi took a deep breath. "From the moment I met Chuck, I felt like I was the only person in the world. He made me feel like I was the center of the universe."

"What about now?" Phil asked.

"I feel like I've been tossed aside. Worn out, used up." Bobbi kept her eyes fixed on Phil. She didn't want to see if her words had any effect on Chuck.

"Can you go back a year or so and tell me how things were between you and Chuck then?"

"Good. We enjoyed each other's company. We talked. What else do you want to know?"

"No complaints at all?"

"Things weren't perfect. We never seemed to have enough time for each other, but I doubt anybody does." Phil nodded slightly. He was giving her every opportunity, every possible opening to attack Chuck. She was her father's daughter, though, and she preferred throwing up emotional walls, bearing her pain privately.

"Bobbi, I'm sure that the one overriding question plaguing you is 'why.' Even though we can make some headway on it, we can never explain it. Even if we could, that wouldn't justify it."

If we can't explain it, why are we here?

"Here's where it gets dicey. Each of you brings a past and a personality into your marriage. Those determine where the trouble spots in your marriage will be."

Phil leaned forward, putting his elbows on his desk. "Everyone has trouble spots in their marriage, even Donna and me. Sometimes they lead to anger, bitterness, or resentment that hang over a couple for years. Many times a husband and wife don't even recognize that they have fallen into discontent."

Was that us? Did I discount all the signs?

Phil looked at her, then at Chuck. "All that is to say, that in order to protect your marriage from future problems, we have to identify and deal with all these issues."

He then fixed his gaze on her alone. "My biggest concern is that you don't come away from this process thinking you were the reason Chuck was unfaithful to you. You didn't cause it. You didn't drive him to it."

Tears began to well up in her eyes. Had Phil convinced Chuck of that?

"Chuck was wrong. No matter what was going on in your lives, in your marriage, committing adultery was wrong."

Chuck's chair squeaked.

"But if things don't change, you may be right back here at some point in the future," Phil said.

I'm not coping this time. We can't do this again.

"Now the flip side," Phil said, turning to Chuck. "Just because Bobbi has been wronged doesn't mean that she is intrinsically right on every issue that comes up. You still have to be the spiritual leader in the household. You can't do that if we completely tear you down. We have to equip you for Christ-like servant leadership."

Chuck, the servant? Not this Chuck.

"Finally, we need to get the two of you on a schedule. Starting out, I'd like to meet with you Monday, Wednesday, and Friday. I know it's a lot, but with you having dinner on the alternate days, that gives us the opportunity to address anything that comes up on those days. Unless you had plans, I included this Monday."

Bobbi murmured her agreement with the schedule, as if she had a choice. Chuck took those choices away from her when he decided to commit adultery. So now, they would talk, three days a week, dredging up everything the two of them ever did wrong. She realized she missed Phil's question, but Chuck was answering.

"Joel is great. I mean, considering everything. He's a peacemaker."

"How do you think Joel is coping?" Phil asked her directly.

"He looks at things simplistically, a black-and-white kind of kid. It's hard for him to understand why things aren't fixed already. He's not the type to hide anything, so I usually know what's going on inside him."

"And Brad?" Phil asked.

"Brad is another story. He's making progress. He'll talk at the dinner table, although not to Chuck." Bobbi glanced at Chuck. He leaned forward in his chair. "It's hard to get an idea what he's thinking or feeling because he's very tight-lipped. There's still so much anger and bitterness toward his dad. He's embarrassed, and he's had to let go of his beliefs about his family."

Bobbi dropped her eyes. "I can identify with a lot of his feelings. He's got a knack for saying exactly what I feel. Some days I'd like to vent that way."

"What stops you?"

"Maturity."

"Do you think it would help Brad if Chuck moved back home?"

"No. If Chuck were home, things would be worse."

"Worse for Brad . . . or worse for you?"

"Just worse," Bobbi said, dodging the question. She checked her wrist-watch with an exaggerated motion. "Gentlemen, I have two boys I need to feed before the game tonight. I hope you understand. Besides, we weren't going to solve it all this afternoon anyway." Bobbi gathered her purse. "Chuck, you don't need to walk me out. Phil, please don't get up. Thank you." Before either man could protest, Bobbi was gone.

"Wow, I hit a nerve," Phil said.

"She said more about her feelings to you just now than she's said to me through this whole situation," Chuck admitted. "She won't talk to me."

"She's coping by maintaining control of the dialogue." Phil rubbed his eyes. "I'm going to have to rethink things a bit before Monday."

"What can I do?" Chuck asked.

"Don't press her. She doesn't feel safe when she's not calling the shots, so continue to be patient with her. It'll be worth it."

Chuck stood up to leave. "Are you going to be okay? You know, the dizzy spell."

"Sure. Watch." Phil leaned forward, grasping the arms of his desk chair. He stood slowly, carefully, paused for just an instant, and then let go of the chair. "See, it's all technique."

"This is nothing serious, right? They can control your blood pressure with medication, can't they?"

"I come from a rotten gene pool. We've been watching my blood pressure since I was in my twenties. I've eaten low-fat, low cholesterol for years. My dad never saw age fifty, and here, I've made it to fifty-six. Don't worry. It's in God's hands, not my doctor's." Phil smiled, and shook

Chuck's hand good-bye.

Chuck walked out of the church building, hoping Bobbi might still be around, and came face-to-face with a sheriff's deputy. His cruiser blocked Chuck's BMW. "Is there some sort of problem?"

"Charles J. Molinsky?" the deputy asked, checking the name on a large envelope.

"Yes."

"You've been served," he said, handing Chuck the packet. Chuck's stomach tightened before he pulled the papers out.

TRACY K. RAVENNA, PLAINTIFF

V.

CHARLES J. MOLINSKY, DEFENDANT

In paragraph four, the words jumped off the page. 'Sexual harassment.' 'Hostile work environment.' On the next to last page, she asked for a quarter of a million dollars punitive and compensatory damages.

After the football game, Bobbi and the boys walked across the deserted parking lot toward her car. Brad recounted every play from his on-field perspective, including his four catches for forty-five yards.

"Not a bad first game," he said, swinging his bag of gear in a wide arc.

Seizing the opportunity as Brad paused to breathe, Joel yelled out, "Hey! That's Dad's car!" and took off at a dead run.

Brad's expression clouded. "I told him not to come."

"Let it go, and get in the car," Bobbi said. She watched Joel talk to Chuck for a minute or two, then he ran back toward them.

"Can you believe he sat in the parking lot through the whole game?" Joel exclaimed as he reached his mother and brother. "He said to tell Brad he had a great game and he'd see us tomorrow."

Bobbi turned to her older son, "See, your dad respected the boundaries you laid down, but he still wanted you to know how much he loves you, and how proud he is of you."

"I'm not proud of him," Brad said, already settled into a pout.

"Mom, Dad said he needed to talk to you over by his car," Joel said. "He said it was important."

Chuck needed Bobbi right now. He needed her to understand, to share his outrage, to take his side. He watched her glance in his direction as she talked to Joel. *Please, Bobbi . . .*

Bobbi looked across the empty lot where Chuck stood outside his car, waiting for her. "I'll be right back," she muttered. Once she got close enough to read his expression, she asked, "Chuck, I'm exhausted. Couldn't this wait until tomorrow?"

"She's suing me!" His eyes blazed, and his neck and face reddened. "That . . . She . . . She says I harassed her and created a hostile work environment! *She* came on to me! I didn't . . ."

"How did you find out? She didn't call you, did she?"

"I got served this afternoon! In the church parking lot!" He clutched a large envelope, holding it up for Bobbi to see.

Across the parking lot, Brad and Joel watched their parents. "He looks mad," Joel said.

Brad reached in his mother's purse, pulled out her phone, and handed it to Joel. "If he touches her, you call the police."

"What are you gonna do?"

"Depends on what he does in the next thirty seconds," Brad said.

Bobbi took the envelope from Chuck and pulled out the papers as he began to pace.

"This is ridiculous! She has no case. She never complained to Walter . . . That's critical in a sexual harassment case, to get the supervisor involved . . . There's no documentation . . ."

Bobbi strained to read by the parking lot lights. Giving up, she opened the passenger door of Chuck's car and sat sideways, using the dome light. She waded through the legal language to the heart of the document. There, Tracy spelled out in unflinching detail what transpired during each of their three encounters. What she said. What he said. Every kiss . . . Every touch . . . It was all a matter of public record.

She rubbed her temple with now icy fingers. *The boys . . . dear God, if the boys ever saw this . . .* 'The defendant placed his hand on the plaintiff's thigh . . .'

"**Mom's throwing up!**" Joel said, poking Brad's shoulder and pointing. "You think I should call an ambulance?" He held the phone ready.

"Easy, Joel," Brad answered. "It's just vomit, but keep watching."

"**Bobbi, I'm sorry** . . ." Chuck panicked. "Let me see if I can find some water or something." He reached behind the seat, then started rummaging through the glove box. "I should have prepared you . . ."

"Pay her." Bobbi wiped her mouth with the back of her hand, grasped the car door to steady herself, and started to walk away.

"I've defended these before. I know what it takes to prove harassment. She's got nothing. Most of what she said is an out and out lie."

"Most if it?" She spun back around to face him. "So some of this is true?"

"Well . . ."

"The conference room? At the law firm? Chuck, that's disgusting!" She stared up into the night sky. She wouldn't give him the satisfaction of seeing her cry. "I didn't think this nightmare could get any worse. I thought you had humiliated me as much as . . ."

"That's just it, Bobbi. I can stop this in its tracks. No judge is going to allow this to move forward once I answer all these claims."

"And I can't risk having my sons exposed to this. Do you want Joel to hear all about the way you unbuttoned her blouse? Pay her, and get rid of her."

"That'll look like I'm guilty. And a quarter million dollars! That's my whole retirement fund. I'll have nothing left."

"Chuck," she snapped, her finger inches from his face. "I'm only going to say this once more. You pay that woman off. If you take this to court, I will divorce you."

CHAPTER 12
QUESTIONS

Saturday, September 3

Bobbi forced her eyelids open, awakening to far too much light. The mantle clock showed a quarter after ten. *Ten? I never . . . Not since the flu . . .* She pulled herself up and checked the clock to ensure it hadn't stopped during the night. It ticked away second by second. *Ten fifteen.*

She wandered through the family room where Joel was playing video games. "Hey, Baby, want some coffee?"

"Have I ever wanted coffee?" he asked, pausing his game.

"Did you get breakfast?"

"I'm okay."

"No signs of life from Brad?"

"You're kidding, right?"

"Yes," she said with a gentle smile. "Thanks for letting me sleep."

"You needed it," Joel said. "Mom, can I ask you something?" He turned his game off, and laid the controller aside.

"This looks serious."

"I know what you said last night about Dad needing to talk about work stuff, but . . ." He frowned and looked away.

"But what? You can say it, whatever it is."

"When you and Dad . . . it looked a divorce starting."

"Oh, Baby . . ." She pulled him close and smoothed his hair. Would she divorce Chuck over the lawsuit? She meant it when she said it, and last night, she would have signed the papers.

"I know you said Dad was the one upset, but you looked like you were just as mad at him."

Bobbi sighed deeply. "I was upset, even angry with Dad." *I can't lie, but I can't tell him the truth either.* "A lot of times Dad gets his mind made up and he doesn't listen to anybody else. I tried to tell him what I thought, and sometimes the only way I can get him to listen is to get just as angry as he is."

"So, did he listen?"

"I think I got his attention, yes."

"Then what made you throw up?"

"I don't know. Just an upset stomach, I guess."

"You have those a lot," Joel said, his eyes narrowing.

"It's nothing, Sweetheart. Just a combination of fast food and aggravation with your dad."

"But you're not getting a divorce?"

There is no right answer to that question anymore. "Didn't Dad tell you we weren't divorcing?"

"Yeah. I guess I was just worrying, you know."

"It's okay. I worry sometimes myself." She kissed the top of his head and left him to his game. In the kitchen, she waited for her coffee to brew, but phrases from the lawsuit crept into her thoughts. *The defendant then said, 'You don't think I wanted you here to work on some ridiculous case?' The plaintiff protested . . .* She couldn't face Chuck for dinner tonight with everything so vivid, so fresh.

He took Tracy to lunch. He called her. He talked to her that Sunday morning he skipped church. And he never mentioned any of it. What else had he neglected to mention?

Then again, Chuck couldn't have done all that Tracy alleged. She made him out to be a virtual rapist. Where was the truth?

When the coffeemaker kicked off, Bobbi poured a large mug and retreated to the study. Her Bible lay on the edge of the desk with her devotional book stuck in the back, open to July 27. She hadn't touched her Bible since that day. Guilt-ridden, she dropped into the desk chair and flipped to the current reading. Psalm 142.

All right, You've got me. I've been avoiding reading, avoiding You. I've already failed as a wife, and I'm failing as a mother. God, I don't think I can handle reading about how I'm failing You, too.

Father, the lawsuit. The details in that . . . I thought knowing he cheated hurt. What do I do next? I told Chuck I would divorce him. The facts make it so much more painful. You know details worse than that about each one of us, and You put it aside and love us anyway. How? How do I put it aside and love him anyway?

I'm tired. I'm tired of hurting. I feel abandoned and alone. Even when I push You away, deep down, I know how much I need You. Don't You leave me, too.

"I cry out to the Lord with my voice . . .
I pour out my complaint before Him;
I declare before Him my trouble.
When my spirit was overwhelmed within me,
Then You knew my path.
In the way in which I walk
They have secretly set a snare for me.
Look on my right hand and see,
For there is no one who acknowledges me;
Refuge has failed me;
No one cares for my soul.
I cried out to You, O Lord:
I said, 'You are my refuge . . .
Attend to my cry,
For I am brought very low;
Deliver me from my persecutors,
For they are stronger than I.
Bring my soul out of prison,
That I may praise Your name . . .
For You shall deal bountifully with me.'"

Tears dropped onto the pages of her Bible. "You do know," she whispered. "You do know. I *am* overwhelmed. I have no refuge left, and dear God, I've never been lower."

She read the psalm again. *There's always hope at the end of a psalm.* She savored the last line, "You shall deal bountifully with me."

"When? When will You deal bountifully with me? Where does the sentence start? 'Bring my soul out of prison, that I may praise Your name'. Out of prison." Bobbi pushed back from the desk and took a long sip from her coffee. "Is Chuck the jailer? Then how do I get out?"

Chuck rounded the corner, beginning the sixth mile of his morning run. Most mornings he stopped at three. His quads and calves burned from the extra distance. Somehow, it made sense to punish his body for all the trouble it caused him.

God, I'm in a no-win situation. Are You testing me? To see where my real priorities are? Well, I'm failing.

Blessed are the peacemakers.

But this wouldn't be making peace. It would be rolling over and dying.

Blessed are you when people insult you and persecute you, and falsely say all kinds of evil against you because of Me.

She's not persecuting me because of You, though. She's trying to ruin me and destroy my marriage. She doesn't want a relationship with me, so why can't she just disappear? And why would she have to hurt Bobbi? Bobbi is innocent.

He'd never seen Bobbi so upset. Even that first night she hadn't threatened to divorce him. She said 'I can't risk exposing *my* sons' and not 'our' sons? Was that a slip?

After his run, he took a long shower, and then rummaged through his tiny kitchen, hoping a bowl of Cheerios wasn't his only option for lunch. He debated all morning whether or not he should skip dinner tonight and give Bobbi some space. She stunned him when she called.

"Chuck, I don't think I can do dinner this evening." She sounded calm, but tired.

"I don't blame you. I know you need to absorb . . . everything. I handled it all wrong." He sighed, then asked, "What did you tell the boys?"

"That you found out some information from work which upset you, and you needed to talk."

"True, but vague."

"They don't need any more specifics."

"I know what you said about how to proceed, but I . . ."

"Chuck, I want you to talk to Phil about this. Get his take, and then we can see about having dinner again."

"Sure," Chuck said, trying not to sound disappointed. Her request was reasonable and pragmatic, very typical of her, but he hated the idea of giving up dinner, even for a few days. "I am sorry for upsetting you last night."

"I don't want to discuss this anymore until you talk to Phil. Goodbye."

Tuesday, September 6

Pulling into the parking lot at his law firm, Chuck felt a nervousness he hadn't experienced since taking his first case. Yesterday, Donna called from the pastor's office and cancelled the counseling session. He never got to discuss the lawsuit with Phil this weekend, and now he had to face Walter Davis unarmed. He took three deep breaths, picked up his briefcase, and walked into Walter's office at exactly eight o'clock.

"Chuck, good to see you," Walter said, standing to shake hands. "How are things?"

Chuck watched for Walter to sit, then he took a seat in one of the office chairs. "Bobbi and I are going through counseling. We're able to talk."

"You've done quite a job keeping up with things here. Maybe I should have you work at home all the time."

"I'm not at home right now."

Walter shifted in his chair, frowning with disapproval.

"Bobbi needs a little time and space, and it's easier for her if I'm not there all the time. I have dinner with her and the boys three times a week. It's amicable, and I'm sure everything will work out in time." Chuck hoped he sounded more confident than he felt.

"I commend you for fighting to keep your family, for facing your . . . responsibilities."

"About that," Chuck said retrieving the lawsuit filing from his briefcase. Handing the papers over, he said, "Tracy has filed suit." Davis' jaw clenched. "She's claiming harassment, but she didn't name the firm. She never complained to you, did she?"

"Never." Walter flipped through the papers, frowning and shaking his head with each new page. "She's obviously mentally ill."

"What?"

Walter rested his elbows on his desk and folded his hands. "This is not the filing of a competent attorney. It's the rambling grievance of a scorned lover. At the very least, she's emotionally disturbed."

Chuck bristled at the word 'lover.' "So you agree she has no case. I expect it to be dropped as soon as I answer it."

Walter scowled and shook his head. "Son, this is a shakedown, and you need to teach her a lesson. I want you to countersue her and destroy her."

"I don't know if that's necessary."

"You misunderstand me. That wasn't advice. You are a partner in this firm, my number two man, and even though she hasn't named the law firm as a co-defendant, there is an association there. I am directing you to file a countersuit and ruin this woman." He stood up, signaling the end of the meeting. "Keep me posted, and I wish you and Bobbi all the best." He shook hands with Chuck once again.

So, it's my wife or my job. Chuck shuffled to his office and collapsed in his chair. *Wonder if Bobbi would like to move?*

He had just turned his computer on when Chad Mitchell knocked on his open office door. "Hey, Chad, come in," Chuck said, motioning him into the office.

"Can I shut your door?" Chad asked, eyes darting toward the hallway. The young hotshot of the firm, charming and full of himself, he constantly pushed the envelope of decorum with Walter, but got away with it because of his competence and his gift for attracting good clients. Nervous agitation replaced that ease and self-assurance this morning.

"Sure. What's wrong?"

Chad shut the door and sat down on the edge of one of Chuck's office chairs. "I wanted to call you, Chuck. I wanted to, but I just didn't have the guts. I am so sorry."

"What are you talking about?"

"All this . . . you and Tracy . . . I was the one who told Tracy you were married. I had no idea . . ."

"You're not making sense."

"Yeah, okay. Tracy met Michelle and me after work one evening, and she said she was waiting for you. I don't even remember what I said, but I mentioned your wife, and Tracy got a real funny look, just for an instant. Then she acted real cool. 'You knew Chuck's married, right?' I said. She said, 'Of course, I asked him for a joke.' I didn't know Chuck . . . about you and Tracy. I would have never said anything . . ."

"It's okay. It's good that Tracy found out."

Chad stopped bouncing his leg. "Now, I don't understand."

"Having an affair was a sin against God, my wife, and family, and Tracy, too. I don't think I could have or would have stopped it unless something drastic happened. You may not believe it, but God used you to keep me from doing even more damage."

Chad smiled and shook his head. "You sound like my grandmother. She used to talk about God being directly involved in her life."

"You don't think He is?"

"If God exists, He surely has better things to do than micromanage my life." Chad crossed his legs and leaned back in the chair. "Anyway, so what's going to happen between you and your wife? If that's not too personal."

"We're going to work through this."

"Just like that?"

"No. I just took five weeks off to go through counseling by myself, and we're going through counseling together. We're still separated, but we love each other, and we're committed to our marriage."

"If I ever cheated on Michelle, you'd find my body parts in trash cans across three counties."

"And that's probably what I deserve, but that's where God steps in."

"And you get away with it."

"Not at all. The consequences don't go away. Things will never be the same between Bobbi and me. My boys have been hurt deeply, and who knows how much damage I did to my reputation. I didn't get away with anything."

"I'll let you get to work. Thanks for understanding."

"Before you go, I may need your help on a very sensitive case."

"If it's Tracy's suit, I can't. I had to file a statement for her. You're on your own on this one."

Chuck turned back to his desk as Chad left. Great. Tracy played the part of the betrayed innocent in front of Chad, and drew him into her game. Flipping through the lawsuit filing again, he had to agree with Walter. It was a slipshod job, not like Tracy at all. She never missed a comma in her documents, and he'd seen her turn down cases because she felt they were too weak, cases he would have taken.

Chuck pulled a legal pad from his desk and scribbled an outline for the easiest way out of this mess. Answer her allegations and let a judge throw it out of court. No trial, no need for a countersuit, and a more than sufficient reproof for Ms. Ravenna. When it was over, Bobbi would understand why he handled it this way.

Friday, September 9

"**Whose interest are** you looking out for?" Phil Shannon asked, as he leaned back in his desk chair.

"It's in everybody's best interest," Chuck said. "My name is at stake. Bobbi will agree with that."

"But she hasn't yet."

"She wanted me to get your opinion first."

"Do you want my opinion?"

"I promised her I wouldn't do anything until I talked to you, but I don't know how else I can get out of this." He braced himself for the 'right' answer.

"Who says you have to get out of it? It's 'yea though I walk *through* the valley of the shadow of death.'" He cut through the air with his hand. "That's the thing. Whatever you face, even though it has the size and shape of death itself, once you go through it, you realize it was only a shadow, and had no real power to harm you."

"So, you think I should fight this? Go to court?" This was more like it.

Phil reached across the desk for his Bible and leafed through it. "You know, my opinion is not worth much. Let me give you a better perspective. Here we go, Jeremiah 15:15. 'O Lord, You know; Remember me and visit me, and take vengeance for me on my persecutors. In Your enduring patience, do not take me away. Know that for Your sake I have suffered rebuke.'"

"I figured that's what you'd say," Chuck muttered.

"I know. I hate for people to start quoting Scripture at me, too, but it's all I have." He smiled and closed his Bible. "And then there's one in the New Testament you've probably heard before. It's in Romans where Paul quotes the Old Testament 'vengeance is Mine' and so forth, but he finishes saying 'don't be overcome with evil, but overcome evil with good.'"

"So I should resign from the law firm and pay Tracy off."

"I didn't say that," Phil said with a slight smile. "Chuck, you are so ready to hear what you want that you don't listen. I want you to overcome evil with good."

"How can I do that without fighting Tracy?"

"By letting God fight this battle. Grab hold of that Scripture and make it your own. You belong to God, and He is more offended than you are by this injustice. He won't let it go. Now, do you think you can handle this better than He can?"

Saturday, September 10

Bobbi kept her promise and invited Chuck for dinner again, although she called for a pizza rather than cooking. It still qualified as dinner. Joel, excited to have his dad there, took control of the conversation during the meal.

Afterwards, Brad collected the plates and salad bowls and carried them to the kitchen. Chuck followed with the silverware and empty pizza box. Brad stunned his father when he spoke. "People are going to think you're psycho if you sit in the parking lot for every football game."

"I hope to see a game in the stadium before the season is over."

Brad shrugged and walked out of the kitchen. Chuck counted it a huge victory that Brad initiated a conversation that didn't end with him storming out of the room. These days, even the smallest victory was precious.

As Chuck set the dishwasher to start, Bobbi came in to refill her iced tea. "No yelling this time," she said.

"Yeah, two whole sentences."

"It's a start."

"I'll take every break I can get." Chuck filled a glass of tea for himself. "You want to sit out on the deck for a little while?" She surprised him when she agreed. He held the door for her, then waited for her to sit in one of the deck chairs before he sat down across from her.

Bobbi silently sipped her tea, so Chuck cleared his throat and spoke up. "Walter Davis is pressing me to file a countersuit, Bobbi. It'll cost me my job if I don't."

"Then you don't have a choice," she said quietly, dropping her eyes.

"I don't know. I'm still trying to figure something out." He wasn't technically lying, but he couldn't risk telling her he was answering the charges. Not yet.

"What did Phil say?"

"He gave me some scripture, but he didn't want to tell me what to do. I think he wants me to work it out for myself."

"I see."

"Look, can we talk about something else?" Chuck asked, sipping his tea. "You left Phil's office in kind of a hurry the other day."

"Did I?"

"You did. What is it about my coming home that upsets you so much?"

"It doesn't upset me. You're overanalyzing everything."

"Then I can come home?"

"No," Bobbi snapped. "I'm not ready yet."

"What is it? What are you waiting for?" Chuck allowed too much of his frustration to show, escalating the tension.

"Why'd you do it, Chuck?" Bobbi blurted out, her voice raw with pain.

"I don't know," Chuck answered quietly.

"That's why you can't come home," Bobbi said, her eyes brimming with tears. "If you really think your affair was just about sex, you're either in denial or you're an idiot!" She closed her eyes, and took several deep breaths before continuing. "Until you understand what you were looking for, what kind of connection you made with that woman, I can't trust you."

"But that's why I'm in counseling. I'm going to figure it out, and I'm going to fix it."

"After Mama died, I was so afraid to get close to anybody. I didn't think I could stand to be hurt again." She looked down. "Until you, that is. I gave you my whole heart, without reservation, because I never doubted how much you loved me. I finally felt safe and secure . . . and I let my guard down." She finished in a whisper.

And he'd squandered the sweet, precious gift of herself that she'd given him that July afternoon eighteen years ago. "How can I even ask you to forgive me?"

"Forgiveness isn't the issue. I can't *not* forgive you. I love you." Tears dropped from her dark eyes. Chuck reached out to hold her hands, hoping she would also let him hold her, but she pulled her hands away. "I can't. I can't touch you right now."

She pushed away from the table and walked a few steps across the deck. "I see your hands . . . they used to be the hands I held, the hands that laid my newborn sons in my arms . . . but now it's 'the defendant placed his hand on the plaintiff's thigh' or whatever."

She wiped a tear away. "I look in your eyes and all I can see in them is that frozen instant when I knew it was true. I've tried to latch onto some other memory, some other image of you, like when you passed the bar exam, or when the boys were born. Those memories, they've been swept away, and I don't know how to get them back."

Her tear-stained cheeks glistened in the soft light. He'd give anything to see her smile again. In spite of her heartache, she carried herself with such grace and strength. Why couldn't he see that before now?

"I think you owe me the time and space I need," she said at last, rejoining him at the table. "I have to figure out how I can live with you again."

"I miss being home. I miss you."

"This separation isn't just hurting you. I hate it, and I hate how it's affecting the boys."

"Then why do it? I don't understand."

"Because it hurts less than betrayal," she answered with unblinking frankness.

Bobbi paced the living room, checking for Chuck's car with each pass by the front window. They were going out for their anniversary. Never mind the fact that they barely spoke to one another this summer. Never mind the fact that he never came to bed until she was asleep. He offered to take her out to dinner and she accepted.

She'd made a promise to herself that no matter what he said, she would not shoot back any sarcastic, recriminating remarks. She wouldn't talk about school. She wouldn't say anything about his hours or his traveling. For three hours, she would be the perfect, supportive wife. If this didn't help, then, maybe their marriage had deeper issues. She wasn't ready to face that possibility.

She saw his car ease into the driveway and her stomach tightened. He strode into the house and set his briefcase by the stairs. Then he saw her. "Oh, you're ready. I'll just be a minute." He took the steps two at a time. No 'happy anniversary'. No kiss. Not even a hello.

He just didn't want to keep her waiting. That's all. She didn't quite believe that, but it was all she could come up with. She could hear the squeaks and creaks as he moved around upstairs. Lord, give me words of grace.

A moment later, she heard him on the stairs. "I, uh, I forgot to make reservations . . . I'm sorry."

"I don't mind waiting."

"So, what sounds good?"

"Italian?"

"Italian, it is." His words, tired and lifeless, matched his eyes. "Oh, wait." He knelt down, unlatched his briefcase, and pulled a small jewelry box out. "Happy anniversary."

She opened the box, and the necklace inside took her breath away, ten or twelve diamonds set in yellow gold. "This is beautiful." She carefully eased it *from the box insert. "Here, help me put it on." She handed him the unclasped necklace and turned around so he could slip it around her neck. It lay perfectly just below her collarbone. "What do you think?"*

"It looks like it was made for you," he said, nodding.

"Thank you." She put a hand on his chest and leaned up to kiss him. Their lips missed, and they kissed each other's cheeks. Still, that counted for something. "You want to see a movie after dinner?"

"I don't even know what's playing."

"It was just a thought." She picked up her purse and followed him to his car. He opened his door and got in. At least her door was unlocked. "It still smells new," she said, when she got in. She picked up more than just a new car scent. Perfume. "Did you get to go out for lunch, today?"

"Yeah." Chuck watched the rearview as he backed out of the driveway.

"I thought I smelled perfume."

For an instant, Chuck looked stricken, but he recovered quickly. "I drove today, and Gina's on ServMed with me."

Gina. Thank God. Gina was safe. Over fifty. Happily married. Utterly professional. It was like taking Rita to lunch. Bobbi wanted to reach for his hand, but the constant shifting made it impossible.

"Speaking of driving, can you have the brakes checked on my car while I'm gone next week? Will you have time to do that?" Then she backtracked. "Wait, are you gonna be home?"

"I'll be in Kansas City . . . uh . . . Wednesday and Thursday, but I'll be back about the time you get home Thursday night." He frowned and she prepared her apology, but he surprised her. "Yeah, Monday maybe. I'll see what I can do. What's wrong with them?"

"I don't feel like they're stopping the car."

"They're mushy?"

"Yeah, I guess."

"May just need fluid," he mumbled.

They rode in silence the rest of the way to the restaurant, but Bobbi was satisfied to have a civil conversation, no matter how short. She took it as a good sign.

Just before eight o'clock, they arrived at the restaurant, and the crowd had thinned. The hostess seated them within a few minutes, and after giving their drink orders, Bobbi snapped the menu open. "I may just go with the shrimp thing, the special, but I feel obligated to at least look at the menu."

Chuck nodded, but didn't respond. Finally, he closed his menu. "I think I'm just gonna get the pasta salad."

"Are you trying to cut back?"

He sipped his water and glanced across the restaurant. "I'm just trying to watch. With all the traveling, it's easy to eat a bunch of junk. And the hotel over in KC has a pretty nice gym, so I try to use it when I'm there."

"Can you still bench . . . what was it? Three hundred pounds?"

He gave her a half smile. "No, that's been a while. Not since I was lugging stuff for Gene."

"You were quite a catch, you know?" She smiled as she poured sweetener into her tea and stirred it. "Big broad shoulders . . . Joel is built just like you."

Again, he didn't respond. He was present in body, but clearly his mind was somewhere else. She wanted to press him, to question him and find out what was going on, but she had promised not to antagonize him tonight.

After several moments of awkward silence, she tried again. "I feel bad not being here Monday for our actual anniversary. We've never spent an anniversary apart."

"Yeah, you're taking all the pressure off me, by breaking the string." He almost smiled again. "I'm glad you're going. You need a break."

Was he being sarcastic? How could he possibly know whether or not she needed a break? He had no idea what she'd been working on the last few months.

"I think when you finally get this case settled, Chuck, we should plan on taking a trip together to celebrate, to reconnect."

"What if you're in school by then?"

"I'll take a personal day. We need this."

"We'll see. A lot can happen between now and then."

CHAPTER 13
EMULATION

FIVE WEEKS LATER
Wednesday, October 12

Brad slouched into his regular Wednesday morning spot at McDonald's, right side, third booth, facing the counter. A moment later, Cooper DeWitt joined him, sliding a loaded tray across the table to him. "So, how are things with your dad?" Cooper asked.

"Are we ever going to eat breakfast without talking about him?" Brad unwrapped his sausage biscuit and took a large bite. Ever since the fight between his mom and dad in the stadium parking lot, Cooper picked him up for breakfast each Wednesday. Every week, they went through the same routine—a McDonald's sausage biscuit and a lame attempt to get him to talk.

He had nothing to talk about, though, because nothing changed between his mom and dad. They counseled with Pastor Phil. They sat through dinner. Some nights, they talked out on the deck, but most nights, his dad left soon after they ate. If he could hang on for two and a half years, he'd go to college and leave this all behind.

Things *were* different with his mom, though. She shocked him when she quit teaching her Sunday school class. She always said that was one of her favorite things. She never nagged him about carrying his laundry upstairs because most days it was still in the dryer. Besides that, it seemed like every week they ran out of something important, like milk or bread. He never thought his dad did that much, but his mom couldn't keep up now that she was on her own.

He took over the yard work when his dad moved out, and Joel helped rake and bag. Joel didn't pester him so much these days. That had to make things easier on his mom.

Brad busted his tail at school, too. He didn't want it to look like he couldn't handle his dad being gone.

"Does your dad still try to talk to you?" Cooper asked, then slurped from an extra large orange juice.

"Yes, but he's still a jerk who thinks everybody should let his affair go because he said he was sorry."

"You still don't believe him?"

"Look, I can say I'm the starting quarterback for the Rams this Sunday, but that doesn't make it true."

"How could we make that true?"

"Starting for the Rams? Like that's gonna happen."

"Seriously, what would it take?"

"I'd have to learn how to play quarterback, put on about sixty pounds, grow about five more inches . . ." He broke into a wide grin. "Then I'd have to lead Missouri to a national championship, get drafted, and make it through camp."

"So, some of it is in your control, like learning the position and gaining weight, but a lot of it isn't in your control at all."

"My lesson alert just went off," Brad said, squinting, grabbing the table to brace himself.

Cooper smiled. "Yep, an incoming lesson has been confirmed." The youth pastor grew more serious and leaned across the table. "Your dad is doing all the things within his control to heal his relationship with your mom and with you."

"I've heard this before, Cooper."

"But what are you doing on your end? Pouting?"

Brad scowled.

"That's what I thought. You're waiting on something. What is it? What does your dad have to do to break through to you?"

"Did somebody put you up to asking this?" Brad's eyes narrowed in suspicion.

"No. What we talk about is completely private. I don't even tell Amy the details."

"What about my mom?"

"Never."

"But she's behind the breakfast thing, isn't she?"

"Yep, she's concerned about you, you know?"

"Here's the deal," Brad said. "I have to be sure he's really put this behind him. I can't watch my mom go through this over some other woman in another year or two."

"Totally reasonable. I'm going to pray that God gives you that evidence and assurance. I know when that happens, you'll be just as powerful an advocate for your dad as you've been in demanding justice."

"Yeah, but if, and I mean if, that happens, I don't want my mom to be pressured into taking him back before she's ready. Just because everyone else is okay with it, that doesn't mean she should rush into it."

"No, but it might help her focus on her own feelings if she knew you and Joel were both reconciled with your dad."

Brad scowled, unconvinced.

"She's a mom. You and Joel are always going to come first. She'll sacrifice her own happiness to make sure you guys are all right. In fact, I'd bet she's doing that right now."

That afternoon, Chuck leaned over his desk, reviewing a contract line by line. It took a moment for him to realize the buzzing noise was coming from his phone.

"The school just called," Bobbi said. "Brad's in the principal's office. He was in a fight."

"What?" Chuck said, rubbing his eyes. "What happened?"

"I don't have any details except that he started it."

"That doesn't sound like Brad. Do you think he'd talk to me if I went to the school?"

"Whether he talks to you or not, you need to go. This is about you."

"Me? Why is it about me?"

"Brad's never been in trouble. What else could it be?"

"Yeah, I guess you're right," Chuck sighed.

"I'll call Phil and cancel us, then meet you there, but you need to be the one to handle this."

Brad sunk a little lower in his chair outside the principal's office as he imagined facing his mother. She'd never yell at him in public. She'd look at him and then drop her eyes in disappointment. Hearing footsteps, he raised his head, and was shocked to see his dad.

"You okay?" His dad sat down in the chair beside his.

Brad nodded. Shame smothered his anger toward his dad. He was grateful for the company. "Where's Mom?"

"She'll be here. What happened?"

"I . . . uh . . . punched a guy in the locker room." He tensed, waiting for the explosion of his father's temper. It never came.

"Just horseplay?"

"No. He mouthed off."

"That's not like you."

"I know," Brad said, burying his face in his hands. "I don't know what got into me. It was like being a different person."

"I know what you mean," his father said. "Son, you're at a crossroad. Your first option is to acknowledge that you've done something wrong, accept responsibility and the consequences, renounce it, and then work to make up for it."

His father looked him in the eye, and for the first time in weeks, Brad didn't look away.

"Or, you harden your heart, put the blame on someone else, and believe that what you did was justified. Then you lash out at anyone who says otherwise. The second fight will be much easier to start, and the third one, easier still. Before you know what's happened, you've lost control of your life."

"You've tried both options?"

His father nodded. "The first choice is hard, really hard, but you don't want to go where the second one takes you. Trust me on this."

Just then, the principal's door opened. "Mr. Molinsky?" he asked, looking to Chuck. Chuck patted Brad's knee, then stood up to shake hands. "Brad, we'll call you in shortly. I just need to talk to your dad first."

Watching his dad disappear into the principal's office, Brad thought back to that confrontation in their kitchen, to his own words, 'I'll never forgive you! I'm ashamed to admit you're my dad!' What if his dad had echoed his words, and matched his anger just now? Instead, his dad showed him compassion and respect and treated him like an equal.

Brad leaned his head back against the wall and strained to hear the discussion inside the Mr. McMillen's office, but it was no use. At least they weren't yelling.

Mr. McMillen motioned Chuck toward a chair and closed the door behind him. "Mr. Molinsky, thanks for coming. You've met Tim Matson, our football coach, correct?"

"Yes," Chuck said, shaking hands with the coach.

"Have a seat, please," The principal said, sitting at his desk. "First off, Brad's one of the last kids I would expect to see in here, and I figure I'll never see him again under these circumstances."

"Thank you," Chuck interrupted.

"In my experience, when kids, good kids, explode like this, they're carrying some kind of emotional load. Are you aware of anything in Brad's life, any atypical behavior that might be a sign he's having trouble dealing with something?"

Chuck sighed. "His mother and I are working through some things in our marriage. We're in counseling, but we're living apart and it's been a strain on Brad, on all of us, really. Everything was my fault and he's carrying a lot of anger at me because of it."

"The thing is, Mr. Molinsky," Mr. McMillen continued, "we can't deal with things on a case by case basis anymore. We have a policy and we have to stick with that for everybody, regardless of extenuating circumstances."

"Meaning?"

"Brad will get a three-day suspension and miss the next football game."

"I understand," Chuck said.

Bill McMillen looked at Coach Matson, then back at Chuck. "Let's get Brad in here, then, and get this over with." He opened the door and motioned for Brad, just as Bobbi arrived. "Mrs. Molinsky, thanks for coming. Brad, come on in."

Bobbi gave Brad a quick smile, but he didn't return it. She followed him into the principal's office. Chuck winked at her and stood up to give her his chair. The principal made quick introductions, then led everyone to sit down. "Brad, do you know why you're here?"

"Yes, sir. I hit another student." His voice didn't waver as he looked squarely at his principal.

"Do you want to give your side of the story?"

"There's nothing to tell. No matter what Owen said or did, I shouldn't have hit him. I want to apologize to you, to Coach Matson, and to you, Mom and Dad." Brad glanced around the room as he spoke. "And Coach, I want to apologize to the team on Tuesday when I'm back at school." Coach Matson nodded. "What I did was wrong and I can't excuse or explain it."

"So, you understand you have three-day suspension coming up."

"Yes, sir."

"And that includes Friday's game?"

"Yes, sir."

"Let's see," Mr. McMillen said, checking the schedule on his desk. "Canfield West. They haven't won a game in years. You won't miss anything but a chance to pad your stats." Brad tried to smile. Chuck knew that missing an unimportant game did little to soften the blow.

"Brad, Mr. and Mrs. Molinsky, I have to say that in all the years I've dealt with discipline issues, Brad's the first 'guilty' student I've ever had in here. No excuses, no finger-pointing. I'm very impressed. You show a great deal of character, Brad."

"I learned it from my dad, sir."

"Mrs. Walcott will have some paperwork for us to sign if you wouldn't care to wait for a few more moments." Mr. McMillen stood and motioned to Coach Matson. "Tim, you want to come with me."

As they left the room, Brad turned to his mother, "Mom, I'm sorry. I don't know what I was doing, what I was thinking."

"It sounds like you've been thinking quite a bit," she said. "Did you mean what you said?"

"Yeah, I did." He looked up as Chuck wiped his eyes. "Dad, I've been a total jerk. I'm sorry." Brad's voice broke, and tears began to form. Chuck reached across the chair and pulled him into a hug.

A moment later, the office door opened again. "Folks," Mr. McMillen began, but he backtracked. "I'm sorry. I didn't mean to interrupt."

"It's okay," Chuck said. "We're okay."

"We just need a couple of signatures and then you folks can get out of here," Mr. McMillen said. Chuck followed Bobbi and Brad out to Mrs. Walcott's desk, where the principal handed Brad a disciplinary report. "All right, read through this and see if it's accurate, especially the details of the incident."

Brad scanned the form. "It's okay."

"Then you need to sign it here, and one of your parents needs to sign it right below that," Mr. McMillen said, pointing to the signature lines at the bottom. With the signatures finished, he took the form, tore off the top copy, and handed it to Chuck. "This one belongs to you and your wife, Mr. Molinsky." He took the second copy for himself. "This last copy is for your file, Brad."

Mrs. Walcott winked at him, and nodded toward Mr. McMillen, still standing by her desk, discipline form in hand. Brad looked up, then watched in astonishment as the principal tore the sheet in half, then in half again. "You'll still serve your punishment, but I don't think we need a record of this. Don't you agree, Coach?"

"Absolutely. I have to get back out on the field. See you Tuesday, Brad." Coach Matson shook hands with Bobbi and Chuck a final time, and left the office with a wave.

"I'll be right out," Chuck said quietly to Bobbi. Once his wife and son were beyond the office door, out of earshot, Chuck shook hands with Mr. McMillen once again. "Thank you. I can't tell you how much I appreciate you cutting Brad some slack."

"Cheryl, I don't know what he's talking about, do you?" Mr. McMillen asked, with a sly smile.

"No idea," she answered.

"Thank you anyway," Chuck said, as he walked out, hoping to catch Bobbi and Brad before they left. He made it outside as Bobbi eased her car in behind his, and Brad rolled down his window. "Dad, want some company Friday night in the parking lot?"

"You bet!" Chuck answered, with a smile and a wave. He watched Bobbi's car until she drove out of sight, then he got in his car and sat for a moment. In the afternoon autumn sun, the bright, warm car interior matched his mood. Closing his eyes, he leaned his head back against the seat. *God, that was incredible. Thank You for giving me my son back.*

Finally, they had the breakthrough they needed. He and Bobbi had reached an impasse. For weeks now, she remained polite, but never made eye contact with him, and until she called today, she never spoke first. Even though he hadn't told her he answered Tracy's allegations and filed the countersuit, he could tell she knew. This afternoon, though, she softened up around Brad. The door opened. Tomorrow night, he wouldn't let Bobbi change the subject or walk away. He'd make her talk to him.

CHAPTER 14
EMPATHY

"Mom, you're late," Joel lectured, his arms crossed across his chest. "Is your phone broken?"

"Something came up." Bobbi swung the front door open wide enough to get around him. She dropped her book bag in the study and began flipping through the mail, while Brad dumped his backpack and football gear at the bottom of the stairs.

"Something came up . . . Let me guess." Joel raised his index fingers to his temples, and closed his eyes. "Brad got in a fight and is suspended for three days."

"Joel, how could you know that? We just left the school!" Brad smacked his brother in the shoulder.

"Brad, Brad, Brad," Joel said, laying a hand on Brad's shoulder. "When are you going to learn? I'm always right, and I know everything." Brad glared at him. "Okay, Nathan Schoenberger. Somebody texted Jeremy. Nathan heard Jeremy talking about it and he sent me a message."

"Great, that didn't take long," Brad mumbled. "Wonder how many other messages are flying around?"

"Did you get three days? Nathan wasn't sure."

"Tell Nathan, yes, including Friday's game," Brad said, wandering into the kitchen for a Coke.

"Guys, how about tacos?" Bobbi followed them to the kitchen, and pulled a pound of hamburger from the refrigerator.

"Tacos would be great!" Joel said. "I'm starved!" Then turning to his brother, he asked, "So who'd you hit?"

"Joel, that's not important," Bobbi said. "It was wrong. Brad admitted that, and he's taking the punishment."

"And Mom forgave you?" Joel asked.

"Yeah, so?" Brad finished off the can of Coke.

"Boy, it would be a lot tougher if you were in trouble here *and* at school. It's a good thing your family accepted your apology and forgave you."

"I've learned my lesson, Joel. You can shut up now."

"So you think forgiveness is the way to go?" Joel asked with a sly grin.

"Yes, Joel. You were right about that, too, okay?" Brad said, rolling his eyes. "I told Dad I've been a jerk. We're cool." He turned and headed up the back stairs, but poked his head back around the corner. "Owen Burcham," he said, and disappeared.

"No way!" Joel scrambled up the steps behind him.

Bobbi shook her head and smiled at the boys. Brad seemed in curiously high spirits for a kid facing a three-day suspension. Of course, she found it difficult to muster any parental anger or even disapproval at him. Who could fault him for reacting to pressures Chuck had brought on all of them?

The hamburger sizzled as it browned in the skillet. *I can't blame everything on Chuck. That's a cop-out.* Brad had the responsibility to walk away from that fight. He knew it was wrong. Just like Chuck.

Dear God, they're the same. They both knew that what they were doing was wrong and they did it anyway. Why can I give Brad a free pass then, and not Chuck?

Thursday, October 13

Bobbi left school by three-thirty and took the long way home so she could stop by the coffee shop, Dear Joe, to pick up a bag of fresh roast. Today hadn't been an especially bad day, but after Brad's suspension yesterday, dinner with Chuck tonight, and parent conferences coming up, she needed a dependable supply of therapy.

She found a parking place close to the door for a change. In the morning, the place was packed, full of professional types, calling out orders, and carrying out gallons of coffee, one cup at a time.

Through the afternoon and evening, though, Dear Joe became more of a coffee house, where college students and an occasional professor would drift in and out for a super espresso. This afternoon, three kids huddled in booths as far away from each other as possible. Each had a stack of books, notebooks, a twenty-four ounce Joe for stamina, and an mp3 player to block out the world. If only it were that simple. If only a midterm was the most stressful thing she had to face.

The owner of the shop, Clay Bartel, looked up from wiping down a counter when she walked in, and flashed his patented million-dollar smile. "I was about to put out a missing persons bulletin on you," he said, tossing the towel to the counter behind him without turning around to look.

"Call off the search party, then. I'm here."

"Hey, my regulars are like family. Are things okay?"

"Fine." She looked in his eyes and knew that somehow news about the affair had made it to the coffee shop. "Just busy."

"Yeah, how's that roomful of monkeys treating you? What are they, second-graders?" A few years younger than Bobbi, full of charm, and with an easy-going manner, she often wondered why he wasn't running a Fortune 500 company instead of a string of coffee shops.

"They are wonderful. Best thing going on these days."

He didn't comment, but his eyes lingered on hers a moment too long. She looked away and he moved on to business. "What can I get for you this afternoon?"

"I just need some fresh roast to take home," Bobbi said, although the richness of the brewing coffee tempted her to have a cup to go as well.

"All of our Europeans are on sale this month, and the Moroccan is our feature."

"I'll take the Bella Florentina, then," Bobbi said. "Can't beat a sale."

"One pound or three?"

"Just one. I'm the only one who drinks it."

"Chuck still hasn't come around?"

"Chuck will never come around." *Not just on the coffee.* Bobbi reached in her purse for her billfold. "Oh, and here's my card, too."

"Chuck doesn't know what he's missing." He looked in her eyes again, then punched a hole in her card. "All right, your total is ten seventeen, and with that filled-up card, you'll get a free pound next time. I also put in a sample of the Moroccan, too, so you can try it."

"Thanks," Bobbi said, taking the bag and dropping her billfold back in her purse. Was Clay Bartel flirting with her, or just being friendly? Had it been so long since she'd received any attention that she no longer knew how to respond?

Forget Clay. Focus on dinner, Bobbi. You gotta figure out something. Chicken . . . That'll work, right? Head down, thoughts a million miles away, Bobbi almost collided with a woman just outside the door. "I am so sorry," she began apologizing, when she recognized Lorraine Kinney.

"No harm done," Lorraine said. "It was a near miss."

"You come here often? I didn't know you were a gourmet coffee fan."

"I didn't either. I stopped on an impulse. Do you have time for a cup?"

Bobbi hesitated and looked at her watch. She didn't want to stay. Making pleasant casual conversation would take energy she needed for dinner with Chuck. Lorraine, of all people, would understand if she opted out.

Then again, running into her, literally, couldn't be just a chance meeting. Lorraine could identify with the pain Bobbi lived with day in and day out. "Sure. Let me put my bag in the car."

Once back inside Dear Joe, Lorraine asked her, "So, what do you recommend?"

"Oh, I don't know. What do you like?"

"I have no idea."

"Try the Gazebo blend," Bobbi said. "Minnie or Molly."

"A Molly what?"

Bobbi smiled. "Those are the sizes. Minnie is small, a normal-sized cup of coffee, then Molly, Bill, and Joe."

"You came back!" Clay said. "Made my day." His blue eyes twinkled and Bobbi almost believed him. "It's the brew, isn't it? Had to have it, right?"

"As a matter of fact, give me a brew and a Gazebo, both Minnies."

"That's the Moroccan. *You* will love it. A strong Turkish base, spiced to perfection."

"You should do commercials," Bobbi said.

"I'll consider it, then." He set the cup on the counter. "Try that and tell me it's not the best cup of coffee you've had this week."

Bobbi took a long sip. "It is very good."

He nodded. "You know, I can tell a lot about a woman by the coffee she drinks."

"How many times have you used that line?" Bobbi lay the money on the counter and picked up the two cups.

"I didn't intend for you to buy my coffee." Lorraine said.

"I know that. Consider it an introductory cup. That's how we get you hooked." Bobbi glanced up at the ceiling. "Don't sit there. The vent will blow down on us."

"You know your way around a coffee shop," Lorraine said, taking a seat at a table away from the vent.

"I've been here once or twice."

"I gathered that much from the guy at the counter."

"Clay? It's in his financial interest to make sure everyone is loved and appreciated." Bobbi glanced back toward the counter. "I never take cream or sugar, so I didn't think to ask if you needed it." Bobbi handed Lorraine a cup and sat down.

"I'm fine. How long have you been a coffee connoisseur?" Lorraine could have passed for Bobbi's mother. Deep lines around her eyes and across her forehead testified to the trials she had faced. While the difficulties in what she called "her real growing up years" hadn't embittered her, they made her reserved and cautious, traits she had in common with Bobbi.

"I've drunk coffee since I was fourteen. In college, I started drinking the flavored kinds, but in grad school, I found the good stuff." An awkward pause hung over the table, signaling the end of small talk. Bobbi resigned herself to the 'you think you have it bad, at least your husband didn't leave' speech. Lorraine surprised her.

"You feel utterly alone, don't you?" Lorraine asked.

"Yeah, I do. Nobody gets it."

"I doubt I do either. I've wanted to talk to you since Chuck went before the church, but the timing was never right."

"I haven't exactly been approachable."

"This is survival. There's no energy for anything else, least of all social graces. You do what you have to do to get through a day and that's all."

"Yeah," Bobbi murmured. "So what was it like when Dean left?"

"I was crushed," Lorraine said, taking a sip from her coffee. She spoke quietly with a gentle humility. "He was such a liar," she said, shaking her head. "I had no idea. I didn't even know he had a secretary." She glanced away, betraying the fact that her own naiveté still embarrassed her. "I had just turned thirty. Todd was seven, Christie was four, and Donnie was two. The first year, I thought I would die, or at least lose my mind. We moved back in with my parents, all four of us in one bedroom. Then I found a decent job, and the kids and I settled into life without him."

"I know it wasn't as easy as you just made it sound."

"No," Lorraine sighed. "But Dean was an adult and he made a decision that I had no control over. I had to live with the consequences, but there wasn't anything I could have changed, or done differently."

"You still love him?"

"It's complicated. I haven't spoken to him more than a half dozen times, and he makes me so angry, I could bite through a nail. On the other hand, he's the father of my children, and I was genuinely happy when we were married." She looked away for a long moment. "I'd like to know if he ever loved me."

"What about forgiving him?"

"It took me fifteen years. I heard a sermon about Samuel when God told him to go make Saul the king. I don't even remember the point of the sermon, but one of the verses was 'they haven't rejected you, they've rejected Me.' That's the summary—Dean didn't reject me, he rejected God. God is my defender and avenger, and this is between Dean and God, not Dean and me."

"So how do you get through it? How do you live with the hurt day after day after day?"

"Honestly, I don't know. When I look back, I don't know how I did it." Then she raised a hand. "Well, I know how I did it—it was all God."

Bobbi sipped her coffee in disappointment. Was that the best anybody could tell her? You just get through it. "Then, when does it stop hurting?" Bobbi asked, hoping for something concrete, something she could grab hold of to get her through this storm. Pray this prayer, or read these verses . . . anything.

"The truth?" Lorraine asked, allowing the slightest smile to form.

"Oh, no," Bobbi said, closing her eyes and returning the smile. "It doesn't, right?"

"No, it doesn't." Lorraine finished off her cup of coffee. "Bobbi, I wouldn't presume to give you advice, but if you'll let me, I want to say two things." She waited for Bobbi's consent before continuing. "God gave Job his family back, but He never removed the pain of the loss from Job's life. Second, Chuck is a good man."

"That's all?" Bobbi asked.

"Anything more would be meddling, and I wouldn't do that for the world." Lorraine smiled and stood to leave. "The coffee was wonderful, thank you. Let me throw your cup away."

Bobbi handed over her empty cup. "Lorraine, I have to tell you, I was a little hesitant to talk with you. I figured you'd tell me I didn't have it so bad, to suck it up, and go on. I'm sorry."

"You know, the Bible says God never puts more on you than you can bear, right? You are carrying as much as *you* can right now. Whether or not that's more or less than what I can handle is irrelevant. Suffering is not a contest."

Bobbi arrived home as Brad started the last lap of the front yard with the lawn mower. She waved at him and went on in the house to start dinner. Joel sat at the kitchen table finishing his homework. "Mom, I need the computer unless you can tell me the top three exports for each of the European Union countries."

"Hi, Mom. How was your day?" Bobbi teased.

"Hi, Mom. How was your day?" Joel repeated, rolling his eyes.

"Fine, thanks," Bobbi answered. "Yes, you can use the computer. Dinner's in about an hour."

"You know," Joel said as he packed up his books, "this would be much simpler if I had a computer of my own."

"Nice try," Bobbi said.

"I have to try," Joel said. "You'd be disappointed in me otherwise."

"Yes, and I have to say no." Bobbi opened the large cabinet that served as her main cupboard. *Chicken. I can fry it and do baked potatoes. Wait, I don't have potatoes. Rice. Have I got any rice?* She moved boxes to the side. *I really need to go to the grocery store soon. Rice, yes!* She pulled the package out and inspected it. Not enough for four people.

It hadn't been so long ago that Bobbi planned meals two weeks at a time so she rarely ran out of anything. Now, if she planned two hours in advance it was an accomplishment.

Breakfast. I'll make pancakes. Surely, I've got eggs and flour. She checked the refrigerator. *Thank God. Eggs and enough milk for dinner.* Now that she had a plan, autopilot kicked in and got her through the preparations.

"**Brad, I'll be** by about six tomorrow so we can eat before the game," Chuck said, as he finished his last bite.

"Okay." Brad began collecting dishes and carrying them to the kitchen. "I cut the grass," he announced before disappearing through the doorway.

"Pathetic," Joel said, shaking his head.

"What?" Chuck asked.

"Dad, he wants television back. Isn't it obvious? No school, no phone, no computer, and no TV. He's going nuts."

"That's up to Mom, not me. She has to live with him."

"He's doomed," Joel said. "Mom, I didn't get finished before dinner. Can I get back online?"

"Yes, and Brad," she said loud enough for him to hear, "you can have television until nine."

"Thanks, Mom!" He stepped into the kitchen doorway, turned and pointed at his brother. "Ha! Joel! You don't know everything!"

"**You look tired,**" Chuck said to his wife once the boys cleared out of the dining room. Since July, the emotional strain had grayed Bobbi's hair, and creased her brow. He wondered if anything could erase the dark circles under her eyes.

"It's been a long week. Well, they're all long these days." She refolded her napkin and set her glass on it. "I ran into Lorraine Kinney this afternoon."

"Oh yeah?"

Bobbi initiated a conversation. He wouldn't bring up the lawsuit if she had something on her mind.

"I nearly knocked her down leaving Dear Joe. We talked for a little while."

"What about?" Chuck could have guessed.

"Dean and you. She said the hurt never goes away." Her eyes began to brim with tears.

"I'm sorry."

"You're always sorry," she said, wiping her eyes.

"What's that supposed to mean?" his jaw stiffened.

"Nothing . . . I don't know. I just hoped for a little more encouragement from her."

"I'm not Dean Kinney. I'm not leaving you."

"No, you just cheated on me. I guess I should be thankful."

"Bobbi—"

"I've got a lot to do to get ready for tomorrow, so can we just call it a night?" She pushed her chair back from the table. "Joel? Hurry up with the computer!"

"Don't do this, please—"

"What?" Bobbi interrupted. "Don't do what?"

"Every time we start to discuss things, you cut it off."

"It's not *things,* Chuck! You were with another woman!" She didn't yell, but her eyes blazed. "You destroyed everything I believed about you, and about our marriage. Every time I think about it, I get physically ill. It's all I can do to keep from throwing up." She crossed the room away from him.

"You told me you loved me in the morning and then you spent the night with someone else." She took a deep breath and continued softly. "You had sex with her, and then came home to me like nothing happened. You're right, Chuck. I *don't* want to talk about it. Not now, not ever." She started to walk out of the dining room, but Chuck intercepted her.

"You've got to face it. That's the only way we can work through it."

"Face it? I can't get away from it!" She swept her hand in front of her in a broad arc. "My whole life is framed by your affair."

Chuck stepped closer. Should he try to hold her? He started to raise his hand, but Bobbi caught sight of the subtle movement. She pointed at him with her jaw clenched. "Don't touch me," she hissed.

"Bobbi, let me—"

"No. Just go, all right?"

"You're not having second thoughts, are you? You're not thinking about splitting, right?" Hadn't they made any progress since July?

"You know Joel's in the other room and can hear us. You expect me to answer that?"

"Yes, I do. You threatened me before. Do you want a divorce?"

"No, but I'll tell you what I do want," she answered, her voice as firm as his. "I want to be able to look people in the eye again. I want to be able to face people, and not wonder what they know." She began to soften. "I want to wake up without the weight of shame and humiliation on my shoulders. I want to love you again without having to justify it to myself or anybody else." She blinked and a single tear spilled onto her cheek as she pointed at his heart. "I want you to deserve to have me love you again."

Chuck stood on Tracy's porch, waiting for her to answer the door. His grip tightened on his toolbox as he glanced down the street. Doing a favor for a co-worker, that's all. It was perfectly normal for him to be here.

And he would tell Bobbi that. If she ever found out. If she ever asked. There was nothing wrong with him being here. Nothing.

He swallowed hard and peered through the window panel in the door, then he checked his watch. Eight o'clock, just like they'd agreed. At last, he heard a click, and the door swung open. His eyes immediately dropped to her white tank top. When she smiled, he knew she'd caught him looking.

She pushed the storm door open, but not wide enough that he could avoid brushing against her as he stepped inside. "Hey, sorry it took so long for me to answer. I was back in the laundry room."

He followed her into the living room, watching her hips as she walked, the way her shorts followed her curves. She was so at ease with herself.

She bent over an open cardboard box in the floor and pulled out a sheet of paper. "For the record, I have handed you the instructions. My responsibility in this is now done."

He laughed and took the sheet, his fingers brushing hers. He walked under the ceiling fan, checking the sheet. "Looks pretty straightforward. Is the lamp on the same breaker?"

"No idea."

He switched the lamp on. "We'll find out. Lead me to the breaker box." He waited for her to pass so he could watch her walk, then turned on the light in the entry hall before following her to the laundry room.

She stretched in front of him and flipped a breaker. "That's the living room. I know that much." She pushed her hair behind her ear. "I've got some stuff to do upstairs, but come get me if you need anything." She reached over and squeezed his bicep. "I really appreciate you doing this for me."

An hour and a half later, he had the new ceiling fan installed, and the old one stuffed in the cardboard box. He walked back to the laundry room to the breaker box, hoping Tracy had come back down to do another load of clothes. She was nowhere around.

Did she expect him to come looking for her? Was she waiting for him in her bedroom? He couldn't . . . That was too obvious. He had no defense against that. He needed some kind of story . . .

He wandered back to the living room. She had to make the first move, otherwise . . .

"Finished already?" She surprised him.

"Ninety minutes, as promised." He nodded toward the new fan. "You want to do the honors?"

"Absolutely." She walked over and clicked the light on, then pulled the chain to start the fan. "Perfect. You do good work, Mr. Molinsky."

"We aim to please."

"Do you?"

What a loaded statement. He had to let it go, though. He couldn't start things. He smiled at her and knelt down and began dropping tools back in his box.

"Here. The least I can do is help." She knelt beside him and dropped his voltmeter in. Every move drew his eyes to her cleavage and filled the air around him with her scent.

As she pulled her hand back, she touched his knee, hesitated for just an instant, then eased forward. He froze until her lips pushed his open. She ran her tongue across his upper lip, and he felt himself relax. He slipped a hand behind her head, and kissed her once, then again.

She pushed away, and he started to protest until she locked her eyes on his. She crossed her arms in front of her, and pulled her tank top over her head. She crushed her body against his, her tongue forcing his teeth apart.

He had to remind himself to breathe. Bobbi . . . Bobbi never . . . it wasn't like this. She tugged at him, and he ripped his shirt off. "Don't worry," she whispered. "I use a patch."

"Want a glass *of wine, or a beer?" Tracy was already on her feet, padding to the kitchen. She was trim and fit, not at all like a woman who'd had two kids. Silhouetted by the refrigerator light, she fulfilled every dream he'd had.*

"I don't . . ." Never mind. He watched her reach in the cabinet for the glasses, admiring the perfect curve of her back. As she walked back to him, she never dropped her eyes. His staring pleased her.

She dropped beside him, poured a glass of red wine, and handed it to him. She poured a second glass, and set the bottle on the coffee table. "I have a bed. We don't have to lay here in the floor."

"I should get going . . ." Suddenly aware of his dry his mouth, he gulped the wine.

"Easy, there." She smiled and arched an eyebrow as she refilled his glass. "You don't want to go, though, do you?"

"Honestly?"

"I knew it." She sipped her wine and set the glass on the table with the bottle. "You always do what you should do." She slid her body against his.

"Just this once, do what you want to do."

"You always do what you want to?"

"Always." She kissed him, the taste of wine still on her lips. He couldn't resist kissing her again, then he stopped for another gulp of the wine, marveling that it was already taking effect. He hadn't had a drop since college, since he became a believer, a believer who knew better than to be with a woman who was not his wife.

He rolled over and sat up. *"Look, I've . . . I need to go . . ."* He reached for his shirt.

"Chuck, you're drunk. You can't drive now. I won't let you."

"I'm not—"

"You've had four glasses of wine in ten minutes. You'll go to jail if you get pulled over."

"It hasn't been . . ." He rubbed the back of his head and blinked. He could remember the first glass and when she poured the second . . . but four? Had he really? *"I'm not drunk. I couldn't be."*

"All right, how many fingers am I holding up?"

"Three."

"One."

He was sure he saw three. Maybe he shouldn't try to drive just yet.

Before Chuck opened his eyes, his brain registered something different. A different smell. Hotel in Kansas City? No . . . He forced his eyes open, and for a split second, he wasn't sure where he was. But then he heard breathing, and it all crashed back into his consciousness.

Tracy . . . He had . . . His life was over. Bobbi would . . . and who could blame her . . . No, Bobbi would never know. And this would never happen again.

He snatched up his shirt and shoes without daring to wake Tracy. Mercifully, her body was covered as she slept on her living room floor, but the pillows and the blankets weren't there when he fell asleep. He knew *that much.*

His toolbox wasn't anywhere close. He'd get new tools. Small price to pay. Wallet. Keys. Get out. But what about . . . what about locking her front door? No. If he woke her up, she'd start all over again, and he wouldn't be able to resist her. Just get out fast.

He checked his watch. Two-twelve. Six hours! How? How could he? He backed out of the driveway without starting the car, or turning on the lights, but as he put the BMW in gear he began to shake, great tremors in his hands, his legs. Freezing and dizzy, he blinked to keep his eyes focused.

He never meant to . . . He just wanted . . . Sweat beaded across his upper lip and across his shoulder blades. And she . . . What was he supposed to do when she . . .? She was so. . . and she knew how to push all his buttons. If Bobbi knew he had any buttons, she didn't care whether she pushed them or not. Tracy . . . it was like water in the desert.

He slapped his face hard. "Bobbi is my wife. I love Bobbi. She's the mother of my sons. We've been married eighteen years, for crying out loud!" But in eighteen years, she never made him feel the way Tracy made him feel. And Bobbi had never, ever made love to him like that. Never.

But he was married. It was wrong. One hundred percent wrong. Totally. Wrong. And if Bobbi ever found out, he'd be paying for these six hours for the rest of his natural life. So, she could never find out. He'd be a good husband from now on, and she'd never have to know. No blood, no foul.

He pulled in his driveway with a quick check around the neighborhood. Not a light on anywhere. Nobody would see him getting home after two-thirty. But even if they did, that was okay. Everybody knew the hours he worked these days. It was perfectly reasonable for him to work late . . . with his wife out of town. Especially with his wife out of town. That way he'd be home more when she was here. Of course. It made perfect sense.

As soon as he stepped through his front door, guilt wrapped around him. He could smell Bobbi's perfume, her coffee . . . He took the stairs two at a time and stripped his clothes off as soon as he got in the master bath, then cranked the hot water faucet until steaming water blasted from the spout.

Clean, that's what he needed. More soap. More hot water. He needed to get clean. He showered until he drained the hot water heater, and the shower ran cold. Condensed water dripped down the walls and fog rolled out when he opened the door. He wiped the face of his watch and frowned. Four o'clock already. His alarm was set for four-fifteen so he could make a ten-thirty meeting in Kansas City.

He sighed and pulled out his razor, the razor that suddenly weighed a thousand pounds, lathered his face and started shaving. At four-fifteen, his cell phone rang, and he nearly jumped through the ceiling. He dug through the pile of clothes at the door until he found it. It was Tracy.

"Hey, you left your toolbox here. Want me to bring it by?"

"No! I mean, it's not that big a deal. I'll uh, I'll get it some other time."

"I can bring it in—"

"Really that's not necessary, and I'll be in KC today and tomorrow, so my office is locked." *And the last thing I need is for everybody to see you bringing in my toolbox.*

"Friday then?"

Bobbi and the boys would be home from Detroit tomorrow night. He couldn't while Bobbi was home. "Friday's no good. If you don't mind it being kinda late Thursday, I'll just grab it then."

"How late?"

"Probably eight or eight-thirty."

"Hardly late. I'll be waiting for you. Thanks again for switching that fan out. And Chuck . . . I'll have trouble concentrating today after last night. You . . . you blew my mind."

"It . . . uh . . . it was good, wasn't it?"

"Yes, it was good."

"I'll see you Thursday."

CHAPTER 15
TRANSPARENCY

Chuck waited as long as he could stand it, hoping his mother still woke before sunrise, when he dialed her phone number. Through the long night, Bobbi's words echoed in his mind. *I want to love you again without having to justify it to myself or anybody else. I want you to* deserve *to have me love you again.* He didn't deserve her love, not when he lied to her, not when he went behind her back pursuing the lawsuit.

"What's wrong?" Ann Molinsky asked as soon as she picked up the phone. "It's ten til seven. You never call this early."

"It's Bobbi, Mom."

"We've been over this before. I'm not getting in the middle."

"I know that. I need you to pray, hard."

"What happened?"

"I can't say exactly. I just . . . I have some critical decisions coming up very soon, and I need some wisdom."

"Psalm 37."

"How can you say that when you don't know what I'm up against? Is that some one-size-fits-all Psalm?"

"No, but it changed your dad's life years ago, and since you are Jim made over, I figure it's a good starting place."

"Mom—"

"Read it first, then call me back if you don't find anything helpful."

"Mom—"

"You need your answer from God, not from me, or anyone else."

"Thanks," Chuck muttered, and hung up. He slouched onto the sofa with his Bible, and found Psalm 37. He mumbled his way through it until the words leapt off the page at him.

"*Commit your way to the* LORD, *trust also in Him, and He shall bring it to pass. He shall bring forth your righteousness as the light, and your justice as the noonday.*"

"I'm gonna hold You to this one, Lord."

Chuck spread the files from Tracy's lawsuit and his countersuit across his desk and read through each one again. Walter Davis made it clear that this topped the list of priorities and he expected a quick resolution.

Tracy's evidence consisted of an answering machine message and a call to his cell phone, the one from that Sunday morning when he picked up his clothes. He couldn't dispute the transcript. 'I know. It was my fault.' and 'I shouldn't have. That was wrong.' She twisted the context, though.

He leaned back in his chair and stroked his chin. Why would Tracy file a lawsuit when she knew it had no merit whatsoever? *It's not the money, because she knows she won't get any, and if it goes forward, she'll end up owing me.*

"God, You promised," he said, then he took a deep breath, picked up the phone, and dialed the bank. "What's the payoff on my house right now?" he asked, once he got through the computer menu to a real person. "Just under eighteen," he repeated, writing the number down in his planner. "Thanks. Now, can you transfer me to investment services?"

A moment later, someone picked up. "Investments. This is Greg Harmon."

"Greg, this is Chuck Molinsky. Where do I stand today?"

"Let me see . . . give me your magic number." Chuck recited his social security number. "You look good. Three-twenty-five, roughly, and early retirement even with college looks very doable. Of course, that's provided the markets stay decent and nothing major happens."

"What if something major happens?"

"Like what?"

"Like I pull out, say, two-seventy-five?"

"Bad things. Like a huge penalty to the IRS. You'd have to pull about three-fifteen to get two-seventy-five, then you'd have to save about sixty percent of your income to retire on time. I think early would be out of the question then."

His stomach rolled. *Everything I've worked for.* "Bobbi has to sign off on that, right?"

"She's on the account."

"How long does it take to get the money?"

"A direct wire takes about ten days, and a paper check maybe three weeks." Greg paused. "Chuck, I don't know what you've got going, but I'd advise against this if at all possible."

"Anybody would. Even so, go ahead and send me the paperwork." He hung up the phone and stared at the numbers he'd scribbled down. *God, there has to be another way out of this.* The alarm on his watch beeped. *Time for Phil already?* He stuffed the sheet of numbers in his pocket. *Maybe after he blows a gasket because I lied to him, he can give me some advice.*

Phil, before we wrap up, I've got something I need to talk to you about." Chuck swallowed hard and looked his pastor in the eye. "When we started all this, you told me I had to be completely honest. I haven't been truthful with you or Bobbi about the lawsuit."

"You're countersuing?" Phil asked.

"I was. I mean, it's filed, but I can't go through with it."

"What changed your mind?"

"Bobbi said something last night. She said she wanted me to deserve her love again."

"She doesn't know about your countersuit at all?"

"I've never told her directly, but I'm sure she does. I hoped I could get it all worked out behind the scenes."

"Behind her back."

"Yeah," Chuck admitted. "She deserves better. I want to be the man she deserves, Phil, and if that means giving up everything I've got . . ." His voice trailed off, and he looked away.

"What do you need from me?"

"I need you to pray. This is going to mean my job. I can pay off our house, but I don't know what will happen after that."

"Do you care if I tell Donna?"

"Please. I already called Mom, and I'm going to talk to Gavin."

"Excellent." Phil smiled broadly. "It may be hard to believe right now, but Chuck, this is like standing on the mountain with Elijah in that moment right before the fire falls. I can't wait to see how God works this out."

"You and me both," Chuck said, wishing for a touch of Phil Shannon's faith.

Since leaving work, Chuck managed to cram in a counseling session and a stop at the doctor's office before picking up dinner for Brad and him. Glancing at his watch as he parked his car, he mumbled, "Only twenty minutes late." When Bobbi opened the door for him, he stepped into the study. "Can I talk to you for just a minute?" He held the test results folder in his outstretched hand.

"What's this?" Bobbi asked taking the folder and flipping it open.

"Those are the results from all the testing you asked me to do."

She snapped the folder shut and handed it back to him. "Here, I don't need these."

"Did you even look at them?" He reopened the folder and held it out to her. "It was all negative. Everything's okay."

"I really didn't think you'd do it," Bobbi said, as she walked past him toward the kitchen.

"So this was just a little test?" He strode to catch up to his wife. "A little hoop to jump through?" His voice cracked as his temper slipped closer to exploding.

"No, I wanted to know that I wasn't facing any future risk." Bobbi pointed at her own heart, her jaw set, then she softened. "At least not any health risks. I don't play games like that. How could you even think that I would do that to you?"

"How could you think I wouldn't go through with the testing? I told you I would do whatever it took to make this right. I meant what I said."

"Yeah, and I thought you meant it when you said you'd be faithful until death."

"Since when do we get to eat in your car?" Brad asked as he moved the fast food sacks from the passenger seat and climbed in the BMW.

"Since now, I guess," Chuck answered. "Sorry I'm late. Phil and I ran over a little. I got super-sized, right?"

"Yeah, and no onions."

"Of course not." Chuck turned on the radio to listen to the pre-game. "They don't give Canfield much hope."

"They don't deserve it," Brad smirked. "If we win by less than three touchdowns, I'll be shocked." They pulled into the stadium parking lot as the band left the field. "Dad, you're not wearing any blue," Brad said, then added with mock disgust, "and you call yourself a fan."

"I have blue eyes," Chuck said.

"Doesn't count." Brad opened one of the sacks. "This one's yours." He turned the volume up on the radio with one hand, and stuffed French fries in his mouth with the other.

Taylor has won the toss and has deferred, so Canfield gets the ball. Taylor's in their home blue jerseys and the Canfield Cougars are in road whites. Aaron Gibbs lines up the ball for the kickoff . . . and we are under-way. High kick fielded at about the twelve-yard line. He makes it about five yards before he's popped by Danny Heatley. Let's see, that was Justin Page on the return for Canfield.

"Yes!" Brad said, pumping his fist. The game proceeded as expected. Taylor scored each time they had the ball, Canfield punted or fumbled, so the first half passed quickly. While the announcer began reading off other local scores, Brad cleared his throat, "Dad, can I ask you something?"

"Sure." Chuck turned the radio down.

"Why'd you cheat on Mom? You knew it was wrong."

"The simple answer—because I'm stupid. Stupid and weak. Stupid for putting myself in a bad situation, and weak for not walking away."

"So what's the complicated answer?"

"If I knew that, I wouldn't still be in counseling with Phil."

"What do you guys talk about? How many times can you go over it?"

"We don't keep going over the adultery part. It's more about what I need to do now, what I should have been doing all along. How to be a man, how to be a good husband, that kind of thing."

"You always loved Mom, though, right?"

"From the moment I met her." Chuck took a long drink from his Coke. He could still picture her that afternoon.

"So, was she hot?"

"Mom? You bet."

"The other woman."

"Let me tell you what she was." Chuck sat up straight in his seat and his eyes narrowed. "She was no different than a prostitute on a street corner somewhere. She just expected to be paid in professional consideration at the law firm." Brad's eyes grew wider as Chuck pointed his finger at him. "I'm not denying that I was one hundred percent responsible for what I did, but she marked me for a fool from the day she walked in that office. Here, let me show you." Chuck reached behind Brad's seat and got his Bible.

"You carry this around with you now?"

"I had counseling today," he answered, flipping through the pages. "Here it is. Proverbs seven." Chuck held the Bible up to catch the parking lot lights. He scanned the chapter, deciding where to start. "Okay, let me paraphrase. Be smart and pay attention to what you're doing, because there are women out there ready to destroy you, and they'll use any means they can, especially sex." He pointed and his voice rose in intensity as he spoke.

Brad held his hands up. "Dad, calm down. You're not in court."

"This chapter is exactly what happened to me. Exactly. Listen . . . here we go, the stupid idiot—that would be me—'took the path to her house in the twilight, in the evening, in the black and dark night. And there a woman met him, with the attire of a harlot, and a crafty heart.'" He looked at his son. "I had no business being at her house after dark. I shouldn't have been there at all, but especially not at night. Nothing good could come out of that." He held his Bible up again. "'So she caught him and kissed him; with an impudent face she said to him . . . I got all this ready just for you. It'll be okay. No one will ever know.'"

"What's impudent?" Brad asked.

"It says shameless in the footnote. Believe me, she was."

"Did she really talk to you like that?"

"Oh, yeah," Chuck nodded, "and it worked, just like in this chapter." He picked up his Bible to read again. "'With her enticing speech she caused him to yield, with her flattering lips she seduced him. Immediately, he went after her, as an ox goes to the slaughter'. Immediately. Not even six months after I met her and I was ruined. 'He did not know it would cost his life.'"

Chuck closed his Bible. "Committing adultery should have cost me everything. If it didn't kill me outright, it should've cost the life I'd made for myself. Your mother should have thrown me out. You guys should have disowned me." Chuck emphasized each point, tapping the gearshift. "I should have lost my job, my health, everything. And for a while, I was sure I had lost it all."

"But you didn't," Brad said.

Chuck smiled at his son's attempt to put a good spin on things. "No, and that's grace. Grace from God, and grace from your mother." Chuck stared off across the parking lot. "I've tried to figure out why God is like that, why He can put up with me that way. I think, maybe, it's so I can plead with you and Joel." He turned and faced his son. "Please, please do everything in your power to make sure you *never, ever* have to look into the eyes of the woman you love, confirm her worst nightmare, and say, 'Yes, I betrayed you, I didn't love you enough to walk away.'" The tears flowed freely now, and Chuck didn't try to stop them or hide them. "I am so sorry," he whispered. "I would give anything to take it back."

Brad shifted in his seat. "I believe you," he said at last. "It's okay, Dad."

"Thanks," Chuck said, wiping his eyes and taking a deep breath. "But it's all up to Mom now. She's got to believe that I've changed, that she can trust me again." Chuck sighed, "So we counsel, and counsel, and counsel some more."

"Oh, you've changed," Brad said. "I can tell."

"How so?"

Giving a sly grin, Brad said, "You're not as big a jerk as you used to be." Brad gulped his Coke, muffling his laughter.

"Thank you, Gavin. Neither are you." He gave Brad a shove in the shoulder.

"Why'd you call me Gavin?"

"Because that's the kind of thing he always says to me. It's like a gift with him."

"Gavin has always been my favorite uncle, you know," Brad smiled. "Seriously, Dad, if I'd gotten in a fight and been suspended *last* year, what would have happened?"

Chuck shrugged.

"If, and it's a big if, you could have contained your temper long enough to talk, you would've stormed into Mr. McMillen's office demanding somebody get fired. Then you would've been mad at me for a month."

"That bad?"

"At least. Ask Joel."

"It's a God-thing, then. Grandma said I didn't have it in me to change that much. She's right again."

They sat in silence for several more minutes. "Joel said you guys had a big fight last night."

Chuck sighed. "Okay, let me explain. First, it wasn't a fight. A fight means we disagreed about something."

"Spoken like a true lawyer."

"Thanks." Chuck rolled his eyes. "There's no disagreement. Mom's right. Period."

"But she's still mad?"

"Well, yeah."

"It never shows," Brad said. "She's very cool."

"That's for your benefit, and Joel's." Chuck took a long drink from his Coke. "Truth is, Mom . . . Mom loves me, and she forgives me, even though I don't deserve it. So . . . she's able to be civil . . . well, more than civil . . ."

"I've never heard you stutter like that."

"I hurt her so much. Every time we talk, I find out there's a new, deeper layer of pain there."

"It'll work out, Dad. I came around, and I never wanted to speak to you again."

Chuck had to smile. "Yeah, it's just a long process. I get impatient sometimes, so I think we're farther along than we are."

"Just be glad you're not married to Aunt Rita."

"Why's that?"

"She hates your guts," Brad said. "Game's starting again." He reached over and turned the radio back up.

Here to start the second half, Taylor will get the ball. Joe Dietrich set to kick it off for Canfield and Garrett Walker deep for the Eagles. Good kick . . . into the end zone, and Walker will let it go. So, the Eagles will start first and ten from their own twenty yard line.

"Kyle Kilburn brings his troops up to the line in a three-wide out set. Danny Heatley, defensive back, in on this one for Brad Molinsky. Brad didn't dress tonight. All right. Kilburn's calling the signal. Still calling, takes the snap, drops back in the pocket looking for his man . . . throws it to Danny Heatley! Heatley's got his man beat! He's at the forty, across midfield. He's got a man moving up on his flank . . . Heatley sidesteps him, and he's gone. Thirty, twenty, ten, touchdown Taylor! Eighty yards Kyle Kilburn to Danny Heatley!

At first Brad beamed, but then Chuck watched as deep dejection pulled his shoulders down, then his eyes, and erased the smile from his face. Danny played in Brad's spot. That would have been his touchdown.

"Wow," Brad whispered, blinking at the radio. "I wish I could have seen it."

"There's no guarantee you would've gotten a touchdown," Chuck said. "Matson could've called a different play. Who knows?"

"Dad, the game's kind of a blow-out. Is it okay if we take off?"

"Sure." Chuck reached up and started the car. "It doesn't help at all, but I'm so proud of you for being a man. Thanks for sitting with me, talking with me."

"You're right. It's not helping."

Chuck gave him a half-smile and headed out of the parking lot.

"You're home early," Bobbi said when Brad shuffled through the front door. Propped in the corner of the sofa, she held a book in her lap, but couldn't recall any of the plot from the hundred pages she'd read.

"Wasn't much of a game," he said, turning the deadbolt. "Where's Joel?"

"Watching television. Is everything all right?"

He dropped into the recliner across from her. "Why does God make it hard to do the right thing?"

"You need somebody smarter than me for that one." She closed her book and laid it aside. "What happened?"

Brad explained about Danny's touchdown. "God didn't have to let Danny do that. I feel like God slapped me in the face after I did the right thing. Why would I ever do things His way again?"

"I know what you mean. Right now, it seems like your dad is doing much better than I am, and he's the one who committed adultery."

"Do you believe him? That he's sorry and everything?"

She weighed her answer carefully. "I'm trying to. If I say I believe him, then my actions have to back that up, and that's where I'm struggling. I guess I don't believe him enough to act like his wife again."

"We had a good talk."

"That's good. You both needed that."

"Can I tell you something else?" He leaned forward, propping his elbows on his knees.

"Always."

"I've never heard Dad talk about you like he did tonight. It was the way a guy should talk about someone he loves."

"Brad . . ." *I don't need this from my son.*

"I don't mean it to sound like I'm pressuring you or anything. It was just different. So is there something you're waiting on? Some sign? Then you'll know?"

"There are a couple of things hanging over us, yes."

"That's why you're still in counseling?"

"Your father doesn't understand why he cheated on me."

Brad flinched when she answered.

"I'm sorry. It's . . . I can't commit to him with that unresolved."

"Yeah, he told me that, too." He stood and stretched. "I'm going on up to bed. Goodnight." He walked over and kissed her cheek, then left her alone.

Bobbi slumped against the arm of the sofa. *Lord, I feel like I've just moved into solitary. I'm getting further from the door rather than closer to freedom. It looks like you're helping Chuck and leaving me to sort this out alone. What am I doing wrong?*

Sunday, October 16

Brad took several deep breaths, and faking confidence as best he could, he stepped into the youth room to face his peers. A couple dozen teens in clusters waited for their worship time to start. Brad wiped his hands on his shirt and hoped his stomach settled before he tried to speak.

Danny Heatley crossed the room to meet him. "So, how's life in the slammer?" he asked.

"I've had it worse. I'm grounded from everything, but I don't get 'the look' every time I come downstairs."

"Man, I can't believe you hit Burcham. That's like something I'd do."

"I just lost it." Brad shook his head and glanced around the room. "So it's all over school?"

"Oh, yeah, but you're a hero. Burcham's needed that for a long time."

"I'm not a hero. I punched a guy."

"I know. I'm just telling you how it's playing."

"I wish I'd seen your touchdown," Brad said. *Even though it should have been mine.*

"I hadn't played offense since junior high. I had an interception that I ran back last year, so this was just my second touchdown. It was awesome. Eighty yards, man."

"I heard it on the radio." Brad did his best radio announcer voice. "Heatley's got his man beat. He's at the thirty, the twenty, the ten, touchdown!" He raised his arms and Danny grinned. "I, uh, listened to the game with my dad."

"Your dad? I thought you were never speaking to him again."

"I changed my mind."

"Guys, finish up your snacks, we're starting in sixty seconds," Cooper

DeWitt announced. He caught Brad's eye, and gave him a nod and a smile.

"Does Cooper know?" Brad asked Danny.

"Are you kidding? He's got more spies at that school than my dad. I don't know how he finds out everything."

"Great," Brad muttered as he and Danny grabbed seats against the wall.

The youth pastor strode up to the front of the room and raised his hands, signaling the start of the meeting. "It's good to see everybody out tonight. Megan's back with us." Cooper pointed to a petite blonde girl off to his right. "You're through with treatments for a while, right?" She nodded.

"I know the end of the quarter's coming up, but all you guys are making straight A's, so it's no big deal." Moans rippled through the group. "Somebody be sure and write that on the prayer wall, then."

Glancing back through the room, Cooper said, "I almost forgot. It's the third Sunday, so we've got Larry and Julie Ayers helping us out. She made those incredible pizza things you guys snatched up." Spontaneous applause and whoops erupted from the teenagers.

Cooper let the clapping go on for a few minutes. "Now, we're going to the throne room of God for an audience with the King. What are we bringing?" He got his notebook out to write down the prayer requests.

Brad listened as several kids shared about family members dealing with illness. He wanted to speak, but he felt like his mouth was filled with sand. He coughed and swallowed, trying to get sound out of his mouth.

"You okay?" Danny whispered.

Brad nodded and resolved to say something after the next request, but a kid started a long story about a friend stealing his grandparents' medications. Brad bounced his leg and waited.

At last, there was a lull and Brad jumped to his feet. "Hey, I've got one," he said, waving a hand. "Pray for my mom and dad. You know what they're going through. They're trying to do the right thing, but it's still hard."

He wanted to stop there, but after a quick glance around the room, he gave the rest of his story. "I was so mad at my dad, I refused to pray for him. I wanted God to zap him, you know? A big lightning bolt or something. But the . . . events . . . of the last few days made me realize I was wrong. I'm going to pray for him, and I want you guys to, too. I want this to be over for them."

From where he stood, Brad could see Cooper grinning like a daddy showing off his favorite son.

CHAPTER 16
CONFLUENCE

"Let's see, I've got the writing folders caught up," Bobbi mumbled as she sorted and restacked the papers on her desk in the after-school quiet. "Next week's book is ready to go, so all I need are copies of the pilgrim thing, and I'll be done. That's if I can *find* the pilgrim thing." At least it was Monday, and she could just go home without the extra pressure of making dinner for Chuck.

"Ah ha!" she said, pulling the Thanksgiving story page from one of her stacks. "I haven't completely lost my mind." Before she could get out of her classroom to the copy machine, her cell phone rang. She dug it out of her tote bag and was surprised to see her sister's name on the caller ID.

"Bobbi, can we push dinner on Thursday back to four o'clock? Kara and John won't be here until that morning, so I don't think I can swing a noon meal." Not the slightest hint of tension.

"Four's fine. What can I bring?" She could pretend as well as Rita.

"Just the boys. I've got everything else. You could let Ann know."

"Ann . . . volunteered to work. She's staying in South Carolina."

"I'm sorry to hear that. I'll miss her."

"What about Chuck?"

"What about him?" The edge returned to Rita's voice.

"He's not invited?"

"I didn't think he would want to be here with things still so strained."

"I have dinner with him three times a week. It's no big deal anymore."

"Even so—"

"Four o'clock, then. We'll be there." Bobbi clicked the phone off, almost hanging up on her sister. With Rita, the issues were black or white, choose her or Chuck.

Bobbi made her copies, locked her desk, and headed home. *Just one more half day.* She longed for the holiday weekend. Teaching sapped every bit of her strength. Her students enjoyed the morning game of reminding Mrs. Molinsky what they did the previous day. If only it were a game.

She let herself in the empty house and dropped her bag by the stairs. The boys had gone home with Jeremy and Nathan Schoenberger, and wouldn't be back until after nine o'clock. Dinner for one required far too much effort, so she pulled one of Joel's vanilla fudge Pop-Tarts from the cabinet. She carried it and a half glass of milk to the living room, and collapsed on the sofa.

She watched as twilight and then darkness overcame the last light in the living room. *Like a heavy, dark blanket . . . a smothering blanket . . .* The mantel clock chimed the half hour. *Time passes, day after day, and nothing changes. Nothing ever changes.*

Bobbi pulled the afghan around her. *This is how Daddy felt, isn't it? Hopeless . . . And he gave up . . .* How tempting. No more fighting. No more trying. No more struggling. But where would Brad and Joel find themselves in twenty or twenty-five years after growing up with a mother who couldn't cope?

She reached for the phone, then hesitated. She couldn't call Ann. Not Rita. Certainly not Chuck. She had one option. She dialed the Shannons, praying that Donna would answer, but after two rings, she hung up. *Donna has enough going on. I just need a good night's sleep.*

Within moments, the phone rang. "Bobbi, I saw where you'd called," Donna said. "Did you need something?"

"No, I dialed your number by mistake."

"Is everything all right, Honey?"

"I'm fine," Bobbi lied.

"Do you want to go get a cup of coffee?"

"Thanks, but I can't. The boys are at a movie and I . . . well, I told them I'd be at home."

"Sure, I understand. You sound like you need some company. Can I bring a coffee to you?"

Could she take that risk? Could she afford not to? "I think I'd like that. Thank you."

Fifteen minutes later, Bobbi answered the door and Donna began apologizing before she even stepped inside. "I got to Dear Joe and realized I never asked you what kind of coffee you wanted."

"It doesn't matter, I'll drink any kind," Bobbi said, trying to smile. "Any kind of *coffee,* that is. All those other things are for sissies."

"I got my two favorites and you can have your choice." Donna opened the bag. "There's hazelnut and cinnamon breakfast."

"Hazelnut. What do I owe you?"

"Not a thing. It's on me."

"At least let me have your jacket, then." She hung Donna's jacket in the hall closet. "We can sit in the living room." Bobbi switched on a lamp and she and Donna settled on opposite ends of the sofa. *Where do I start? How do I begin?*

Donna rescued her. "How are you?"

"The truth?"

"That's up to you. I could probably guess, though."

"So I'm not doing such a good job hiding everything after all."

"You might be. Let's just say I have an inside track."

"Phil?"

"No, Phil never tells me what you discuss in counseling. He either says, 'we had a good session' or 'keep praying for Bobbi and Chuck.'"

Bobbi stared into her coffee cup. "I feel like I'm losing my sanity. I can't remember anything. I can't concentrate. It's all I can do to get through a day."

"How are things with Chuck?"

"I don't see how it's ever going to be resolved."

"Does it seem kind of pointless to keep going through counseling?"

She couldn't tell her counselor's wife, 'yes, it's pointless.' "It's not Phil's fault. He's gracious and understanding, but we're not getting anywhere. I know he's aggravated with me."

"No, he's not, but he does know you're not making a lot of progress." Donna took a long sip from her coffee. "Honey, can I be real honest with you?"

"Of course." She set her coffee on the end table, hoping that meant Donna had the answer.

"You're holding on to something. I'm not sure what it is, but until you let go of it, you're stuck right here."

"But I've done all the right things. I told Chuck I loved him. I encouraged Brad and Joel to forgive their dad. I've even defended him to Rita . . ." Emotion choked off her words.

Donna slid down the couch and took her hand.

"I want to forgive him. I told Chuck I forgave him, but I can't go back to how things were." Bobbi wiped her eyes.

"You're still angry, but not just at Chuck. Who else has betrayed you?"

"No one."

"What about God? You're angry with Him for pulling the props out from under you, for not protecting you from this."

How could Donna know? Yes, God had betrayed her, but she never dared to form that thought, much less voice it. That was heresy, to accuse God that way, wasn't it? Bobbi clenched her jaw, as if to physically prevent the words from escaping her lips.

Donna dropped her head, almost apologizing. "Honey, you can't heal your marriage until you deal with this."

"Deal with this?" Bobbi stood, paced away from the sofa, and spoke to the living room ceiling. "I'm supposed to go to God and say, 'You know, I expected a little more out of You. Chuck's just a man, after all. I expected him to let me down.'"

"Yes, just like that," Donna said with a smile.

"I can't talk to God like that."

"But He already knows your thoughts. It's freeing to be that honest and real with God."

"So you want me to yell at God?"

"No, I want you to bring all that stuffed emotion into the light. Own it, so He can heal it. He won't heal what you try to hide from Him."

Bobbi shuffled back and dropped on the sofa. *He's not going to heal anything, period.* She snatched her coffee cup off the end table and gulped half the contents.

"You haven't told Chuck any of this, have you?" Donna asked. "That's not fair to him."

"I don't have a choice." Bobbi took the last drink from her coffee, giving her the chance to push things down deep inside once again.

"You absolutely do have a choice. What are you afraid of?"

"Excuse me?"

"You're not being honest with Chuck or anyone else because you're afraid of something."

Afraid to trust Chuck . . . Afraid things will never get any better . . . Afraid my boys are scarred . . .

"You don't have to tell me. That's not the point, but you can't go on like this. I've struggled all my adult life with depression and the things you've said, or left unsaid, are as familiar to me as my own thoughts."

"Depression?" That was for neurotics. She might be irritated, frustrated, or angry even, but she was *not* depressed.

"It started when I was twenty-four years old. Phil was in graduate school, nearly finished, trying to discern if he was being called into the ministry or not. His dad had just died unexpectedly. David was a baby. I had a complete emotional collapse."

Donna stared off across the living room. "Phil was a psychology major, and he saw it all coming, bless his heart. I think he understood more about what went on inside my head than I did. He ended up dropping out of school just short of his master's degree, and by the time I was straightened out, he'd decided on seminary."

"Phil was a psychology major?" Bobbi asked, trying to divert the conversation.

"He surely was," Donna said with a smile. "He wanted to go into marriage and family therapy of all things."

"And here he gets all that, plus pastoring a church."

"Now I know where you're going with this." Donna chided, pointing a finger in a teasing reproof. "There is nothing that Phil would rather be doing than working with you and Chuck."

"Well, we're putting him through his paces."

"He can handle it." Donna finished off her coffee and set the cup on the floor beside the sofa. "Now, despite your attempts to change the subject," Donna teased, then her smile faded, "you're in a spiritual and emotional crisis. Please, get some help before things get worse."

"How could they possibly get worse?"

"Depression won't let go of you." Donna's sincere intensity unnerved Bobbi. "It will take you from wishing this would all go away, to thinking things would be so much easier if you weren't around, maybe to the point of making plans."

"Plans? You mean suicide?"

Donna nodded. "You won't shock me if you've thought about it."

Bobbi had wished this would all go away, more than once. How many times had she been out driving, and just for a fleeting instant, hoped a big truck would cross the centerline in front of her? A tear made its way down Bobbi's cheek. Donna pegged her.

"Honey, listen to me. You need to take care of yourself first and foremost. There's no sense trying to go through marriage counseling right now. You need to see a doctor, and you need to tell Chuck . . . everything."

"Chuck doesn't deserve—"

"Bobbi, don't you wish your daddy would've shared his heart with you and Rita?"

"Of course," Bobbi whispered.

"Because you love him."

Bobbi nodded, tears flowing now.

"Honey, Chuck loves you, and I believe you love him. Let him walk through this with you."

Before Bobbi could protest or offer excuses, the front door opened. "Hey, Mom!" Brad called.

Bobbi wiped her eyes and swallowed all traces of emotion. "In here. How was the movie?"

"Better than homework," Brad said, then he waved at Donna. "Oh, hi!"

"Hi boys," Donna said, standing. "I'll get going, Bobbi. Do you guys have school tomorrow?"

"Just a half day," Joel said.

"Well, enjoy your break." Donna took her jacket from Bobbi.

"Thank you for coming over," she said. "I mean that."

Donna gave Bobbi a gentle hug. "Think about what I said. I speak from experience. I know it's hard and it seems like it's never going to change, but it can, and it will. Phil says 'even the longest day has its end.'"

Tuesday, November 22

Bobbi surprised Chuck when she suggested eating out so close to Thanksgiving. He'd carried retirement fund paperwork around with him for weeks, watching for the right opportunity, but the longer he waited, the more he wavered. He had to get Bobbi's signature tonight.

The restaurant's big screen televisions playing basketball and hockey ruled out any substantive conversation. Before Bobbi could escape to her car, Chuck caught up with her in the parking lot. "Can I take you for a cup of coffee?" he asked.

Bobbi looked at him and checked her watch, then glanced over toward the car and her sons. There wasn't a believable excuse on earth she could give him.

Chuck followed her back to the house and waited while she got Brad and Joel safely inside. As she locked the front door, he got out and opened the passenger door for her. She slipped around him without a word, got in the car, and pulled her door closed.

Three blocks from the house, Chuck broke the silence. "You haven't said anything bad about my car yet." He smiled, trying to see her face and still watch the road.

"Those days are gone, Chuck, when your car was the biggest dispute between us."

At Dear Joe, Chuck held the door for his wife, then every muscle tensed when the guy behind the counter looked up and smiled at Bobbi.

"Don't tell me—" the guy said.

Bobbi nodded. "It was his idea, even."

"Bobbi?" Chuck's jaw tightened.

"Chuck, this is Clay Bartel. He owns Dear Joe."

Chuck reached to shake hands, but Clay continued wiping his hands on a dishtowel. "You seem to be good friends with my wife."

"She's my best customer. I try to take care of her." He set a cup on the counter in front of Bobbi. "That's the Moroccan you liked so well. My treat. Now, what can I get you?" He waited for Chuck to answer his challenge.

The menu board made less sense to Chuck than the Spanish owner's manual for his cell phone, but he couldn't let Coffee Boy know that. "Turkish," he said, and enjoyed the hint of surprise on the guy's face. Turkish was the only kind of coffee he could remember Bobbi drinking.

"That's a pretty strong blend. Not for wimps. Sure you don't want to try it first?"

"It's Bobbi's favorite. That's good enough for me."

"What size?" Another challenge.

He scanned the menu board. *Minnie . . . Molly . . . What? Sizes, gotcha.* There was no way Chuck was ordering a girl size. "Uh, Bill."

The corners of the coffee guy's mouth turned up as he poured the cup then snapped the lid on. "That'll be three-twenty-five."

Chuck laid a ten dollar bill on the counter. "I'll buy my wife's coffee, thank you." He gulped from his cup without taking his eyes off Clay Bartel. The coffee, thick and bitter, caught in his throat, and he had to bite his tongue to keep from coughing and spitting. "You . . . you keep the change."

They had Dear Joe to themselves, so Chuck led Bobbi to a booth in the corner and took the seat facing the counter. "Is that guy always like that?"

"Clay? Like what?" She glanced back toward the counter and Chuck bristled.

"All hitting on you," he said.

"Hitting? Please. That's the most ridiculous thing you've ever said to me." She nodded her head toward Chuck's cup. "And I can finish that if you need me to."

"I don't need you to finish my coffee," he huffed, choking down another gulp. "So, what's the plan for Thursday?"

"Dinner's at four." She never looked up.

"What? What's the matter?"

"I don't think you should go."

"Did Rita put you up to this?" The back of his neck warmed.

"Don't start on Rita." Bobbi rubbed her temple as she sipped her coffee.

"No, she's doing everything she can to force you to choose—either her or me. Can't you see how she's manipulating you?"

"And you're not?"

"I've given you the time and space to sort all this out. Rita needs to back off and give you that same space." He took a long slow breath. "When we got married, nobody could make that decision for you. It was yours and yours alone. This has to be the same way."

"So, I can't talk to anybody else?"

"I didn't say that. I want you to make your own decision, from your own heart, and not base it on what you think someone else wants you to do."

She sipped her coffee in silence. "What if that decision isn't what you want to hear?"

"If it's what *you* want, I can live with it."

She frowned, and rolled her eyes at him.

"Okay, I'll prove it to you," he said. "You tell me what *you* want me to do for Thanksgiving. Go or not. Your decision."

She looked him in the eye and her voice never wavered. "I don't want you to go."

"All right then. That's settled. I'm not going." Bobbi chose Rita. How much longer before she took her sister's advice and divorced him? Then Coffee Boy could swoop in . . .

He drove Bobbi home, knowing if he said anything right now, it would be the wrong thing, and would only make matters worse.

When they got back to the house, Bobbi didn't even give him a chance to turn off the car. "I can let myself in," she said, without looking at him.

"Are you sure?"

"Yeah. You're okay with Thanksgiving?"

Would she change her mind if I said 'no'? "I'll be fine."

Bobbi nodded and got out of the car. He watched her walk in the house and close the front door, then he slammed his hands against on the steering wheel. "This is two against one, God." Tears of frustration left dark dots on his slacks. "I can't win this."

Wednesday, November 23

Chuck answered his mother's call before the first ring faded. "I got your message," she said. "What's wrong? You sounded agitated."

"It's just . . . We . . . It's Rita. She's poisoning Bobbi's mind. I don't stand a chance. From a woman's perspective, okay? Not my mother's perspective, but from a woman's perspective, what can I do? What does Bobbi need to see from me to get rid of whatever picture Rita's painted for her?"

"What happened? I thought you were making progress."

"Were. Until Bobbi started being manipulated."

"Manipulated? Or manipulated by someone other than you?"

"Mom! I need help, not more accusations!" Silence. "I'm sorry. I haven't slept. She . . . she doesn't want me there for Thanksgiving."

"Son, I know you're devastated, but this solution has to be yours, not mine."

"But I don't have any answers."

"Maybe you're trying to solve the wrong problem. This is between you and God, not you and Bobbi, or even you and Rita."

"Why can't you be like other mothers and just interfere, and tell me what to do?" He was only halfway kidding.

"Because then you'd be like other sons and completely ignore my advice, and blame me when everything went wrong."

"That's all I'm going to get out of you, isn't it?"

"Today, yes. I'll talk to you soon, and I'll be praying hard."

"Thanks." Chuck slouched onto the sofa with his Bible, and found Psalm 37 again, but different verses caught his eye this time.

"Rest in the Lord, and wait patiently for Him;
Do not fret because of him who prospers in his way,
Because of the man who brings wicked schemes to pass.
Cease from anger, and forsake wrath;
Do not fret—it only causes harm . . .
The steps of a good man are ordered by the Lord,
And He delights in his way.

Though he fall, he shall not be utterly cast down;
For the Lord upholds him with His hand."

Chuck exited the interstate and twisted in his seat so he could pull his phone from his pants pocket. He needed to let Tracy know he'd be at her place right on time, but before he could dial, his phone rang. It was Bobbi. "Hey, almost home?"

"I wish," she said. "It looks more like eleven or eleven-thirty. How about you?"

"About the same, maybe a little later. I'm not quite to Columbia yet."

"How'd things go?"

"Good. I think we'll wrap this up ahead of schedule." His call waiting beeped. "Hang on. I've got another call."

"Go ahead and take it. I didn't have anything else. I'll see you at home."

"Tell Gavin to drive carefully." Chuck picked up the other call. "Hello?"

"Where are you?" Tracy asked.

"About fifteen minutes from your place."

"I was getting anxious."

Me too. For two days now, scenes from Tuesday evening replayed in his head, slipping into his memory in the most unexpected moments, like in the middle of the meeting with Tom Conrad.

And she was anxious. It had nothing to do with making sure he got his toolbox. No, she was anxious to be alone with him again. Incredible. He wasn't going to her place with the intention of having sex again. He just . . . he wanted to see her, talk to her, that's all. Enjoy some intelligent conversation.

He pulled into Tracy's driveway and untied his tie. He got out of the car and tossed his suit jacket on the passenger seat with the necktie. Casual. Low-key.

He rang Tracy's doorbell and worked to roll up his sleeves while he waited, but he only got the left one before she opened the door. When he saw her, he *forgot the toolbox, forgot he had sleeves, forgot he had a wife, forgot everything. She was dressed like a Victoria's Secret model, in sheer black lace lingerie, with a short, silk robe. Her hair fell down to her shoulders, and his jaw dropped.*

She smiled and opened the storm door for him. He stepped inside, never taking his eyes off her cleavage. She pushed the door closed, then pinned him against the wall, pressing her hips against his. She kissed him hard, sending a shiver down his spine.

He thought he heard the deadbolt, as he slid his hand around to her back. He felt her breath on his ear, caught her scent. "Make love to me, Chuck." Then she pulled back, twisted away from him. He forced an eye open. He was alone in the foyer of Tracy's house.

'Make love to me,' she said. Tough to do when he couldn't find her. He rubbed his eyes, then looked in the living room, the dining room, and the kitchen. She was upstairs. He stood with a hand on the post, looking up the long flight of stairs. If he followed her upstairs, he couldn't explain that one away. He was consciously choosing to be unfaithful to his wife. He glanced at his watch. It wasn't nine o'clock yet. Plenty of time. He grasped the banister and took the steps two at a time.

At a quarter *past midnight, Chuck pulled into his own driveway. He had showered before he left Tracy's so her scent didn't linger on him. Strange soap he could explain. Strange woman . . . not so much. One thing was absolutely certain. He could not be with Tracy Ravenna again. He couldn't. He was a married man. A father . . . He went to church . . . Just this past Sunday. He sat there in church beside his wife. That had to count for something.*

Granted, he crossed a line tonight. He chose. He chose Tracy, but if he stopped now, there was no real harm done. He could choose to end it, and it would end now. He'd go in there and be Bobbi's husband from now on. He draped his suit jacket and tie across his arm, and grabbed his briefcase. He'd get the garment bag from the trunk in the morning. And the toolbox.

Bobbi left the front door unlocked for him. That meant she hadn't been home long. What if she was still awake? His pulse quickened and he ducked in the downstairs bathroom. He carefully inspected his face. He didn't think Tracy was wearing any lipstick, but he couldn't risk it. He washed his hands, so his sweaty palms didn't give him away, then he stole upstairs.

Thank God, she was asleep. The bathroom light was on, so he could see to change clothes. He hung his suit on its hanger, and grabbed a pair of pajama pants from the dresser.

"Welcome home," Bobbi said. Her voice, soft and gentle, startled him so that he had to grab the corner of the bed.

"I thought you were asleep. You scared me."

"I missed you this week."

"Missed me? But I'm gone all the time."

"I was gone this time. I felt like I'd abandoned you."

He flipped the bathroom light off, then pulled the covers back, and climbed in bed beside her. "You had a good time, though?"

"I did, but . . . I don't know. It just really hit home how much I missed you." She surprised him, laying a hand on his chest, then leaning over to kiss him on the lips. "I wish it was a different . . . uh . . . week of the month, you know."

"I'll give you a rain check. We're both exhausted, anyway."

"I intend to collect . . . soon as possible." She nestled beside him, once again laying a hand on his chest.

"Goodnight, Bobbi." He didn't move a muscle until he heard her breathing grow slower and deepen. He had to think. This was Thursday. He was going to be out of town next week until Thursday evening. If he made it a point of being with Bobbi this weekend, then he could see Tracy Thursday. That would work. He'd have things to catch up on so it would make sense for him to stay late at the office. Thursday it is.

CHAPTER 17
CAPITULATION

Thursday, November 24, Thanksgiving Day

Chuck settled in front of the television and arranged Styrofoam containers from his carryout dinner on the coffee table. *The most pathetic Thanksgiving ever.* Before he could get the first bite down, the ring of his cell phone startled him. He glanced at the caller ID. *Rita and Gavin?* "Hello?"

"Hey, Dad, is Mom there with you?" Brad asked.

"No. What's wrong?"

"I don't know . . . Mom didn't come to Thanksgiving. She was sick. All day yesterday, too. Aunt Rita called to see if Mom was feeling better, and she couldn't get an answer at home. She just left to go check on Mom."

"It's probably nothing. You know how hard your mom sleeps if she takes cold medicine, or maybe she went out to the drugstore or something." Chuck tried to hide his rising worry. This wasn't like Bobbi. "I'll see what I can find out. Thanks for letting me know." Chuck shifted the phone from ear to ear as he put on his jacket.

Thirty seconds later, Chuck jerked his BMW in gear and headed home. He took advantage of the light traffic, rolling through stop signs and anticipating green lights.

A half a block from his house, he saw Rita's car in Bobbi's spot in the driveway. She sat in her car, talking on her cell phone. Chuck parked behind her, then got out and tapped on her window.

"What are you doing here?" she asked as soon as the electric window slid open.

"Brad called me. Have you tried Bobbi's cell phone?"

"I just did. No answer. Where could she be?"

"I don't know. Let's go inside. Maybe we can figure something out."

"You still have a key?" Rita asked, getting out of her car.

"Yes, I still have a key," Chuck answered without trying to hide his irritation. He unlocked the door and dashed from room to room, surveying the house. He met Rita back in the entry hall. "Nothing looks out of place, but I didn't see Bobbi's purse anywhere."

"Her phone was in the kitchen," Rita said, handing it to Chuck. "Wherever she is, she doesn't want to be disturbed. When was the last time you talked to her?"

"Tuesday night."

"Same here. Did she sound okay to you?"

"Yeah, I guess." Chuck closed his eyes and rested the side of his fist against his lips. Bobbi was tired Tuesday, didn't say much, but that seemed to be the new normal. "Try the Shannons. Sometimes Bobbi talks to Donna. It's all I can come up with right now."

While Rita called, Chuck paced through the house. Bobbi filled every empty spot on the wall, every flat space on the shelves and tables with framed pictures. Most of the photos were of the boys, but here and there, she mixed in a few photos of the two of them.

Off to the side of one of the shelves in the built-in bookcase sat a small rock. He smiled and lifted it from its spot. Only Bobbi would keep a rock from the Dixson Lake boat ramp. *No pictures of the lake . . .*

"I know where she is!" he said, and bolted for the front door.

"Donna hasn't talked to her, but now she's worried, too." Rita said, as Chuck blew past her toward the front door. "Where are you going?"

"I know where Bobbi is. I'll call you." He slammed the front door behind him before Rita could protest or volunteer to go with him.

Chuck pushed his BMW to its limits on the drive to Dixson Lake State Park. She had to be okay. Bobbi wasn't the irrational type . . . and she hadn't left any kind of note or anything . . . *Don't even go there. She*

wouldn't . . . She was exhausted, that's all. She was exhausted, and she was at the lake. She had to be at the lake.

It made perfect sense. Everybody wanted something from her. Everybody was pressuring her. Even him. Especially him. She was using all her energy to take care of her family, and neglecting herself. She reached a breaking point and felt like she needed to get away. That had to be it.

As he rounded a bend and caught his first glimpse of the boat ramp, his chest constricted. A heavy chain and padlock hung on the gate of the deserted boat ramp with a sign 'closed for the season.' He lost the strength to keep his foot on the brake and his car inched forward. He'd been so sure he'd find her here.

He pulled his hand back up to the steering wheel and left the boat ramp. He remembered a spot a little further down the gravel road that should be wide enough for him to turn his car around. He wheeled the BMW in a wide circle, then threw it into reverse. As he looked over his shoulder, he caught a glimpse of a color that didn't belong among the sparse trees and brush. A deep metallic burgundy . . . Bobbi's Camry!

He jerked the car back on the road, throwing gravel, fighting to keep it straight as he accelerated through the bend. Bobbi stood, leaning against the front fender of her car, hands thrust deep into her coat pockets. *Oh, thank God, thank God, thank God.* He fumbled to get his phone from his pocket. Rita answered before the first ring faded. "I found her," he said, swallowing to keep Rita from hearing him cry. "She's okay."

"Where are you?"

"Never mind that. You can stop worrying, and let Donna know she can, too. I'll make sure Bobbi gets home safe." Even though he could hear Rita trying to ask him more questions, he hung up. When she called right back, he turned his phone off. He parked his car behind Bobbi's, blocking it in. Now she couldn't leave before he did.

It was hardly a picnic area, just a table and a cast-iron grill mounted on a pipe set in a slab of concrete, but Dixson Lake stretched before them. Bobbi stared off into the lake, wisps of hair blowing across her face in the gentle wind. If she heard him, she didn't turn around. Chuck got out of his car and pushed the door shut with a soft click. He scuffed his feet against the gravel so he didn't startle her.

"You're good," she said, catching him off guard.

"If I was good, you wouldn't be out here alone on Thanksgiving." He eased up as close to her as he dared. *Don't shut down now.*

"Have you ever wanted to just disappear?" Her eyes never moved from the lake.

"Right after I picked up that phone message from you." He stared out across the gray water along with her.

"Why'd you come home then?" She turned and looked at him, her eyes filled with sad confusion.

"I couldn't imagine my life without you. I had to see if you loved me enough to give me another chance."

"I want to, Chuck," she said, dropping her head. "I really do."

"But?"

"This is killing me. I can't sleep. I'm barely getting by at school—"

"What is it?"

She raised her head, but her dark eyes flitted away from his, landing on the brush behind him, the gravel at her feet, and finally back on the lake. Telling him wasn't safe. *Tell the water then, but Bobbi, say it, please.*

"I'm afraid." She blinked several times, then words tumbled out. "I'm afraid you're going to hurt me again, but I'm afraid of losing you. I'm afraid of being abandoned again . . ." Her voice trailed off and a single tear slipped down her cheek.

Chuck leaned in and slid his right arm around her, then he folded her body against his, anchoring her with his left arm. When she didn't push him away, erasing the months he ached to hold her, he cried with her.

All this time, he thought the turmoil came from resisting reconciliation while claiming forgiveness. She was struggling with much more than his infidelity. Deeper than anger, hurt, or even betrayal, he had shaken her to the very core of her soul, touching off her deepest, most primal fears.

As she cried, Chuck kissed her lightly. "I love you," he whispered. "It'll be all right, I promise."

After several minutes of sobbing, she raised her head, and wiped her eyes. "I'm sorry I ruined your Thanksgiving."

"Are you kidding? I've never been so thankful in my entire life." She trusted him again, trusted him enough to show him her heart. Chuck kissed her once more and wiped a tear from her cheek. "You're freezing. Let me take you home." Chuck felt her body tense. "Please, Bobbi."

"But my car—"

"I'll get Gavin or somebody to come back with me tomorrow to get it." She relaxed against him and he walked her back to his car. He opened the passenger door for her, then reached across and started the engine. "I'm going to set the brake on your car and lock it up."

As he walked around to Bobbi's car, he turned his phone back on. It alarmed, indicating a message and several missed calls from home. He hit redial and Rita stunned him when she let it ring once before answering.

"You jerk! Why'd you hang up on me?"

"Don't you want to know how Bobbi is?"

"Of course! Where was she?"

"I'm bringing her home now, but you have to be out of the house."

"No, I want to talk to her."

"Rita, you and I can have this out later. Right now, Bobbi's very fragile, and I don't want her to know how worried we all were. I'll have her call you in the morning."

For a long moment, she didn't respond. "I'll keep the boys at my house tonight," Rita said. "You'll stay with her?"

"I won't leave her . . . ever."

CHAPTER 18
COMMUNICATION

Bobbi felt like they chased the daylight all the way back home, only to have it escape. Clouds obscured the moon and stars in the dark sky. They arrived at their dark, empty street, welcomed by their dark, empty house. But her dark emptiness had evaporated.

For Bobbi, her husband's touch ended the exile her head had imposed on her heart. In spite of the tears, maybe because of them, she began to relax. She had missed him so much. She missed the way he loved her, not just through the months of their separation. It had been years since he loved *her*. Nestled against his old leather jacket, the one she bought him, she felt comfortable, secure, safe.

He knew her well enough to find her, and loved her enough to come after her. For the first time since that wrenching morning in July, she had hope.

She let Chuck open doors for her and walk her inside.

"Are you hungry?" he asked, flipping on the entry hall light.

"No."

"Will you eat anyway? Please?"

"I haven't been to the grocery store in a while. Our only option may be peanut butter and jelly." She walked toward the kitchen, but in the time it took her to cross the room to turn on the light, Chuck swung the refrigerator door open.

"Looks like some elves have been here, then." Chuck pointed to a complete Thanksgiving dinner in labeled plastic storage containers.

"Rita. She's been here. She knows I was gone. How am I gonna explain everything to her?"

"Don't worry about it tonight." Chuck took the storage containers out of the refrigerator, inspected them, and set them on the counter. "I talked to her already, and promised you'd call her tomorrow."

Her eyes narrowed in disbelief. "Rita . . . my sister . . . talked to you?"

"Rita and I will be fine. We both want the same thing. We just have a difference of opinion on how to get there." He put a container of mashed potatoes in the microwave and punched in the cook time.

"What is it that you both want, then?" Bobbi watched Chuck get plates and silverware ready. Apparently, he did know where she kept them.

"We want to make sure no one ever hurts you again."

"A little unrealistic."

"But worth shooting for."

He continued reheating vegetables, turkey, dressing, and bread. Bobbi took a seat at the breakfast table and Chuck arranged the containers in front of her. Microwaving more than one item was slaving in a kitchen for him, and now he was serving her. Of course. She scared him so now she merited the 'complete basket case' treatment.

"Tea?" he asked.

"Just water."

Chuck filled two glasses with ice water, and sat down across from her. He held out his hand so he could ask the blessing on the meal. She hesitated, then slipped her hand into his. She felt the slightest, hopeful squeeze as he bowed his head.

"Father God, I can't thank You enough for letting me be here with Bobbi for this meal. Thank You for bringing us this far, and I ask for Your help the rest of the way. In Jesus' name, amen."

No one could compete with Rita's cooking, even reheated, and Bobbi savored every forkful, until she felt eyes on her. Chuck's silverware lay across his plate. He watched her as if he had never seen her before.

"What?"

"You asked a question out at the lake, and instead of answering it, I should have kept my mouth shut and let you talk. Can we go back to that question?"

"About disappearing?"

"Is that how you feel?"

"Felt. I couldn't see how I was going to get out of this."

"This what?"

"Life. I can't do my job. I'm not taking care of the boys. I'm just sleepwalking through my days. Something has to give." She took a long drink from her water glass. "I reconsidered divorce, but that would create more problems than it would solve. And, honestly, death . . . started to have some appeal." She glanced away from him, shamed by the admission.

"You went to the lake to commit suicide?" He shuddered.

"No. I went to the lake because I knew there had to be another alternative. God doesn't want me divorced and I don't think He wants me dead, but beyond that . . ." She twisted her fork in her mashed potatoes. "There are too many questions that I don't have answers for anymore," she said, a weary resignation in her voice.

"This is about more than just me, isn't it?"

Bobbi rolled her eyes up toward the ceiling. "It would be so easy to lay all of this at your feet, blame you for everything." She looked at him with the slightest smile. She still loved him. "I think you would take the blame even, but no, it's not just you."

She took a sip from her water. "That lake has meant a lot to both of us, our first date, our engagement . . . I wanted to go back, to start over, so I drove out there and I asked God to meet me there."

"Did He?"

"It was so real, like He was right there. I've felt like I was in prison, trapped by circumstances, and God said, 'No one ever locked the door. You can walk out any time.' I protested that God had to change things first. 'No,' He said. 'I want to change you. I want you to stop trying to go through this in your own strength. I want you to trust Me.'"

"Sounds familiar," Chuck said.

"We're quite a pair, aren't we?"

"Are we?"

"A pair? Somehow, yes, we are still a pair. I haven't figured out the details—"

Chuck held up a hand. "Don't need details. That little reassurance was enough."

"I'm making you nuts, aren't I?"

"That's beside the point. How can I help you?"

"I don't know if you can. If I can't trust God now, when things are so hard, and so painful . . . what other alternative do I have? Where else can I turn?" She took another drink from her water glass, wiping the bottom of the glass on her napkin before setting it back on the table. "I told the Lord everything I was afraid of."

Chuck reached across the table, and took Bobbi's hands in his. "I will never hurt you again. You don't have to be afraid of that."

"You sound pretty sure."

"I am. I've learned so much in the last few months, counseling with Phil and studying on my own. The Bible talks about how husbands should love their wives the way Christ loved the church, even giving Himself for it. That means more than just being willing to die for you."

He pushed back from the table. "I'll show you. Let me grab something out of the car." She watched him walk out, and wondered if she should pinch herself. In eighteen years of marriage, Chuck never treated her with such consideration. Phil Shannon must be some kind of teacher, or Chuck was an incredible actor. Either way, it unnerved her too much to enjoy the attention.

When Chuck came back in the kitchen, he carried a manila envelope under his arm. He dropped it on the table and took his seat again. "Jesus spent every moment, all His energy, equipping His disciples, making sure they could fulfill what God had given them to do. Even now, He's preparing a place for us, and interceding for us. That's the way I want to pour myself into loving you, the way you deserve, the way I should have all along."

He pushed the envelope toward her. "I will do anything it takes to prove this to you. Open it."

She slid the packet of papers out and leafed through them. The first group was from the investment firm, with the spots for her signature highlighted. Chuck had signed them back in October. The next sheets were legal documents settling the harassment lawsuit with Tracy. The last sheet was a letter of resignation.

Bobbi looked up in wide-eyed disbelief. "Chuck, you can't. Your dad started that firm. You can't—"

"My dad is dead," he said, taking her hands again. "You are my life. You are worth more to me than my job, more than everything else I have. I have to protect you first."

"I don't . . . I don't think I can deal with this right now." Bobbi pulled her hands away and pushed the envelope to the side.

"Of course. There's no rush."

"Do you have another job lined up?"

"Not yet. I figured we'd pay off the house from the extra in the withdrawal, then we could afford to live on your salary until I found something. That's assuming I can sell my car at a decent price."

"Chuck . . .?"

"God will work it out." He pulled her empty plate closer and stacked the plastic containers on it, but before he could get them to the sink, the phone rang. He snatched it off the cradle. "Hello? . . . She's fine. Hold on just a moment." Chuck held the phone against his shoulder. "It's Donna. Do you want to talk to her?"

She held out a hand for the phone. "Donna, it's Thanksgiving. You should be spending time with your grandkids."

"Oh, I am, don't worry. I'm glad Chuck is there with you. Are you okay, really?"

"I think I've turned a corner, yes. I'm sorry they dragged you into this. Which one of them called you?"

"I'll never tell." Donna's smile came through in her voice. "I won't keep you. I just wanted you to know we love you, and we pray for you, and Chuck, and the boys every day."

"That means a lot. I, uh, I think I'll take your advice about seeing a doctor. Who would you recommend?" Bobbi watched Chuck's face fall as she asked.

"My doctor, Neil Craig. He's excellent—a good, Christian man. He teaches and writes these days, so he only works off referrals. If you don't mind me telling Phil, he can give the referral, and then the doctor's office will call you to set things up."

"Thank you."

"You're welcome, Honey. You let Chuck take care of you, now."

"I will." Before Chuck could make any comments about the doctor, she explained. "Donna stopped by Monday and recommended I see a doctor. Phil is going to give me a referral."

"What kind of doctor?"

"I don't know. Neil Craig is his name."

Chuck frowned and picked up the phone book. "Oh, Bobbi." He looked up from the listing in the yellow pages. "He's a psychiatrist."

"I probably need one."

"I highly doubt that."

"Chuck, I can't think straight. I can't remember what I teach from one day to the next. I've become a liar to cover everything up, to hide it from Brad and Joel. I don't eat. I don't sleep. I'm just . . . numb."

"Let me run a hot bath for you."

"What?"

"A bath. You know, hot water?" He disappeared up the back stairs, but came back a few minutes later, carrying a towel, the cordless phone, and Bobbi's bathrobe. He handed her the phone. "I'm going to put your towel and robe in the dryer, and you just push the 'intercom' button on the phone when you're ready for them."

"All right, that does it," Bobbi said, smacking her hand on the kitchen table. "Who are you? What do you want?"

"You want me to go?"

"No, but this is very weird, Chuck. I don't understand why you're treating me this way. Am I that messed up?"

"Of course not. I didn't mean to smother you."

"It's not . . . it's just . . . it's too new. You're going to have to take things a lot slower."

"Slower?"

"You can't be this nice to me all of the sudden and not expect me to be a little freaked out."

"If I promise to tone it down, will you still take the bath?"

"Always a negotiation with you," she muttered heading up the stairs.

Friday, November 25

Chuck woke to the sound of Bobbi's even breathing and for a split second, forgot that he fell asleep in the armchair, watching her rather than beside her. He rolled his shoulders and neck to loosen the stiff muscles, then slipped into the kitchen to start the coffee.

He ran his tongue across his teeth and decided he needed something stronger than coffee to get rid of the taste of last night's dinner. He rummaged through the cabinet in the downstairs bathroom hoping to find an extra toothbrush, but settled for a bottle of mouthwash.

When he returned to the kitchen, the coffeemaker had finished, so he poured a cup, and slipped into one of the breakfast nook chairs. The last time he enjoyed a cup of coffee in his own kitchen was that Monday morning in July, the morning he left for Kansas City, the Monday before Bobbi found out the truth about his affair.

"I'm going to have a cup of coffee and enjoy the peace while the boys are still asleep," she had said. "You're welcome to join me."

He looked at her, at the door, checked his watch, then frowned and set his bags down. A cup of coffee would take less time than arguing with her.

"This is just normal coffee, right? Not that weird gourmet stuff?"

"It's grocery store coffee, out of a can and everything." She poured two cups and carried them over to sit with him in the breakfast nook. "So why are you flying to Kansas City anyway? You've driven all the other times."

"Two reasons. We want the union to think we're sparing no expenses, that we're serious about negotiations."

"That's why you're wearing the serious black suit, right?"

"No, it was just the next one in the closet."

"Of course it was."

"Second," he admitted with a smile, "we're not paying for it. The client is, so why not?"

"It just seems wasteful, almost dishonest to me."

"It's just how things are done. It's no big deal."

"So now you're okay with skirting the edge of ethics to make a buck?"

"This isn't skirting anything. Is it unethical to dress up for a job interview? No! This is no different."

"So as long as things look good, they are good?"

"What is with you?"

"With me? I'm just trying to understand how these big million-dollar deals work."

"Well, you sound sarcastic."

"That wasn't my intent." Bobbi hid behind her coffee. He didn't believe her at all. She accused him of arrogance all the time, but never saw it in herself. She had a sanctimonious moral superiority that dripped from every word. "Oh, before I forget, where should I take my car to have the brakes changed?"

"What's wrong with your brakes?"

"Chuck . . ." She used that same tone of voice with Joel when he forgot to take out the trash. "I asked you to have them looked at before I left for Detroit."

She wasn't going to hang this on him. Not this morning. "Are you sure you didn't just think about asking me? I don't remember you mentioning them."

"That doesn't surprise me," Bobbi muttered. "We talked about it on the way to dinner for our anniversary."

"Can it wait until Friday when I get back?"

"Not unless you want me to be in a horrible, fiery crash on the highway. I don't feel safe driving on them."

"Why does everything have to be a big drama with you?"

"Why does everything but ServMed irritate you?"

"I'm not gonna get into this again."

"Good, because I don't want to hear it again."

"Bobbi, you invited me to have a cup of coffee with you, and you're using it as an opportunity to attack me."

"I am not attacking you. I just don't need to hear how important ServMed is. I got it the first ninety-seven times." She walked to the sink and rinsed her cup out and set it in the dish drainer. "You know, I wish you'd put as much energy into being a husband and a father as you do into being an ego-driven workaholic."

"And I wish you'd treat me with the same consideration you show the little kids at school."

"When my kids are obnoxious and selfish, they get a timeout."

"Fine," Chuck said, not bothering to hide his aggravation. "I will take a timeout in Kansas City for the week." Chuck finished his coffee and looked at the wall clock. "We'll take my car." He saw Bobbi wince at the suggestion. "What?"

"I hate your car, Chuck. It screams, 'I'm a jerk with too much money!'"

"You just said yours was unsafe to drive." Chuck slammed the coffee cup on the counter. "It's a great car. Besides, I am a jerk and before the week's out, I'll have too much money, so it's a perfect fit."

"And that doesn't bother you?"

"What? That people think I'm a jerk?"

"That's not what you said. You said you were a jerk. That's different."

"You call me a jerk all the time. I'm used to it." Chuck stalked back to the entry hall, pausing at the hall mirror and turning his head slightly, trying to see the back of his head.

"It's not noticeable," Bobbi said.

"That's not what I was doing," he lied.

"Chuck, you check that thin spot every time you leave this house. Nobody can see it but you."

"Can we go? If I miss my plane because you had to start an argument with me—"

"I . . . started an argument with you?" She picked up her purse and shook her head. "Then don't bother to call when you get there because I surely wouldn't want to distract you from all-mighty ServMed." She slammed the door, leaving him alone in the foyer.

He picked up his bags. "Timesaver."

He'd give anything to have that morning back. He got up to pour a second cup of coffee when Bobbi came in the kitchen. "You didn't sleep in that chair, did you?" she asked. "That wasn't necessary."

"I didn't want to leave you." He set a cup of coffee on the table for her. He leaned against the sink and took a long drink from his cup. "I'm going to go get your car. Will you be okay?"

"I'll be fine." The phone rang and Bobbi's irritation with his hovering came through in her 'hello.'

Chuck sipped his coffee and waited to see who called. He realized he forfeited the courtesy of knowing who talked to his wife, but after last night, he wasn't leaving unless she made him.

"I have a four o'clock doctor's appointment," Bobbi announced, and hung up the phone.

"Can I drive you?"

"I've been driving for myself for years, now."

"Please?"

"Whatever."

"Thank you. I'll be back soon with your car." Chuck had to fight off the urge to kiss her before he walked out.

Rita rushed to answer the doorbell without checking the driveway. Who on earth? She swung the door open and her jaw dropped. "Chuck?" She recovered quickly. "Where's Bobbi?" She glanced past him toward his car.

"Bobbi's at home. She drove out to Dixson Lake yesterday, and we left her car so I could drive her home. I was hoping Gavin could go with me to pick it up. Is he here?"

"No, he's not. They all went to the mall to stand in line to buy some video game. I have no idea when they'll be back."

"Thanks anyway," Chuck said, turning to leave.

"Wait, I'll go with you," Rita said. "If you don't mind."

"Uh . . . no," Chuck said, unable to hide his surprise.

"Let me get shoes and a coat." She shut the front door, then returned a moment later, locked up and followed Chuck to his car. The tiny interior of the two-seater dictated that Rita sit with her shoulder almost touching Chuck's. No wonder Bobbi hated this car.

Rita tried to focus on the road ahead, but she couldn't help glancing over when Chuck shifted gears. This sudden concern had to be an act. Gavin claimed that it was best for Chuck to stay with Bobbi last night. She shot back that if Bobbi was that vulnerable, Chuck was the last person she needed. Through the night and into this morning Rita beat back every protective instinct in her, and she'd stood it as long as she could.

"Why did Bobbi drive out to the lake?" she asked.

"She just wanted to get away and think about things."

"What kind of things?"

"What do you think, Rita?" Chuck said, irritation in his voice. "Our marriage, her life . . . lots of things."

Rita couldn't hold back any more. The sentence she said to herself so many times in the past few months came out with all the accusation and venom she felt. "You don't have any idea how much you hurt her, do you?"

She stiffened, ready for him to lash back and defend himself. Instead, he began outlining his case, his voice rising as he ticked off his points.

"Let's see, I stripped away the sense of security she so desperately needed since losing her mom and dad. Two, I have instilled a paralyzing fear of hurt and rejection in her that has prevented us from accomplishing anything in counseling. Three, I've made her question her judgment and her intuition, because I blindsided her with my affair."

"Chuck—"

He held his hand up. "I'm nowhere near finished. Four, I stole the joy that should have come from having her own class. Five, I've driven her to withdraw from everyone and everything she loves, including you. Six, I have forever tainted the memory of our anniversary. Seven, I've created a burden of guilt in her because she feels like Brad and Joel have been shortchanged as we have tried to work through my infidelity."

He paused just a moment as he watched his rearview mirror. "Let's see. Where was I? Oh, yeah. Eight, I shook her faith in God. Nine, she hasn't had a decent night's sleep since July, and she's lost weight from not eating right. Now, to top it all off, she has an appointment with a psychiatrist this afternoon that is one hundred percent my fault. Did I leave anything out? You want to add anything?"

Rita sat in silence with no rebuttal.

"You can say a lot of things about me and I deserve all of them I'm sure, but I live every minute of every day with the full knowledge of how deeply I hurt Bobbi, and for the most selfish and disgusting reason."

He didn't bother to hide his tears. "But you know what?" He whispered. "She still loves me."

"Chuck, I owe you an apology. Gavin told me you had changed, but I didn't believe him."

"You don't owe me anything. I don't blame you for wanting to protect Bobbi. She needs you right now. She needs your support and your presence. There's still a hard road ahead."

"You mean with the psychiatrist?"

"Donna recommended she see one."

"For what?"

"Any number of things, depression, anxiety, sleeping on the sofa—"

"She's still doing that?" Rita asked.

"Still?"

"I don't think she's slept in her bed since . . . since all this started."

"Great, that's number eleven," Chuck muttered. He found Bobbi's car just where he left it. He handed Rita his extra keys and she opened her door to get out.

"Do you think I could stop in and see Bobbi for a minute when we get back?"

"She'd like that."

"See you back at the house then," Rita said, closing the car door.

You could have gone on in," Chuck said when he met Rita in his driveway.

"Yeah, I know. Just check with Bobbi first."

Chuck knocked as he opened the front door. "Bobbi! I'm back!" Not 'I'm home.'

"I'm in the kitchen."

Chuck found her at the breakfast table with a cup of coffee. "Rita ended up going to the lake with me." Bobbi's eyebrows arched in surprise at the mention of her sister's name. "She wanted to see you, but she asked me to check with you before she came in."

"Tell her to come in. Good grief."

"I'm going to go get a shower and change clothes, but I'll be back by three," Chuck said, before heading back out.

"See you then," Bobbi said as he left.

Rita paced the front sidewalk, but snapped around when she heard the front door open. "Bobbi's in the kitchen," Chuck said, motioning toward the house.

"Listen, Chuck, why don't you and Bobbi come for cake tomorrow evening about seven? That is, if she's up to it, and you can stand to be around me."

"Are you inviting me to your home, for your birthday? Are you sure?"

"I'm sure, you jerk." Rita smiled and punched him in the arm.

Chuck hugged his sister-in-law. "Now get in there. Bobbi needs you."

Rita eased the door open and walked back to the kitchen. For the first time in months, Bobbi looked rested. "How are you this morning?"

"Better, thanks," Bobbi said. "Thank you for letting my boys freeload. Again."

"Don't mention it. I don't have to entertain Danny when they're at the house."

"You want some coffee?"

"No, thanks." Rita took a deep breath. "Bobbi, I need to apologize to you. Instead of being supportive while you work through this with Chuck, I've been an additional problem for you to deal with—"

"You just want to protect me," Bobbi interrupted.

"That's no excuse. Chuck and I talked on the way out to the lake. I apologized to him, and I don't want things between Chuck and me to be another burden for you. I'm sorry I let that happen."

Bobbi reached over to hug her sister. "I've missed you."

"So, how are you, really?" Rita asked.

"Better than I've been in weeks."

"Chuck says it's depression, not food poisoning." Rita crossed her arms and raised an eyebrow.

"You caught me," Bobbi admitted. "I think things are turning around, though. Chuck and I should be able to take some real steps forward now."

"Yeah, who was that guy, anyway? I almost asked for his driver's license."

"He was so sweet to me last night and he insisted on driving me to the doctor's appointment this afternoon."

"Just guard your heart. Don't let Prince Charming cloud your judgment."

"Rita—"

"Wasn't it President Reagan who said 'trust but verify?' That's all I'm saying."

CHAPTER 19
PALLIATION

Bobbi poured herself another cup of coffee and retreated to the study to enjoy a few moments of peace before Chuck returned. She needed all the soothing she could get right now.

God, is this what trusting You means? A psychiatrist? Is this a test? Like, 'are you going to trust Me even if I ask you to do something uncomfortable?'

Then, for the third time this afternoon, she reached for the phone to call and cancel the appointment. Nobody she knew saw a psychiatrist. No one . . . except Donna Shannon.

Chuck's car pulled into the driveway and she took one long last drink from her coffee. By the time he knocked on the door, she stood at the hall closet, checking herself in the full-length mirror inside the closet door. *I hope this is how you're supposed to dress to go see a psychiatrist.* She smoothed her sweater against her slacks, grabbed her coat, and slung her purse up to her shoulder.

Chuck eased the door open. "Ready?"

"No, but we can go." She locked the door and glimpsed Chuck's car. "Do you care if we take my car?"

"Would you rather drive?"

"It's not that. It's silly, but . . . I don't know . . . I'd rather go in my car." She fished her keys from her purse and handed them to Chuck.

He unlocked the car and opened her door for her. Her eyes met his as she got in. *He thinks I'm a nut case already.* Chuck closed her door and then got in.

"Did you have a good afternoon?" he asked.

"I've had enough coffee to float a barge."

"Nerves?"

"Ya think?"

"It won't be as bad as you think," he said.

"How many psychiatrists have you seen?"

"Well, none."

"Then don't patronize me."

Dr. Neil Craig met Bobbi with a warm handshake, then he took the stack of papers his receptionist asked her to fill out. Tall and slender with salt and pepper hair and wire-rimmed glasses, the kindness in his eyes reminded her of Phil.

"Please," he said, motioning toward a brown leather armchair. He sat down in a chair across from Bobbi and glanced through her paperwork. "In the interest of full disclosure," he began, smiling slightly, still flipping pages, "Mrs. Molinsky, I have to tell you I've known Phil Shannon since college. He's an excellent counselor and had he just written a thesis, he would have a master's degree. We've consulted professionally for years, and he feels that your situation has acquired a medical dimension that requires more than just counseling." He reached back, laying the stack of papers on his desk, then looked Bobbi in the eye. "What can you tell me about what's going on in your life right now?"

"My husband had an affair this summer," Bobbi said, trying her best not to look away.

"Did you discover it, or did he confess it?"

"I discovered it." *My whole evening is free again* . . . "But he didn't deny it."

"Was he forthcoming with the details?"

"As forthcoming as I could stand." *The defendant then kissed the plaintiff's neck* . . .

"Was there any discord in your marriage leading up to the affair?"

"No." The doctor shifted in his chair. *He doesn't believe me.*

"Did he suggest, or do you believe, that you did anything to push him into an affair?"

"No."

"He came with you today?"

"He insisted." Was that a good thing or a bad thing?

"So you've reconciled?"

"We're separated."

"But you're able to talk."

"We've made progress, yes."

"How long have you been married?"

"Eighteen years."

"Do you have children?"

"Two sons, fifteen and eleven."

"How did they handle the revelation? That is, if they've been told."

"We told them from the beginning. Brad, our older son, was angry and bitter for quite a while, but he's made peace with his dad. Joel's biggest concern was whether we were divorcing or not. Once he was sure we intended to work through this, he's just waited for life to get back to normal. I think, all in all, they've handled it very well."

"Good. That's good to hear. Do you think your husband is serious about counseling?"

"Probably more than I am."

"You don't have much faith in counseling?" he asked, slowing down his rapid-fire questions.

"It's not that, and Phil's wonderful, but it's all I can do to get through a day."

"No energy, motivation, that kind of thing?"

She nodded. "Donna Shannon suggested it was depression, and recommended that I see you."

"What do you know about depression?" The gentle sympathy in his voice put Bobbi at ease.

"Not much, I guess."

"It's a multi-faceted disease, with biochemical, emotional, behavioral, and cognitive dimensions. In other words, how you feel, act, and think work in conjunction with your brain chemistry, and they are interdependent. They affect each other, and are affected by each of the other dimensions." He smiled at her. "I have to sound like a doctor every so often."

"Of course."

"Can we do a quick screen just to get an overview of how you are right now?"

"Do I have a choice?"

"You always have a choice." He looked over the rim of his glasses and smiled. "But this will save us about three weeks of therapy."

"Then by all means, do the screen." For the first time, she let her back touch the chair.

"It's a quiz." He pulled a sheet of paper from his file cabinet. "It's like one of those magazine quizzes. You choose the statement that best reflects how you've felt in, say, the last week or two. The score will give us a quick assessment, and we'll go from there." He handed Bobbi the sheet, a clipboard and a pen. "I'm going to step out for just a moment, so I don't make you uncomfortable."

Within ten minutes, Bobbi finished the assessment and the doctor returned. She handed him the clipboard and he began to scribble on her paper. Her palms dampened as he tapped the sheet with the end of his pen, scoring her answers.

"All right, this quiz is a pretty reliable indicator of depression and its relative severity. Based on a person's answers, that severity will fall into one of five categories: typical, that is, no mood disturbance, borderline, moderate, severe, or extreme," Dr. Craig said, counting off on his fingers. He laid the clipboard across his knees. "Your score falls in the severe range."

Bobbi's eyes grew wide. *I am a basket case* . . . "So what does that mean? What do I do?"

"First of all, let me put you at ease. Depression is common, treatable, and defeatable, but it's also pernicious and relentless. A diagnosis of depression doesn't mean you are a weak person, or a bad person. I assume you're from Phil's church?"

Bobbi nodded.

"It also doesn't necessarily mean that God is punishing you, or that this is a sin or faith issue. Notice, I said 'necessarily.' We'll have to get farther into therapy to determine that for sure. Generally, it comes from a cycle of warped thinking that probably began years ago, coupled with some out of balance brain chemistry."

"Warped? How warped?"

"Not 'howling at the moon' warped, just . . . normal warped." He smiled and adjusted his glasses. "For example, if you thought you deserved to have bad things happen to you, and this affair was more proof, that would be warped."

Bobbi frowned and nodded.

"You don't think that, do you?"

"No."

"Good. I get that one a lot." His eyes twinkled, and Bobbi understood why Donna liked him so much.

"I mentioned therapy," the doctor continued. "I'd like to see you next week, then biweekly, then monthly for a while so we can identify some of this warped thinking and redirect it. You don't seem to be a risk for suicide unless you lied on the assessment." He paused, looking over his glasses at Bobbi. She shook her head. "So hospitalization isn't necessary. I'm also going to give you a prescription for an anti-depressant."

Medication . . . great. Bobbi frowned and sat up straighter in her chair. "Is that necessary? I don't even like to take aspirin."

"I understand, but these aren't habit-forming, and have very few side effects. It's not going to change your personality, or make you feel or seem drugged. It will just moderate your emotions, kind of make it a fair fight."

Bobbi didn't respond.

"I've had good results with my patients using them," Dr. Craig said.

Bobbi didn't budge. "If you were diabetic, would you take insulin?"

Bobbi let out a sigh. "If you say that's what I need, then I'll do it."

"Thank you. That said, I also have found that sometimes the first choice of medication may not give us the desired results, so don't get discouraged if it takes a few weeks to get it lined out."

"I knew there was a catch," Bobbi muttered.

"Trust me, at least for a few weeks," he smiled. "Let me ask you this. Do you believe you and your husband will reconcile, genuinely, and not just out of obligation or expectation?"

"I believe Chuck is sorry, and he's doing everything Phil has advised to rebuild his relationship with Christ, with me, and our sons. He's made great strides."

"I detect a but."

"I'm still afraid and I wrestle with trying to bring my heart and head together. I had an epiphany of sorts yesterday." Bobbi described for Dr. Craig her time at the lake the day before. "I need to let go and trust God first, and I think trusting Chuck will naturally follow."

"I was optimistic about your likelihood of responding to therapy and treatment before you told me about that experience, and now I'm even more so. Based on your assessment, you don't have many of the issues I would expect with infidelity, like guilt, or feeling responsible for the affair. I think you're engaged in your own treatment and have a good, realistic understanding of the process. What about support from your family and friends?"

"I'm sure they will be there for me." Bobbi relaxed her shoulders, sensing the end of the session.

"Good. That's extremely important. Finally, do you work?"

"I teach second grade."

"Do you enjoy it?"

"I should."

"But you don't?"

"It's a job. All this with Chuck hit, and teaching has been more of a burden in some ways."

"Can you take any time off? If it's at all possible, I'd recommend you take at least a week off."

"I suppose," Bobbi said. She didn't want to draw the attention of her coworkers and students.

"Treat it like a vacation. Don't start any household projects, or try to catch up on any chores or anything like that. Get out of town for a few days, if you'd like."

"What about Chuck? Can I see him or not during this week?"

"Do you want to see him?"

If he's the Chuck who came to the lake yesterday . . . "I think so, yes."

"Do it on your terms, and don't try to fix your marriage in this week. I'd also like for you to drop everything else for the time being, clubs, committees . . . everything. And make sure Phil gives you a break on marriage counseling. You don't need anything else vying for your attention."

"Then just what am I supposed to do all day?"

"Set one goal each day, and that's all. The rest of the time, do things you enjoy, or used to enjoy." Bobbi frowned again. "You don't think this will work?"

"No, I trust you," she said. "This is all new. I just need to adjust. I'll be fine."

"Yes, you will be."

Bobbi caught Chuck glancing at her a half dozen times on the drive home, but he never asked what happened in the doctor's office. She knew it was killing him, though, so she tossed him a cookie. "The doctor wants me to take a week off to kind of regroup."

"That's a great idea. You need a break." He reached for her hand and she let him hold it.

"I'm not sure Mr. Henneke will see it that way."

"Let me talk to him."

"Chuck—"

"I know you're more than capable, but here's my concern. You are emotionally exhausted and I'm afraid that if he challenges you at all, you'll drop your request just to keep everybody happy."

"I need to explain—"

"No, you don't. Your doctor said you needed a week off. That's all Henneke needs to know." He pulled his cell phone off his belt. "What's his number?"

Bobbi could hear Donna from last night, *'let Chuck take care of you,'* and she relented. "I'll get it for you when we get home."

Chuck went straight to the phone in the study once Bobbi unlocked the door, while she headed to the kitchen for a bottled water.

"You're all set," Chuck said, catching up with her in the kitchen. "One week, almost no questions asked. He said Molly Griffin would be your sub, and he gave me her number if you want to talk to her." He handed her a slip of paper with the phone number. "I'll be by about seven forty-five to get the boys Monday morning."

"Thank you."

He glanced at his watch. "You want me to get you some dinner before I go?"

He was fishing for an invitation to stay, but things were going well, and Bobbi didn't want to blow that. If he stayed, he wouldn't resist the impulse to bring up coming home, and when she put him off again, they would end the day angry and frustrated. "I can manage, thanks."

"You sure? I could fix you something."

"Since when do you cook?"

He tugged at his waistband. "Since my pants barely fit from eating take-out all the time."

"Will wonders never cease?" Bobbi shook her head. "I think I'll pass tonight."

"But you will eat something."

"I promise." Bobbi held her left hand up, and placed her right hand on her heart. "Rita should bring the boys home soon. I'll eat with them."

"Speaking of Rita, she asked us over for cake tomorrow evening."

Bobbi snapped upright in her chair. "I completely forgot her birthday! I'll have to hit the mall in the morning . . . Wait. Did you say *us?*"

"I did." Chuck smiled.

"Wow. Life may return to normal, after all."

Bobbi heard him say under his breath on his way out, "I can't wait."

"No pressure," Bobbi muttered as she dropped the phone number slip on the stack of mail on the kitchen counter. The envelope Chuck gave her Thursday evening lay beside the stack. She waited until she heard the front door close, then she pulled the papers out and read through them line by line.

Was he bluffing, overplaying, hoping she'd back down? A month ago, two days ago even, she would have said yes without hesitation. But now . . . He wouldn't have carried the papers around for weeks if he were bluffing. No, he would have brought them in with all the drama he could muster, making sure she understood the sacrifices he was making. Instead, he trusted God, trusted her, and risked everything. How could she do anything less?

Saturday, November 26

Bobbi, Brad, and Joel arrived at Rita's house moments after Chuck. "Wait here just a minute, guys," Bobbi said. "I need to talk to your dad before we go in." She pulled the envelope from between her seat and the armrest and got out of the car.

A verse from her morning devotional from Psalm 119 ran through her mind. 'I cling to Your testimonies; O Lord, do not put me to shame!' *Your testimonies, Lord, not mine, not Chuck's, just Yours. Please . . . work this out.*

Before Chuck could close his car door, she handed him the envelope. "I want you to have these before we go inside."

"Thanks, but there was no big rush." He smiled and took the papers out for a quick glance. His smile melted into puzzlement. "You didn't sign anything."

"I know what I said, what I threatened . . ." Her eyes flitted to her own wedding band. "But trust has to start somewhere. Don't settle with her. She doesn't deserve your money, or anything else from you."

"I . . . uh . . . wow, this is a big change."

"**So what's in** the envelope?" Brad asked his brother without taking his eyes off his parents.

"No idea. Mom got up too early for me to dig through it."

"You're slipping."

"I know. It was the turkey and the pie. Looks like good stuff, though."

"What?"

"In the envelope." Joel slapped his brother's shoulder. "You'll never be a spy if you can't stay focused."

"**You're sure about** this?" Chuck asked.

Bobbi nodded. "This time, yes. I have peace about it. I actually slept last night. Do you know how long it's been?"

"About four months, I'd guess."

"Something like that."

"Thank you. Bringing the papers back, taking this step." He tapped the envelope against this car door and she thought he might cry, so she rescued him.

"So what now?" she asked. "You're still countersuing, right?"

"Yes." He tossed the envelope onto the passenger seat of his car.

"Well, this should be good," she said with a resigned sigh. "I can't wait to see how God works this one out."

"Me either," Chuck grinned, then reached in his car again and pulled out a fall flower arrangement.

"What's that?"

"Birthday present. How should I know what to get your sister?"

Bobbi shook her head.

"What?"

"You've never brought *me* flowers for my birthday."

"I took that into consideration." He twisted around and produced a second vase of Asiatic lilies from the car. "Will you accept these with my apologies?"

"Now, you're scaring me," Bobbi teased, taking the flowers and inhaling deeply. "They smell wonderful. I love lilies. You remembered that?"

His nod became an awkward shake. "Ye . . . no. Lucky guess, but your flowers are bigger, prettier, and they smell better."

"You did good. Thank you." She motioned to Brad and Joel to get out of the car. Chuck fell in step beside her, his hand in the small of her back, steadying her as they stepped up on the porch. It felt comfortable, natural, and when he kissed her cheek before ringing Rita's doorbell, she never protested.

Monday, December 5

Bobbi sat at her desk, reading Molly Griffin's notes from last week. She kept the kids on task and on schedule, accomplishing everything in the lesson plan, and even the choral reading scheduled for today. *The kids probably didn't know what to think.*

The feeling of inadequacy, the one Dr. Craig warned her to guard against, crept into her thoughts. She was embarking on a fresh start, he said. Her hands weren't this sweaty and cold in August, though.

As the morning progressed, she fell into her teaching rhythm, and all the other issues in her life dissolved away. Until Chuck slipped into her classroom. Just before lunch, he came in without a word, waved, and took a seat in the back of the room.

The children buzzed with curiosity and Bobbi knew none of them, herself included, would be able to stay on track until they knew what was going on.

"Boys and girls, this is Mr. Molinsky," she said, motioning toward him. Several students waved, while a little girl in the back covered her mouth and giggled. "Why don't you take a few minutes for silent reading while I see just what he's up to?"

She felt dozens of eyes on her as she walked to the back of the room to the door. Chuck took the cue and followed her out in to the hallway. "What's wrong?" she asked, her hand still on the door handle.

"Nothing. Tracy's dropped her lawsuit. She's gone."

CHAPTER 20
CRYSTALLIZATION

"What do you mean Tracy's gone?"

"Left town, no forwarding address or number," Chuck said. "Nobody knows where she went."

"And she dropped the suit?"

"The court called this morning." His blue eyes twinkled. "We were on the docket for next week."

"I don't understand."

"There's nothing to understand! God answered our prayers. We all prayed for God to bring this to a resolution, and now, we try to forget we ever heard of Tracy Ravenna."

It can't be that easy. It's never that easy. There's got to be a catch. Why doesn't he see that? Bobbi folded her arms across her chest. "You sure she's not gonna show up at the law firm and shoot everybody, starting with you?"

"Only men do that," he said with a dismissive wave of his hand. "Which reminds me, you have a very conscientious office staff."

"What are you talking about?"

"I had to leave my suit coat and I had to tell them exactly why I was here before they'd let me come to your room. Mr. Henneke almost frisked me."

Bobbi's eyes opened wide and she raised a hand to cover her mouth. "I'm sorry. I'll smooth it over with everybody."

"I'm glad they watch out for you like that." He pointed toward her classroom door. "I didn't mean to disrupt things. I thought you'd want to know."

"Thanks," she said, pushing the door handle down.

"I don't think I've ever seen you actually teaching before."

"There's nothing magical about it." Bobbi swung the door open and turned back to her class.

Saturday, December 10

Chuck stood in the cold wind, holding Christmas trees upright for Gavin to inspect and size up. He wanted a nine-foot tree, without a lot of branches close to the ground, full, but still with the triangular evergreen shape. Rita insisted on a strongly scented tree, but it couldn't be too sappy.

Chuck rubbed his hands together, then he grabbed the next prospect with one hand, shielding his face with the other. "You ever think about an artificial tree?"

"I'll pretend you didn't say that," Gavin stretched his tape measure out in front of the tree. "I think we have a winner!"

"Hallelujah! I don't know which one was going to kill me first—the cold or the lack of food!"

"Let me pay for this and I'll buy you lunch." It took Gavin, Chuck, and one of the farm employees to wrestle the tree up on top of the SUV and get it tied down. Gavin then drove to a diner a few miles away. "They have great chili here."

"It's inside," Chuck said, blowing into his cupped hands. "I don't care what they have to eat." The place bustled as waitresses moved between their tables and the kitchen, so lunch arrived soon after they ordered.

Gavin asked the blessing, then began mixing shredded cheese and diced onions into his chili. "How's Bobbi?"

"She went back to work this week, but there's still something hanging over her. When I went to tell her about the lawsuit, I got no reaction out of her at all. You have any ideas what the problem could be?"

"You."

"Me? But I fixed this."

"Not yet, you haven't. I made you mad that day on the golf course when I suggested there was more to your affair than just sex. Has Bobbi asked you why you cheated?"

Her agonized words echoed in his head. *Until you understand what you were looking for, what kind of connection you made with that woman, I can't trust you.* "Yeah, we've discussed it."

"I know you're frustrated and you feel like she's being difficult, but there's a method in what she's doing."

"Then enlighten me."

"Trust is the key issue here, right?" Gavin glanced at him, and waited for his nod. "Even if she forgives you and you reconcile, Bobbi will not go back to the way things were before."

"I understand that. I've changed."

"I'm not denying that. I think Bobbi wants you to spell out what you wanted from Tracy so she knows you came up with it on your own. She won't believe you if she thinks you're parroting somebody else's idea."

"But I don't have the answer."

"What's Phil doing with you?"

"Making me list everything we've ever argued about to see if there's a pattern."

"And?"

"It's mostly stupid stuff."

"What was the most recent thing? Before the affair?"

"The BMW."

"Bobbi made you buy it?" Gavin grinned at him.

"Funny. She hated everything about that car from the minute we pulled on the lot."

"That's significant. Why?"

"We were on our way to a restaurant for her birthday."

"A little inconsiderate."

"Yeah . . ." Chuck stared out the window, trying to recall where they ate dinner that night.

"Wait," Gavin interrupted. "You bought that car in March. When did Tracy start at the firm?"

"February. Why?"

"You bought that car to impress that woman, didn't you?" Gavin squinted at Chuck over the rim of his glasses, and Chuck knew he used the tone of voice reserved for the seventh graders who ended up in his office.

Chuck raised a hand to protest, but he knew better. Gavin nailed him. "Bobbi said it sent all the wrong signals. I convinced myself she meant the cost." By the time he bought the BMW, he'd decided Tracy's opinion of him mattered more than his wife's. The affair had already begun.

"So what else have you argued about?"

"The biggest one was when Bobbi decided to stay home after Brad was born. It was a long, protracted disagreement that flared through the pregnancy."

"You didn't want her to stay home?"

"She just finished her master's degree, like a week before. It seemed like a complete waste of everything she had worked for."

"So Brad wasn't worth it?"

"That's not what I meant! Bobbi is brilliant, much smarter than I am—"

"Obviously."

"Can I finish, please?" Chuck asked. Gavin motioned for him to continue. "Bobbi could do anything. It's a waste for her to use her talents to change diapers and burp babies. Even teaching school, she's not reaching her potential."

"So you want her to be the high-powered executive type?"

"She certainly could," Chuck said.

Gavin laid his spoon down and looked over the top of his glasses at Chuck. "You want Bobbi," he said, "but you want her to be Tracy."

Chuck glared at him in stunned silence, but Gavin didn't stop. "Your relationship with Tracy gave you the best of both worlds—a charming, devoted wife to take care of your family, and a successful, dynamic mistress to share your professional ambitions."

Chuck's grip on his spoon tightened until his hand shook. From the very beginning, he tried to remake Bobbi, mold her into his ideal. She fought him every step of the way, so he gave up trying to love her. Then Tracy came along, and she fit his vision, but she didn't love him. Bobbi loved him. He needed both women.

"I'll be outside," he said, dragging his coat behind him.

Chuck staggered over, sank onto the running board of the Explorer, and buried his face in his hands. His coat dropped onto the ground, forgotten. *Dear God, this is despicable. How can Bobbi forgive this? How can You?*

Hearing the crunch of gravel, Chuck raised his head to see Gavin holding the car keys. "Let me unlock the car for you." Chuck labored to put his coat on, then climbed inside, and leaned his head back against the headrest. "I didn't say that to hurt you," Gavin said before he started the car.

"I know," Chuck said. "It's true, though. I thought I understood what happened, but you just crystallized everything." He blinked back tears. "When Phil first started counseling me, he had me go through the gospels, and make a list of everybody Jesus came in contact with and how He treated them." He took a deep breath and blew it out slowly. "John the Baptist was first, and I said Jesus validated his ministry. Phil asked me what Bobbi's ministry is. I couldn't answer him."

"It's raising her sons, and teaching her kids, isn't it?"

"Yeah, she just lights up when she talks about the boys. And I saw her in her classroom Monday. That's her gift . . . and I've undermined her for years. I told her she didn't have a real job, that there was nothing magical about teaching kids—"

"Ouch."

"It's worse. Monday, she said those very words back to me, 'there's nothing magical about teaching,' and I didn't catch it. I can't imagine how deeply I wounded her." He rubbed his eyes and sighed. "How do I fix this? How do I validate her?"

"You listen to what she's not telling you."

"That makes no sense."

"She's Tony's daughter, and I never got a straight answer out of him. He'd say, 'Got big plans this weekend?' I'd answer him and he'd drop it. Years later, I realized he wanted me to ask him the same question. Then he'd tell me what job he had planned so I could ask him if he needed help. That was the whole point. He needed help with something and would not, could not, bring himself to ask."

"So Bobbi's not being straight with me?"

"Yes and no. She won't invest the effort to talk to you if you're only listening on a very superficial level, so she's gonna test you. Like, she comes home and says she's exhausted. What do you think she means?"

"She's tired?"

"Too shallow. She means, she doesn't want to have to fool with dinner, but she feels guilty about not fixing a homemade meal, so she won't ask you to go out to eat. She's hoping you'll pick up the signal and suggest a restaurant. Then she has no guilt, and you get to be the hero."

"You're serious? All that from 'exhausted?'"

"Yep."

"That's insane. You know that, don't you?"

"Maybe, but this is how Tony operated."

"Rita does this?"

He laughed. "Rita blurts things out, and then regrets them later."

Chuck couldn't wait to tell Bobbi the things he and Gavin talked about, but throughout dinner she seemed tired, not ready for a heavy discussion. *Gavin says she'll ask again when she's ready. Wait for her.*

As he began loading the dishwasher, Bobbi handed him a red envelope. "Here, this came for you."

"It's from work." He tore open the end of the envelope. "Christmas party invitation—a wasted stamp." He tossed it in the wastebasket.

"You're not going?" Bobbi asked.

"I'm not going by myself."

"Aren't you usually supposed to take your spouse to those kinds of things?"

"You *want* to go?"

"Your whole office knows what happened. I think we need to go. Together."

"But we're not—" Chuck snapped his fingers as he looked for the right words.

"Back together? I know that, but I need to face these people."

She knew what was in the envelope all along. She was setting me up to ask her to the party. Gavin was right. "I'll pick you up at seven-thirty Friday."

The timer buzzed and Bobbi pulled the pie from the oven, and set it on a hot pad on the counter. Blueberry, Chuck's favorite, made with fresh Michigan blueberries she bought at a roadside stand on the way home Thursday. Everything was ready. Potato salad, baked beans, steak fries, even homemade bread. With Chuck home on a Saturday, it was cause for celebration, and she went all out, even asking him to handle the grilling. He frowned and shook his head, but he eventually relented, and stood out there right now, flipping the T-bones. Brad held the basketball over his head playing a personal game of keep-away with Joel.

She could see Chuck look over at the boys, and then get that characteristic twitch in his neck. The boys were simply behaving like boys, like brothers, but he would lose it if she didn't intervene. She wanted Chuck to have a perfect day at home, so the two of them could enjoy an evening together. She'd bought a silk and lace gown in Detroit, and she was dying to model it for him.

Tonight she intended to command his undivided attention.

Chuck jabbed the fork into one of the steaks. She had to act fast. She grabbed a tablecloth and headed out to the deck. "Hey, guys! Things are about ready. Why don't you go wash up."

Brad dropped the basketball and jogged toward the deck.

"That's not where that goes," *Chuck snapped, pointing at the ball.*

"But we're coming right back after dinner."

"And you can get it out of the garage. Discipline, Brad."

"It's a waste of time to put it up if I'm gonna get it right back out in twenty minutes."

"I'll get it," *Joel said.* "I'm closer."

"Joel, don't touch that basketball. Brad, come back here, pick up that ball, and put it in the garage."

Bobbi nodded at Brad. He huffed and rolled his eyes, but trudged back across the yard.

"Can I open the garage door for him, Dad?" *Joel called.*

"Are you trying to be smart, Joel?" *The back of Chuck's neck reddened.*

"No, Dad, I'm trying to speed this up. I'm starving."

Chuck turned back to the steaks without answering, and Joel yanked the garage door up. Bobbi winked at the boys as they passed her to go inside, then she spread the tablecloth out on the picnic table. "The steaks smell wonderful."

"Thanks." *Chuck carefully transferred them to the platter.* "Are the boys like that when I'm gone?"

"Like what?"

"Disrespectful."

"Disrespect—?" *Bobbi stopped herself. She wasn't going to argue with him today.* "The boys are on their best behavior when you're gone."

"Good." *He set the platter on the table and stretched a leg over the seat of the picnic table.*

"I made tea and lemonade."

"I'll just have water."

Bobbi walked back into the kitchen and began pouring the drinks, muttering under her breath. "I said 'I made tea and lemonade.' I made it—"

"Mom, how soon is Dad leaving again?" Brad asked as he shuffled back in the kitchen with Joel close behind.

"Guys, be patient with him. A few more weeks and this case will be over."

"And then he'll be here all the time. Great." He slumped against the counter.

"Brad!"

"Mom, you heard him. That's psycho."

"I'll talk to him." She pointed across the counter. "Grab the potato salad and take it outside. Joel, you get the baked beans."

"I'd rather get the pie."

"Yes, I know. I'm guarding the pie myself."

"Rats."

After carrying everything outside, they sat down to eat. Chuck picked up his knife and began trimming the fat from his steak.

"Aren't you gonna pray, Dad?" Joel asked.

"Oh . . . yeah . . . sorry." Chuck laid his knife across his plate and bowed his head. "Uh . . . Lord, thank You for this food, for the hands that prepared it. Bless it in Jesus' name. Amen."

"Short and sweet. Yes." Joel reached for the basket of fries. "Make sure you eat a lot, Dad, so you're way too full for dessert."

"What's for dessert?"

"Something yucky. Mom brought it from Michigan. I'm sure it's no good anymore."

Bobbi shoved Joel's shoulder and smiled. "I made a blueberry pie."

"Wow, how did I rate that?" Chuck asked.

"I hadn't made one in a long time. You're overdue."

They ate in near silence for several minutes, with only a few comments about the food. Chuck reached for a second helping of potato salad. "Hey, how's baseball going, Brad?"

"Uh . . ." He looked at Bobbi in a panic. "Uh . . . well . . ."

"Brad's not playing baseball this summer," Bobbi said.

"He what?"

"He wanted to concentrate on football."

"So all the gear, all the camps . . . that's just thrown out the window?"

"May I be excused?" Joel said.

"Yes." Chuck never took his eyes off Brad. "What's the story, Brad?"

"I . . . Well . . . I went to . . . uh . . . spring practice, and Coach said . . ."

"Does he have a name?"

"Coach Matson said he thought I could play varsity at wide-out if I worked at it."

"Varsity, as a freshman?"

"I'll be a sophomore."

"So, nine years of baseball, all-star at second base, all down the drain for a hint of a promise from a coach who probably says the same thing to every kid?"

"Dad, I like football better, and you said to focus on one thing and go after it."

"I put you up to this?"

"No, sir, it's just . . . I thought you'd be okay with it."

"That's why you didn't tell me, right? If you thought I'd be okay with it, why didn't you tell me months ago?"

"Mom said . . ." Brad looked in her eyes, then back at his dad. "I mean—"

"No need to lie, Brad. Mom told you not to tell me. It's okay." Chuck leaned up on the table. "Why don't you finish your dinner inside."

Brad slowly gathered his silverware, apologizing to Bobbi with his eyes. He carefully balanced his plate on his glass and walked inside.

As soon as the door clicked, Chuck started. "Why did you keep that from me?"

"Because you're extremely busy right now, and don't need to worry about every little household detail. I can manage."

"But this is a major parenting decision. I think I should have a part in that."

"It's baseball, Chuck. It's not major."

"It's abandoning a commitment! I don't understand how he could walk *away from something that had been such a big part of his life . . . since he was six, for crying out loud!"*

"He's a kid! He doesn't have to be locked into this for the rest of his life." She stood and started to gather the dishes.

"What else haven't you told me about?"

"What?"

"What else are you keeping from me?"

"Chuck, make up your mind. Do you want me to call you for every little thing, or do you want me to let you focus on this case?"

"I don't want to be purposefully left out of the things going on in my own house!"

"Fine, I'll get the checkbook, my calendar, and the mail from the last month. You want to check my e-mail, too?"

"Will you stop mocking me? Why is it every time I make a legitimate request or ask a question, you come back with the sarcasm?"

"I am not getting into this right now." She carried a carefully balanced stack of dishes into the kitchen, with Chuck close behind her. "I wanted two days. Just two days where we could be like a normal family."

"And it's my fault your fairytale didn't come true again." He threw his hands up in the air. "I can't win."

"That's because you're playing a completely different game." She stormed outside and gathered the rest of the dishes. He stood and watched her fumble with the door handle. She slammed the dishes on the counter. "I have tried my best to make your home a refuge for you where you could escape the pressure that everyone else was putting on you. I wanted this to be a place where you knew you were loved and respected. But apparently, I'm doing it all wrong. I can't please you. The boys walk on eggshells when you're home—"

"See, this is where you just don't understand—"

"Then tell me! I am begging you. I want to understand."

He just shook his head.

"What? You won't open up, or you don't think I'm capable of understanding?"

"Bobbi—"

"No, you hold on just a minute. Do you love me?"

"What kind of question is that?"

"Answer me."

"Bobbi . . ." He rolled his eyes and huffed.

"Chuck." She folded her arms across her chest. She was not losing this one.

"Yes, all right? Yes. Of course I love you. Are you satisfied?"

"I'm gonna tell you something, and I want you to get it with both ears. I love you. I will be here when you get through this . . . midlife crisis or whatever it is you're going through right now. But I will not be part of some plastic picture-perfect family that you can show off without it interfering with your life in any way."

"That's not—"

"You decide whether you want to be part of my family." She pointed a finger at his chest. *"You decide. Because I am through begging, through humiliating myself."* In one quick motion, she swept the blueberry pie into the trash can. *"I'm through trying to make you happy."*

She stormed out of the kitchen, but Chuck couldn't respond. She'd never . . . Then she slammed the bedroom door, causing the dishes on the counter to rattle.

He had to act fast. *"Bobbi! Wait!"* He charged up the stairs after her and knocked on the bedroom door. She had a point. He'd beg her forgiveness and show her how much he needed her. *"Bobbi?"*

"Go away!"

"Is the door locked?" Silence. *"Is the door locked, Bobbi?"*

"No." Her soft, gentle voice invited him.

He turned the knob slowly and eased the door open. She stood in the doorway of the master bath, her arms tight across her chest. She clutched a wadded-up shirt in her hand, and she wiped her eyes with the palm of her other hand.

"I'm sorry." He crossed the room and took her in his arms. "I'm sorry. You're right. I just . . . I lost sight of everything." He kissed her, then whispered, "You are a wonderful wife. I'm sorry I take for granted everything you do for us." He kissed her cheek and then lingered over her lips.

"Listen, Mister." He kissed her in between words as she tried to speak. "I don't want you . . . to think . . . you can just . . . come in here . . . and kiss me . . . and it's all better."

"I would never think that." He raised her hand, the one with the wadded shirt in it. "What is this?"

She unfurled a silk nightgown, the color of brown sugar, trimmed in lace. "I picked this up in . . . in Windsor."

"It's beautiful."

"I . . . uh . . ."

"Would you try it on?"

"Now?" She glanced toward the door. "But . . . the boys."

"Are old enough to take care of themselves." He stepped back and locked the bedroom door.

CHAPTER 21
LOYALTY

Friday, December 16

Bobbi leaned in close to the mirror in the master bathroom and applied her lipstick with long, deliberate strokes. Her sleek, black dress flattered her. Her haircut and color banished all traces of gray for at least six weeks. She slipped her earrings in and then inspected herself in the mirror one more time.

Not bad. She smoothed her dress and pushed her hair behind her ears. *I can do this. I can be Mrs. Chuck Molinsky.* If she could survive the evening, and if Chuck behaved more like a husband and less like a law partner, she'd have him come home.

She dropped the lipstick tube into her beaded clutch purse and headed down the back stairs to the family room. A World War II video game commanded Brad's undivided attention, but Joel saw her walk in the room. "Wow, Mom! You look great!"

"Thanks, Buddy. You guys will be okay, right?"

"I'll watch out for Brad. Don't worry." Brad threw a pillow from the sofa at his brother, without missing a beat on the video game.

"You know the rules, no visitors, and if anyone calls, do not tell them you're here alone. My phone is charged and the firm's number is by the kitchen phone." She double-checked her purse for her cell phone. "Oh, Aunt Rita and Uncle Gavin had plans this evening, but the Shannons are home if you need anything."

"Crud!" Brad exclaimed as his turn ended. "So close!" He dropped his controller on the floor in front of the television. "Mom, just go. We'll be fine."

"Are you in a hurry to get rid of me? What are you going to get into?"

Bobbi asked, her eyes narrowing in mock suspicion.

"We only have three islands to go to defeat the Japanese, so we'll be right here when you get back."

"I know, I know. You'll be fine." Bobbi kissed Brad on the cheek, and turned to kiss Joel on the top of his head. "I thought I heard your dad. Is he here?"

"I am," Chuck said from the entry hall behind Bobbi. "I put the pizza in the microwave." When Bobbi turned to face him, she saw a look in his eyes that rivaled his first glimpse of her on their wedding day. "You look . . . incredible."

"Thanks." Bobbi felt her face flush. "I need to get my coat." She pointed past him to the front closet.

Chuck stepped aside and opened the closet, then took out Bobbi's coat and held it for her as she slipped it on. Two steps onto the porch, she stopped dead in her tracks and stared at the nice, new, but unpretentious, grey sedan in the driveway. "What is this?"

"It's a Chrysler," Chuck said. He took her by the arm, and walked her toward the car.

"I can see that. Where's your car?"

"That *is* my car."

"No, really. Where's your BMW?"

"I traded it." Chuck opened the sedan's door for her.

"But you loved that car," Bobbi said as she got in.

"No, I love you, and you hated that car. I bought it for all the wrong reasons." Then he smiled and patted the car's hood. "Besides, this one has a four hundred and twenty-five horsepower engine." He closed her door, walked around the car and got in. "Are you positive you want to go to this party? Because we can just go to dinner or something, if you'd rather."

"I want people to know you still have a wife."

Bows, ribbons, wreaths, and evergreen branches hung in every corner at

Benton, Davis, & Molinsky. Soft string music played in the background. The rich aromas from the buffet met Chuck and Bobbi as soon as they entered the building. Among them, Bobbi thought she recognized Dear Joe's Moroccan coffee.

"What's wrong?" Chuck asked.

"Nothing. It just . . . it smells like . . ."

"Like what?"

"Moroccan coffee."

"Not everybody drinks liquor," Chuck said, reaching for her coat.

"And nobody else drinks imported coffee."

"What's your point?" He hung her coat on the rack, then slipped his overcoat off. "You don't think we should try to accommodate our guests?"

"Guest, singular."

"I happen to love Moroccan coffee," he said.

"You threw half of the Turkish blend away."

"Fine," he pouted. "I had the caterers get it special for you. Sue me."

She smiled and arched her eyebrow. "You should know better than to say that in a building full of lawyers."

"Yes, but don't hold that against us." Walter Davis slipped up behind her and took her hand. "It's good to see you. I hope you're able to enjoy the evening." He leaned forward, kissing her cheek.

Bobbi stiffened and held her breath to keep from choking on the strong scents of cigars, Old Spice, and bourbon. "I'm sure everything will be fine," she said once he stepped away.

Walter pumped Chuck's hand. "The food's back towards the conference room like last year."

The words 'conference room' stabbed Bobbi. Could she do this? Could she push from her mind all the things she knew happened in this building, and be the wife she took a vow to be? *Dear God, stick close to me tonight.*

"Where's Helen?" Chuck asked, glancing back through the lobby.

"She's not here. Her sister broke a hip a week or so ago, and Helen is staying with her this weekend."

"I'm sorry to hear that."

"Well, Pat's healing, and it means no one is counting what I have to eat and drink this evening." He slapped Chuck on the back, then wandered off to continue his hosting duties.

"I'd say Walter's had a couple already," Bobbi said.

"You think?" He slipped his hand around hers. "Can I get you a cup of that coffee?"

"I'd like that." They walked across the lobby toward the conference room and Bobbi felt eyes on her. Before she could turn around to see who it was, Chuck began reintroducing her.

"Bobbi, you remember Eva Tamashiro, one of our paralegals."

Bobbi reached out a hand, but the other woman mumbled a hello and walked away. "Frosty."

"Eva didn't like me before and now she hates me. All the women here hate me, except Christine, our receptionist. She still speaks to me."

"What did you do to get in her good graces?"

"Nothing. She prays for us every day."

"Tell her thank you."

"You can tell her yourself. Come on." He led her across the room to a young blonde woman with sparkling blue eyes. "Christine, I'd like you to meet my wife."

"Mr. Molinsky, Merry Christmas!" She smiled and reached her hand out to Bobbi. "Mrs. Molinsky, I'm very glad to meet you." She pulled the elbow of the young man next to her. "This is my husband, Brian. He's a paramedic."

Brian shook hands. "I drive the ambulances you guys chase."

"Sorry," Chuck said. "That's not us. You're thinking of Carter Gilman. We're all business law."

"Chuck, it was a joke." Bobbi rolled her eyes at her husband. "Christine, I wanted to thank you for your prayers. We need them."

"My heart did a little flip when I saw you guys come in together," she said, raising a hand to her chest.

"We're making progress, but don't mark us off your prayer list yet."

Christine took a step toward Bobbi and lowered her voice. "Can I be really honest with you, Mrs. Molinsky?" As if on cue, Brian stepped forward and directed Chuck toward the buffet.

"I know Mr. Molinsky was wrong," Christine said, "completely, totally wrong, but he didn't stand a chance. That woman was determined to . . . take advantage . . . of somebody. Mr. Davis was probably the only one safe, and I'm not so sure about him." Christine shook her head. "She was awful. She insinuated herself into everything Mr. Molinsky tried to do—"

"And now she's gone, and we're trying to move on with our lives," Bobbi said.

"Oh, of course, I'm sorry." Christine's cheeks flushed.

Bobbi dropped her head, frustrated for shaming the one ally she had in the building. "You have a very kind heart, and I appreciate you being Chuck's friend."

"Yes, ma'am, but he spelled out the boundaries after he came back to work. He told me not to come to his office, but to call him out front, and to make sure he never has a meeting alone with a woman. Sometimes, that's a real trick to schedule."

"It means a lot that you go to that much trouble for us," Bobbi said. Chuck never mentioned any of this, even though it would have benefitted him.

"Oh, it's kind of fun sometimes. One time, he asked me to sit in on a meeting, so it wouldn't be just him and a lady client, you know. I carried in a big ole stack of folders and notebooks, and just acted like I knew what they were talking about." Christine smiled. "Thankfully, nobody asked me any questions or anything. I would've been dead."

"No, trust me, lawyers are all talk. I'm sure you could've faked it." Bobbi glanced around the room. "I don't think there are too many people standing in line to help Chuck out these days."

"No, ma'am. It's a shame, too. Mr. Molinsky is a really nice guy."

"That's one I don't hear very often. You and Brian are newlyweds, right?"

"Is it that obvious?" Christine smiled, and blushed again. "We got married in July. Brian's a goof, but I love him to death."

July . . . when my marriage was falling apart.

"I hope you and Mr. Molinsky and your boys are able to enjoy Christmas. Don't let that woman steal that from you," Christine said, as Brian and Chuck returned to rejoin the conversation. "If you would kindly excuse us, I need to introduce Brian to Mr. Weinberg. He's our newest partner."

Bobbi leaned close to Chuck. "I thought Pete was Jewish. He comes to the Christmas party?"

"This is purely a social event for him. Here, I brought your coffee."

Bobbi took the cup from him and savored the aroma before taking a long drink. "How long has he been a partner?"

"Walter moved him up in late July."

"How late?"

"The Friday after I got back from Kansas City."

Bobbi watched Chuck as he dragged his shrimp through the cocktail sauce on his plate. "Was Walter punishing you by moving Pete up?"

"Pete's earned it. He works hard."

"You didn't answer my question. What else did Walter do to you?"

He looked up from his plate. "Walter made some management decisions that he believed were in the best interest of the firm as a whole."

"You are *such* a lawyer," she said, rolling her eyes. For the first time, Bobbi considered what the affair cost Chuck professionally. Tracy Ravenna, however, walked away unscathed. What was she really after? Partnership? "Did you consider Tracy for partner?" Bobbi asked.

"What?" Chuck coughed to keep from choking.

"You heard me."

"No, I never recommended her."

"Her plan didn't work then, did it?" Bobbi said, raising her eyebrow in the slightest a hint of a smirk.

Before Chuck could answer, a balding man in his late fifties broke in between them and seized Chuck by the shoulder before he fell over. He reeked of whiskey and once he regained his balance, he slurred, "Chuck, you have great taste in women."

"Walker, this is my wife." Chuck set his plate down on a nearby table and took a step closer to her. "Bobbi, this is Walker Prescott. He's a client." She forced a smile and shook the man's hand.

"Your wife!" Walker clutched his heart and staggered backwards a step. Off to the left, a couple glanced in his direction and moved further away. "You cheated on this woman? Then you're just plain stupid."

"That's the consensus," Chuck said, his eyes darting past Walker. Bobbi knew he was looking for an escape, some way to get rid of Mr. Prescott before the conversation degenerated.

"The other one must have been a goddess. Do you still have her phone number?" he asked Chuck with a leering wink.

Chuck's eyes flashed, and he reached out in what appeared to be a handshake, but with a quick twist, he locked Walker's wrist.

"What are you . . . doing? I have . . . tendinitis . . ."

"You're drunk," Chuck hissed. "That's the only thing saving you right now—"

"Mr. Prescott, have you met Will Hines?" Chad Mitchell tugged Walker's free arm and Chuck let go. "He just joined us in April." Chad gave Chuck a quick 'got your back' nod.

Chuck returned the nod, then faced Bobbi without raising his eyes to hers. "I'm sorry. I lost it. He . . . None of that . . ."

"I should go congratulate Pete," she said, ignoring his sputtering. He was defending her, defending their marriage. How could she fault him for that?

"Walker didn't know where he was, much less what he was saying—"

"Chuck, shut up. Let it go."

"Only if you will."

"It's gone," she said, then smiled at him. "But what was that wrist thing?"

"My dad learned that in the army. I didn't want you to think that I'm like Walker at all."

"I don't."

Just before nine-thirty, Walter Davis called everybody to the lobby. He recounted the year's accomplishments, congratulated Pete, thanked the staff for their hard work, and wished everyone a Merry Christmas. The party was over and Bobbi let herself breathe again. She survived.

Before she could escape, Walter Davis motioned at her from his office. "Do you know what Walter wants?" she asked Chuck.

"No idea." He took her hand and crossed the lobby.

"I'd like to speak with you for a few moments," Walter said, leading them into his office. "Do you have time?"

"I guess," Bobbi said.

"Please, have a seat," he said as he shut the door behind them, then took his seat behind the desk. "Bobbi, the last thing I want to do is to pry into your personal life, so don't feel obligated to say anything, but I've never seen anything like this in my life."

"Like what?"

"Like Chuck. Like you. It's as if nothing happened between you, and to top it off, Chuck doesn't yell at the staff any more. He's more focused, gets more done in fewer hours, and is more helpful to the younger attorneys. It's the opposite of what I expected. Did you give him some kind of ultimatum or something?"

"I didn't do anything. It was God."

"But you seem to get along better than most married couples I know. That's what I don't understand." He scowled and stroked his chin. "I've been around church people all my life and they were no different from me. They faced the same challenges, made the same decisions—sometimes, poor ones—and had the same flaws." Walter shook his head. "But the two of you, this is either completely genuine or you're both insane."

"A few months ago, I would have picked insane," Bobbi said. "But with some struggle and lost sleep, we've made it to this point."

Walter pushed his chair back and sighed. "Helen . . . She talks about God the way you do, like He's real. I thought she was the exception."

"I promise He's real. Jesus Christ is real, and the changes are real." Bobbi felt a gentle nudge in her spirit. *God, You're not serious.* She'd explained the basics about salvation, about Jesus' death, to her Sunday school class and to her sons, but never to another adult. The nudge became stronger until she heard herself say, "Do you want to change, Walter?"

"I'm past seventy years old. I can't change."

"Jesus changes you. All you have to do is ask Him to, and believe that He will."

"Nothing is that easy, my dear." Walter held his hands up and shook his head again. "There's always a catch."

"There was a catch for Jesus. He had to die for it." She saw Chuck smile and nod. "Walter, I don't want to patronize you if Helen has explained this before."

"I've heard it, the whole spiel." Walter's sour skepticism hadn't changed.

"Then the decision rests with you," Bobbi said.

"It's like a class action lawsuit," Chuck said, leaning up to the desk. "All the negotiating has been done, the details all hammered out. The payment fund has been established for the members of the class. In order to receive the benefits of the settlement, you just have to identify yourself as part of the class. Once you're part of the class, you're entitled to the grace and forgiveness of God, which grants you life with Him once this life is over. God made all the arrangements Himself. You just have to decide to participate."

After what seemed like a very long silence, Walter relaxed, his scowl disappeared and he said, "All right."

"What?" Chuck asked, and Bobbi almost laughed. The great negotiator was stunned he'd persuaded someone.

"I want what you and Bobbi and Helen have. Tell me what to do."

"You just have to pray." Chuck looked to Bobbi. "That's it, right?" She nodded, and bowed her head. "There aren't any special words you have to say. You tell God what you know, and what you want Him to do about it."

"God, this is Walter Davis. I know that You're real because these kids couldn't go through this without You doing something. I don't understand it, but I know I don't have anything like that. Chuck says I can have it if I ask. Well, if You'll have me, I want You to change me like You changed them." He raised his head and looked at Chuck. "Did that do it?"

"Did it?" Chuck asked.

"Yes," Walter said with a grin spreading across his face. "I believe it did." He wiped a tear away and picked up his phone. "I should call Helen."

As Bobbi listened to Walter, she marveled that God could take something as ugly as adultery, use it as a means to bring a man to Himself, and allow her to be part of the process.

When Walter hung up the phone, he wiped another tear away. "Helen said to tell you this is an answer to fifty-two years' worth of prayers."

After promising to meet Walter for breakfast Monday morning, Chuck took Bobbi's hand and walked with her toward the lobby's coat rack. "You were incredible tonight. You stood by me. You were gracious and charming, and then with Walter—"

"I was a nervous wreck."

"It didn't show. You said all the right things." He pulled her coat from its hanger. "A tremendous evening, I'd say."

"There's one more thing before we go." She turned and motioned across the lobby to the conference room. "I faced everyone, but not . . ."

He dropped her coat on a chair as they walked by. "Do you want me to leave you alone?"

"I think so," she said, stepping into the conference room doorway. *God, right here . . . In this room . . . The scene of the crime against me, against my marriage.* She felt warmth in her cheeks and her pulse thundered in her ears. *'The defendant shoved the plaintiff against the table . . .' That table . . .* Her heart raced, her chest tightened, and she couldn't get enough air into her lungs.

"You okay?" Chuck asked.

Words wouldn't form into an answer and her feet refused to take her away from the conference room. She recognized that feeling in her jaws, though. "Trash can," she whispered, scanning the corners of the room. She found one behind the door, dropped to her knees, and vomited.

Chuck was there, steadying her, strings of words spilling out of his mouth. He pulled her to her feet and shielded her view of the table. The table. "Come on. I'll get you some water or something."

"I'm sorry," she whispered. "I thought I could . . ." She let him lead her to a sofa in the lobby. She pressed and rubbed her icy hands together. *No progress . . . All these months, all the counseling, and it still makes me throw up.*

Chuck knelt in front of her with a Styrofoam cup. "You're getting a little color back."

She sipped the water, then held the cup in both hands. "I'm, uh . . . I thought I was a little farther along."

"No one has you on a schedule."

"But I set a goal for myself, and failed."

"And you're going to forget every good thing that happened tonight because of that."

"Don't lecture me—"

"All I'm saying is give yourself the same grace you've given me."

"This isn't about grace. Do you have any idea what just happened? Any idea?" She slammed her cup on the glass-topped table beside the sofa, splashing water out.

"Going in the conference room upset you. I understand—"

"How dare you suggest you understand what I feel." She stood and snatched her coat off the arm of the nearby chair. "How arrogant! How presumptuous!"

"What choice do I have when you won't tell me what's going on inside you?"

"I'm the one paying for your sin, Chuck! I'm the one who doesn't sleep at night. I'm the one seeing a psychiatrist. I'm the one who vomits every time it confronts me. You aren't suffering at all!"

"That's not true!"

"All I hear is you're a great guy, working so hard, making all these changes, just the perfect husband." She jabbed her chest with her finger. "But I wasn't worth that. You had to cheat before you became the husband I should have had all along."

"You're right. I failed you for eighteen years. I admit that. I've admitted it to everybody I know. What else do you want me to do?"

"I wanted to get through this evening . . . I was going to have you come home if I could pull this off, but I'm not ready, and frankly, I wonder if I ever will be."

CHAPTER 22
SOJOURN

Chuck caught Bobbi's eye at a red light, but she turned her head toward the window. Such a fantastic evening, a taste of what life together could be like, destroyed in an instant. He turned on to Ashley Drive, dreading the next stupid thing he was bound to say. Bobbi gave him a break.

"Can we call a truce?" she asked, without looking him in the eye.

"Sure." He pulled the car in the driveway and turned the engine off, but didn't move to get out.

"We proved tonight that we can . . . handle a social situation." She fidgeted with the clasp on her purse while she spoke. "Can we put all the other stuff aside until after Christmas?"

"What stuff do you want to put aside, exactly?" He knew, but he wanted to hear her say it.

"I don't want to discuss our marriage." Now she raised her head and faced him. "I don't want to try to work anything out, or solve anything, until the holidays are over. Can we maintain the status quo until then?"

He twisted around to face her. By the porch light, he could see a tear. He'd give anything not to make her cry again. "I'd rather maintain the eight o'clock-ish status quo, before I screwed up again." She ignored the opening.

"I want the boys to have a good Christmas, and I don't want your mother to worry."

"Is she staying here?"

"She wouldn't give me an answer." Bobbi unbuckled her seat belt, then opened the car door. The dome light came on, but it seemed that she wanted that. "I mean for you to stay here, too."

"Stay here?"

"Christmas Eve. You need to be here with the boys. Spend the night Christmas Eve. Just don't . . . you know, assume that it means anything more than that."

"Of course not. Thank you for the invitation."

She eased out of the car, then leaned over for one more word. "I'll . . . uh . . . try to take your advice."

"What's that?"

"About not forgetting the good things that happened this evening. Good night, Chuck."

She shut the car door and he watched her until she disappeared into the house. "Now, that's some progress."

Friday, December 23

Chuck set his mother's suitcase down and fumbled with the key to his apartment. "It'll put you in mind of that place I had in Evanston," he said, pushing the door open.

Ann stepped through the door and surveyed the living room, then she glanced in the small kitchen and down the hallway toward the bedrooms. "This is a nice place."

"This is a rotten place." He set her suitcase against the wall and slipped his leather jacket off. "My wife and sons are somewhere else. I hate this place."

Ann motioned for him to sit with her on the sofa. "I didn't come Thanksgiving, and I almost didn't come for Christmas, because I knew if I saw you and Bobbi apart, I wouldn't be able to deny what you'd done any longer." She sighed and looked around Chuck's living room. "To walk into an apartment and not your house . . . it pained my soul in a way you'll never understand."

"I'm sorry," Chuck said, but she raised a hand and cut him off.

"You and Bobbi and the boys are all I have. I was terrified that you ripped them away from me, and I'm not sure I could live through that. For weeks, I turned over in my mind what your dad and I could've said, could've done differently . . ."

Ann took a deep breath to regain her poise. "Your dad was the most stubborn, difficult man I have ever known." Chuck had to smile. "But he had tremendous integrity and honor. Tremendous. And you were the light in his life." Chuck looked away. If she intended to guilt him, she'd found the perfect button. "I thank God he didn't have to see this. It would have destroyed him."

"Don't you think I know that?" He stood and paced toward the kitchen, then he whipped back around to face his mother. "Every day when I go into that building, his building, I know I dishonored his memory, his name, his reputation, everything he ever taught me. If I could undo it all—"

"How could you even do it in the first place?" Ann picked up a throw pillow, and slammed it against the back of the sofa. The calm poise in her voice gave way to pained anger. "I was nineteen years old before I ever heard anybody say 'sex' out loud, and an affair was sordid and shameful."

"You think I'm not ashamed?" Chuck asked, matching his mother's tone. "The closer we get to working things out, the shame gets worse." He stared at the ceiling until he had his temper under control. "Bobbi loved me more than I ever grasped before all this, and now . . ." His voice trailed off, as he searched for words. "She's risking everything to love me still."

Ann straightened the throw pillow and nodded. "She's a remarkable woman. I don't know if I could've forgiven your dad if he'd . . ." Chuck rejoined her on the sofa, and she took his hands in her own. "This is going to be a difficult Christmas for me. I came because I've never missed Christmas with my grandsons."

Chuck leaned back and rubbed his eyes. "I was so deluded. I thought I could get away with it, that I was different somehow. No one would ever find out, and no one would get hurt. I can't think of anybody I haven't hurt."

Saturday, December 24, Christmas Eve

"Mom! They're here!" Joel called. Bobbi left a sink full of dishes, tossing the towel on the counter, and made it to the entry hall as Joel swung the front door open. He threw his arms around Ann's neck, then, still beaming, he hugged his father. "What took you guys so long?"

"Grandma's slow," Chuck muttered.

"But my hearing is perfect," Ann said, frowning at Chuck, then she looked down the hallway toward the kitchen. "Where's Brad?"

"Showering," Bobbi said. "It was almost noon before he got moving this morning." She pushed the front door closed and pointed up the stairs. "Chuck, you can take your mom's things up to our bedroom."

It was such a simple phrase, "our bedroom," and it rolled off her tongue, but it sounded strange, almost foreign. She looked away and took a step backward. She hadn't meant anything by the remark at all. *Please, Chuck, just let it go.* He picked up the bags and headed upstairs without a glance in her direction.

Bobbi watched him disappear, then turned and gave Ann a long hug. "I am so glad you're here," she whispered.

"It was hard." Ann inhaled deeply. "You've been baking. Cookies."

"Chocolate chip, and oatmeal, and peanut butter," Joel said with a grin. "And Brad missed it all, the lazy bum."

Bobbi put a hand on his shoulder. "My taste tester and I got started this morning. I figure we've got two big meals in two days, and I don't want to cook all day tomorrow."

"You need help," Ann smiled. "Lead the way." The women settled in the kitchen amid bowls, cookbooks, and measuring cups. For a long time, they made small talk, then at last, Ann spoke. "Bobbi, I can't thank you enough for the grace you showed my son. I don't know many people who could have forgiven him.”

Bobbi looked up from the chopped celery and laid the paring knife down. Had she misread her mother-in-law all these months? That didn't sound like a mother siding with her son. “He hurt me so much, and hurt so many other people but . . .” She looked down and pushed the celery aside as she stalled. “I couldn't add unforgiving bitterness to the other pain. I had to forgive him, for my own sanity as much as anything.”

“Things seem to be improving.”

“They are.”

“But?”

“I don't know. He's dying to come home, and the boys want him home.”

“You're not ready.”

“It would be dishonest to let him come home as long as I'm unsure. Coming home would mean it was over, all over.”

“Honey, when you say you're unsure, are you afraid he's going to cheat again?”

“It's not that. I can't explain it.”

“Then how will you know when it's time?”

“He doesn't understand why he did it, so how can I be sure, how can *he* be sure it won't happen again? I need to know what he was thinking, what he was looking for.”

“Are you certain you want to know all that?”

“Why wouldn't I?”

“Because it will reopen the wounds you've tried so hard to heal. For Chuck to sit down and say, ‘Sweetheart, here's why I wanted this other woman and not you’ . . . no good can come of that.”

Bobbi scooped the celery bits into a nearby mixing bowl. “So stop dwelling on the sin.”

“In a way, but it's bigger than that. Listen to me very carefully, because I don't want you to misunderstand me. Chuck hurt you, he sinned against you, but he ultimately answers to God.” Ann paused and added, "And not you."

"I know that." Bobbi rinsed her paring knife and tapped it against the sink. "But I think he owes me an explanation."

"Understanding the sin is not going to prevent it from happening again. The Bible never says we need to know more about sin. If you and Chuck fixate on the steps leading to adultery, it will make you suspicious, it will beat him down, and it will tear apart this fledgling trust you're rebuilding." Ann walked to the sink to wash the dishes so they could start the next round of cooking. "I'm through meddling now."

"It's not meddling. I wish you'd been here through this whole mess. There were so many times I wanted to sit down and talk with you."

"I've thought about that myself. This really scared me, and I hated that helpless feeling." She glanced back toward the kitchen doorway. "I picked up some real estate catalogs this morning. I'm moving back."

Bobbi turned to hug her mother-in-law. "How soon?"

"As soon as I can find a place that suits me," she said, then a mischievous smile spread across her face. "I'm a little particular, you know."

The Molinskys attended the candlelight Christmas Eve worship service as a family, complete and intact. After church, the five of them drove around town looking at the Christmas lights and decorations. Rita sent over a pecan pie, a pumpkin pie, and a chocolate cake, and after a late snack, Ann and the boys said goodnight and headed upstairs to their bedrooms.

Chuck settled in the corner of the family room sofa, finishing his glass of milk.

"Do you care if I sit with you?" Bobbi asked. So far, Christmas was low key, just as she hoped. Now the test. Could Chuck maintain the truce? Could he sit here with her, and not bring up their marriage?

"I'd love it," he said, tossing a pillow to the floor. "Thank you."

"For what? Sitting with you?"

"That and for letting me be here."

"Good grief," Bobbi said, rolling her eyes.

"I'm serious. You could have divorced me, and been perfectly justified, but you didn't. I will never take that for granted."

"I couldn't divorce you." She pulled the afghan from the back of the sofa and spread it across her legs. So much for the truce. "And it's not because I'm some super-forgiving person."

"Phil says women have a much better understanding of the tender heart of God because of the things they face in life. You have been grace to me when everyone else called for justice. I can't thank you, or thank God for you, enough." Chuck shifted and fished in his pants pocket, pulling out a small, unwrapped box. "Here," he said, placing the box in Bobbi's hand.

Bobbi slid away from him on the sofa. "You promised we wouldn't get each other anything for Christmas."

"It's not what you think. Just open it."

She frowned and opened it. "It's your wedding band. I don't understand."

"Keep it for me, until you're ready for me to come home again. I don't feel right just putting it on and wearing it."

"I wear mine. You don't 'feel right' wearing a wedding band?"

"It's not that," he said. "I don't want to assume a commitment from you that you aren't ready to make."

"So I won't commit? Are you honestly suggesting that it's my fault we aren't reconciled?"

"Not at all! I'm doing this wrong." He rubbed his eyes and let a long slow breath go. "I wanted it, the ring, to symbolize when this was over. That's all. Like a new beginning."

"Does it fit?"

"Better than the day you first gave it to me."

"I don't know how much longer it'll be." She slid the lid back on the box. "There's more to coming home than just bringing your clothes back. We have a history here." She glanced around the room. "Everything is tainted now."

"Let's move then." He moved closer to her and took her hands. "Let's move, or build a place." His eyes twinkled and he nodded. He'd made his mind up already. "Get a fresh start."

"It's not the house. It's the memories."

"Then we'll make new ones. Rita can find us the perfect place!"

"What about the boys? This is the only home they've ever known."

"Honey, when they hear the reasoning behind it, they'll be all for it."

"Well . . . what about our finances?"

"You know them better than I do. This house has tripled in value since we bought it, and it's nearly paid off. With the equity built up in it, we'd come out ahead unless we bought something outrageous."

Sunday, December 25, Christmas Day

Bobbi poured a scoop of Indonesian coffee into the basket of her single cup coffeemaker, pushed the button, and waited while it brewed. Chuck and Ann had gone back to his place, and the boys disappeared upstairs. The house was quiet again at last. *Lord, we did it. We got through Christmas. Thank You.*

Before the coffeemaker kicked off, the phone rang. "Hey, Baby, how did things go?" Rita asked. "Good Christmas?"

"Yeah, just a couple of weird moments, but this morning was good. The boys were totally blown away by their laptops. How's the Heatley tribe?"

"Two of Gavin's brothers are gonna be granddads, and one of his nieces is engaged. So, what kind of weird?"

"Chuck . . . He wants me to keep his wedding ring until we reconcile. Said he didn't want to just wear it."

"You're wearing yours, aren't you?"

"That's what I told him. Not only that, he thinks we should move."

"Because?"

"Because he's tired of waiting on me, and he's pressuring me to drop my very legitimate protests, just like he's done on everything for eighteen years."

"He said that?"

"I'm inferring. I said we had a history here, and he wants to start over somewhere else."

"He may have a point."

"I'm sorry, you have a wrong number. I thought this was my sister calling."

"Baby, think about it for just a minute. You won't sleep in your bed because of what it reminds you of. You have too many triggers in that house."

"That's crazy."

"Which coffee mug were you drinking out of the morning you found Chuck's e-mail?"

"The lighthouse one."

"Have you used it since then?"

"No."

"But it's still in your cabinet, and you see it every day, and you think, 'that's the cup from the day I found out Chuck cheated,' don't you?"

"You're really obnoxious, you know that?"

"I think it would help you move on."

"I'm not sure I can handle the stress right now."

"What stress? I'll find the house, and Chuck can hire professional movers. All you'll have to do is unlock the front door on your new house."

"I don't know—"

"Let me start the process. You can shut it down at any time before the offer."

"Ask Gavin. If he thinks it's a good idea, then . . . start the ball rolling."

Thursday, January 5

After a hectic morning with her students still wound up from Christmas break, Bobbi enjoyed the peace of a working lunch in her classroom. Just a few minutes into the lunch period, though, her phone rang. "Hey, you want to sell your house this week? I have a highly motivated buyer."

"Rita, I'm at school. I can't do this now."

"It's lunch time, isn't it?"

"Well, yeah."

"Okay, then. Like I said, the buyer is highly motivated. They'll pay the asking price, no questions, no conditions, and they want it as soon as possible."

"No inspection, even?"

"Nothing."

"Who in the world is it?"

"It's a young couple. He's being transferred here, and they need a place fast, but they don't want to rent."

"This sounds vaguely familiar . . . At Thanksgiving, didn't Kara say that John was taking a new sales territory with the chemical company?"

"She did."

"You're selling my house to Kara and John?"

"Listen, they were all over it when they found out you were selling. If you still like the house on Danbury, we can close this in a couple of weeks."

"No, they don't need that kind of house payment. I couldn't do it in good conscience."

"John's going to put down sixty percent. Their payment will probably be less than yours."

"I doubt that."

"Maybe not, but he also said if you'd come down twenty-five grand, he'd pay cash."

"Where did they get that kind of money?"

"John's parents gave them a huge chunk of change when they got married, which John invested, and they've put every dime of Kara's salary in mutual funds. That boy is loaded."

"This is too fast," Bobbi sighed. "The house has only been on the market for a week."

"You're not having second thoughts, are you?"

"No. I guess I'm not mentally prepared to sell yet. I'll talk to Chuck, but I can't imagine that he would have any objections. If they're sure—"

"They're positive. Call me after you talk to Chuck, and we'll start the paperwork."

Bobbi clicked her phone off and dropped it back into her purse. Chuck expected her to have everything resolved when they moved. That was the purpose of moving, after all. With a good offer on her house, she was running out of time.

Friday, January 6

Donna set her coffee down and waved when Bobbi bustled into Dear Joe for their weekly cup.

"It's not after four, is it?" She dropped her bag on the floor under the table. "Ted called a staff meeting . . . On a Friday! Let me grab a cup, then I have some questions for you."

"Thanks for the warning." Donna watched as Bobbi stood at the counter for a few seconds, then a young man, who bore more than a passing resemblance to Chuck, pushed through the double doors from the back of the shop.

"Hey, Beautiful." He flashed a smile and leaned on the counter. "Where've you been?"

This was not typical customer-shop owner banter, and as Donna watched the conversation, she began to rack up questions of her own.

"I was here last week," Bobbi said.

He hung his head. "I was over at the Forest Park shop. Definitely my loss. You look great."

Oh, Bobbi, don't you see what's going on?

"Thanks. I feel good."

"Lemme guess, a Molly Moroccan."

"Sounds good. You have me hooked on that, you know." She pushed her hair behind her ear and smiled, then counted out the dollar bills for her coffee.

The young man set her cup on the counter and swept up the money. He punched a button on his cash register and drew out several coins from the cash drawer. He reached over, held Bobbi's hand in his right hand and dropped the coins in her palm with his left.

"Baby, your hands are freezing!" he said, dropping his left hand down to cover hers. "I need to get you a second cup just to hold." Donna cringed.

"I'll warm up. Thanks, Clay." Bobbi picked up her coffee and joined Donna at the table.

Lord, give me wisdom. "You had some questions?" Donna asked.

"Phil gave me some homework." She pulled a notebook from her bag, and laid it on the table. She sipped her coffee as she leafed through it. "Here we go. He had me read Hosea."

"Oh, that's the perfect story."

"But is it telling me I'm supposed to accept things, take Chuck back, and go on? God didn't give Hosea any options about buying his wife back from the slave market, even though she'd left him to become a prostitute. That's asking a lot."

"God asks us to love the way He does, unconditionally, with grace and forgiveness."

"I don't know if I can do that. I love Chuck. I will honor my vow to him, but is that enough? It feels like I'm acting out of obligation."

Donna took a long drink from her coffee and relaxed when the shop owner disappeared through the double doors. "First of all, this struggle is a wonderful thing. You want an authentic marriage, and God will honor that."

"So we haven't blown our opportunity?" Bobbi asked.

"Of course not." Bobbi said 'we.' She was already reconciled in her mind, yet she resisted it with everything she had. "Is that the problem?" Donna asked. "Are you afraid God won't bless your marriage now?"

Bobbi shook her head. "It's more than that. This is such foreign territory for me, I don't know how to . . ." She dropped her eyes. "I can't trust God that Chuck won't do . . . something like this again. He's challenging me to, I know He is, but—"

"What do you want from Him?"

"I want proof Chuck understands what he did, and he won't do it again."

"Bobbi, can I share some observations that might be difficult to hear?" Donna pushed her coffee cup aside and leaned up to the table. Bobbi nodded. "Chuck has a weakness. I don't think there's any question about that. What I hear, though, is there is no grace for Chuck, but you want every accommodation for your insecurities and weaknesses."

Bobbi snapped back in her chair as if Donna had slapped her. "That's not true at all."

"Let me explain. That man at the counter was flirting with you. Relentlessly. He was out of line."

She rolled her eyes. "You sound like Chuck."

"Chuck has seen him?"

"Yes, and he was defensive and jealous."

Donna smiled. "Chuck reacted that way because he could see what was happening . . . because it happened to him."

"Chuck committed adultery because a woman flirted with him? That's ludicrous."

"Lust is not your weakness, Bobbi. You don't see how enticing it is.

You didn't even recognize what was going on."

"Because nothing was. You're both overreacting."

Donna raised a finger and smiled. "However, your weakness is doing everything yourself because you don't trust another soul."

"I trust you . . . and Phil . . . and Rita and Gavin—"

"And there are two glaring omissions from that list."

"Chuck and God." Bobbi frowned and gulped her coffee.

"Honey, you're demanding a guarantee that Chuck cannot give you, and that God will not give you."

"After all this, he can't promise he'll be faithful? What have we been doing for six months, then?"

"Hey, Hotshot. Gonna grace us with your presence for a day or two?"

Chuck swiveled his office chair around and smiled at Tracy. "This afternoon and all day tomorrow."

"Gone next week?"

"Flying out Monday, and staying til it's finished. Round the clock if we have to."

"Flying? You are the man, now."

"It's a commuter hop. Hardly big time."

"Even so, Gina's not flying over there." She walked over and dropped a folder on his desk. "I got the background on Burke County. If you're good with the angle, I can take care of the details."

"I'll take a look at it." He pulled the folder onto his stack. He could smell her perfume. She'd gotten her hair trimmed, maybe. No suit jacket today, just a sleeveless cotton sweater that accented her tan and her well-defined upper arms. She must go to the gym every day. She had plenty of stamina, that was for sure.

"Hey, are you with me?" she said, waving a hand. "I bet you're having trouble remembering where you slept last."

No, he remembered that perfectly. An empty hotel room with just a television for company, and every woman on every show reminded him of her.

He thought being with Bobbi this weekend would rid his mind of Tracy, and everything about her. Far from it. Bobbi loved him, but Tracy wanted him, and he . . . wanted her.

He tapped the folder on his desk. "I'll get back with you before the day's out on this."

"I'll look forward to it."

His eyes followed her out of his office and back down the hall. She had great legs. So did Bobbi. Bobbi. He never called her when he got into the office. He snatched the phone up and dialed his home number.

He had tried his best during the past week to stay on Bobbi's good side. He called her every night from Kansas City. He made sure he asked about the boys, about school, even about Rita. He wanted to give her every reassurance. On the fourth ring, she picked up.

"You're back in town?"

"Yeah, if you don't care, I'm gonna go ahead and stay late tonight to get everything caught up. That way I'll get home on time tomorrow night."

"Caught up? What else is there? I thought ServMed was all you had right now."

"Well, I had a couple of things come up with my regular clients, and Walter's got me on a new case with one of our young attorneys."

"Can't anybody else do that? You're too busy as it is."

"Yeah, but I don't have to do much on this one, just offer some guidance."

She sighed. "You want me to save you some dinner?"

"No, I have no idea what time I'll get home."

"I'll see you later, then."

He held the receiver, ready to dial again, when his eyes fell on the framed picture sitting to the left of his computer. His family. Beautiful, devoted wife. Handsome sons. He reached up and lay the picture face down. As long as he didn't get greedy, they'd never know, they'd never get hurt.

He dialed Tracy's extension. "Is there any way I can convince you to stay late this evening?"

"Well, I had plans, Chuck."

"Sure. This is short notice. I understand." He leaned over his desk, ready to hang up.

"Is there something in particular that you need? Maybe I can take care of it right now."

"Uh . . . no."

He reached over, ready to hang his phone up once again when she spoke. "Your office?"

"Conference room."

"I have an appointment, but I'll be back by six-thirty."

"I'll make sure the door's not locked."

CHAPTER 23
DISCLOSURE

Monday, January 16

Bobbi followed Dr. Craig into his office and settled into the now familiar chair across from him.

"Let's get right into this session," he said. "We left off talking about your dad, and those years between your mom's death and his death. How do you feel about your dad?"

Bobbi uncrossed her legs and sat up a little straighter in her chair. So many complex emotions, too much to deal with today. "Disappointed."

"You love him?"

"Of course."

"But he let you down."

Bobbi nodded.

"How? I could guess, or I could tell you, but I want you to answer it."

"I needed him, and he didn't even try."

"What did that do to you?"

She swallowed hard and waited a long moment before responding. He was asking for words she'd never told another person, never spoken aloud. "I felt like I wasn't worth the effort."

"That's not true," Dr. Craig said, a gentle quietness in his voice.

"What my head knows and what my heart believes are not always in agreement."

"And you are not alone in that. With young women, especially, so much of their self-image depends on their father, and in your case, your coping skills have all come from him."

"Or lack of them."

"I was getting to that," the doctor said with a slight smile. "He passed on several things that you need to un-learn, the sooner the better."

"Such as?"

"He taught you that everyone, God included, will leave you to fend for yourself. He taught you to guard yourself, to accept injustice without fighting back, without standing up for yourself."

"Wait a minute, I don't think I'm a doormat."

"No, but you would rather absorb a wrong than redress it."

"I don't think so."

"Bobbi, have you ever argued with your husband? Before the affair."

"Nobody agrees on everything all the time."

"Do you ever challenge him?" He leaned forward and looked over the top of his glasses at Bobbi.

"I don't know what you're getting at."

"Give me a minute." He adjusted his glasses and shifted in his chair. "When you found out he had been unfaithful, and confronted him, did you yell at him?"

"We both raised our voices."

"Are you afraid to be angry?"

Bobbi flinched at the question. "No." She leaned back, crossing her legs, doing her best to distance herself.

"I think you are. I think you're afraid of that 'out of control' feeling that comes with anger, and I believe you're afraid of what your husband will think of you if you get angry."

Bobbi couldn't argue with him. She hated when he did that.

"Anger is not a sin, Bobbi. It's easy to sin when you're angry, but the anger itself is not a sin. Unresolved anger becomes bitterness, and it will eat away at you, your sanity, and your health until it destroys you."

Bobbi fixed her eyes on a spot on the wall behind Dr. Craig. She sat motionless, debating, could she trust him? Could she admit to him . . .? At last, she murmured, "What if he leaves me?"

"Your husband?"

Bobbi looked Dr. Craig in the eyes. "What if I vent all this anger, and he leaves me?"

"What makes you think he would?"

"He cheated on me. That's the first step to leaving, isn't it?"

"Not necessarily, but I can't speak for your husband. I don't know what pushed him to infidelity."

"Neither do I. He's never been able to explain it." She stared past the doctor again, returning in her mind to that first confrontation. "That first night, I told him I hated him. He said it was a mistake to have come home, and he walked out. I was panic-stricken."

"So you pushed all that anger down, and you forgave him." He paused, then spoke with a sympathetic gentleness she hadn't heard in her adult life. "Bobbi, that's not forgiveness. That's denial. Forgiveness is letting it go—completely. You have to be able to look at your husband as if the affair never happened, and you can't forgive him until you deal with this anger." For a long, uncomfortable moment, he left her hanging, then leaned forward in his chair. "Let me make a few summary statements, and you tell me if they are accurate or not. First, your husband sinned against you by committing adultery. Accurate?"

"Yes."

"If he willfully abandoned you, that would also be a sin against you. Correct?"

"Yes." Where was he going with this?

"You have a right to be angry when you have been wronged unjustly."

"Okay." She crossed her arms and mumbled, "I hate this game."

"But you play it so well," he said with a smile. "I know expressing anger is confrontational, and that's scary to all of us. I also know that being alone is one of the most basic fears humans have."

"So I'm stuck."

"How so?"

"Face my fear. Express my anger or live in marital limbo forever."

Dr. Craig nodded. "Simply put, yes. I don't think you can move forward until this is taken care of. This is the key."

"What did you say?"

"I said, this is the key."

The words of Psalm 142 ran through Bobbi's mind. 'Bring my soul out of prison, that I may praise Your name.' The key.

Wednesday, January 25

Chuck sat in one of Phil's office chairs, watching the door, waiting for Bobbi. "She'll be here," he said. "I've never known her to miss an appointment with anybody."

"I'm not worried," Phil said.

"I'm afraid selling the house is putting extra pressure on her."

"We can discuss that." He made a note, then looked up and smiled. "Good to see you, Bobbi."

"I'm sorry I'm late. Ted called one of his notorious last minute meetings." She dropped her bag in the floor behind her chair, and slipped her coat off.

"Here, let me get that," Chuck said, reaching for her coat. She let him take it, and almost smiled at him. He hung it on the coat rack behind Phil's door, and the uneasy feeling about today's session intensified, squeezing his chest.

After an opening prayer, Phil pushed back from his desk. "Don't hesitate to correct me, but I feel like we're at an impasse. I've been reviewing my notes, and we've covered everything more than once." He shifted in his chair and looked at each of them. "Well, everything except one issue." Phil dropped his eyes down to his notebook.

"The why," Bobbi said.

"I think it's time," Phil said. "Bobbi, you've said from the very beginning that you needed an explanation. Is this still the case?"

"I'd like to hear it from you, Chuck," she said, turning toward him, "rather than relying on my imagination and the speculations of others.

I'm sure you didn't wake up that morning and decide to commit adultery. I want to hear the process."

Chuck swallowed hard and nodded. She wasn't ready, despite what she said, or what Phil believed, but he didn't know how to postpone it without looking like a weasel. *God help me.* He dragged his chair around so he could face her.

"Let me say first, that things have changed. I love you in a way I didn't comprehend before, let alone practice. My feelings have changed. My priorities have changed . . . Just don't use the past to project the future, please."

He took a deep breath, and glanced at Phil. His pastor's nod did nothing to calm him. "It started because I was in a stagnated routine." Bobbi squeezed the arm of her chair, so he tried to explain, to soften the blow.

"That was my fault, I know. I understand now that if I love you the way I should, that can't happen, but I didn't. I thought that was what marriage was like after that many years."

Bobbi's eyes bored into him and he felt sweat beading across his back and chest. "When Tracy began working at the firm . . ." Bobbi flinched when he said Tracy's name. "I was immediately attracted to her, and because I was emotionally compromised, I didn't recognize the danger in that. I watched her walk. I noticed what she wore every day. I looked forward to being in meetings with her." He took another deep breath and dropped his eyes. *Please, Bobbi, don't explode.* "And I began to imagine what it would be like to be with her."

"You mean you began to fantasize about having sex with her," Bobbi said with sharp disgust.

"Yes," Chuck whispered. Her eyes narrowed and her grip on the arm of the chair tightened. "This is hard enough. Please, let me get through it."

"No, I *asked* to hear this." She waved her hand for him to keep going.

"The . . . lust . . . was a mental compromise. Added to the emotional compromise I'd already made, it was just a matter of time before I made a physical compromise, too. Tracy flirted with me, fed my ego."

Bobbi's jaw flexed and her eyes locked on his with an unblinking glare.

"I thought things like, 'Bobbi doesn't listen to me like this.' I looked for any excuse I could find to justify my thoughts. 'She's all wrapped up in her career now. She doesn't even need me.'"

"I cannot believe you!" Bobbi slammed her hands against the arms of the chair. "This is the best you come up with? All this counseling, and it comes down to I didn't make you feel needed, so you slept with the first girl that flirted with you!"

"That's not what I said! You've got to hear me out. You owe me that much."

"I don't owe you anything," Bobbi spit at him, jabbing a finger toward his chest. She grabbed her bag and stood up to leave.

"Bobbi, sit down!" Phil spoke with a force Chuck had never heard, even in the fieriest sermons. The tone in his voice stunned Bobbi and she did sit back down, her face flushed. Phil let out a sigh of frustration. "I'm sorry. I shouldn't have . . . I'll leave if you'd rather talk to Chuck alone, but I'm not letting you walk out of here. This can't go on."

Bobbi didn't say anything and she didn't move her eyes from Phil's as he spoke. "I warned you both from the beginning that this would be hard, that it would hurt, but you have to deal with all of it." When Bobbi dropped her eyes, Phil turned to Chuck. "All right, go on."

Chuck's pulse pounded. It would get much worse before he finished. He took another deep breath and wiped his palms on his pants. "It wasn't much of a stretch to go to a physical compromise next. I took a lot of stupid chances, working late with Tracy in the building, calling her at home to ask her questions. I sent all the wrong signals."

Bobbi shook her head, but didn't say a word.

Chuck glanced at Phil, but found no subtle encouragement in his pastor's eyes today. He cleared his throat and continued. "She gave me a set-up. She told me about this ceiling fan in her living room. She wanted to add a light fixture to it. She asked me for the name of an electrician, knowing I'd volunteer to do it. You were out of town, so I had the perfect opportunity. I thought I could get it out of my system."

"You mean the lust," Bobbi said. "You were going to get the lust out of your system."

A single bead of sweat trickled down between Chuck's shoulder blades to the small of his back.

Bobbi crossed her arms and tilted her head. "So, did you at least get the light fixed?"

"Yes."

"Now I get it," she said, raising a hand. "You so thoroughly impressed her with your abilities, she just had to show her appreciation the only way she knew how—"

"It wasn't like that!"

"Then what was it like? Eighteen years, Chuck! Didn't our life together mean anything to you? How you could jeopardize it for something so cheap? How could you think you could be with her, and go on like nothing happened?"

"I've tried to explain how things slid—"

"Is this the first time you've been unfaithful or just the latest?"

"This is the only time I have been with someone else."

"But it's not the first time you've thought about it, is it?" The question hung for several uneasy moments. "Answer me."

He had to tell her the truth. "No."

"I can't believe this! I was so afraid you would leave me. You left me some time ago."

"What? Afraid I would leave you?"

"I loved my mama and she left me. I loved Daddy and he left me, but he abandoned me emotionally before that. I thought when I met and married you that *finally* I could be safe and secure, that *you* would always love me and be there with me."

Chuck closed his eyes and raised the side of his fist to his mouth, trying to push the guilt out his mind so he could listen to his wife. She didn't speak until he looked at her again.

She spoke quietly, but with an unwavering firmness. "The fear never went away, though. It lurked in the back of my mind. Now I find out that the one thing I feared most has happened." The firmness gave way to sad gentleness as she closed her eyes. "You *have* left me. We just haven't filed the paperwork yet."

"Bobbi, if you would just listen to me for a minute—"

"Just . . . stop. Everything I believed about you, about us, has been destroyed. You say things have changed, so I should ignore your little indiscretion, is that it?"

"No, I just wanted a second chance."

Bobbi didn't respond, but stood up and walked across the room, and stared out Phil's office window. "And what was it? Two days before you were with her again?" She turned to face him again. "Didn't you feel the least bit guilty?"

"Yes, I was disgusted with myself."

"Not disgusted enough to stay away from her."

"Bobbi . . ." He knew she wouldn't believe him. "This . . . It's like an addiction."

"That's pathetic."

"When I was in college, before I became a believer, I was with a lot of girls, and I never forgot that rush. I figured faith and being married would be enough to control those impulses. I depended too much on my own strength and resolve."

"We see how much of that you had." Contempt. That's what clung to her words. Just like that first night. "But now you're fixed. Everything is fine and we'll live happily ever after, right?"

"I can't imagine how much this hurts."

"That's the most believable thing you've said this afternoon!"

"You know how things have changed between us in the last few weeks. We're almost there."

"Phil," Bobbi said, ignoring him. "I think I've had enough for today. Can we just wrap it up here?"

"Yeah," Phil said. "Chuck, you go ahead. I want to speak with Bobbi. And don't follow her, trying to explain things. Let her sort this out on her own."

Chuck grabbed his leather jacket from the back of his chair. "I told you the truth this afternoon. The truth about what happened in the past. That's not true for the present, and it's not going to be for the future, either." She didn't answer him, didn't even to look at him.

"I said that's enough for today." Chuck had heard that tone from his dad plenty of times, but never from his pastor. He gave Phil a half nod and walked out without taking his eyes off Bobbi.

Phil watched Bobbi, waiting several long moments for her shoulders to relax and her jaw to unclench. "Can I make you some coffee?"

"It's gonna take more than a cup of coffee."

"You did well."

If she heard him, it never registered. "I'm sorry, Phil, I need to get out of here." Her hands shook when she let go of the chair.

"Of course, let me walk you to your car," he said. He grasped the corner of his desk and pulled himself up.

"You look like you're in pain."

"Old age. I'll be all right once I get going." Bobbi slipped her coat on, picked up her bag, and followed him outside. "Now you know why he did it. How does that change things?"

"It's worse than I imagined. I hoped maybe he would tell me it was all her fault, that she led him astray."

"That would be easier to believe?"

"No, easier to accept. I can't love him any more than I have. If I couldn't keep him before, how can I now when he's seen how easy it is to find someone else?"

"Nobody said you had to do the keeping."

Bobbi picked her keys out of her purse and unlocked and opened her driver's side door. She threw her purse across to the passenger seat and got in. "What is there to stop him now that he didn't have before?"

"You should ask him," Phil said. "The thing is, Chuck has done everything you've asked him to. He's answered every question, taken time off from work, counseled, studied, even seen a doctor. If he hasn't satisfied your requirements now, he never will." He paused and rested his hand on her car door. "If you don't trust the evidence you've seen yourself that Chuck has genuinely repented of this, then I don't know what else we can do."

"So I either take him back or divorce him?"

"It may be that black and white, I don't know," Phil sighed. "Just don't make a decision based on the emotion of this afternoon." He reached in his back pocket and pulled out a small envelope and handed it to her. "Give yourself a few days before you read this. We'll talk about it next time." Bobbi put the envelope in her purse, with a scowl. "Trust me," Phil said, closing her car door.

The bags on the passenger seat and the smell of French fries proved that Bobbi had been through the drive-thru at Wendy's, although she didn't remember it. Her memory was locked on a loop of Chuck's sorry explanations. If he wasn't any better at making a case than that, it was a wonder the family hadn't starved. Did he think she was stupid enough to buy the 'I couldn't help myself' defense? Outrageous.

As she turned the corner onto her street, she saw a car in the driveway, and Chuck standing beside it, waiting for her. "Great," she muttered as she pulled in. She grabbed the food sacks and her bag, then got out, slamming her door. "What are you doing here?"

"I want to talk to you."

"I don't want to talk to you."

"That's fine. Just listen to me for five minutes."

"I've heard enough from you today, Chuck. Go away!" Bobbi tried to brush past him, but he took hold of her upper arm. She growled at him,

"Take your hand off me." He jerked his hand back. "You have five minutes," she seethed and stormed into the house.

She stayed two steps ahead of him until he cornered her in the kitchen. "Bobbi, you've got to understand that all those things I said were in the past. That's not how I feel now."

"I heard that! I get it!" She slammed her purse on the kitchen table. "You said you loved me, but that didn't stop you from cheating on me!" She didn't care that Brad and Joel would hear the blowup. "You said you loved the boys, but that didn't stop you!" She counted off on her fingers emphasizing each point. "You said you loved God, but that didn't stop you! Not even your fixation with your image stopped you! Nothing that you ever claimed to mean anything to you made you think twice about committing adultery, Chuck! Nothing!"

"Things are different now."

She pushed past Chuck to the stairs. "Brad! Joel! I brought dinner!"

"What about all those things you said about not fighting and trusting God?"

"What about Phil saying to leave me alone? Your five minutes is up."

"This is not over," Chuck said, as he turned to leave.

"Yes, it is."

CHAPTER 24
RESTORATION

Bobbi left the boys eating in the kitchen and thanked God they didn't mention the argument. They pretended to believe her story about having a lot of paperwork to catch up on for school, leaving her alone in the study. She slumped into the desk chair, leaned her head back, and closed her eyes.

Phil said they'd been through everything. He couldn't add anything else, so it rested with her. She had to decide. Forget the affair, or divorce him. Some choice.

She reached for her Bible and notebook, and flipped open to the notes she made on Hosea. God did everything for Israel, and still they rejected Him. Even worse, Israel chose false gods, incapable of loving in return. Didn't Chuck choose a false wife who would never love him?

In chapter three, God said for Hosea to 'go again and love,' just like He did with Israel. That's what He expected her to do. *I can't do it, God. I can't love the way You do. He hurt me too much, and I'm too afraid to trust him again.*

Dr. Craig said she had a pattern of absorbing hurts, but she told herself months ago only a fool would absorb this. Chuck Molinsky would not make a fool out of her again.

With tears dropping on the pages of her notebook, she chose a third option. She'd have Chuck draw up formal separation papers. She couldn't divorce him, but she couldn't live with him as his wife, either. At least with a separation, there would be some resolution. Everybody would know where they stood, and maybe sometime later, much later, they could try counseling again. Sealing the decision in her own mind, she slid her wedding band and engagement ring off, and dropped them in a side pocket of her purse.

Thankfully, they hadn't closed on the house on Danbury Court yet. Kara and John could wait a little longer before taking ownership of this house, long enough for Rita to find a place for her and the boys in her price range.

As Bobbi stuck her notebook back in her Bible, her eyes fell on some verses in chapter eleven of Hosea that she had marked years earlier.

"How can I give you up, Ephraim?
How can I hand you over, Israel?
My heart churns within Me;
My sympathy is stirred.
I will not execute the fierceness of My anger;
I will not again destroy Ephraim.
For I am God, and not man,
The Holy One in your midst;
And I will not come with terror."

Thursday, January 26

Bobbi sat at the kitchen table, sipping her second cup of coffee, pondering how she would tell Chuck her decision, when the phone rang. Startled by the early call, she answered before the second ring.

"Bobbi," Rita said, her voice weak. "Gavin just got a phone call. Phil Shannon had a massive stroke this morning. He's . . . he's dead."

"What?" Bobbi whispered. She heard the words, but they made no sense.

"Yeah, I guess a blood clot made it to his brain, and caused the stroke."

"I just, we just saw him yesterday afternoon. How . . .? I'm . . . I'm stunned." Her vision blurred as tears welled up. Phil couldn't . . . "Phil?

Phil Shannon? You're sure?"

"Are you going to be all right? I can come over if you need me to."

"What?"

"Are you going to be okay?"

"I just need a few minutes." Her knees threatened to buckle under her, so she slid into the nearest chair. "A stroke, you said?"

"Yes."

"Did he have any symptoms?"

"I don't know. David told Gavin he was gone before the paramedics got there."

"Oh, poor Donna."

"Listen, I won't keep you on the phone. Gavin has some more calls to make. My schedule is clear today if you need me."

"Thanks, thanks for calling, for letting me know." Bobbi hung up the receiver. Phil Shannon couldn't be . . . He married them. He baptized her boys. Baptized Chuck. If she and Chuck couldn't reconcile with Phil's help, what hope was there now? What was God doing?

"Mom, what's wrong? What happened?" Brad asked, and Bobbi realized she never heard him come in the room.

"Where's Joel?"

"He was right behind me." Brad walked to the back stairs and yelled, "Joel! Downstairs now!"

Joel tromped down the stairs. "Brad! You're . . . Mom, what's wrong?"

"Guys, Phil . . . Pastor Phil . . . He died this morning. He had a stroke."

"I didn't even know he'd been sick," Joel murmured.

"Honey, strokes happen all of the sudden. You don't get a lot of warning."

Brad crossed his arms and slumped against the kitchen counter. "He's . . . Pastor Phil's the only pastor we've ever had. It's gonna be weird at church without him."

"Yeah, I can't . . . I can't imagine . . ." She squeezed a sob back down her throat.

"Mom, are you and Dad going to be okay?" Joel asked. "Pastor Phil's counseling you and everything, and things didn't sound so good last night."

"I'm sorry you heard all that. We'll . . . Dad and I . . . we'll be fine. We'll work something out." Bobbi sipped from her coffee cup and glanced at the microwave clock. Twenty after seven. She had twenty-five minutes to pull herself together.

The morning drive passed in near silence. Should she call Chuck? No, he'd want to talk, and that's the last thing she wanted from him right now. At school, she shepherded her students through the morning routine. A week off playground duty meant a few precious moments of peace and quiet during morning recess. She got her cell phone and made a quick call.

"Dr. Craig's office," the receptionist said.

"This is Bobbi Molinsky. Is there any way on earth I can see Dr. Craig today?"

"He had a twelve-thirty cancellation. Would that work for you?"

"That would be perfect. Thank you." Her students went to lunch at twelve-fifteen, then straight to P.E. She'd just have to find someone to get her kids after lunch and escort them to the gym.

Chuck stared at a set of incorporation papers, resorting to following each word with his finger to try to stay focused. All night he told himself Bobbi only meant the conversation was over, the conversation, and not their marriage. He'd feel better hearing her say that, though. Four times already, he'd picked up the phone, but chickened out before he got the number dialed.

"Chuck, can I see you for a moment before you get started this morning?" Walter Davis stood in the doorway. He never came to anyone's office. This was a bad sign.

"Sure," Chuck said, and followed Walter to his office.

"Go ahead and close the door and have a seat," Walter said, glancing into the lobby. Another bad sign. "Chuck, I'm seventy-two years old, and I've worked for almost sixty of those years. I want to enjoy what time I have left in this world." He folded his hands on the desk in front of him, then looked straight at Chuck. "What I'm saying is, it's time for me to step down. I'm retiring, and I want you to take over the firm."

"This is kind of sudden," Chuck said.

"Not really. I wanted to retire last year, but I wasn't sure you had the mettle to run things here. I have no doubts now."

"I don't know."

"It's what your dad would have wanted. It's what Jim Benton would have wanted, and it's what I want. You've earned it."

"What kind of timetable are you looking at?" He couldn't deal with any of this until things were settled with Bobbi.

"Oh, let's say March first. I think that will be plenty of time to get you up to speed on the management end of things."

"How can I say no?"

"You can't," Walter said with a smile. He stood up and shook Chuck's hand across his desk.

"Thank you, Walter. I appreciate the vote of confidence. It came at a good time." Chuck nodded to Christine on his way back to his own office, but she waved him over to the desk.

"Mr. Molinsky, Mr. Gavin Heatley is on the line." She handed him the phone.

Chuck frowned and took the receiver from her. "Gavin, what's up?"

"We just got some terrible news."

Immediately, Chuck's stomach tightened. *God, please, not Bobbi.*

"Phil Shannon had a stroke this morning. He didn't. . . It . . . It was fatal."

"Oh, no." Chuck grasped the corner of the reception desk, weak in the knees. "What happened?"

"I don't have a lot of details. I didn't want to keep David on the phone. He said Phil had a blood clot that broke loose, and went to his brain. Phil probably never knew what hit him."

"Gavin, I was in his office yesterday . . . He was fine. He seemed fine." He leaned over the desk and tried to take in a long slow breath. Suddenly, his brain jumped back six years. He could hear his mother's voice, and he remembered every syllable. *Chuck . . . your dad . . . I'm . . . It was peaceful. He's not in any more pain.* But with his dad, they knew. They had time to prepare. It didn't sucker-punch him this way.

"Does Bobbi know?" He couldn't muster more than a whisper. Could Bobbi even handle the news after yesterday? Was it just yesterday?

"Rita called her."

"Was she okay?"

"I think she was still going to school."

"We had it out yesterday in Phil's office. She was so angry with me . . . I don't know how we can put this back together without Phil."

"You finally hit on why, didn't you?"

"Yeah. She hinted at divorce, said I'd already left her. Like the last six months never happened."

"Give her a few days."

"That's, uh, that's what Phil said." He pushed a hand back through his hair. "Gavin, this is like losing my dad again."

"You wanna grab a cup of coffee or something?"

"Thanks anyway. I'm gonna head back to my office. I need to sit down."

"You sure you're okay?"

"Yeah. Thanks. Thanks for calling." Chuck set the receiver back on its cradle, and blew out a deep breath.

"I'm so sorry, Mr. Molinsky," Christine said gently.

"Thank you. Would you hold the rest of my calls today? You know, unless it's family or something."

"Sure thing."

He walked slowly back to his office. *God, this doesn't make any sense. Why Phil? Why now?*

"I kind of expected to see you today, Bobbi," Dr. Craig said as he closed his office door.

"You heard, then . . . about Phil." It didn't sound any more real to her than when Rita called.

"Yes, a mutual friend called this morning right after I got in the office. It was quite a shock." He took a seat and looked Bobbi in the eyes. "So, what do you want to talk about today?"

She closed her eyes and shook her head slowly. She practiced on the drive over here, but the words refused to come unless they dragged tears with them.

"Take your time," Dr. Craig said. "I understand."

"I don't . . ." She swallowed and raised her eyes to the ceiling in a vain attempt to prevent tears from streaming down her cheeks. "I don't understand."

"I doubt anyone does. When did you see Phil last?"

"Yesterday. Yesterday afternoon. We, uh, . . . Chuck finally told me why he committed adultery. He tried to tell me."

"Did you get angry?"

"Yes, but that's beside the point."

"Did you express that anger?"

"I think Chuck is afraid I'm going to divorce him now. He got the message."

"Good." Dr. Craig nodded. "Not that your husband thinks you want a divorce, but that you weren't afraid to express a justified emotion." He blinked slowly and nodded. "But this was beside the point."

"We need Phil now more than ever. We're just beginning the hard part of reconciliation."

"So you're reconciling?"

"Maybe."

"You weren't wearing your rings. I wasn't sure."

"You noticed that?"

"It's part of my job to notice little things, little changes," he said. "So maybe you're reconciling." He waved his hand, passing the conversation back to her.

"All the ugliness has been brought to light, and now maybe we can start to put things back together. Well . . . we could have." Bobbi shook her head. "I don't understand why God would take Phil from us. And that doesn't even begin to touch on how much Donna and the rest of his family and the church still need him."

"Apparently, you don't need him," Dr. Craig said.

"Excuse me?"

"I don't want to sound cavalier about it, but if God took Phil home while he still had a lot of work to do, then God would have a big mistake to answer for, right?" Bobbi had to agree. "And we know that's not the case."

"So, what is?"

"Look at it from a different angle for just a moment. Was Phil a good and faithful servant of God?"

"Of course."

"Doesn't he deserve to hear that from God, and receive his reward?"

Bobbi nodded slowly. Phil deserved the best God had to offer him.

"It could also be that God took Phil to save him and Donna from greater suffering. What if Phil's stroke had been debilitating rather than fatal, and he lived for years, unable to speak or take care of himself? Would that really be easier on him or his loved ones?"

"That's hard to say."

"It is, but I've found in dealing with death, that simplistic explanations are useless. People's lives are too complex, too interconnected, to say with confidence why someone died when they did."

"But I trusted Phil . . ."

"And you should." Bobbi looked away, on the verge of tears. "Bobbi, what is it?"

"Did . . . Did God do this because I trusted Phil . . . more than I trusted Him?"

"God doesn't work that way." He looked away for a moment. "Phil's death will work God's purpose in the lives of the hundreds of people that knew him. I can't presume to know what all those purposes could be, but I know that ultimately God is good, His love is sure, and His timing is perfect according to *His* purposes."

"But here's the other thing," Bobbi said, wiping her eyes. "The whole time I've been dealing with these issues in my marriage, I've felt God telling me over and over to trust Him. Trust Him for what? How can I trust Him when He does something like this?"

"I don't think trust comes with limits or qualifiers."

"So I should reconcile completely, unequivocally?"

"Do you think that's what God is telling you?"

"I'm not sure."

"Tell me about your last devotional or study time, when you felt God speaking to you."

"I was going back through some notes I'd made on Hosea, but I can't love Chuck the way God loves Israel. Restoration happened because of a change of heart on Gomer's part and on Israel's. How can I be sure there has been a change of heart in Chuck?"

Dr. Craig sat for a few moments, staring across the room, then he smiled. "Who brings about a change in the heart of man?"

"God."

"Who initiated the restoration?"

"God did."

"What about with Gomer and Hosea?"

"Hosea did. I don't like where this is headed."

Dr. Craig smiled. "Could it be that God is encouraging you to trust Him to bring about the necessary changes in Chuck's heart? Or perhaps to trust that He's already done it? Or to trust Him enough to initiate reconciliation?" He leaned back and dropped his hands to the arms of the chair. "God, many times, wants us to make a move in faith, then He is right there beside us once we take that first step."

"You sound like Phil," Bobbi said.

"I take that as a high compliment."

Sitting in her car, Bobbi leaned back against the headrest. "You know what this is like, God? This is just like when we went to Florida, to Disney World when Joel was four. Chuck called out to him from the pool. 'Come on, Joel. Jump. I'll catch you.'

"He let him go under, God. Chuck caught him, but he intentionally let Joel go underwater. And he was terrified . . . If I jump, I'm afraid You're going to let me go under."

She sighed and opened her purse to find her car keys when she saw the letter Phil gave her yesterday afternoon. She opened the envelope and pulled out a sheet written in Phil's neat block printing.

WITH APOLOGIES TO THE APOSTLE PAUL AND PHILEMON–

PHIL SHANNON, PASTOR OF PRESTON ROAD COMMUNITY CHURCH AND DONNA, MY BELOVED WIFE AND PARTNER,

TO BOBBI OUR BELOVED FRIEND AND FELLOW LABORER:

GRACE TO YOU AND PEACE FROM GOD OUR FATHER AND THE LORD JESUS CHRIST. I THANK MY GOD, MAKING MENTION OF YOU ALWAYS IN MY PRAYERS, HEARING OF YOUR LOVE AND FAITH, WHICH YOU HAVE TOWARD THE LORD JESUS AND TOWARD ALL OF US. FOR WE HAVE GREAT JOY AND CONSOLATION IN YOUR LOVE, BECAUSE OUR HEARTS HAVE BEEN REFRESHED BY YOU, OUR SISTER.

THEREFORE, THOUGH I MIGHT BE VERY BOLD IN CHRIST TO COMMAND

YOU, YET FOR LOVE'S SAKE I APPEAL TO YOU FOR MY SON, CHUCK, WHOM I HAVE COUNSELED, WHO ONCE WAS HEARTRENDING TO YOU, BUT IS BELOVED TO YOU AND TO ME. I AM SENDING HIM BACK. YOU THEREFORE RECEIVE HIM, THAT IS, MY OWN HEART. BUT I DIDN'T WANT TO DO THIS WITHOUT YOUR CONSENT, THAT YOUR RECONCILIATION MIGHT NOT BE BY COMPULSION, BUT VOLUNTARY. CHUCK DEPARTED FOR A WHILE AND GOD HAS WORKED IN CHUCK'S HEART, SALVAGING GOOD FROM HIS SIN AGAINST YOU, ACCORDING TO HIS DIVINE PURPOSE, THAT YOU MIGHT BE RECONCILED TO HIM FOREVER.

IF YOU COUNT ME AS A PARTNER, RECEIVE HIM AS YOU WOULD ME. IF HE WRONGS YOU AGAIN, PUT THAT ON MY ACCOUNT, SO GREAT IS MY CONFIDENCE IN HIM. BOBBI, HAVING CONFIDENCE IN YOUR OBEDIENCE, I WRITE TO YOU, KNOWING THAT YOU WILL DO EVEN MORE THAN I SAY. THE GRACE OF OUR LORD JESUS CHRIST BE WITH YOUR SPIRIT. AMEN.

"Phil," Bobbi whispered. He took Paul's letter to Philemon and rewrote it for her, assuring her, on his own character and reputation, that it was safe to take Chuck back. Besides that, he was confident she would do it.

The words she read last night ran through her mind. 'How can I give you up, Ephraim? How can I give you up?'

Rereading the letter, the pieces began to fall into place. God met her at the level of her trust. She trusted Phil Shannon, so God promised her through Phil that the changes she saw in her husband were genuine. She didn't have to be afraid. She could take that step into her Father's arms. He wouldn't let her go under.

She searched through her purse until she found her rings and slid them on. "Phil, I'm sorry you didn't get to see this."

As soon as the bell rung that afternoon, Bobbi drove straight to Chuck's office. "Mrs. Molinsky, it's good to see you!" Christine smiled and waved when Bobbi walked into the law firm's lobby. "Do you want me to call Mr. Molinsky?"

"Yes, but tell him it's Mary Roberta Petrocelli," Bobbi answered. She imagined the puzzlement on Chuck's face as Christine relayed her maiden name.

"He'll be right out," Christine said.

Chuck strode into the lobby before she hung up the phone. "What's going on?" In spite of his quick response, Bobbi could read him. Mental and spiritual exhaustion pressed on him.

"I need to talk to you," Bobbi said.

"Of course, come on back." Chuck motioned her towards his office. He followed her and closed his office door as she took a seat. "You, uh, caught me off guard using your maiden name. Are you trying to tell me something?"

"First of all, did you hear . . . Phil . . . about Phil?"

"Yeah, Gavin called me. Are you okay? After yesterday, I was afraid the news about Phil might be a little too much."

"I can't believe that was just yesterday," she said, then looked into her husband's eyes. "It hit you hard, too, didn't it?"

He looked away for a moment. "It's like when my dad . . . Phil . . . I owe him a lot." He exhaled sharply and blinked several times before meeting her eyes again.

"Chuck, I want to apologize to you—"

"You don't need to apologize to me."

"Yes, I do. I said I forgave you, but I couldn't let go of the anger, and the hurt, and the fear that it would happen again. That wasn't forgiveness. Then I made you chase a moving target when it came to reconciliation."

She paused and glanced up at the ceiling, trying to prevent tears from spilling onto her cheeks. "Yesterday . . . it hurt like that first day, hearing you say it . . . but I also know it could've been worse. If you wanted to have an affair, it would have been much easier after I made you move out." She shifted in her chair and took a deep breath. "What I'm trying to say is, I believe you love me and you want to make our marriage work—"

"Oh, thank You, God!" Chuck knelt down in front of her, eyes brimming with tears, and took her hands. "I was so afraid after yesterday I was beyond forgiveness. I prayed God would give you whatever it took to see my heart now, not what I did to you."

"Wait, I still . . . I need to know, what's changed, what's going to be different from now on."

"Sure," Chuck said, wiping his eyes, and slipping back to his seat. "For starters, I'm making a job change."

"You can't leave this firm. We discussed that already."

"I'm not leaving it. I'm, uh, running it."

"Are you serious?"

"Walter's retiring March first. Now I won't have to travel, and I'll have control over my workload. Plus I won't have to worry about impressing my boss anymore." He smiled at her. "I'll have the freedom to devote the kind of time to you and our marriage that I should have been doing all along. I always made a point of carving out time for the boys, but never for us. That was stupid."

"I put the boys before us, too. I figured they were ours for such a short time, they had to come first."

"I also promise not to be alone with a woman again. I promise to let you know when I'm struggling with temptation instead of keeping it inside. I want to continue with some sort of counseling or mentoring or whatever, so I never drop my guard on this again, and I promise to thank God every day for giving me the grace of a second chance."

"Be patient with me. I've shut you out. I've been unreasonable . . . There are things I need to change, too, for us to have the kind of marriage God intends." She studied his face for a moment, and then reached into her purse ignoring her tears. She took out a small jewelry box, and when Chuck saw his own wedding band, he began to cry as well. "I believe that God has changed you, and I want to start fresh. That's why I gave Christine my maiden name."

She took Chuck's left hand and slid the ring on his third finger. "Charles James Molinsky, I want you to come home. I want you to be my husband, and I want to be your wife. Until death do us part."

Chuck took Bobbi in his arms and kissed her, held her, and then kissed her again. Several minutes later, their emotions exhausted, Bobbi said, "I want us to go see Donna."

"Of course," Chuck said, as he shut his computer down. "I'll let Christine know I'm gone for the day." While he closed folders, stacked files, and cleared his desk, Bobbi called home.

"Mom?" Brad answered. "Are you okay? I didn't think you were going to be late today."

"I stopped by Dad's office. We're going to go see Donna for a little while. Will you guys be okay until we get home?"

"You and Dad are going together?"

"Get used to it."

"I'll tell Joel."

"Make sure he understands 'we' will be 'home' later."

"Gotcha. Oh, Grandma called. She said everything went through at the bank, and she changed her plane ticket so she could be here for Pastor Phil's funeral."

"Dad or I will call her when we get home. We shouldn't be too long. Love you."

"Love you, too, and Mom, I'm really happy for you."

CHAPTER 25
VINDICATION

"You're staring," Bobbi said, as she eased her Camry to a stop in front of the Shannons' house.

"I can't help it," Chuck said. "I've pictured this day for months, and it's finally here."

"Well, I don't want to climb over the gear shift, so you'll have to loosen that death grip on my hand so I can get out of the car."

"If I have to," he muttered, but took her hand again as soon as he made it around the car.

She let him lead her onto the porch, and they waited several long moments after Chuck rang the doorbell. At last, David Shannon opened the door. "Bobbi," David said, leaning down to hug her, then he turned and shook Chuck's hand. "Chuck, good to see you. Thanks for coming."

"We should have called." Bobbi said.

"Nonsense." He held the door open for them. "Mom's inside."

"She's up for visitors?"

"She's a very strong, courageous woman, and she would hang me if I didn't bring you in." He smiled and ushered them around to the living room where Donna sat in the corner of the sofa with a little boy on her lap engrossed in a book, while his toddler sister played in the floor nearby. "Mom, Bobbi and Chuck are here."

Donna looked up and patted the little boy's leg. "Grant, let Nana up for a minute." She lifted her grandson, and set him on the sofa by himself.

As soon as she stood, Bobbi crossed the room and hugged her. "I am so sorry."

"Thank you, Honey. I don't know what I'll do without him." When they let go, Chuck gave Donna a gentle hug as well. Wiping her eyes, Donna said, "You know David, I guess. These are his little ones. Grant is four, and Maddie is fifteen months." She glanced toward the hallway and back in the kitchen. "Jan is around here somewhere. She's been on telephone duty most of the afternoon. And Cooper, bless his heart, he showed up at the hospital by five-thirty, and he's been at the church the rest of the day."

"I can't believe David's babies are this big," Bobbi said. "They'll be Brad's size before you know it."

"They've grown since Christmas," Donna said, watching Maddie play with a Noah's ark set. "Michael and Stacy will get here tonight. Their little boy is walking now." Grant had climbed down from the sofa and stood behind his grandmother, watching Bobbi and Chuck.

"Grant, this is Mr. and Mrs. Molinsky." Donna slipped a hand to the boy's back, guiding him forward. "They go to church with Papa and me."

"My Papa is in heaven." Grant inched closer and held his hand out.

"Yes, he is," Bobbi said. She shook his hand, then knelt down to Grant's eye level. "Mr. Chuck and I love your Papa very much. He's a very special man."

"Daddy says we'll see him again someday." Grant turned to shake hands with Chuck.

"We sure will," Chuck said.

"Grant, you have such pretty red hair," Bobbi said, smoothing his bangs.

"He gets it from his Papa," Donna said, laying a hand on her grandson's shoulder. "My boys got my blonde hair, but my grandsons are both red-headed like their Papa. Did you know Phil when his hair was still red?"

"It was already gray when you came," Bobbi said.

"Oh, you're right," Donna said. "He went completely gray, oh . . . before he turned thirty, I guess."

"Donna, we won't stay long," Chuck said. "We just wanted to tell you how sorry we were, and how much you and Phil mean to us. We couldn't have gotten through the last few months without you."

"Thank you," Donna said, then smiled as Grant wriggled away and climbed back on the sofa. "We love you and your boys so very much."

"When Rita called this morning," Bobbi said, shaking her head. Rising emotion choked off her words, and she didn't want to fall apart in front of Donna.

Donna nodded. "Phil's health was much poorer than anybody realized, and the doctor cautioned us a stroke or something was a real possibility. You remember back—when was it—Labor Day? When we had to cancel one of your appointments?"

Bobbi nodded. It all made sense now.

"After the doctor checked things out, he determined it wasn't just a blood pressure or medication issue. Phil had several blood clots. His doctor didn't want to risk surgery, for fear Phil wouldn't make it off the table, so we did several rounds of different clot-busting drugs. None of them helped. The whole time, the doctor warned us that if one of the clots moved, and hit his heart, or his lungs, or his brain, it would almost surely be fatal."

Donna looked away, and her voice weakened. "He . . . woke up a little before four this morning, and said he had a tremendous headache, and before I could get the light on . . ."

"I'm so sorry. We had no idea."

"Phil wouldn't tell anybody, wouldn't let me tell anybody," Donna said wiping her eyes. "He didn't want to cause a fuss. He wanted to just keep working, and if God wanted to heal him, He would, but if God was ready for him to come home, that was just fine, too. We had told our kids the situation, but I don't think another soul knew."

"Donna, is there anything you need?" Chuck asked.

"No, thank you. With the kids here, I'll be fine. Just pray for David. He's going to preach his daddy's funeral Monday. It'll be hard."

"We should go," Bobbi said, looking at Chuck. She had planned to tell Donna that she and Chuck reconciled, but after seeing Donna in person, it seemed the wrong time. The news would keep. "We love you," she said giving Donna another quick hug.

Chuck moved his left hand to Bobbi's back to walk out, but before he could take a step, Donna spoke. "Is that a new piece of jewelry, Chuck?"

Chuck turned back around and smiled. "I just got it today."

"So, is it official?" Donna's eyes twinkled.

"I'm sorry Phil didn't get to see us together," Bobbi said.

"Honey, he knew it was going to happen."

"Wednesday . . ." Bobbi said and glanced away. Shame gripped her heart for the anger and bitterness she vented yesterday afternoon. "He knew just what I needed." She searched through her purse for Phil's letter, and handed it to Donna.

Donna opened the letter, pausing to wipe away tears as she read. "I can hear him saying that," she whispered at last. She folded the letter carefully, gently, and slid it back in its envelope. "Thank you for sharing it."

"I could not have done this without you and Phil," Bobbi said, taking Chuck's hand.

"Yes, you could have," Donna said with a gentle smile. "God just allowed Phil and me the blessing of being part of it. Now you go bless somebody else and we'll call it even."

Out of the corner of her eye, Bobbi watched Chuck wrinkle his brow in confusion as she drove past the turnoff to their street. "Trust me," she said and reached over to pat his hand. When she pulled into the parking lot of his apartment building, he smiled and kissed her cheek.

"I'll help you carry things," she said as she unbuckled her seat belt.

"You don't need to. I won't try to get it all today." He opened the car door then paused. "I'd rather spend my first evening back at home actually at home, and not moving boxes."

Bobbi watched him disappear inside the apartment building, then she leaned back against the headrest. *Lord, I doubted we would ever see this day. You worked a miracle, though. Thank You for bringing things back to normal.* Normal wasn't exactly the right word, however. *Thank You for a second chance.*

Later that evening, Chuck awoke to the news playing on the television in the family room. The Missouri-Iowa State basketball game had ended, and Brad and Joel had cleared out. He stretched, then clicked the television off. The emotional intensity of the last two days caught up with him. Maybe he could sleep in tomorrow. How bad would it look if he slid in to work late the day after being named sole managing partner?

He walked through the kitchen, locked the back door. He checked Bobbi's coffeemaker, making sure it was ready to go in the morning. He sighed and glanced around the room one more time before turning out the light, his eyes brimming with tears. He was home.

"Thank you," he whispered, then flipped the switch, and made his way toward the front stairs.

Bobbi called to him from the living room. "Where are you sleeping?"

He wondered that very thing himself, but decided to sleep in the guest bedroom just as he had done at Christmas. That is, unless Bobbi had other ideas. "Wherever you tell me to," he said.

"Don't you have a bed?" She switched the living room lamp off, picked up her pillow and blanket, and crossed the room to him.

"Don't you?"

"I do," she said, handing him her blanket and pillow, "and I have a husband worth sharing it with."

Sunday, January 29

The Molinskys slipped into the morning worship service, almost unnoticed, just after the music started. As much as Bobbi wanted to be there as a family, she experienced a painful awkwardness when she walked in the sanctuary. By coming in late, she hoped to insulate herself from the uneasiness.

A heavy stillness hung over the people, over the very space inside the building. No one spoke above a whisper. No one had the heart to sing the hymns. For Preston Road Community Church, Phil Shannon's funeral had already begun.

Bobbi whispered a prayer for Cooper DeWitt, seated alone on the front pew. He had to walk the church through the devastating grief, to preach this morning in Phil's place. With a fresh haircut and a tailored suit, he looked fifteen years older. As the last hymn finished, Bobbi saw him drop his head for just a moment before standing and taking his place behind the podium. Opening his Bible seemed to take all his strength. He laid a sheet of notes to the side, swallowed hard, then lifted his head.

"Folks, seminary certainly didn't prepare me for a day like today. I doubt all the experience and wisdom in the world would be much help after a loss like this." He scanned the crowd. "Miss Donna . . . I spoke with her yesterday afternoon . . . just, uh . . . just pray for God's supernatural comfort on her. David and Michael convinced her that the service this morning on top of the visitation and funeral might be a bit too much, so she's not here."

But Donna was there. Everyone was so focused on the young man in the pulpit, so determined to do this well for Phil's sake, they never saw Donna Shannon steal in from the back.

Her boys had done their very best to persuade her to stay home, to consider her own health, and not subject herself to the emotional strain of being in a worship service without her husband. With the visitation tonight and the funeral tomorrow, she needed her energy, they said. Everyone would understand.

Perhaps, but David and Michael didn't understand that she craved a feeling of comfort and closeness with Phil, a feeling she could only find at church, Phil's place.

Cooper looked toward his wife, the same way Phil always caught Donna's eye before he preached. Then Cooper began to speak with conviction and resolve. "In First Corinthians eleven, Paul instructs the people, 'Imitate me just as I also imitate Christ.'" Cooper described the way Phil taught him how to pastor, how to study and pray, and served as his role model in every facet of ministry, all because Phil followed Christ.

Chuck slipped an arm around Bobbi's shoulders. She glanced up at him, and tried to smile. The longer Cooper spoke, the more her stomach churned. Sweat beaded across her chest and back. With her pulse pounding in her ears, Bobbi closed her eyes. *Dear God, help me get through this service. Just a few more minutes.* Relief never came, though. The blood drained from her hands, leaving them icy white. She glanced at Chuck again, but he never took his eyes off Cooper.

A moment later, Chuck shifted to stand up. Cooper had given an invitation. Thankful to stand, Bobbi gripped the pew in front of her. Everything would be over soon. Then from behind her, in her right ear, she could have sworn she heard a voice.

'Bobbi, Chuck confessed his sin in front of all these people. You need to vindicate him in front of them.'

Not today. With Phil . . . it wouldn't be right.

'I wouldn't ask you if it wasn't the right thing to do . . . today. Trust Me.'

She sighed and touched Chuck's hand so he would let her out of the pew. She made her way down the outside aisle, rounded the front pew and knelt down. She sensed someone beside her and felt a hand on her shoulder. Chuck. Her heart ached and tears began to well up in her eyes. She had walked out on him when he faced their church.

A moment later, Rita knelt beside her and took her hand. "I love you. Everything's going to be all right."

"There's something I have to do. Pray for me." Bobbi slipped away and took Cooper's hand. She poured out her heart, while he nodded and then smiled. He hugged Bobbi, and then directed her to sit in the corner of the front pew across the aisle, then he slipped back up to the podium and pulled a small black book from the pulpit. As the musicians finished the chorus of the invitation hymn, he raised his hand, and the music faded away.

"Folks, have a seat. You know the struggle that Bobbi and Chuck have been going through. We've all been praying for them, doing our best to hold them up to the Father. Bobbi wants to speak to you about that."

He motioned for Bobbi, then he sat down beside Chuck. Bobbi watched the two men whisper back and forth, with Chuck nodding the whole time.

She took a deep breath, stood, and faced her church. Her stomach tightened immediately. Talking to eight-year-olds every day hadn't prepared her for this. She looked out over her friends and family, and just before she began to speak, she saw Donna Shannon smile and nod.

"The last few months have been the most difficult in my life, testing my commitment to my marriage and my faith in God, at the deepest levels. My Father is an amazing God, and He did something only He could do." She looked at Chuck seated on the front pew and smiled. "He brought reconciliation to my marriage." A slight murmur passed through the crowd and Bobbi wiped away a tear. Off to her left, Chuck did the same.

"Thank you for your prayers. They worked." She smiled and blinked away another tear. "Chuck repented, he's changed, and I've completely forgiven him. I want this to be the end. I don't want anyone to ever bring it up again, or hold over him what he did. Jesus Christ died to pay for it. It's under His blood and through His work in my heart, it's gone." She glanced at Cooper and he joined her at the altar, carrying the small book from the pulpit.

"How fitting to see such a tangible legacy that Pastor Phil left," he said, motioning for Chuck to join them. "God did the hard work, but Phil, in his wisdom and compassion, pointed them in the right direction, and encouraged Chuck and Bobbi to be obedient to God's Word in the face of such a challenge."

He motioned to the boys still seated in their pew. "Brad and Joel, why don't you join your folks up here?" Joel exploded into the aisle. Brad followed close behind, no less excited, but far more reserved than his little brother.

Joel reached his dad first and hugged him with such energy Chuck had to take a step back just to keep his balance. "I knew it, Dad!" he said. "I knew it all along."

Chuck kissed his son's forehead. "You were the only one who did, Buddy."

Bobbi took Joel's hand, pulling him close, then kissed his cheek. "Thanks for not knocking me down," she whispered. Brad hugged her and Chuck, and then took his place beside his dad.

With her sons standing by, Bobbi faced her husband at the altar of Preston Road Community Church. Chuck took her hands, just as he did almost nineteen years earlier.

Cooper DeWitt cleared his throat, opened the small book, and spoke. "Dearly beloved, we are privileged to be here in the sight of God, to witness as this couple reaffirms their marriage commitment to God and to each other. Chuck, do you believe that marriage is a covenant, a lifelong commitment?"

"I do." Chuck's face radiated pure joy.

"Will you then vow to remain steadfast in sacrificial, unconditional love for Bobbi, your wife, to seek reconciliation in times of trial, to remain pure in your relationship with her in mind and body, and to seek personal and spiritual growth in your marriage relationship?"

"I will," Chuck said. Cooper then turned to Bobbi and repeated the questions. Her answers were clear and firm. She trusted her husband and his pledge, and had no hesitation in returning that promise.

Cooper then asked the congregation to stand, and he addressed them. "As you have witnessed Chuck and Bobbi renew their vows, will you support and encourage them to walk in obedience to God in this marriage covenant so long as they both shall live? If so, answer, 'We will.'"

A resounding 'we will' echoed through the sanctuary. Cooper smiled and winked at Bobbi. "Chuck and Bobbi, inasmuch as you have been obedient to God through repentance, forgiveness, and reconciliation, and have sought to reaffirm your covenant vows, may God bless you as you live before Him as husband and wife until death alone comes between you."

Chuck didn't wait for Cooper's signal before he leaned in and kissed Bobbi.

Cooper Dewitt looked out on the congregation and prompted them. "And all God's people said . . ."

"Amen!"

EPILOGUE

SIXTEEN MONTHS LATER

Chuck and Bobbi Molinsky
&
Big Brothers Brad and Joel
Welcome

Shannon Hope Molinsky

May 22 9:44 p.m.
6 lbs 11 oz 19 ½ inches long

Tuesday, July 17

"You're right, the Kenyan coffee is excellent," Rita Heatley said as she set her cup down. "Of course, I can't believe I'm at a coffee shop in the middle of summer. We should be getting ice cream." Just then, Shannon Molinsky began to whimper. "Here, Miss Shannon, let me get you out of that seat. Does Mommy make you sit in here all the time?" Rita lifted her niece out of her carrier and snuggled her close.

"You'd better get practiced up, Grandma," Bobbi teased.

"I've got plenty of time. Kara's not due for six more months." Rita turned Shannon around on her lap so she could manage her coffee cup. "Do you know that woman?" Rita asked.

Bobbi eased around. An attractive redhead in her mid-thirties, smartly dressed, with a satchel slung over one shoulder, stood at the counter. "I've never seen her. Why?"

"She keeps looking over here." Rita said.

"Maybe she knows me from school." Bobbi sipped her coffee. Shannon began to fuss, so Bobbi took her from Rita and began to pat the baby's back.

Just then, the woman at the counter approached their table. "Aren't you Chuck's wife?" she asked. "What a beautiful little girl." She smiled and waved at Shannon.

"How do you know Chuck?" Bobbi asked, as her stomach tensed up.

"I've worked with him. He's a very lucky man." The woman waved at Shannon once more, then walked away. Before she disappeared through the coffee shop door, Bobbi caught sight of the monogram on her satchel—TR.

CONTINGENCY
Discussion Guide

1. Is *Contingency*, Bobbi's story or Chuck's? (In other words, which character grows and changes most significantly?) Discuss how their stories parallel even though Bobbi is the victim and Chuck is the transgressor.

2. Bobbi struggles throughout the book with the idea of divorce. Is divorce called for in her situation? Why or why not? What circumstances warrant divorce for a believer?

3. Rita presents a stark contrast to Bobbi in temperament. Did you ever find yourself agreeing with Rita? Are there times when her tough approach is appropriate? How is she good for Bobbi? Do you ever seek counsel from those who might challenge your course of action? Is it wise to do so?

4. Phil explains, "There's an irresolvable tension that exists between God's sovereignty and man's free will. He never forces man to act or prevents him from acting. God is never caught off guard by our choices, and His purposes are always fulfilled in spite of our interference." Do you agree? How could this offer hope to Bobbi?

5. During counseling, Phil says, "Each of you brings a past and a personality into your marriage. Those determine where the trouble spots in your marriage will be." Is he right?

6. What made Tracy so dangerous to Chuck, and why was he so blinded to the threat? What might he and Bobbi have done to protect their marriage from infidelity? Are the trouble spots Phil mentioned also blind spots?

7. Chuck and Bobbi were each deeply affected by their relationships with their fathers. How did those relationships factor into the affair and their responses to it? Several characters stepped in to

become surrogate fathers for Chuck and Bobbi. How did they contribute, helping get the couple back on track? Consider the role your own father plays in the issues you face. Do you have surrogates to turn to if necessary?

8. In chapter 4, Gavin challenges Chuck's idea of grace, saying he can't condone infidelity or let it slide. What is grace? What examples of grace are displayed in the story? Read Hosea 1:2, 2:14 and 3:1-2. What elements in the Biblical story of Hosea might have led Phil to recommend it for Bobbi to study?

9. Phil is unwavering in his belief that confession is critical for Chuck's restoration. Do you agree with Phil? Although hers are private, what confessions does Bobbi make that clear the way for reconciliation? Have you experienced a restored relationship through making or hearing a confession?

10. Psalm 37 and Psalm 142 become emotional and spiritual refuges for Chuck and Bobbi. Read through each psalm and discuss how they fit the character's situation. What psalms do you turn to in times of crisis?

11. Bobbi and Chuck each experienced a critical moment of surrender. What were they and how did those moments set up the final resolution between them? Think back to a time when God brought you to a point of surrender. What was the result? Is He challenging you now to let go of something?

12. In a coffee shop meeting with Bobbi, Donna Shannon explains, "God asks us to love the way He does, unconditionally with grace and forgiveness." How do events work together to help Bobbi risk taking that step? Has God ever challenged you to love and forgive unconditionally? Did you wrestle with that challenge like Bobbi did? Have you, like Chuck, ever needed unconditional love and forgiveness? Was it difficult to be patient and wait for God to work in another's heart?

Please enjoy a sample from the second book of the
Covenant of Trust Series

INDEMNITY

Available 2011 from
MINDSTIR MEDIA

PROLOGUE

Two minutes. Wait two minutes before reading the results. She set the alarm on her wristwatch for five minutes, just to be sure, and left the bathroom.

In the kitchen, she paced between the refrigerator and the doorway, a dozen, then two dozen times. She was never late. She had to be pregnant this time. At thirty-two, her ever-ticking biological clock grew louder and more urgent with each passing month.

For months she researched, planned, and when the time came she executed it flawlessly. As soon as he introduced himself to her, she knew he was the one. Just like Mr. Dailey, he was intelligent, successful, driven, but he was also a man of character and integrity. Granted, she wore him down, and led him to compromise some of that integrity, but he would recover. Most importantly, he would never leave his wife for her.

Once or twice, she allowed herself to wonder what might have happened if she'd met him ten or fifteen years ago. Maybe things would have been different. Maybe she would be different.

The alarm on her watch beeped. She rushed to the bathroom, and snatched up the plastic stick. Positive! She was pregnant. She fumbled to find the package instructions and reread them slowly and carefully. Two lines just like in the picture. She *was* pregnant.

Lightheaded and unsteady, she sat down on the edge of the tub, and focused on her breathing. "Be calm," she coached, but then she indulged in a moment of pure satisfaction. She did it. She was going to be a mother. This was her one chance to redeem herself, to prove that she wasn't completely messed up.

After one more deep breath, she stood and checked the calendar. It was July now, that meant . . . April, or maybe early May. A spring baby. A boy. A boy with his father's square jaw and broad shoulders. She smiled, and gently lay a hand low on her belly.

First things first, however. She had to get rid of Chuck. He could never know about the baby. That would protect him, and prevent anyone from getting to her through him. He was leaving town this morning for Kansas City, giving her a day or two to set things in motion. She would tip off Chuck's wife that he strayed, and then play the part of the scorned lover. Chuck would have to marshal all his energy and attention to appease his wife. He would be more than glad to let her fade out of his life.

Just for safety's sake, she would file a lawsuit accusing Chuck of harassing her. It was utterly groundless, but it would keep him from contacting her. He wouldn't want anything to do with her ever again. By the time she began to show, she would drop the suit, and simply disappear.

CHAPTER 1
REAPPEARANCE

SEVEN YEARS LATER
Thursday, August 2

"This is going to be a miserable day," Bobbi Molinsky muttered to herself as she got out of her air-conditioned car. Thick, heavy air blanketed her, and shimmering waves of heat rose from the asphalt parking lot. She headed up the sidewalk along the short side of the playground, thankful the teachers' lot was close to the building.

Hearing giggling over the rhythmic squeaking of the swings, Bobbi glanced back at the playground. A small boy swung in a wide arc. "Emma! I'm gonna jump!" he teased in a sing-song voice. "One! Two! Three!" The woman gasped in mock horror, satisfying the boy, who never left the swing. "Fooled ya!"

Bobbi shook her head and smiled as she passed. He sounded like Joel. In fact, except for his dark, reddish hair, he could have passed for Joel's little brother. *Bobbi, your baby boy is a college freshman now. Let him go.* Besides, her nest was hardly empty. With Shannon entering kindergarten, she and Chuck were starting over.

Inside the school building, mothers and grandmothers with children in tow, clutched papers, filled out forms and hustled in and out of the office. Of course. Open registration for transfer students. That explained the boy on the swings. Maybe he would end up in Shannon's class. Or hers.

Bobbi slipped into the school office, picked up her mail and headed down to her classroom. A wall of cardboard boxes surrounded the desk, giving the room the look of a warehouse. After spending the morning unpacking boxes and arranging the room, she dropped into her desk chair, and began reviewing her class roll while her computer booted. *Wade . . . Carmella . . . Kaylee . . . Brayton . . . Brodie . . . I think I had Brodie's brother. Ashton is a boy, not a girl . . .* The last name on the list, a handwritten addition, was Jackson Charles Ravenna.

Ravenna.

Seven years ago, Chuck had an affair with Tracy Ravenna. Surely, this couldn't be . . .

"Dear God, please," Bobbi murmured. "Not again." She quickly flipped through her students' information sheets until she found Jackson's. Round, loopy letters confirmed her fears.

Jackson was Tracy's son.

Emotions Bobbi locked away for the last seven years churned to the surface. In spite of the counseling, the changes Chuck made, and the reconciliation, searing pain surged through her, almost as fresh and real as the day she looked in Chuck's eyes and knew he'd been unfaithful.

Would Tracy try to reestablish contact with Chuck? Is that what she was after? Had he done enough to protect his heart and mind from her in these intervening seven years? Seven years . . . Jackson was six years old. She ran her finger down the sheet looking for a date of birth. April eighteenth. She counted backward on her fingers. April meant July.

He was conceived in July. Chuck was with Tracy on the eleventh, the fourteenth and the twenty-first . . . Pain gave way to bitter shame. Jackson Charles Ravenna wasn't just Tracy's son.

He was Chuck's son.

She wiped the sweat beading across her forehead. The air conditioner was on, wasn't it? Light-headed and nauseous, Bobbi leaned over, and breathed deeply, dragging the wastebasket closer as a precaution.

They quit counseling altogether because everything was good. They were solid. She loved him, and she trusted him. She asked Chuck point blank if Tracy was pregnant, and he said no. If he lied . . . If he knew about this boy all these years . . . If he kept this a secret . . .

Clutching the class list, she bolted back outside to her car. She couldn't wait for Chuck to come home to discuss this. She had to know now. She jerked her car out of the parking space, her tires squealing as she sped out of the parking lot.

******

Chuck sighed and gave up squinting through the Thursday updates. He reluctantly pulled his glasses from his shirt pocket and slid them on. Bobbi didn't need glasses yet, much less bifocals, but then, Bobbi wouldn't be fifty this fall either.

He reached across his desk and picked up the photo of his wife. He took the picture on their second honeymoon on Maui, moments after he stopped a complete stranger to ask him if he'd ever seen a more beautiful woman. He captured her shy smile, with the self-conscious tilt of her head.

A few weeks later, with that same expression, she whispered, "Chuck . . . I'm pregnant."

"What? How?"

"Well, Sweetheart, when a husband and wife love each other, there are many special ways to show that—"

"Bobbi! I'm not talking about mechanics!"

She smiled that smile again. "I guess God wants to give us a reconciliation gift." God gave him more than reconciliation gift. Shannon Hope Molinsky proved God forgave him.

He smiled and set the picture back on his desk, and glancing out through the glass walls of his office, he nodded to Christine, his receptionist. He adjusted his glasses, and began reading again. Before he finished two pages, he caught movement out of the corner of his eye.

Bobbi charged across the lobby, her jaw set, fire in her eyes. Before he could react, she banged his office door closed behind her. "So help me, God, if you knew about this, Chuck, I will divorce you right now!" She threw a packet of papers across the desk.

"What are you talking about? If I knew about what?"

"I asked you!" Bobbi leaned across his desk, pointing a finger at him. "I asked you specifically if she was pregnant!"

"Who? Tracy? She wasn't."

"Read that last name on my class list! It's her son!"

Chuck picked up the papers without taking his eyes off his wife. He swallowed hard and adjusted his glasses, then skimmed the top sheet until he found 'Jackson Charles Ravenna'. A wave of squeezing pressure hit his chest. "How do you know—?"

"Next to last page," she snapped.

He looked away from her icy glare and carefully turned pages. This had to be a misunderstanding, a mistake of some sort. His eyes ran down the sheet looking for 'Jackson Charles Ravenna.' He immediately recognized Tracy's handwriting. Before his mind blasted in a thousand directions, he looked back up at his wife, battling to maintain calm in his voice. "Now Bobbi—"

"Don't patronize me!" She slammed her hand down on his desk. "You look me in the eyes and tell me the truth. Did you know about this boy?"

"No." He locked eyes with her. "I'm as shocked as you are."

"I doubt that," Bobbi shot back. "She hasn't tried to contact you?"

"No."

"Have you tried to contact her?"

He could feel heat rising under his shirt collar, and his pulse began to pound.

"Chuck . . . answer me," Bobbi seethed with quiet fury.

Chuck wished she were still yelling. "When I split the firm and sent Pete to open the Kansas City office . . ." Her clenched jaw twitched ever so slightly. "I checked with the Missouri Bar to see if she was there." Bobbi dropped her head and huffed. "That's all, I swear. I've never, ever tried to find a phone number, an address, nothing."

"Say it without blinking."

"I haven't had any contact with Tracy in seven years."

"That's about to change," Bobbi smirked, and pointed at the class list. "He's yours, isn't he?"

"He couldn't be. She told me she took care of everything."

"And of course she wouldn't lie." Bobbi rolled her eyes at him, and jabbed a finger toward the packet. "Look at his birth date."

"April eighteenth. So?"

"Do the math."

Chuck's blood ran cold as he counted backwards nine months. He looked up from the paper, into his wife's eyes, as her anger gave way to fear and uncertainty.

"Bobbi, I don't know what to say . . ." He wanted to cry, yell, throw something, punch something, then rip the papers up in little tiny pieces.

"Almost to the day, isn't it?" she said quietly.

He rested his hand on his desk, so she couldn't see it shake, and slowly pushed his chair back from his desk.

"What are we going to do?" Bobbi slumped into one of the office chairs.

"I don't know," Chuck answered, his voice just above a whisper. "I can't think right now." Tracy . . . was pregnant . . . "That lyin' . . ." He clenched his fist, crumpling the papers still in his hand. "How could she . . .? Pregnant . . ." He stood and reached for his suit jacket.

"What are you doing?" Bobbi stood between him and his office door.

"I'm gonna go straighten this out."

"Now?"

"She owes me an explanation! I think she intended to get pregnant all along—"

"Chuck! You're six years too late! We're not dealing with a pregnancy anymore. She has a son. A little boy—"

"Then I need to find out if he's mine."

"His middle name is Charles. I think that's a fairly good indicator."

"What if she's just playing games?"

"No, I saw this kid today. I'm sure it was him. He looks just like Joel, except his hair is the same color as his mother's."

"You saw him? Where was Tracy?"

"I don't know. He was with an older woman. He called her Emma."

"Emma? Who's Emma?" He pulled his jacket on. "I'm gonna get to the bottom of this."

She grasped him by the arm. "Are you insane? In the first place, I will not sit by and let you go see your mistress—"

"She's NOT . . ." Chuck turned away and took a deep breath. "Bobbi, how could you . . . how could you say that? I thought we were past—"

"It's not past anymore." She held her hand to her face. "It's all right in front of me again. You have no idea what you're walking into. Get some help on this before you do anything. Before *we* do anything."

At least she corrected herself, and said "we." He needed to get his wife some reassurance, quickly, before the trust between them deteriorated further. "Call Rita. See if she and Gavin can meet us at the house in an hour or so."

"Kara's working today. Rita's got her girls and Shannon."

"We'll send the kids outside or something. I'm gonna call Glen." Bobbi crossed her arms across her chest and paced away from him while punched numbers on his cell phone.

Pastor Glen Dillard picked up quickly. "This is kind of a strange time to call. Is something wrong?"

"Yeah, Glen. I mean, nobody's hurt or anything, but something's come up. Can you meet us at the house in about an hour?"

"Sure, but can you give me a little to go on?"

Chuck glanced at his wife and lowered his voice. "The woman I had the affair with is back. I'll explain the rest at the house."

"How's Bobbi?" The seriousness in Glen's voice encouraged Chuck in an odd way.

"She's okay. I think she'll be okay."

"Can I call Laurie at work just to have her start praying?"

"Tell her 'thanks'."

Bobbi turned Chuck's desk phone around so she could use it. "You just dial like a normal phone, right?" she asked before pushing any numbers.

"Dial a nine, first." Chuck reached across the desk, and pushed the buttons, turning on the speakerphone.

"I hate speakerphones."

"I want to hear what Rita says."

"You may change your mind on that." They waited three long rings before Rita answered. "Hello? Chuck?"

"No, it's me," Bobbi replied. "I'm at his office."

"Why? What's wrong?"

"Are you sitting down?"

"You're scaring me. Tell me what's going on."

"Listen to me very carefully before you go off, all right? I picked up my class list today, and there was a Jackson Charles Ravenna on it."

"No. . . Tell me it's not . . ."

"It is." Bobbi swallowed hard, and looked at him with a mixture of sadness and accusation. "And he's almost certainly Chuck's." There was dead silence on the line.

"Did Chuck know about this?" Rita asked at last, each word sharper.

"Not until I told him."

"And you believe him?"

"Yes."

"You took a little while to answer that," Rita said. Chuck closed his eyes and shook his head.

"I have to believe him."

"What do you need me to do?"

"Can you and Gavin meet us at the house in about an hour?"

"Of course. Kara was off today after all, so she came and took the girls to her house."

"Perfect. Start praying, and I'll see you soon."

"Baby, I am so sorry. I thought this was over for you."

"It will never be over, Rita. Never." Bobbi returned the office phone receiver to its cradle.

"Do you believe me?" Chuck asked.

She looked past him to the photos on the bookcase behind him, then her eyes darted to the crinkled papers on his desk. "It felt just like that

morning I read her e-mail. All I could think was that you'd lied to me."
Chuck rounded the desk to take her in his arms. "I don't have the
strength to go through this again," she whispered.

"You don't have to. I didn't lie."

"I know. I know you didn't." She relaxed against him.

"Bobbi, I can't do this without you."

****

Across the lobby, Christine Gardner tried not to watch the Molinskys
through the glass walls. When Mrs. Molinsky tore through the lobby
without speaking, Christine knew something happened. Seeing the angry
confrontation, and hearing the raised voices, confirmed it was something
extraordinary. She could only think of one person who could get that kind
of reaction from Bobbi—Tracy Ravenna.

Chad Mitchell, Chuck's right hand man, passed through the lobby and
caught her stealing glances at the couple. "What's going on?" he asked,
nodding toward Chuck's office.

"I'm not sure."

"But you've got a gut instinct, right?"

"I can't say anything. I might be wrong."

"I'd bet my life on your instincts."

"Please don't breathe a word of this, but Mr. Mitchell, I think Tracy is
back."

About The Author

After working several years as research chemist, Paula Wiseman was blessed the opportunity to stay home with her children and follow the writer's path. She has been published in several *Cup of Comfort* devotional books and in *Life Savors for Women*. She blogs on matters of life and faith at www.paulawiseman.com. *Contingency* is her first novel. She enjoys small town life in Illinois with her husband, Jon, and three children.

CPSIA information can be obtained at www.ICGtesting.com
Printed in the USA
BVOW071846300512

291416BV00002B/31/P